MATT CHRISTOPHER®

The #1 Sports Series for Kids

✳ LEGENDS in SPORTS ✳

JACKIE ROBINSON

Text by Glenn Stout

LITTLE, BROWN AND COMPANY

New York ✷ Boston ✷ London

Little, Brown and Company

Time Warner Book Group
1271 Avenue of the Americas, New York, NY 10020
Visit our Web site at www.lb-kids.com

www.mattchristopher.com

First Edition: March 2006

Matt Christopher® is a registered trademark of
Matt Christopher Royalties, Inc.

Text by Glenn Stout

Library of Congress Cataloging-in-Publication Data

Stout, Glenn.
    Jackie Robinson / text by Glenn Stout. — 1st ed.
        p.   cm. — (Matt Christopher legends in sports)
    ISBN 0-316-10826-X
    1. Robinson, Jackie, 1919–1972 — Juvenile literature.   2. Baseball
players — United States — Biography — Juvenile literature.   I. Title.
II. Series.

GV865.R6S86   2005
796.357'092—dc22   2004020153

10 9 8 7 6 5 4 3 2 1

COM-MO

Printed in the United States of America

Contents

✤ CHAPTER ONE ✤

1919–1937

The Sharecropper's Son

Jackie Robinson changed America. Before he broke the color barrier and became the first African American to play major-league baseball in the twentieth century, American society was segregated, which means that people of different races were kept apart and rarely lived or worked together. African Americans were not permitted to use the same restaurants, hotels, schools, or even the same drinking fountains as white Americans. They were not allowed to live in certain neighborhoods or do certain jobs. Many white Americans simply didn't believe that African Americans were as smart or talented as white people were.

No African American had played major-league baseball since 1884, when Moses "Fleet" Walker briefly played in the American Association. Many of the men who ran professional baseball had prejudiced attitudes toward African Americans. They decided that blacks would not be allowed to play in the majors. This decision was never a written rule, for such a rule might have been challenged in a court of law. Instead, they made a secret agreement among themselves that none of them would sign an African American player.

But that didn't stop African Americans from playing the game. They organized their own teams and barnstormed around the country, playing other African American teams and semipro clubs. Later they formed their own leagues, known as the Negro Leagues. The stars of these leagues, like slugging catcher Josh Gibson and speedy Cool Papa Bell, were heroes in the African American community. When African American teams played exhibition games against major-league teams, they more than held their own. They all knew they had the ability to play in the major leagues. All they needed was an opportunity.

In 1947 a twenty-eight-year-old African American named Jackie Robinson was given that opportunity — and when he took it, he made sports history.

✾ ✾ ✾

Jack Roosevelt Robinson was born on January 31, 1919, in Cairo, Georgia. He was the fourth son and fifth child of Jerry and Mallie Robinson.

Jerry Robinson was a sharecropper. He worked on an old plantation owned by a white man named James Sasser. Although Sasser paid Robinson and other African Americans to work his fields, the money they earned wasn't enough for them to live on. Robinson and the other sharecroppers had to borrow money from Sasser to buy food and pay rent. It was difficult for them to work enough to pay back what they owed, so most were doomed to live in poverty for their entire lives.

Jerry Robinson married Mallie, the daughter of a former slave, in 1909. Soon after, they started a family. First came three sons, Edgar, Frank, and Mack, and then a daughter, Willa Mae.

Through hard work, Jerry managed to get out of debt and became a "half-cropper," which meant that he was allowed to keep a small portion of his crop to feed his family and to sell at a profit. As a result, he often had some money in his pocket. At first he used the money to take care of his family. But as time

3

went on, he started spending it on having fun in Cairo.

When Jackie was six months old, Jerry told Mallie he was going to Texas to visit his brother and find a job. He promised to send for her and the children. Instead, he went to Florida with another man's wife, never to return.

Fortunately, Mallie's family came to her rescue. Her brother, Burton McGriff, worked for a doctor in California. He told Mallie that there were jobs in California for anyone willing to work hard, including African Americans. In 1920 Mallie moved her family to Los Angeles, where she got a job as a maid to a white family.

By 1923 she had saved enough money to buy a small house in Pasadena. Unfortunately, her family was not welcomed by their white neighbors. Some people spread rumors that the Robinson children were vandalizing other houses. Others circulated a petition that called for them to move. One night a wooden cross was burned on their front yard, a symbol of a hate group known as the Ku Klux Klan (KKK). The Klan considered African Americans to be subhuman and did not believe they should live or work near whites. Klan members terrorized African Americans, sometimes even killing them. By burning a cross on their lawn, the KKK hoped to scare the Robinsons out of the neighborhood.

But Mallie Robinson refused to be intimidated. Eventually, her neighbors accepted the family.

Meanwhile, at the local playground, Jackie was learning that on the playing fields, color didn't matter as much as ability. Jackie, like all the Robinson children, was a fine athlete, excelling at football, basketball, and baseball. Once the neighborhood kids realized that he was the fastest runner and best athlete at the playground, they often bribed him to play for their teams. But prejudice still existed. As soon as the game ended, many of his white teammates behaved as if they didn't even know him.

Jackie attended Grover Cleveland Elementary School. After school, he helped support the family. He sold newspapers and hot dogs and shined shoes, turning his earnings over to his mother. Only when he was done with work was he allowed to play.

When Jackie was old enough, he joined a band of boys who called themselves the Pepper Street Gang. His brother Mack was also part of the group. They challenged other Los Angeles gangs to games of football and other sports, often for small sums of money. But they also committed small crimes, like stealing golf balls from a local golf course. As a result, boys from the Pepper Street Gang were sometimes in trouble with the police.

Fortunately, sports helped keep Jackie, Mack, and the other Robinson children out of serious trouble. Edgar, the oldest, was a talented softball player and bicyclist. Frank was a sprint champion. And in high school Mack excelled in track and field.

In fact, Mack was so talented that he had high hopes of winning a track scholarship to college. But in those days few colleges gave scholarships to African American athletes. When Mack didn't get a scholarship, Mallie, Frank, and Edgar saved money to send him to Pasadena Junior College. At PJC, he set a national junior college record in the long jump. After two years at Pasadena, he won a track scholarship to the University of Oregon.

Jackie followed Mack's lead. While attending Washington Junior High, he played baseball, football, and basketball and also ran track, helping to lead each team to the league title. He even won a citywide table tennis tournament. At Muir Technical High School he continued to play sports, including baseball, which at the time was his least favorite sport.

Meanwhile, in the summer of 1936, Mack earned a spot on the United States Olympic track team. He traveled with the team to Berlin, Germany, to compete in the Games. Jesse Owens, an African American from Ohio, was the big star of that Olympics, winning four gold medals. Mack finished second to Owens in the 200-meter sprint and earned a silver medal.

Today, the winner of an Olympic medal is usually honored by his hometown. But when Mack returned to Pasadena, no one would even give him a decent job. He was finally hired as a manual laborer by the City of Pasadena. But a short time later, he and every other African American employed by the city were fired as part of the city's protest against ending segregation at a public swimming pool.

Mack's experiences left him bitter. They also made it clear to Jackie that even famous and respected African Americans didn't have it easy. His own experiences on the high school football field taught him the same bitter lesson.

Jackie was one of only a handful of African Americans playing in his high school league. His position was running back, which meant he handled the ball on most plays. Practically every time he had the ball, he was targeted by the other team. The opposition hammered him, hitting him hard even after the play was over. Between plays, they insulted him with racial slurs.

Jackie was far less accepting of such treatment than Mack had been. When Jackie was taunted, he talked back, and when he was pushed, he pushed back. Many white people were not accustomed to seeing a young African American man stand up for himself. Stellar athlete or not, Jackie was pegged as a troublemaker with a poor attitude.

In the final football game of Jackie's high school career, Muir met archrival high school Glendale for the league championship. The game was played at the Rose Bowl in Pasadena. Glendale knew that in order to beat Muir, they had to stop Jackie Robinson.

Jackie took the opening kickoff and made a dash up the field. Glendale players stopped him after a short gain. The referee blew the whistle, signaling the end of play. Jackie got to his feet to join the Muir huddle.

Then, all of a sudden — *Wham!* A Glendale player slammed an unsuspecting Robinson back to the ground. Hard.

This time, Jackie didn't get up. The cowardly attack left him with two broken ribs and forced him from the game. Without Jackie, Muir couldn't score. Glendale won 19–0.

As his broken ribs slowly healed, Robinson learned that many of his teammates and opponents had won scholarships to play college football. But even though he was clearly the best player in the league, no school offered him a scholarship. The rib injury, his attitude, and the color of his skin caused college recruiters to ignore him completely.

Jackie was frustrated by the slight. As far as he was concerned, his athletic career was over. After graduation, he planned to look for a job.

But his mother and brothers wouldn't let him quit. They pooled their resources and sent him to Pasadena Junior College. Mallie Robinson hoped her youngest son would become a doctor or a lawyer, but Jackie didn't share those dreams. He knew that as an African American, his chances of succeeding in either field were slim. He agreed to attend the two-year college for one reason — to play sports — and planned to major in physical education.

He didn't know it at the time, but his long journey to the major leagues would soon begin.

✦ CHAPTER TWO ✦

1937–1941

Jackie Robinson, All American

Jackie was looking forward to playing football for PJC when he started college in the fall of 1937. But on the first day of football practice, he broke his ankle. In the weeks that followed, he watched from the sidelines as the team struggled without him.

With six games left in the season, Robinson returned to the lineup. Suddenly, Pasadena became a powerhouse. Robinson was all over the field, returning punts and kickoffs, running with abandon in the backfield, and proving to be a tough defender in an era when football players were expected to play both offense and defense. With Robinson in the lineup, Pasadena went undefeated, winning five games and tying one.

As soon as football season ended, Robinson tried out for the basketball team. He was an instant star, leading the team in scoring. Unfortunately, as one of only a few African Americans playing collegiate sports in California, Robinson once again found himself a target.

In a game against Long Beach, a defender named Sam Babich played Robinson roughly, banging into him over and over again. When Robinson complained, his opponent walked over to him and asked, "You want to make something of it?"

Robinson's eyes blazed. "Sure," he said.

With that, Babich took a swing at Jackie, hitting him on the temple. Robinson lost his cool. He threw a punch that knocked Babich to the floor. Moments later, fights broke out all over the gym.

Once Jackie cooled down, he was embarrassed by his behavior. He approached Babich, holding out his hand in friendship. But Babich refused to shake the hand of an African American. It was not the first time, or the last, that Jackie's offer of friendship was to be rebuffed.

After basketball season ended, Robinson tried out for the baseball team. But the track coach also wanted him to compete in track and field. So Jackie joined that team, too. Throughout the spring, he often

practiced both sports on the same day. On at least
one occasion, during the conference track-and-field
championships, Jackie competed in his specialty, the
long jump, and then hustled over to Glendale to play
in a baseball game. And through it all, he attended
classes and kept up with his homework.

Few other student athletes could have handled
Jackie's rigorous sports schedule. But at Pasadena,
he was spectacularly successful. On the track, he
recorded a long jump of 25 feet 6⅝ inches, breaking
Mack's old junior college record. On the baseball
diamond, he led Pasadena to the league championship, playing shortstop, stealing twenty-five bases
in only twenty-four games and hitting .417.

That spring, he also had an opportunity to measure himself against big-league competition. The
Chicago White Sox held spring training in Pasadena
and agreed to play an exhibition game against Jackie's
junior college team to help raise funds for the
school's athletic department.

Jackie wasn't intimidated. He smacked out two
hits and made several strong plays in the field.
White Sox manager Jimmy Dykes was impressed.
"If that kid were white," he said after the game, "I'd

sign him right now." But of course signing Robinson was impossible because he was black.

Jackie began his sophomore year with stellar play on the football field. In almost every game, he broke free for at least one long run. He helped his team to eleven straight wins, and he himself gained more than 1,000 yards and scored seventeen touchdowns.

But it was during the final game of the season, a match against Compton played at the Rose Bowl, that Jackie made his most memorable play. As Compton lined up to kick off, Robinson retreated to his own goal line to return the kick. The ball was booted high into the sky and tumbled end over end toward him. Jackie backed up into the end zone, caught the ball, and started running.

Once Jackie got a full head of steam, no one could catch him. He started and stopped, darting first one way and then another, avoiding tacklers and then sprinting straight down the field. He raced 104 yards for a touchdown.

He was no less dominant on the basketball court. Although teams of the era struggled to score 50 points a game, Jackie averaged an astounding 19 points per contest. He earned all-state honors and helped PJC win the California Junior College Championship that year.

In the spring, he resumed his double duty in track and baseball. That year, he led the baseball team to the league title and was named the Southern California Junior College Most Valuable Player.

At Pasadena, Robinson proved he wasn't just a good athlete — he was one of the best in the country, the kind of player who could make a good team great. His performance attracted the attention of the four-year colleges that had ignored him during high school. Some colleges were now so eager for him to attend their institution that they made offers that were illegal, promising him money, cars, and other benefits if he came to their school.

Jackie knew that accepting such offers was wrong and that if he got caught, he would pay the price. His brother Frank helped him weigh his options. He advised Jackie to accept a scholarship from nearby UCLA. The school had both a fine academic reputation and a strong athletic program. Jackie took his brother's advice.

Sadly, Frank didn't live to see his brother flourish at UCLA. In 1939, he was killed in a motorcycle accident. Jackie was devastated by the tragedy.

A few months after Frank's death, Jackie was arrested when he tried to break up a fight between his friend and another man. He and his friend had been going for a drive. The friend, who was black, got into an argument with the driver of another car, a white man. The police arrived, and because Jackie was an African American, they arrested him. Fortunately, his baseball coach from Pasadena heard about the incident and interceded. The charges were dropped, and his coach advised Jackie to put the episode behind him.

Jackie did, but he had learned another bitter lesson about the way society treated African Americans. It wasn't enough to be as good as everyone else. He had to be better — and behave that way, too.

When he entered UCLA in the fall of 1939, Jackie felt out of place. Once again, he was one of only a few African Americans at the school. Most of his white classmates were far better off financially. Only when football practices began did he start to settle in.

The UCLA Bruins football team was already a

potential powerhouse. Another African American player, Kenny Washington, was one of the best runners and passers in the country. But since the Bruins didn't have another threat, opponents were free to focus their attention on Washington. The UCLA coaching staff hoped Jackie Robinson would give the opposition another player to worry about.

He did. In his second game, Robinson broke loose, returning a punt 65 yards for a touchdown. Although he was often used as a decoy and touched the ball only eight or ten times that season, whenever opponents keyed on Washington, Robinson was left free. He made the most of every opportunity. Despite missing two games with a sprained knee, he led the nation with an astounding average of 12.3 yards per carry from the line of scrimmage and was one of the best punt and kickoff returners in the country. He helped Kenny Washington average more than 100 yards passing and rushing per game. That year, the Bruins were among the top teams in the country.

Soon after football season ended, Jackie joined the UCLA basketball team. Among players of mostly mediocre talent he shone. Despite being double-teamed by the opposition, he led the southern division of the conference in scoring.

In the spring of 1940, Jackie planned on competing in both track and baseball as he had done at Pasadena Junior College. But the demands of practice, games, meets, and his college course load were too much. After appearing in only one track meet, he quit the team to concentrate on baseball, promising to return to the track after baseball season.

Much like their basketball team, UCLA's baseball team wasn't very good. But Jackie Robinson was not destined to be a star baseball player for the Bruins. After making the team and earning the position of starting shortstop, he struggled.

The highlight of his season came in a 6–4 win over Los Angeles City College. Robinson collected four hits and used his speed to steal four bases. One of those steals is noteworthy, for it provides a glimpse of the kind of player he would eventually become.

Midway through the game, Robinson banged out a hit and then made his way to third base. As the next batter stepped in and the pitcher began his windup, Jackie took his lead and faked a dash to home.

The opposing pitcher glanced over at him and

forced Jackie to move back. Then he prepared for his pitch. It never crossed his mind that Robinson would actually try one of the rarest and most exciting plays in the game — a steal of home.

But Jackie was determined to do whatever he needed to do to help his team win. Over and over, he danced off the base, all the while timing the pitcher's windup. Finally, he was ready. The hurler toed the rubber and reared back for his windup. Robinson took off.

When the catcher realized what was happening, he yelled to the pitcher. The pitcher rushed through his windup to fire the ball to the plate. Jackie was already beginning his slide, twisting away from the catcher and reaching his right leg out to home plate. As the dust settled, the umpire threw his hands out and yelled, "Safe!" Jackie Robinson had stolen home! The crowd buzzed with excitement.

It was a great start to his career. The local press, already aware of his exploits on the football field and basketball court, predicted that Robinson would soon be a star baseball player as well. But things didn't work out that way at first.

When the Bruins began playing in the California

Collegiate Baseball Association, their opponents included powerhouses like Saint Mary's, Santa Clara, and Stanford. Robinson found those teams much tougher than Los Angeles City College. He had trouble getting hits. And since he wasn't reaching base, he had few opportunities to use his greatest weapon, his speed. He also struggled in the field, making a series of errors. For the first time in his life, Robinson couldn't seem to play the sport.

The Bruins finished the year with a disappointing 6–9 record. Robinson had only one more good game, an exhibition game against a team from a Marine base in San Diego. Frustrated by his failure to get base hits, Robinson bunted the ball three straight times and managed to beat the throws to first for base hits.

Despite that performance, his record for the season was dismal. He made ten errors, scored only nine runs, and knocked in only one. In sixty-two at bats, he collected only six hits, for a batting average of .097.

At the end of the season, he rejoined the track team as promised. There he had much better success, winning the league and NCAA titles in the broad jump. And he found time to compete in other sports as well, earning the league title in golf and a national Negro tennis tournament and earning a reputation as the best table tennis player at UCLA.

In short, despite his failure on the baseball diamond, he was still one of the greatest all-around athletes in college sports at the time. He earned varsity letters in football, basketball, baseball, and track, becoming the first athlete in UCLA history to letter in all four sports during the same year. Already some people were calling him the best all-around collegiate athlete since the great Native American Jim Thorpe. Thorpe had been a multisport star at the Carlisle Institute before winning the decathlon championship at the 1912 Olympics. Later, he had played both pro football and major-league baseball.

Jackie also found fulfillment off the diamond. A mutual friend introduced Robinson to a quiet, serious young African American nursing student named Rachel Isum. At first Rachel wasn't interested in Jackie. She knew that he was a big sports star and assumed that he was stuck-up. But when the two began to talk, she learned that away from the playing fields he was quiet, thoughtful, and gentle. Jackie and

Rachel started dating at UCLA and would remain together for the rest of their lives.

Jackie looked forward to his next year at UCLA, but he would not enjoy the same success as in his first year. Kenny Washington had graduated, and now UCLA's football opponents quickly learned that if they could stop Jackie Robinson, they could stop UCLA. Every time he touched the ball, it seemed as if the entire defense were waiting for him. Despite making two long scoring runs of more than 60 yards, his rushing average plunged from 12 yards per carry to just over 3 yards. He was most effective in the open field, returning punts, where he led the nation with an average of 21 yards gained per return. UCLA finished the season with only one victory in ten games.

Robinson and the Bruins were a little more successful on the basketball court. Although Robinson averaged more than 12 points a game, the team finished with a 6–20 record.

Robinson's frustrations were not limited to athletics, however. He had become increasingly aware of and sensitive to the plight of African Americans.

Although he encountered little direct prejudice at UCLA, he realized people treated him better than most blacks because he was a well-known athlete. He'd heard from African American friends who had graduated that even with a college degree, it was almost impossible to find a good job. Most employers preferred to hire a white man even if an African American candidate was more qualified.

That reality plus other considerations made Jackie begin to question his reasons for staying in school. He couldn't help feeling guilty that his family worked so hard to make ends meet and provide him with money while he spent most of his time playing sports. By the spring of 1941, Jackie had decided his education wasn't worth such hardships. As he later wrote, "I was convinced that no amount of education would help a black man get a job. I could see no real future in staying at college and no real future in athletics."

Professional sports, at least on the major-league level, simply weren't an option. The National Football League was struggling to survive, and only a handful of African Americans had ever been allowed to play in the league. The National Basketball Association didn't even exist. The Olympics had been canceled due to World War II. Major-league baseball wasn't an option for any African American. Even if it had been, Jackie's disappointing performance at UCLA did not mark him as a likely candidate for the diamond.

In the spring of 1941, Jackie's background as a physical education major led to a job offer from the National Youth Administration (NYA), a government-sponsored camp program designed to help impoverished or troubled children. It was looking for qualified counselors. Jackie accepted the job and quit school.

At age twenty-one, his athletic career seemed over.

★ CHAPTER THREE ★

1941–1945

G.I. Jackie

Jackie Robinson left UCLA and moved to the NYA camp in Atascadero, a town midway between Los Angeles and San Francisco. His new life was a far cry from the one he had led at UCLA, but he enjoyed working with the kids, and he played on the camp baseball team. Then in midsummer the program was abruptly canceled, and Jackie Robinson found himself unemployed.

Fortunately, some people still remembered him as a football star. He received an invitation to play for the College All-Star team in an exhibition against the NFL champion Chicago Bears in Chicago. Although he wouldn't be paid, he would receive three weeks of free room and board. That was enough for Jackie. He was still in great shape, even though he hadn't played football in more than six months. Although the collegians lost to the Bears, 37–13, Robinson played well and caught a touchdown pass.

After the game, he was invited to play football for the semipro Los Angeles Bulldogs of the Pacific Coast Professional Football League. Unlike the NFL, the league was integrated — in fact, his former teammate Kenny Washington played for the team. Jackie accepted their offer of $100 per game plus a job during the week.

Just as the season was about to begin, the team relocated to Hawaii. Jackie followed them there and finished the season. Then, before he could figure out what to do next with his life, world events intervened to make the decision for him.

Two years earlier, war had broken out in Europe. By late 1941, nearly every major world power except the United States was involved. Then, on December 7, 1941, the Japanese bombed Pearl Harbor in Hawaii. In response, the United States entered World War II.

Before the bombing of Pearl Harbor, Jackie had a deferment from the draft because he was considered the sole supporter of his mother. But now that the United States was at war, he could be called for duty at any time.

That winter he made pocket money playing semi-pro basketball for the Los Angeles Red Devils. He wanted to get a coaching job, but there were few opportunities for African Americans. With little else to do, he spent much of his time in Pasadena, playing sandlot baseball and softball. His prowess on the diamond earned him an invitation to play in an exhibition game against a barnstorming, or traveling, team of white major leaguers.

It may be that someone in the major leagues saw something in Robinson during that game. On March 22, 1942, the Chicago White Sox held spring training at Brookside Park. Under circumstances that to this day are not precisely clear, the White Sox agreed to give Jackie and another African American, pitcher Nate Moreland, a tryout for the team.

Robinson performed well at the tryout. White Sox manager Jimmy Dykes, who remembered Jackie from the exhibition game years before, said, "Personally, I would welcome Negro players on the White Sox."

adding that if Robinson were white, he would be worth a $50,000 bonus. But Dykes didn't have the authority to sign Robinson. Besides, despite the tryouts, the major leagues remained closed to African Americans. Still, those tryouts were the first time ever that African Americans had been allowed to demonstrate their abilities for a major-league team.

Soon after, Robinson was ordered to join the army. On April 3, he was sent to Kansas for basic training.

At the time, the United States military was segregated, meaning African American soldiers were assigned to their own units. Jackie was in the cavalry division. He hoped that his years of college would help him get into Officer Candidate School (OCS), but he was rejected because of his color.

As it turned out, however, heavyweight boxing champion Joe Louis, an African American, was assigned to the same camp. Robinson told him of his plight. Louis used his influence to arrange for Robinson to attend OCS, where he was soon named a morale officer, in charge of keeping the soldiers in good spirits.

Yet Jackie had trouble keeping his own spirits high in the midst of the racism that surrounded him.

In the summer of 1943, he tried to join the camp baseball team, which already included two major leaguers, Pee Wee Reese and Dixie Walker of the Brooklyn Dodgers. He showed up at practice one day, only to be turned away by another officer, who told him he would have to play for the "colored team." When he asked about the colored team, he was told there was no such team.

Another racial incident occurred later that fall. At that time, many military bases around the country were forming football teams. The teams would play one another to entertain the troops. The base commanders took the competition very seriously — so seriously, in fact, that they were willing to play an African American like Jackie Robinson.

At first, Jackie agreed to join the team. But then his superiors told him that he would be left behind when they played in the South. Humiliated again, Jackie quit.

He was quickly developing a reputation in the army as a troublemaker — that is, an African American soldier who wouldn't be pushed around. In retribution for his behavior, Jackie was assigned to an African American tank battalion and sent to Camp

Hood (later known as Fort Hood), Texas, usually the last stop for soldiers before being sent overseas.

In Texas, Jackie continued to resist the racism that was so pronounced in the military. On June 6, 1944, he got on a bus at Camp Hood. On base, buses were still segregated. African Americans were supposed to sit in the back and were not allowed to share seats with white passengers. When Jackie boarded, he sat next to a light-skinned African American woman, the wife of one of Robinson's fellow officers.

The bus driver slammed the bus to a stop. He thought the woman was white and ordered Jackie to move.

Jackie refused. Then the driver ordered him off the bus. Again Jackie refused. He didn't tell the driver that his seatmate was African American. It was the principle of the matter that caused Jackie to resist.

The bus driver returned the bus to the depot, where Jackie Robinson was arrested for insubordination. The army decided to court-martial him.

Word of his arrest reached the African American press. Robinson, because of his athletic career at UCLA, was already well known throughout the African

American community. Newspapers started publishing outraged articles about the incident.

When Robinson's white battalion commander refused to pursue the court-martial, the army transferred Robinson to another battalion whose commander would press charges.

But as the outcry from the press grew louder, the army became embarrassed. Before long, they wanted nothing more than for the incident — and Robinson — to disappear. But they couldn't just drop the charges. Finally, a military official looked at Jackie's medical records and noticed the broken ankle he had suffered at PJC. All of a sudden, the army decided that the ankle made Jackie unfit for military service. In November he received an honorable discharge due to "physical disqualification." He was out of the military, but he was also out of a job.

Football season was already over, so he didn't have the opportunity to join a semipro team. Semipro basketball didn't pay enough for Robinson to live on. So Jackie began thinking about baseball. He already knew several Negro League players. Although Robinson hadn't played much baseball since leaving UCLA, his battle with the army had made him well known throughout the African American community. That helped earn him an invitation to try out for the Negro League's Kansas City Monarchs in March of 1945.

The Monarchs were one of the best teams in the Negro League. Their roster included the most famous African American player in America, pitcher Satchel Paige. Fortunately for Jackie, so many experienced players had entered the military that the Monarchs were in need of new talent. He made the squad. He never imagined what a turning point it would prove to be, not just in his own life but also for all Americans.

✦ CHAPTER FOUR ✦

1945

Trials and a Tryout

When Jackie Robinson first joined the Monarchs, he hadn't played a serious game of baseball since leaving UCLA. No one, including Robinson himself, knew if he would become a good baseball player.

That spring, the Monarchs played a number of exhibition games against local teams. Robinson played shortstop. He had a good glove and was a speedy runner and an adept bunter, but he struggled to hit for power and his arm was weak. Although he didn't earn a position in the starting lineup, he was a solid utility infielder. In addition, his name was so well known that he drew crowds wherever he played.

Then Jackie Robinson got lucky. First, Monarchs starting shortstop Jesse Williams was sidelined with a sore arm. Robinson took Williams's place on the field, earning valuable playing time. Soon after this, Robinson received the opportunity of a lifetime.

There had always been men and women of courage and conviction who fought to break down the barriers that prevented African Americans from taking their rightful place in society. With World War II nearly over, some of these activists were beginning to question how the United States could ask a man to risk his life for his country, as thousands of African Americans did, and then deny him the rights that most white Americans took for granted. Pressure increased to end what were known as Jim Crow practices in the workplace, regulations that prevented African Americans from getting certain jobs. Some progressive members of Congress were pushing for fair employment legislation that would make it illegal to deny anyone a job due to race.

The African American media had been arguing for these changes for years. Now, some white politicians, activists, and journalists joined their fight. Sportwriters, too, began to speak out against segregation. Dave Egan of the *Boston Record* and Jimmy Cannon of the *New York Mirror* wrote that African

Americans deserved the right to play in the major leagues.

In Boston, a city councilman named Isadore Muchnick agreed. Each year, the National League Boston Braves and the American League Red Sox needed permission from the Boston city council to play baseball on Sunday. Normally, this was granted without debate. But Muchnick told both teams he would block the agreement unless they agreed to hold a tryout for African American players.

Both teams resisted. The Red Sox even told Muchnick that African Americans were welcome to try out for the Red Sox, but "none had ever asked to try out."

Then sports editor Wendell Smith of the *Pittsburgh Courier,* an influential African American newspaper, told Muchnick that he could provide three players. Outfielder Sam Jethroe had led the Negro American League in hitting in 1944 with a .353 average. Second baseman Marvin Williams had hit .338 in the Negro National League. Jackie Robinson was the third player.

Even though Robinson had played only a handful

of games in the Negro League, he was well known throughout the nation. He had not only the physical skills to succeed, Smith believed, but also the social skills to survive as the first African American player in professional baseball.

In mid-April the three players traveled with Smith to Boston. On April 16, Robinson, Jethroe, and Williams worked out for a handful of Red Sox coaches, including manager Joe Cronin. They all performed well, but no one more so than Jackie Robinson. He later recalled that he hit the ball "good to all fields." Muchnick saw the tryout, too. "You never saw anyone hit the wall the way Robinson did that day," he later reported.

But after an hour or so, a voice rang out over the field at Fenway Park: "Get those niggers off the field!" No one has ever been able to identify the speaker, long rumored to have been either Boston Red Sox owner Thomas Yawkey or general manager Eddie Collins. Some have even questioned whether the incident took place. Jackie Robinson himself never mentioned it and rarely talked about the tryout later.

Robinson said he never got the impression that

the ball club intended to sign any of them to a contract. Yet the tryout was important, for it increased pressure on the major leagues to lift the color barrier. Then, in 1944, one man led the charge that finally broke through.

Branch Rickey was president and general manager of the Brooklyn Dodgers. Decades before, Rickey had served as baseball coach at Ohio Wesleyan College. One of his players, an African American named Charlie Thomas, had been refused a room at the team hotel. "That scene haunted me for many years," said Rickey later, "and I vowed that I would always do whatever I could to see that other Americans didn't have to face the bitter humiliation that was heaped upon Charlie Thomas."

Now, nearly forty years after the incident, Rickey was finally in a position where he could make a difference.

The Brooklyn Dodgers had long been the laughingstock of the National League. Of the three New York teams, which also included the Yankees and the Giants, the Dodgers were the least successful. If they were ever to compete with these rival teams, the Dodgers needed an edge.

Branch Rickey's feelings about racism and his need to improve his ball club coincided with the social pressures to change major league baseball. Rickey quietly began making plans to sign an African American player to the Dodgers. It was not only the right thing to do, he felt, but also what was necessary to make the Dodgers a better team.

Rickey first learned of Jackie Robinson through Wendell Smith and his colleagues. He knew that the first African American ballplayer would have to be not only a great player but also a great person, for he would be under tremendous pressure and certain to face ugly episodes of racism. He sent scouts to see if Robinson was that player.

The scouts came home impressed with Robinson's athletic skills. Additional background checks on his personal character showed him to be strong-minded, controlled, and intelligent. When Rickey heard the scouts' reports, he felt certain he had found his player.

In August, scout Clyde Sukeforth met one-on-one with Robinson. He didn't tell Robinson of Rickey's true plans, saying instead that the Dodgers manager was thinking about creating a Negro League team. Soon after, he asked Robinson to accompany him to Brooklyn to meet with Rickey. On August 28, 1945, Robinson and Rickey met for the first time.

Robinson expected Rickey to quiz him about his baseball career, but Rickey surprised him by peppering him with questions about his personal life. Then Rickey asked Robinson if he knew why he had been asked to come to Brooklyn.

Robinson said he assumed Rickey wanted him to play for his new Negro League team. Rickey told him he was wrong. What he wanted, he said, was to sign Robinson to play for the Brooklyn Dodgers.

Robinson was stunned. He knew that he was being offered an extraordinary opportunity. But he also knew that if he took it and failed, it might be years before another African American would receive such a chance. If he succeeded, however, if he could prove on the baseball field that African Americans were equal in ability to white Americans, he could advance the cause of civil rights in a way no other action had before.

Rickey, meanwhile, wanted to make certain that

Robinson knew what he would be up against if he accepted the offer. He began to act out various situations Robinson might face, calling Robinson every racial slur he could think of and trying to goad him into a fight.

Robinson was puzzled. "Mr. Rickey, what do you want?" he asked. "Do you want a player who is afraid to fight back?"

Rickey replied, "I want a ballplayer with the guts *not* to fight back!" He then described a situation in which a ballplayer slid into Robinson with his spikes high, hurling racial epithets and throwing a punch at Robinson's face.

His voice booming with emotion, Rickey asked, "What do you do now, Jackie? What do you do now?"

Robinson understood. "I get it, Mr. Rickey," he said. "I've got another cheek."

That was precisely the kind of response Rickey had hoped for. He pushed a contract across the table, promising Robinson a $3,500 bonus and a salary of $600 a month to play the 1946 season for the Montreal Royals, the Dodgers' top farm club. If he accepted the deal, Robinson would become the first

African American in more than sixty years to play baseball outside the Negro Leagues. If he succeeded in Montreal, he would then have a chance to play for Brooklyn in the major leagues.

A great experiment was about to begin.

⋆ CHAPTER FIVE ⋆

1945–1946

A Royal Beginning

When Jackie Robinson walked out of the Dodgers' office, he could scarcely believe what had just happened. And the only person he could tell was Rachel! Rickey made him promise to keep his plans a secret, for the Dodgers president knew there were still significant obstacles to overcome before Jackie could even step onto the playing field. So Robinson joined the Monarchs, finishing the season with a .387 batting average.

Rickey made Robinson's signing public on October 23, 1945. Robinson traveled to Montreal and was introduced at a press conference.

News of the deal sent baseball reporters scrambling. There was immediate speculation that Rickey would bring Robinson to the major leagues, but the Dodgers president downplayed that scenario. Robinson still had to prove himself in the minors.

Meanwhile, neither the major-league owners nor baseball commissioner Albert "Happy" Chandler commented publicly on the event. For the time being, they considered it a minor-league matter.

In November, Robinson traveled to Venezuela for a barnstorming trip with other Negro Leaguers. Most of the other players wanted him to succeed, although a few wondered why Robinson, of all the players in Negro League baseball, had been selected to test the color line.

While Robinson honed his skills in South America, Branch Rickey signed another Negro League player, pitcher John Wright. Wright wasn't much of a prospect, but Rickey didn't want Robinson to be the only African American at spring training with the Royals. He later signed three more Negro Leaguers, pitchers Don Newcombe and Roy Partlow and catcher Roy Campanella, to minor-league contracts.

When Robinson returned to the United States, he married Rachel. He was in love and realized that he needed and wanted her strength and support in the days ahead.

Robinson was told to report to the Dodgers' minor-league training camp in Sanford, Florida, on March 3.

Before he arrived, Rickey warned all 150 players in the Dodgers' minor-league system that he wanted no trouble. He told Montreal manager Clay Hopper the same thing. Hopper, a native of Mississippi, was very narrow-minded about racial issues. But he realized that if he didn't give Robinson a fair chance, he could be out of a job.

The residents of Sanford were not as cooperative. They didn't approve of black men and white men playing baseball together. Only two days after Robinson arrived at spring training, they forced the Royals to move their camp to an African American section of nearby Daytona Beach.

Robinson got off to a slow start. He didn't throw well enough to play shortstop and was shifted to second base. But he still played poorly. Many of his white teammates whispered to one another that if Robinson were white, he wouldn't even have made the team.

It wasn't until the end of spring training that Robinson finally performed up to expectations. In the club's last exhibition game against the major-league Dodgers, he had two hits and a stolen base, and he played second base perfectly. Thanks to this game, he earned a spot in Montreal's starting lineup.

Yet most of his teammates held him at a distance. While no one was openly hostile to him, few had ever been around an African American. They were unsure of how to behave. After every practice, Robinson left the ballpark alone.

The club traveled to New Jersey for the first game of the International League season against the Jersey City Giants. The stands were packed to over-flowing with more than twenty-five thousand specta-tors, the vast majority of them white and curious to see Robinson play. No one who attended the game has ever forgotten the experience.

Robinson's day started quietly. He grounded out his first at bat. In the second inning the Royals scored twice. Robinson came to bat with two men on base. Jersey City pitcher Warren Sandel didn't want to be the first pitcher to give up a hit to Robinson. Unfortunately, he didn't get his wish. On the first pitch, Robinson swung. *Crack!* The ball shot off the bat toward left field and soared into the stands for a home run!

The crowd erupted with cheers. With that homer, Robinson had won them over.

Robinson ran around the bases, too excited

to jog. He wasn't sure how manager Clay Hopper, coaching third base, would react, but Hopper slapped him on the back as he would have any other ball-player. In fact, the manager would soon become one of Robinson's biggest supporters.

According to baseball tradition, a batter who homers is greeted with a handshake by the next hitter. Robinson didn't know whether George Shuba would shake the hand of an African American. But as Robinson reached home, Shuba held out his hand for Jackie to shake. Incredibly, it was the first time in the modern history of baseball that a white hand had clasped a black hand to offer congratulations. Moments later, his teammates crowded around him, patting him on the back and shaking his hand. Although a few would continue to treat him distantly, the vast majority had been won over.

Robinson's first day got even better. In his next at bat, he unveiled his greatest asset, his speed. He dropped a bunt and beat it out for a base hit. Then he stole second. When the next batter hit a ground ball to third, Robinson acted as if he were returning to second base. But as the third baseman threw to first, Robinson turned around and dashed to third, beating a return throw from the first baseman. Now he was only 90 feet from home plate.

As the pitcher took the stretch position, Robinson danced off base. Three times the pitcher threw to third, and three times Robinson scrambled back in time. But after each throw, he stretched his lead out a little more.

Then, midway through his motion on his fourth pitch attempt, the pitcher thought he saw Robinson break for the plate. He stopped his motion. The umpire immediately threw up his hands. Once a pitcher starts to throw a pitch, he is not allowed to stop. But Robinson had rattled him so badly, he had done just that. The umpire called a balk — an illegal motion by the pitcher — and Robinson cruised on home.

The Jersey City crowd went wild. For this day at least, Robinson was their hero. And the day wasn't over yet.

Robinson played the rest of the game as if he were taking out the frustration of every Negro League player who had ever been denied the chance to play organized baseball. In the seventh inning, he singled, stole second base again, and scored on a hit. And in the eighth inning, he reached base on another bunt. The next batter hit a ground ball. As the throw to first base got the batter out, Robinson ran to second — and kept going. He beat the throw to third, advancing two bases on a ground ball out!

The Jersey City players were completely rattled. Once more Robinson bluffed a dash toward home and caused the pitcher to balk.

Not even Hollywood could have imagined a better beginning to Robinson's career. In five at bats, he had collected four hits, scored four runs, knocked in three, stolen two bases, and forced two balk calls. One Montreal sportswriter was so impressed by the performance, he described it as equal to "another Emancipation Day for the Negro race."

Of course, Robinson couldn't play quite so well in every game — no player could. And neither would he always be welcomed as he had been in Jersey City. In nearly every city he played, there were racial incidents of one kind or another. A player for the Newark Bears asked to be sent to another league rather than play against Robinson. In Syracuse, fans taunted Robinson mercilessly, and someone let a black cat onto the field. Pitchers threw at Robinson's head, and base runners slid into him roughly.

Robinson was facing precisely the kind of behavior that Branch Rickey had foreseen.

But Robinson kept turning the other cheek. Although it was never easy for him, he tried to put all his energy into his play on the field.

Fortunately, in the Royals' home city of Montreal, Robinson was welcomed by French-Canadian fans. African Americans were accepted in Montreal as they were not in many cities of the United States. Jackie and Rachel, now expecting their first child, felt comfortable setting up a home there.

By midseason, Jackie was leading the league in hitting and stealing bases at will. The Royals finished the regular season in first place, with a record of 100–54, eighteen and a half games ahead of second-place Syracuse. Robinson led the league with a .349 batting average and 113 runs scored.

In the playoffs, the Royals dumped both Newark and Syracuse to win the International League. The victory earned the team the right to play American Association champion Louisville in the Little World Series.

Before the first game even took place, Robinson was the story of the series. No African American had ever played baseball in Louisville before. When the first game started, the overwhelmingly white crowd greeted Robinson with boos and racially charged jeers. The Louisville Colonels took two of the first three games.

Montreal sportswriters let their home fans know just how poorly Jackie Robinson had been treated in Louisville. When he took the field in Montreal for game four, local fans came out in droves to show him their support. Every time Robinson showed his face or touched the ball, they cheered wildly. The game entered extra innings, and Robinson thanked the crowd for their support by knocking out the winning hit.

The victory tied the series. In game five Robinson scored the go-ahead run after slugging a triple and secured the win with a squeeze bunt in the ninth. Then he knocked out two hits in game six. Montreal won to capture the minor-league championship.

After the last game, the crowd refused to leave. They poured out onto the field, chanting, "We want Robinson," in English and singing in French, "*Il a gagné ses épaulettes* [He has won his spurs]."

They refused to leave until Robinson made an appearance.

As soon as he emerged from the dugout, they swarmed over him. He attempted to leave the park, only to find his way blocked by thousands of joyous fans. Police were powerless to keep the people at bay. Robinson finally broke away — and started running, pursued by hundreds of fans. After three blocks, a stranger pulled alongside Robinson in a car, motioned for him to get in, and drove him home.

Reporter Sam Maltin of the *Pittsburgh Courier* watched the entire scene. He wrote later of the behavior of the Montreal fans: "To the large group of Louisville fans who came here with their team, it may be a lesson of goodwill among men. That it's the man and not his color, race or creed. They couldn't fail to tell others down South of the riots, of the chasing of a Negro — not because of hate, but because of love."

Soon, the entire nation would hear the same message.

★ CHAPTER SIX ★

1947

The First

Robinson's first season with Montreal made it clear that he was ready for the major leagues. As Sam Maltin wrote at the end of the year, "He's strictly Brooklyn. He never belonged in this league."

Robinson remained busy in the off-season. He went on tour with an all-black team, and in January he and Rachel celebrated the birth of their first child, Jackie Jr.

Meanwhile, Branch Rickey was working to bring Robinson up to the Dodgers. To help the transition, he decided to hold spring training for the Royals in Cuba, far from the segregation and limelight of Florida. Then, at a secret meeting of all sixteen major-league owners in January of 1947, he announced his plan to promote Jackie Robinson to the Dodgers. He spoke for a long time, hoping to convince the others to support him publicly and abandon their decade's-old "gentlemen's agreement" that barred African Americans from the major leagues.

After he finished speaking, every other owner declared his opposition. Then Rickey asked for a secret vote. He hoped that some owners actually supported his plan and would show their support in a secret ballot. But the vote against Robinson remained fifteen to one. Rickey left the meeting not knowing how he could possibly bring Robinson into the major leagues.

A few days later Rickey asked to meet with baseball commissioner Happy Chandler. Although Chandler had attended the meeting in New York, he had remained silent. Rickey hoped the commissioner would support him.

Once again, Rickey argued for Robinson's promotion. He told Chandler that it was the moral thing to do, and that if baseball didn't allow Robinson to play, it might even spawn riots in the African American community.

Chandler listened in silence and then spoke. "I'm going to have to meet my Maker someday," said Chandler, a religious man, "and if he asks me why I didn't let this boy play and I say it's because he's black, that might not be a satisfactory answer. So bring him in."

Chandler had realized that since there was no official rule banning African Americans, the vote by the other owners was meaningless. The commissioner told Rickey he would approve Robinson's contract just as he approved hundreds of others each year. In fact, under the written rules of baseball, Chandler concluded that it would be illegal if he did not approve the contract. After all, the "gentlemen's agreement" had never been an official rule. As commissioner of baseball, Chandler was legally responsible only for enforcing the written rules of the game.

With that hurdle out of the way, Rickey's plans began in earnest. The ideal situation would be for Robinson's Brooklyn teammates to see him play and be so impressed that they would ask Rickey to bring him up to Brooklyn. But that hope was naive.

First, there wasn't an open position for Robinson to play. Pee Wee Reese and Eddie Stanky, two established stars, ably filled both shortstop and second base. And while both the third- and first-base jobs were up for grabs, there were already many candidates on the Dodgers roster. Besides, Robinson had very little experience at either position. Still, Rickey had Brooklyn first baseman Howie Schultz secretly tutor Robinson in first-base play.

But little went according to plan. Some Dodgers players made it clear that they weren't eager to have Robinson as a teammate and began circulating a petition announcing their opposition to him. Brooklyn manager Leo Durocher learned of the ploy in the middle of the night. He roused his players from their sleep and ordered them to meet with him in the kitchen of the team hotel.

Durocher was blunt. "If the old man [Rickey] wants him to play, then he's going to play." The players who opposed Robinson, such as outfielder Dixie Walker and pitcher Kirby Higbe, were told that if they didn't care to play with Robinson, the Dodgers would gladly trade them. The petitioners backed off, although Walker did let the Dodgers know that he preferred to be traded rather than play with Robinson.

Then the front offices of the Dodgers and Yankees started bickering. Yankee general manager Larry MacPhail took offense at a newspaper column written by Leo Durocher that suggested that Mac-Phail was friends with gamblers. MacPhail demanded that commissioner Chandler take action. Just before the start of the season, Chandler shocked the Dodgers when he suspended Durocher for the season for "conduct detrimental to baseball." Coach Clyde Sukeforth temporarily took over.

In early April, the Dodgers were still working to put together their team. They continued to shift Robinson from first to second base. They also had another new player to worry about, African American catcher Roy Campanella.

Things were not yet settled when both players took the field in Brooklyn wearing the uniform of the Royals. Before the game, Rickey told Robinson it would be his last game in a Montreal uniform. Robinson told no one and tried to concentrate on the game at hand.

In the sixth inning, with a man on first base, Robinson tried to bunt the runner over to second base. But he made a rare mistake and bunted the ball directly back at the pitcher, who was able to start a double play.

As Robinson jogged back to the dugout, he was

surprised to see his Montreal teammates giving him a standing ovation. They met him at the dugout and swept him up in their arms.

Only then did Jackie Robinson learn what had happened. Branch Rickey had released a brief statement that read, "The Brooklyn Dodgers today purchased the contract of Jack Roosevelt Robinson from the Montreal Royals. He will report immediately."

Those two sentences are perhaps the most important in the history of major-league baseball. An African American would finally play in the major leagues.

Robinson had precious little time to celebrate. On April 11 the Dodgers began a three-game exhibition series with the Yankees. Then the regular season would start.

Prior to the first game, Robinson moved his gear from the visitors' clubhouse to the Dodgers' locker room in Ebbets Field. When he first entered the locker room, he was both afraid and nervous. He was confident of his athletic ability, but he knew that the real challenges would come when he first faced his teammates in the locker room and the fans and opposing players on the field. Although he knew many of the Dodgers players by sight, there wasn't a man on the team whom he considered a friend. Whereas the other Dodgers expected support from one another when they struggled, Robinson knew that he would have to earn his teammates' respect.

He also knew that if he didn't succeed on the field, it might be years before another African American received a chance to play in the majors. With that in mind, he was determined to live up to his promise to Branch Rickey to turn the other cheek, no matter how angry he became or how uncomfortable he was made to feel. Failure to succeed — in any way — simply was not an option.

The Dodgers won only one of the three games versus the Yankees. Crowds at both Ebbets Field and Yankee Stadium were understandably curious, but they treated Robinson relatively well. Robinson played first base, and although he wasn't the big star in any of the three contests, he played decent games. With the exhibition games behind him, it was time to step up to the plate for the real thing.

Robinson made his debut on April 15 at Ebbets Field in Brooklyn against the Boston Braves. The crowd was large, but there were still several thousand

Jackie Robinson, the man who broke baseball's color barrier, poses in his Montreal Royals uniform on April 18, 1946.

AP/Wide World Photos

After rounding the bases in a game in 1946, Jackie Robinson is congratulated by teammate George Shuba. The handshake is significant because few white players were willing to accept Robinson—yet.

April 10, 1947: Jackie Robinson signs the contract that made him a Brooklyn Dodger—and a historic figure as the first black player in the major league.

After a long, hard year, Robinson takes his place among his teammates, winners of the 1947 National League pennant.

The winner of the 1949 National League MVP award at home with his trophies.

AP/Wide World Photos

Hoping to break up a double play, Dick Sisler of the Phillies slams into Robinson at second base during a National League playoff game. (The Dodgers won, beating out the Phillies to go on to the World Series.)

Speed and smarts combined: Robinson steals home past Yankees catcher Yogi Berra during the 1955 World Series. The Dodgers won the series, their first in club history.

Jackie Robinson poses in his Dodgers uniform prior to the start of the 1956 season—his last.

empty seats. Before the game, some vendors sold buttons outside the park that read, "I'm for Jackie."

Robinson began his career quietly. He went hitless in the Dodgers' 5–3 win. In the Dodgers' second game of the season, he did manage to collect his first hit, a bunt single, but he did little else in Brooklyn's 14–6 victory. After that, he began to relax, cracking a home run in his third game and collecting three hits in the fourth. Then the Philadelphia Phillies came to Brooklyn.

Philadelphia manager Ben Chapman was from the South and an unapologetic racist. He didn't think Robinson should be in the big leagues, and he ordered his team to put the African American to the test; in his words, he wanted them "to see if he [Robinson] could take it."

Although the Dodgers swept the series, the results of the game were secondary to what went on in the dugouts and on the field. The Phillies and their manager kept up a nonstop stream of insults directed Robinson's way. Dodger Howie Schultz later recalled that the things they said were "as bad as you can imagine. If they said those things today, it would cause a Civil War."

Teammate Eddie Stanky had not supported Robinson, but over the course of those three games, even he was offended by the Phillies' behavior. He knew that Robinson was not allowed to retaliate. He became the first Dodger to stand up for Robinson. In the third game, he approached a couple of Phillies players between innings and told them bluntly to "pick on somebody who can fight back."

After the series, National League president Ford Frick ordered the Phillies to stop taunting Robinson. Frick's order may have stopped the Phillies, but opposition to Jackie was growing throughout the league. The Chicago Cubs reportedly voted to go on strike rather than play against him. Frick informed them that if they did, they would be barred from baseball for life. They didn't strike, but one of the Cubs pitchers repeatedly threw at Robinson every time he came to bat.

Fans, too, joined in the attacks. Wherever he played, Robinson was greeted with jeers and insults.

Robinson kept turning the other cheek, but the pressure was getting to him. He wasn't playing as if he belonged in the major leagues anymore. He was hitting barely .200, and since he wasn't getting on base, he was unable to use his speed. Fortunately, the Dodgers got off to a quick start, winning nine of their first twelve games. Otherwise, Robinson may well have been returned to the minor leagues.

In early May, Robinson broke out of his slump. Then the St. Louis Cardinals came to town. Like the Cubs, the Cardinals appeared ready to go on strike rather than play against Robinson. Once again, Ford Frick stepped in. According to *New York Herald Tribune* writer Stanley Woodward, Frick told the Cardinals players, "I don't care if half the league strikes . . . All will be suspended, and I don't care if it wrecks the National League for five years." The Cardinals backed off.

But the other teams kept trying to intimidate Robinson. When he traveled with the Dodgers to Philadelphia, the Philadelphia ballplayers tried a new tactic to distract Robinson. They obeyed Frick's order not to taunt him, but a number of players still made their feelings very clear. Whenever Robinson came to bat or took the field, they held their bats as if they were rifles and pointed them in his direction.

After that series, the Dodgers traveled to Cincinnati. Robinson received so many death threats that the FBI searched rooftops near the ballpark for snipers. In the locker room, manager Burt Shotton told the other Dodgers of the threats. Outfielder Gene Hermanski broke the tension when he suggested, "Why don't we all wear the same number — forty-two?" in an attempt to confuse a potential sniper. Everyone laughed.

Robinson's teammates were beginning to understand what he was going through and to appreciate the strength of his character. Also, after their quick start, the Dodgers were stumbling, and they knew that if they were going to win the pennant, they needed Jackie Robinson's help. They began to view him not as an African American but as a teammate. And, ever so slowly, some began to regard him as a friend.

When the Dodgers returned home after their first road trip, things began to settle down. The crowd at Ebbets Field was still on Robinson's side and greeted him warmly. He and Rachel and their young son moved from a hotel into an apartment in Brooklyn, where they were welcomed by their neighbors.

So far, Robinson had faced everything the opposition could throw at him and had survived. Now it was time for him to show them that he truly belonged in the major leagues.

In June, Robinson began to heat up. He channeled his anger and frustration into his play on the field. When an opposing pitcher threw at him, Robinson usually made him pay by knocking a base hit. In fact, he collected a base hit in twenty consecutive games, lifting his batting average to above .300. His hot streak helped the Dodgers pull into first place.

On July 3, Robinson learned that his trials were not in vain. Owner Bill Veeck of the Cleveland Indians signed Negro League infielder Larry Doby. Thanks to Robinson's cool head and hot bat, the major leagues were starting to open their doors to African Americans.

In the second half of the season, the Dodgers took command of the pennant race, and Robinson demonstrated that he was one of the best players in baseball. His bat stayed hot, and he began to take liberties on the base paths, stealing and taking extra bases whenever possible. For opposing pitchers, the most frightening sight in baseball was Jackie Robinson on base, then dancing down the base path.

In September, *The Sporting News*, the most influential baseball publication in the country, named Robinson major-league baseball's Rookie of the Year. When the Dodgers returned home from a road trip a few days later, thousands of fans met the team at New York's Pennsylvania Station. In a scene that reminded many of what had taken place in Montreal the year before, police officers had to help Robinson make his way through the crowd of adoring Brooklyn fans.

The Dodgers clinched the pennant on September 22. The next day, the club celebrated "Jackie Robinson Day" at Ebbets Field. Robinson received an automobile, a television, and other gifts from appreciative fans.

He finished the regular season with a .297 batting average and led the league with 125 runs scored and twenty-seven stolen bases. Furthermore, with his twelve home runs, he was tied for the most on the team, and he finished fifth in the balloting for league MVP.

But the biggest challenge was still to come. The Dodgers faced the heavily favored New York Yankees in the World Series.

Robinson introduced himself to the Yankees in his first at bat. With one out, Robinson singled. Then he stole second. When teammate Pete Reiser tapped back to the pitcher, Robinson got caught in a run-down that went on long enough for Reiser to reach second. Robinson was out, but moments later Reiser scored on a single to put the Dodgers ahead.

Robinson was the Dodgers' most dangerous player throughout the series, leading the team in hits. But the Yankees were still the Yankees. They defeated Brooklyn in seven hard-fought games.

Although the Dodgers fell one victory short of a world championship, in every other way the season had been a success. The team had won the pennant, and Robinson had proven that not only could an African American ballplayer succeed in the major leagues, he could be a star.

Civil rights leaders began to cite Robinson's example on the baseball field when they argued against Jim Crow policies in other areas of American society.

Millions of Americans came to see that African Americans were deserving of the same rights and privileges as any other American.

Jackie Robinson may have been only the first African American in the major leagues, but in his wake, millions of Americans would eventually have a better life.

✳ CHAPTER SEVEN ✳

1948

Fighting Back

In the months following his first season in the major leagues, Jackie Robinson was busier than he had ever been in his life. He helped Rachel raise Jackie Jr., appeared at dozens of banquets and other speaking engagements, and, with the help of newsman Wendell Smith, wrote his autobiography and agreed to collaborate on a movie based on his life. Although many fans were still against him, Robinson had become one of the most popular players in baseball.

As a result of his involvement in so many activities, Robinson didn't play any baseball in the off-season. He didn't have time for regular workouts either. When he arrived for spring training in 1948, he was fifteen pounds overweight.

Despite reaching the World Series in 1947, Branch Rickey wasn't satisfied with his team. The Dodgers had a great deal of young talent in the minor leagues, and Rickey decided it was time to make room for those players in the majors, even if it kept the Dodgers from winning the pennant in 1948. Rickey traded second baseman Eddie Stanky and moved Robinson from first to second, believing that although Robinson had played well at first, second base would suit him better. Young Gil Hodges would eventually become the new Dodgers first baseman.

Rickey also kept a close eye on two other African American players in the Dodgers' minor-league teams. Catcher Roy Campanella had had a fine season the previous year and was knocking on the door, as was pitcher Don Newcombe.

As Robinson tried to play his way into shape, the Dodgers went on a long barnstorming trip through the South. Rickey hoped the trip would help integrate professional baseball in cities like Dallas, Oklahoma City, and Tulsa.

Robinson agreed with Rickey's goals, but the trips were difficult for him. He usually wasn't allowed to stay in the same hotels as his teammates, and there were still some fans who greeted him with hostility.

Robinson and the Dodgers got off to a slow start in 1948. Jackie found the extra pounds hard to lose, and he and the Dodgers' new players needed time to adjust to their positions. Although Robinson hit over .300 in the first half of the season, he wasn't the same threat on the base paths that he had been in his rookie year.

In late May, the Dodgers were in last place. Then they brought up Roy Campanella and made him their starting catcher. The Dodgers immediately began playing better.

In midseason, they finally rallied to become a threat for first place. Robinson lost his extra weight and in August was once again a terror on the bases. At the end of the month, he enjoyed the greatest day of his brief career. In the first game of a double-header sweep of the Cardinals, Robinson hit for what is called the "cycle," collecting a single, double, triple, and home run in the same game. He also stole a base, scored three runs, and knocked in two others. The two victories pushed the Dodgers into first place, but, unfortunately, they faded in September and finished third.

In every way but the final standings, the season had been a success for Robinson. Statistically, he had nearly equaled his performance in 1947; he had also knocked in nearly twice as many runs. But his real achievement came in the Dodgers clubhouse.

Over his first two seasons, he had developed some real friendships among the Dodgers players. None was more important than his relationship with Dodgers captain Pee Wee Reese.

Reese had been born and raised in Louisville, Kentucky. Growing up, he adopted the same attitudes toward African Americans as most other whites who lived in the South. When Robinson first joined the Dodgers, Reese wasn't certain he liked the idea of having Jackie Robinson as a teammate. He knew that when he returned to Louisville, his old friends would harass him for playing baseball with an African American.

But Reese was the Dodgers' team captain, and he took that responsibility seriously. He quickly saw that Robinson was a great ballplayer and could help the Dodgers win. Over time, he also realized that Robinson was an even better human being. Reese knew that few ballplayers of any color could put up with the horrendous treatment Robinson faced regularly.

Reese began to reach out to Robinson, asking him to play cards on bus and train rides and inviting him to join in trips to the movies and to dinner. Several times during Robinson's first two seasons, when hostile crowds verbally abused Robinson, Reese made a point to stand next to Robinson and place his hand on his back, letting everyone know that Reese considered him a friend as well as a teammate.

Reese and many of the other Dodgers grew as human beings by having Robinson as a teammate. For most of them, Robinson was the first African American they ever knew personally. As they got to know him, they realized that many of their beliefs about African Americans had been incorrect and that apart from the color of his skin, Jackie Robinson was the same as they were. He loved to play baseball and laugh, work hard, and spend time with his family. On the field, no Dodger tried harder to win. Robinson didn't care about his own statistics; he cared only about the score at the end of the game. Off the field he was friendly and compassionate, always ready with a kind word for a teammate in a slump.

Just by playing baseball, Jackie Robinson was teaching Americans that despite differences in culture, upbringing, and race, people are far more alike than they are different. Ever so slowly, fans and players were looking at Jackie Robinson as simply another human being.

❉ CHAPTER EIGHT ❉

1948–1953

The Boys of Summer

After two hard seasons in the major leagues, Jackie Robinson relished the thought of his third season. Although not every team was integrated, most clubs were now signing African American players. As a result, Branch Rickey lifted his restrictions on Jackie Robinson's behavior. He didn't have to "turn the other cheek" anymore. He could just concentrate on playing baseball. As Robinson told a reporter, "They better be rough on me this year, because I'm going to be rough on them."

In the 1948 off-season, Robinson did his best not to repeat the mistakes he had made the previous year. Instead of attending banquets, he took a job at the Harlem YMCA, working with children. He exercised regularly, too, so when he reported to the

Dodgers' new training camp in Vero Beach, Florida, he was in the best shape of his life.

Once again, the Dodgers barnstormed through the South. They drew immense crowds, and although Robinson was still greeted with hostility in some places, in most he was cheered, even by white fans. Children, both black and white, were particularly enthralled with Robinson.

Although the Dodgers started off slowly, two weeks into the season Robinson got hot. He carried Brooklyn with him. In May, batting fourth, known as the "cleanup position," in Brooklyn's potent lineup, he hit over .400 to pull the Dodgers into first place. Pitcher Don Newcombe, who became the Dodgers' third African American player, helped him out. The performances of Robinson, Campanella, and now Newcombe made it clear that by being the first team to integrate, the Dodgers had an edge. Even those teams that would still have preferred to remain all white began to realize that if they didn't soon sign African Americans, they would lose out on some potentially great players.

Meanwhile, Robinson was hitting for average and power, fielding flawlessly, and running strong on the bases. And with Rickey's approval, he was playing aggressively without worrying that it would cause trouble. Now, when he felt he had been wronged, he stood up for himself. If a base runner slid into him with his spikes high, Robinson would return the favor when he ran the bases. When umpires made a call he felt was incorrect, he argued. And players throughout the National League suddenly heard Jackie Robinson's voice from the Brooklyn dugout. He could "apply the needle" to the opposition just as effectively as they had done to him, although without the racial ugliness he himself had faced.

And for the first time Robinson began to speak out publicly about racial issues. When he was asked how he felt about civil rights issues, he made his support crystal clear for those who were fighting for equality. In the second half of the season, the Dodgers and the St. Louis Cardinals battled it out for the pennant. In a more personal race, Robinson and Cardinals outfielder Enos Slaughter fought for the batting title. Neither contest was decided until the final game of the season.

To win the pennant, the Dodgers needed to beat

the Phillies, and to win the batting title, Robinson needed a hit. In the third inning, Robinson took a step toward accomplishing both tasks by singling in the Dodgers' first run, then stealing second, and later scoring to key a five-run Dodgers rally that put them ahead 5–0. Brooklyn held on to win and take the pennant — and Robinson edged Slaughter for the batting title .342 to .336.

Yet once again, the Yankees stood between the Dodgers and a World Series championship. Brooklyn was no more successful in 1949 than they had been in 1947. The Yankees won in five games.

But the off-season provided another measure of progress. A few weeks after the end of the series, the result of the vote for the Most Valuable Player of the National League by the baseball writers was announced. Earlier that year, a sportswriter named Tom Meany had indicated which way he would vote when he asked in his column, "Who would you pick as the most dangerous player in baseball today?" After discussing Boston Red Sox slugger Ted Williams and star outfielder Stan Musial of the Cardinals, Meany concluded, "The most dangerous player in baseball is . . . Jackie Robinson," whom he accurately described as a player who can "beat you in more ways than any other player in the game today." Meany's colleagues apparently agreed, for they selected Robinson as league MVP. Only three short years after reaching the major leagues, Robinson was recognized as one of the best players in the game.

Just after the first of the year, Rachel Robinson gave birth to a daughter, Sharon, and soon afterward, Robinson went to Hollywood to star as himself in the movie version of his life, *The Jackie Robinson Story.* Then it was back to baseball.

The Dodgers appeared primed to repeat as National League champions. The club was a virtual all-star team. In addition to Robinson and Reese, the Dodgers lineup also included sluggers such as centerfielder Duke Snider and first baseman Gil Hodges, and the league's best catcher, Roy Campanella. All but Hodges have since been inducted into the Baseball Hall of Fame.

Although Robinson got off to a great start, 1950 just wasn't the Dodgers' year. In midseason, Dodgers co-owner John Smith died. Branch Rickey and another co-owner, Walter O'Malley, didn't get along and started to wrestle for control of the team. A string of nagging injuries in the second half bothered Robinson, and the Dodgers lost the pennant to the Phillies on the final day of the season.

A few weeks later Branch Rickey decided to sell his portion of the Dodgers to Walter O'Malley. Robinson knew he would miss Rickey. Not only had Rickey been responsible for bringing him to the major leagues, but he had also remained Robinson's strongest advocate and a great friend. Playing for the Dodgers would never be quite the same for Robinson without Rickey around.

Under new manager Charlie Dressen, Robinson and the Dodgers got off to another great start in 1951. By midseason it appeared as if the Dodgers would run away with the pennant. Although the New York Giants had been the pick of many to win the pennant, the Dodgers dominated New York throughout the first half of the season.

The two clubs had been rivals for almost fifty years. Pitchers on both teams often threw at batters on the other team. Robinson was a frequent target, not because of his race, but because the Giants knew that in order to defeat the Dodgers, they had to stop Robinson. As a result, there was nothing Robinson enjoyed more than beating New York.

In one memorable contest in 1951, Giants pitcher Sal Maglie brushed back Robinson several times. Although throwing inside is part of baseball, throwing at a batter's head is dangerous. And Robinson was particularly sensitive about being thrown at. He remembered how often he had been a target when he first entered the league.

Midway through the game, Robinson had had enough of Maglie's treatment. So the next time Maglie threw him a decent pitch, Robinson dropped a bunt down the baseline, forcing the first baseman to field the ball and toss to Maglie at first base. Robinson dashed down the line as fast as he could. Maglie took the throw and tried to step on first base.

Robinson wanted to do more than just make it to first. He wanted to make it clear to Maglie that he was tired of being thrown at. As Maglie stepped toward first, the former football star lowered his shoulder and crashed into Maglie like he was throwing a block on an end run. The pitcher went flying, and the Giants charged from the dugout toward

Robinson. The Dodgers came to his defense, and soon there was a big argument on the field. It took the umpires several minutes to calm things down. Robinson was out, but he had made his point.

By August 13, the first-place Dodgers led the Giants by thirteen and a half games. Dodgers manager Charlie Dressen even pronounced, "The Giants is dead."

Then, all of a sudden, the Dodgers' archrival woke up. For the rest of the season, the Giants played as if they had forgotten how to lose. The Dodgers didn't play badly, but the Giants simply played better. With one day remaining in the regular season, both clubs had identical records of 95–58. Each team had one game left to play.

The Giants played first and beat the Boston Braves 3–2. In order to tie for the pennant and force a playoff game, the Dodgers had to beat Philadelphia.

The Phillies jumped out quickly to take a 6–1 lead. The Giants listened to the game on the radio as they prepared to board a train back to New York. As a few Giants started celebrating the pennant, another teammate cautioned, "Robinson is there — anything can happen."

It did. The Dodgers fought back to tie the the game and send it into extra innings. In the twelfth, the Phillies loaded the bases with two outs. A hit would win the game. First baseman Eddie Waitkus stepped to the plate and belted a screaming line drive up the middle.

Jackie Robinson reacted. He dove to his right, parallel to the ground, and reached out and stabbed at the ball with his glove before crash-landing. But he held onto the ball. Waitkus was out, and the inning was over!

The play knocked the wind out of Robinson. He stayed on the ground for almost a minute, his glove tight around the baseball. Even though the play cost the Phillies a chance to win, the Philadelphia crowd, which only a few years before had treated Robinson poorly, couldn't help but applaud his play.

Two innings later, Robinson came to bat against Philadelphia's ace pitcher, Robin Roberts. Robinson watched the first two balls pass by. On the third pitch, he swung. *Crack!* The sound of the bat meeting the ball echoed through the park. Roberts and the Phillies watched helplessly as the ball rattled into the upper deck in left field to put the Dodgers ahead. Robinson was mobbed by his teammates as he crossed home plate, and when the Phillies went down without scoring, the Dodgers escaped with a 9–8 win, earning the right to play the Giants in a three-game play-off to decide the pennant.

The two teams split the first two games, setting up a one-game showdown at the Polo Grounds. The result was one of the most memorable games in baseball history.

Unfortunately, it didn't go Robinson's way. The Dodgers carried a 4–1 lead into the ninth inning, but the Giants rallied to draw to within two runs. Then, with two out and two on, Giants third baseman Bobby Thomson cracked a home run to win the pennant for the Giants. He ran around the bases, jumping and leaping. Every Dodgers player put his head down and trudged off the field.

Every one except Jackie Robinson, that is. As Thomson toured the bases, Robinson watched him closely, making sure he touched every base.

In the off-season, the Robinson family expanded again when Rachel gave birth to another son, David. Then it was back to baseball.

At first, the Giants looked as if they would run away

with the pennant, but in late May, their star center-fielder, Willie Mays, was drafted into the army. Mays, an African American, was one of the best young players in baseball and an example of the impact integration was having on the game. Without him the Giants struggled, and the Dodgers charged to the pennant. Robinson had another good season, even cracking a home run in the All-Star game.

Once more Brooklyn faced the Yankees in the World Series. Robinson got off to a great start. In the first inning of game one, he put the Dodgers ahead with a home run, and in game three, he scored all the way from second base when a pitch got away from Yankees catcher Yogi Berra. Nevertheless, the Yankees again managed to defeat the Dodgers in seven games. Once more, Brooklyn fans were forced to look forward to next year.

At the start of the 1953 season, it soon became clear that Robinson's career was nearing the end. With each passing year, he had trouble keeping his weight down and arrived at spring training heavy. Meanwhile, rookie second baseman Jim Gilliam was ready for the major leagues. To make room for Gilliam, Robinson moved to third base. If he was disappointed, he didn't let it show. "Whatever is good for the club goes," he said of the lineup change.

Gilliam gave the lineup a spark. Robinson, after starting the season at third, filled in wherever needed, playing every infield position before settling into left field for the remainder of the year. He finished with a .329 batting average, ninety-five RBIs and seventeen stolen bases.

The Dodgers ran away from the league and once again captured the pennant. But despite another terrific series by Robinson, the Yankees again defeated them in the World Series.

Robinson knew that despite his fine performance in 1953, his days as a ballplayer would soon come to an end. After all, he was thirty-four years old. So far, in his seven-year major-league career, he had been Rookie of the Year, an annual All-Star, and league MVP. Arguably, over that time period, he had been one of the greatest players in the game. One cannot help but wonder what he would have achieved had he been able to begin his career years earlier.

But even more important, in the years since he had broken the color barrier, dozens of other African Americans had followed Robinson into the major leagues. On the Dodgers alone, his African American teammates included Campanella, Gilliam, and Newcombe. The Giants were led by outfielders Willie Mays and Monte Irvin. Sam Jethroe, who had tried out with Robinson for the Red Sox in 1945, had reached the major leagues with the Boston Braves. Larry Doby and the great Satchel Paige had starred for the Cleveland Indians. Moreover, many of the teams that continued to resist integration, such as the Boston Red Sox and Detroit Tigers, were starting to pay a price on the field and struggled to remain competitive. Clearly, there was no turning back.

The Dodgers, who had often been the laughing-stock of the major leagues during much of their history, were now considered a powerhouse. But despite winning four pennants since Robinson had joined the team and finishing second twice, in their long history the Dodgers had never won the World Series.

Before his baseball career came to an end, Jackie Robinson was determined to change that.

★ CHAPTER NINE ★

1954–1956

Champions

Dodgers team owner Walter O'Malley surprised everyone in 1954 when he replaced manager Charlie Dressen with Walt Alston. Alston, who had long served the team as a minor-league manager, sized up his new squad. Every player in the heart of the Dodgers lineup — Robinson, Reese, Hodges, Campanella, and Snider — was over thirty years old. When the team got off to a slow start, Alston shook things up.

Although Robinson was hitting well, Alston moved him around in the batting order and back and forth between the outfield and third base. Then Robinson injured his heel and had a hard time running. Late in the game, a better defensive player often replaced him. Even so, he hit .311 for the season.

The Dodgers finished in second place, five games behind the Giants. Many people believed that with players like Robinson and Reese, Brooklyn's chance of winning a world championship was gone.

But the next season, the Dodgers surprised everyone. It was as if all the older players looked around and realized it was now or never for them. The club jumped ahead quickly and ran away with the pennant. Robinson, however, was now little more than a part-time player. Young Don Hoak got much of the playing time at third base, and Sandy Amoros seemed ready to take over in left field. Robinson had a hard time adjusting to his secondary role and played in barely half the Dodgers games, hitting only .256, the worst of his career.

But at the start of the World Series, the Dodgers turned to Robinson. In game one against the Yankees, he played third base. Entering the eighth inning, Brooklyn trailed 6–3. Then outfielder Carl Furillo led off with a hit, bringing Robinson up to bat. He smashed a ground ball to Yankees third baseman Gil McDougald. The ball careened off McDougald's knee for a two-base error as Furillo went to third and Robinson made second. When Don Zimmer hit a sacrifice fly, Furillo scored to make the score 6–4. Robinson stood at third.

As Robinson took his lead off third base, he noticed that Yankees pitcher Whitey Ford hardly gave him a second look. In fact, he didn't even bother to pitch from the stretch position to keep Robinson close to the base.

Robinson understood. After all, he didn't steal many bases anymore, much less home. But this was the World Series, and Robinson was tired of losing to the Yankees.

He started thinking about stealing home.

It was risky and went against usual baseball strategy. Up at bat, Dodgers pinch hitter Frank Kellert represented the winning run. If Robinson were called out, the Dodgers' rally would come to an end and everyone would blame Robinson for squandering Brooklyn's chance to win the game.

But Robinson was thinking about more than game one. As he looked over to the Dodgers' dugout, he saw a team that didn't look like they expected to win the game *or* the series. If they were to get fired up, they first needed a spark. He decided to give them one.

Robinson made certain not to give away his inten-
tion. As Ford stood on the mound and took the sign,
Robinson took a safe lead and tried to look as if stealing home was the last thing on his mind. But as soon
as Ford began to move to start his windup, Robinson
broke for home, running as fast as possible.

Yankees catcher Yogi Berra yelled to alert Ford.
The crowd at Yankee Stadium jumped to their feet.
Ford tried to hurry his windup and threw the ball
home as quickly as possible.

Robinson bore down on home plate, his legs
churning and his teeth clenched. Berra rose from
his crouch to catch the ball and prepare for a colli-
sion at home. Robinson began his slide just as Berra
caught the ball. The catcher dropped to his knees
and held the ball with both hands as Robinson slid in
feet first, stretching his body out as far as possible.
His right leg touched home plate in a cloud of dust.

Umpire Bill Summers stood and leaned over the
two men to make the call. He hesitated for a moment, then flung his arms out. "Safe!" he called.
Berra jumped in the air in disbelief and started
arguing. Meanwhile, amid thunderous applause,
Robinson calmly rose and pulled off his cap, which

had come loose. As he trotted over to the Dodgers' dugout with his hat in his hand, it was obvious to all that his hair contained more gray than black. Yet for an instant he had still been able to turn back the clock, reliving the time when pitchers worried about his stealing home.

Unfortunately, the Yankees held on to their one-run lead to win. They won again in game two. It appeared as if Robinson's effort had been for naught.

But when the two clubs went to Brooklyn for game three, Robinson turned the clock back one more time. As Brooklyn roared to an 8–3 win, Robinson doubled down the left-field line. But he ran hard through second base and made a wide turn.

Yankees outfielder Elston Howard thought Robinson was too far off second. As Robinson slowed to run back, Howard quickly threw behind him, hoping to catch him off base.

That was just what Robinson wanted. The play was one of his favorite old tricks. As the throw came in to second base, Robinson turned on a dime and sprinted to third, easily beating the relay from second. Earlier in his career he had relied on his athleticism. Now he used his brains to make the play.

The win gave the Dodgers some momentum. They won the next two games to move ahead in the series three games to two, only to see the Yankees fight back and take game six. The series would be decided in the seventh and final game.

Unfortunately, Jackie Robinson would not be available. Somehow, perhaps while running bases, he had reinjured his heel. On the morning of game seven, he could barely walk.

He sat on the bench for the most important game in Brooklyn Dodgers history, watching as rookie pitcher Johnny Podres shut out the Yankees, and Gil Hodges knocked in the only two runs the Dodgers needed in the 2–0 win that finally made them World Champions.

Even though he didn't play in the final game, the victory was still satisfying for Jackie Robinson. He had accomplished everything he set out to do in baseball. The 1956 season was a struggle for him. He felt tired all the time, and it sometimes showed. He didn't know it yet, but he was beginning to suffer from diabetes.

Even so, in September, as the Dodgers and the Braves fought it out for the pennant, he was perhaps the Dodgers' most valuable player. Throughout the month, he was again the same daring and aggressive base runner he had been in his younger years. He took the extra base at every opportunity, beat out infield hits, and worried pitchers to distraction. The Dodgers won the pennant by one game.

Entering the World Series, Robinson knew his career would soon end. Although he hadn't told the Dodgers yet, he had already made the decision to retire.

Robinson had a great series. He hit a home run in the first game and keyed Dodgers rallies in games two through four as the two clubs split the first four games. But in game five, Yankees pitcher Don Larsen threw a perfect game shutout to put New York within one win of the championship.

Game six entered extra innings with the score at 0–0. Then Jim Gilliam walked. Pee Wee Reese sacrificed him to second. Then the Yankees intentionally walked Duke Snider to pitch to Robinson.

That was a mistake. With two outs and a man on second, Robinson pulled the ball deep to left field, over the outfielder's head. Gilliam scored and the Dodgers won 1–0.

Unfortunately, there would be no miracle for the Dodgers in game seven. New York jumped ahead early. In the last of the ninth, they led 9–0 with two out when Jackie Robinson came to bat.

He struck out, but Yankees catcher Yogi Berra dropped the ball. Any other player in baseball would have just stood there and allowed Berra to tag him to end the game.

But Robinson had never been "any other player." From the first day he reached the major leagues to his last, he had fought and hustled and tried just as hard as he possibly could. He had never taken the easy way out before, and he wasn't about to now.

As soon as he saw the ball bounce free, he took off, running as hard as he possibly could. Berra threw the ball quickly to first base, and Robinson was out, but he didn't stop running hard until he was past first base. Only then did he slow down, turn, and jog back to his teammates amid the Yankees celebration.

His baseball career was over. But there was still much more Jackie Robinson wanted to do.

☆ CHAPTER TEN ☆

1957–1972

Outside the Lines

When many baseball players retire, they choose to stay in the game as a coach or scout or in some other capacity. But Jackie Robinson was different.

When he looked at America, he saw a society in which African Americans still faced an uphill battle for equality. He had done all he could to help level the playing field during his years in baseball. Now Robinson chose to become a pioneer for civil rights off the field.

He had met a man named Bill Black who owned a large chain of coffee shops called Chock Full O' Nuts. Many of the restaurant employees were African American. Black wanted Robinson to become the company's director of personnel.

Robinson knew it was a unique opportunity. Very few African Americans were employed as business

executives. He decided to take the position and an-
nounce his retirement from baseball in a magazine
article.

But before the article appeared, the Dodgers
shocked Robinson by trading him to the Giants.
Brooklyn fans were stunned. Team owner Walter
O'Malley had already made it clear that he was planning to move the team to Los Angeles. That, combined with the trade of Robinson, made Brooklyn
fans feel betrayed.

When Robinson's article came out, however, the
two teams canceled the deal. Jackie Robinson was
officially out of the game of baseball.

But at the same time, he was everywhere else. By
the end of the 1957 season, more than fifty African
Americans had played in the major leagues. Another
hundred were playing in the minors. Only a few
teams, such as the Red Sox and Tigers, had yet to
play an African American in the majors, but both
had signed African Americans to minor-league contracts.

Yet in a sense, Robinson's accomplishments had
come at a certain cost. The integration of the major
leagues had led to the collapse of the Negro Leagues.

Although now there was opportunity for African Americans in organized baseball, only the very best players were being signed. The integration of baseball had come too late for many African American players.

Within a few years of his retirement from baseball, Robinson became active in the National Association for the Advancement of Colored People (NAACP), a national civil rights group. He soon became a member of their board of directors. He also hosted a radio show that discussed racial matters and wrote a column in the *New York Post*. Robinson knew that although baseball was integrated, the battle for civil rights was far from over.

In 1962, in his first year of eligibility, Robinson was elected to the Baseball Hall of Fame, breaking the color barrier at that institution. At the ceremony he said humbly, "I feel quite inadequate to this honor. It is something that never could have happened without three people — Branch Rickey, who was like a father to me, my wife, and my mother. They are all here today, making the honor complete. I don't think I'll ever come down from cloud nine."

Yet in the years that followed, Robinson's star

started to dim. As the civil rights movement continued to grow, new African American leaders, such as
the Reverend Martin Luther King, Jr., emerged and
pushed the cause throughout the nation. Robinson
was relegated to the sidelines, and many younger
Americans nearly forgot who he was.

As it happened, Robinson needed his time to tackle
problems in the Robinson household. His eldest son,
Jackie, was drafted and sent to Vietnam. When he returned, he was battling a drug problem. Robinson
stood by his son and supported him in his fight.

Robinson left Chock Full O' Nuts and tried to take
advantage of other business opportunities, working
for a while for another restaurant chain and dabbling in both the construction industry and banking.
Robinson believed that African Americans had to
take part in the business world to help themselves
economically. He hoped others would follow his
example.

Then Robinson's health began to fail. Diabetes af-
fected his eyesight and sapped him of energy. For
a while, his doctors even considered amputating
his leg. To make matters worse, in 1971 Jackie Jr.,
who had successfully battled his drug problem, was

killed in a car accident. His death hit Robinson hard, and over the next year, his health deteriorated.

In 1972, baseball recognized the twenty-fifth anniversary of Robinson's debut in the major leagues. He made his final public appearance on October 15, 1972, in a television interview before the second game of the World Series between the Oakland Athletics and the Cincinnati Reds in Cincinnati.

Major-league baseball was celebrating the progress it had made in regard to race. The interviewer asked Robinson how he felt about this progress. Robinson didn't mince words. Although there were many African American players on the field in baseball, very few worked in positions of authority in the dugout or in the front office. Time and time again, retired African American players were passed over for jobs in baseball. Robinson let baseball know how he felt.

He was pleased with the progress, he told the interviewer, but then he added, "I'll be more pleased the day I can look over at third base and see a black man as manager." His words angered some officials, who felt Robinson had embarrassed baseball. But he was only speaking the truth.

Two years later, former player Frank Robinson

became the first African American manager in the game, and many teams began hiring African Americans in the front office. Today, African Americans are employed throughout the game, including as owners of teams.

That was Jackie Robinson, fighting to the end and using his fame to continue to push for civil rights. It was to be his last fight, however. Nine days later, on October 24, 1972, he passed away of a heart attack. Jackie Robinson left a world that he had helped change for the better. He didn't just break the color barrier — he shattered it to pieces so it could never be reconstructed again. By doing so, he helped destroy similar barriers in all phases of society. When Robinson first signed with the Dodgers, racial segregation was the norm in America, and African Americans enjoyed few rights. By the time of his death, segregation was no longer acceptable. That was a victory far greater and far more important than any Robinson won on the baseball field. His impact and his legacy still live today in all people who believe in equal rights and opportunities for everyone.

Baseball has not forgotten him, either. In every

major-league baseball stadium, his number, 42, has been retired and is on display. The Rookie of the Year Award is now called the Jackie Robinson Award. Every April 15, the anniversary of his debut for the Dodgers, baseball celebrates Jackie Robinson Day to recall his memory and the game's commitment to his cause.

More than two thousand people attended Jackie Robinson's funeral. The Reverend Jesse Jackson delivered the eulogy to a crowd that alternately cried at Robinson's loss and cheered his accomplishments. At the end of his speech, Jackson noted that Jackie Robinson's tombstone would read "1919 dash 1972." "On that dash," Jackson said, "is where we live."

His voice rising with emotion, Jackson went on to express how many people felt about Robinson then and how many feel about him today. After each sentence the crowd roared its approval.

"On that dash he snapped the barbed wire of prejudice!" Jackson cried.

"His feet danced on the base paths!"

"But it was more than a game!"

"Jackie began playing a chess game!"

"He was the black knight!"

"In his last dash Jackie stole home and Jackie is safe!"

"His enemies can rest assured of that!"

"Call me nigger, call me black boy! I don't care!"

Every mourner knew that when Jackie Robinson heard those harsh words on the fields of play, he turned the other cheek. And by doing so he had proven to the world that the measure of a human being lies not in the power of his bat, the speed of his feet, or even the color of his skin, but in the strength of his character. Jackie Robinson went to bat for African Americans across the nation — and he hit each of them a home run.

Matt Christopher®

Muhammad Ali

Lance Armstrong

Kobe Bryant

Jennifer Capriati

Jeff Gordon

Ken Griffey Jr.

Mia Hamm

Tony Hawk

Ichiro

Derek Jeter

Randy Johnson

Michael Jordan

Mario Lemieux

Tara Lipinski

Mark McGwire

Yao Ming

Shaquille O'Neal

Alex Rodriguez

Babe Ruth

Curt Schilling

Sammy Sosa

Venus and Serena Williams

Tiger Woods

The #1 Sports Series for Kids

Read them all!

*Previously published as Crackerjack Halfback

Lacrosse Face-Off

Line Drive to Short **

Long-Arm Quarterback

Long Shot for Paul

Look Who's Playing First Base

Miracle at the Plate

Mountain Bike Mania

No Arm in Left Field

Nothin' But Net

Penalty Shot

Prime-Time Pitcher

Red-Hot Hightops

The Reluctant Pitcher

Return of the Home Run Kid

Roller Hockey Radicals

Run For It

Shoot for the Hoop

Shortstop from Tokyo

Skateboard Renegade

**Previously published as Pressure Play

Skateboard Tough

Slam Dunk

Snowboard Champ

Snowboard Maverick

Snowboard Showdown

Soccer Duel

Soccer Halfback

Soccer Scoop

Stealing Home

The Submarine Pitch

The Team That Couldn't Lose

Tennis Ace

Tight End

Top Wing

Touchdown for Tommy

Tough to Tackle

Wheel Wizards

Windmill Windup

Wingman on Ice

The Year Mom Won the Pennant

All available in paperback from Little, Brown and Company

Discover the magical worlds of

Enid Blyton

Enid Blyton

More Wishing-Chair Stories

Mollie and Peter are home for the mid-term break, and Chinky and the Wishing-Chair are ready to whisk them away to magical lands.

They'll meet brownies, visit the Land of Wishes and even find gold at the end of the rainbow. But best of all will be what happens when they meet Santa Claus on Christmas Eve . . .

The third magical Enid Blyton Wishing-Chair adventure.

Discover the magical worlds of
Enid Blyton

Mollie and Peter are home for the holidays and they long to see their pixie friend, Chinky, and the magic Wishing-Chair.

But then the Wishing-Chair is stolen! Whatever will Mollie and Peter do now?

The second magical Enid Blyton Wishing-Chair adventure.

Discover the magical worlds of

Enid Blyton

When Mollie and Peter go to buy their mother a birthday present, they discover the most extraordinary thing: a chair that can fly and grant wishes!

The Wishing-Chair takes them on some marvellous adventures — to the Land of Dreams, to a giant's castle where they must rescue Chinky the pixie, and to a disappearing island!

The first magical Enid Blyton Wishing-Chair adventure.

Discover the magical worlds of
Enid Blyton.

Joe, Beth and Frannie are fed up when they hear that Connie is coming to stay – she's so stuck-up and bossy. But that won't stop them from having exciting adventures with their friends Silky the fairy, Moon-Face and Saucepan Man.

Together they climb through the cloud at the top of the tree and visit all sorts of strange places!

One day, Robin and Joy read about the Magic Faraway Tree in a book and decide to go meet Joe, Beth and Frannie themselves. The five children have all sorts of exciting adventures together, including being captured by the Enchanter Red-Cloak in the Land of Castles, a birthday treat for Joy in the Land of Wishes, and a delicious visit to the Land of Cakes!

Discover the magical worlds of
Enid Blyton.

Joe, Beth and Frannie move to the country and find an Enchanted Wood right on their doorstep! And in the wood stands the magic Faraway Tree where the Saucepan Man, Moon-Face and Silky the fairy live.

Together they visit the strange lands which lie at the top of the tree and where they have the most exciting adventures!

Rick thought it would be dull in the country with Joe, Beth and Frannie. But that was before he found the magic Faraway Tree!

They only have to climb through the cloud at the top of the huge, magical tree to be in the Land of Spells, or the Land of Topsy-Turvy, or even the Land of Do-As-You-Please!

Are We There Yet?

The Family Series

Also by Enid Blyton

The Enchanted Wood
The Magic Faraway Tree
The Folk of the Faraway Tree
Up the Faraway Tree

Naughty Amelia Jane!
Amelia Jane is Naughty Again!
Amelia Jane gets into Trouble!
Amelia Jane Again!
Good Idea, Amelia Jane!

The Adventures of the Wishing-Chair
The Wishing-Chair Again
More Wishing-Chair Stories

Enid Blyton

Are We There Yet?

The Family Series

EGMONT

EGMONT

We bring stories to life

Cover and interior illustrations by Mark Beech

The Caravan Family first published in Great Britain 1945
The Saucy Jane Family first published in Great Britain 1948
The Pole Star Family and *The Seaside Family* first published in Great Britain 1950
The Buttercup Farm Family and *The Queen Elizabeth Family* first published in Great Britain 1951
This edition published 2016 by Egmont UK Limited
The Yellow Building, 1 Nicholas Road,
London W11 4AN

ENID BLYTON ® Copyright © 2016 Hodder & Stoughton Ltd.
Text copyright for *The Caravan Family* © 1945 Hodder & Stoughton Ltd.
Text copyright for *The Saucy Jane Family* © 1948 Hodder & Stoughton Ltd.
Text copyright for *The Pole Star Family* and *The Seaside Family* © 1950 Hodder & Stoughton Ltd.
Text copyright for *The Buttercup Farm Family* and *The Queen Elizabeth Family*
© 1951 Hodder & Stoughton Ltd.

ISBN 978 1 4052 8270 3

A CIP catalogue record for this title is available from the British Library

Typeset by Avon DataSet Ltd, Bidford on Avon, Warwickshire

Printed and bound in Great Britain by the CPI Group

59771/1

The
Caravan
Family

Contents

1

Round the next corner

Daddy had been away for two long years, and now he was back again! Mummy smiled all day long, and the three children were happy too.

Soon Daddy and Mummy began to talk about where they were going to live. 'We can't live with Granny any more,' said Daddy. 'We must have a home of our own.'

'A dear little house in the country!' said Mike, the eldest.

'Called Cherry Cottage,' said Belinda, who was next.

'And let's keep cows,' said Ann, the youngest.

'We'll try and find all you want,' said Daddy, and he laughed.

So they tried. They heard of cottages here and houses there, but oh dear, when they went to see them, they didn't like them a bit!

'Well, whatever are we to do?' said Mummy. 'We really can't all live at Granny's for the rest of our lives!'

Then they found one dear little cottage with roses growing all the way up the walls. It was set on a hill and had a lovely view.

'We'll have this!' said Mummy. But the price was very high, and Daddy hadn't enough money to buy it. So that was no good either.

They came away from the cottage feeling rather sad. 'We shall never find a home,' said Mummy, and she looked so miserable that Daddy put his arm round her and gave her a hug.

'Don't give up hope!' he said. 'Why, you may find a home round the very next corner!'

'Things like that don't happen, Daddy,' said Mummy, but she laughed.

'I wonder what's round the next corner,' said Belinda. 'It would be funny if Daddy's words came true!'

'We'll see what houses there are when we come to the next corner,' said Mike. So they all looked hard when they came to it.

There were no houses to be seen at all – only two old caravans, set in the corner of the field!

'They're empty,' said Mike. 'Can I get over the gate and have a look at them, Daddy? I've never seen a caravan really close to.'

The three children climbed over the gate, while Mummy and Daddy leaned against it, waiting. Ann was the first at the caravans. 'There are steps to go up into them,' she cried. 'Shall we go up? There's no one here!'

But the doors were locked. The children couldn't get inside. They stood on one of the wheels and

peeped through a window.

'They're quite big inside!' said Belinda. 'Look! – that's where the stove is – and the smoke comes out of the little chimney-thing at the top. It's awfully dirty inside, though.'

The children had a good look at the two caravans. They had once been painted a gay yellow and blue, but now the paint was dull and cracked. The shafts into which horses had once been backed, to pull the caravans along, slanted to the ground, and there were no horses to be seen.

'How I wish *we* lived in a caravan!' said Ann, longingly. 'Just think of it, Mike! When we got tired of living in one place, we could put in the horses and go off to another!'

'A house on wheels!' said Belinda. 'Mike – why *shouldn't* we live in a caravan? After all – we can't get a house!'

'Let's go and ask Daddy!' said Mike, and the three of them sped off to the gate.

'Daddy! Daddy! Why can't we live in a caravan?' cried Belinda. 'Why can't we? Do you suppose these would be for sale?'

Daddy and Mummy laughed. 'Live in a *caravan*! Oh no, darling, we couldn't do that.'

'But why not?' said Ann. 'I can think of all sorts of good reasons why we should, and not a single reason why we shouldn't!'

'Couldn't we live in a caravan for the summer – just till we find a house?' said Mike, suddenly. 'It would be a kind of holiday, Mummy – and you did say you'd like to go off for a holiday, a long one, now Daddy is home again.'

'Well,' said Mummy and Daddy together, and looked at one another. A holiday – in caravans – just till they could find a house? It wasn't a bad idea at all!

A big burly man came walking along the lane. Daddy spoke to him. 'Good afternoon! Could you tell us if these caravans are for sale?'

'They are,' said the farmer. 'They belong to me. I bought them off some gipsies last year. Why, do you want them? You can have them cheap.'

Suddenly everyone felt very excited. The caravans were for sale – cheap! *Oh Daddy, Daddy, do buy them*, thought all the children, looking at him with big eyes.

'Well – I'll come along and talk to you about them,' said Daddy. And he went along with the farmer. Will you believe it? – when he came back, he had bought both the caravans! The children hung on to his arms, laughing and shouting in excitement.

'Oh Daddy! They're ours, they're really ours! When can we move in? Oh, our new home *was* just round the corner after all!'

'The caravans will have to be well cleaned, repaired

and re-painted,' said Daddy. 'That will take three weeks. And we must buy two horses. My goodness – we're going to have some fun!'

'We shall be the Caravan Family!' said Belinda. 'What adventures we shall have!'

2

The two caravans

Granny held up her hands in horror when she heard that Daddy had bought two caravans.

'My *dear!*' she said, 'what *can* you be thinking of? Don't do a thing like that. You can stay with me for always.'

'No, Granny dear,' said Mummy. 'You have had enough of three noisy children in your little house. You deserve a little peace and quiet now. We shall be very happy in the caravans.'

Of course, Granny had to go to and see them. She thought they were dreadful. 'You'll live like gipsies,' she said. 'I can't bear it.'

'Come inside and have a look,' said Belinda, slipping her hand into Granny's. Daddy had the keys now, so the caravans could be unlocked. Granny and Belinda went up the steps to the door of the caravan. It was a funny door. You could open all of it at once if you wanted to – or you could open just the top half and leave the bottom half shut.

'Isn't it a good idea?' said Belinda to Granny. 'None of *your* doors open like that, Granny. Now see what

a lot of room there is inside this caravan. This will be Mummy's and Daddy's.'

Granny looked round. She saw what looked like a big wide room, with two little windows at the front, and a bigger window down each side. There were no curtains, of course. There was an old stove at one end and a very old and dirty sink, with taps.

'Good gracious!' said Granny. 'You can even have running water. I didn't know that – and cook too. Well, well, well – it really might be rather exciting.'

'Daddy is having two bunks made on this side just like a ship has,' said Belinda. 'One, the lower one, can be used as a couch in the daytime, and the other will fold down flat against the wall, and be out of the way.'

Granny began to get excited. 'It *could* be made very nice,' she said, 'yes, very nice. You can have cupboards or lockers built against the walls to keep your things in. Pretty curtains at the windows. A flap-table built against the wall, that lets down flat when you don't want it. Gay rugs on the floor – and thick cork carpet underneath to keep out the cold and damp.'

'All this sounds as if it would cost rather a lot of money,' said Mummy, coming in too.

'I shall help you,' said Granny, at once. 'I didn't like this caravan idea – but if you are set on it, we'll do everything as nicely as possible. I shall help you!'

Well, of course, that made things more exciting

than ever, for Granny's ideas of helping were very generous. She took the children shopping with her, and they chose gay blue and yellow rugs for their caravan floor, and a very gay piece of stuff for curtains. Granny got them blue and yellow blankets for their bunks and a blue eiderdown each.

'I'm simply LONGING to live in our caravan!' said Mike, hopping about. 'I can't wait. Three weeks is a terribly long time.'

It was. But there was a great deal to do. Two men arrived one day to repair the caravans. They put a new wheel on one. They mended the chimney of the other. They took out the old stoves ready for new ones to be put in. They mended the rotten old floorboards.

'Everything is all right now, sir,' they said to Daddy. 'We can get on with the cleaning and painting.'

Then what a to-do there was, cleaning the caravans. They were scrubbed well, even the wheels. Then they were ready for the painting.

'What colours shall we have?' said Daddy.

'Red,' said Mike.

'Green,' said Belinda.

'Blue, yellow, orange and white,' said Ann.

'Silly!' said Mike. 'Mummy, what do *you* want?'

'Let's have yellow and red,' said Mummy. 'Yellow for the sun that we hope will shine down on us this summer, and red for the roses it will put into your cheeks.'

'Oh yes,' said the children. 'Red and yellow!'

So red and yellow it was. The men let Mummy choose the colours and she chose a ladybird red, deep and clear. She chose a creamy yellow.

Then the men began the painting. They painted the caravans yellow, with red round the windows, and a red edge to the roof. The chimneys were red and yellow and the spokes and rims of the wheels were painted red. The door was yellow, and the shafts were blue.

'The caravans look lovely, lovely, lovely!' cried Ann. 'Oh Daddy, oh Mummy, aren't they the finest homes in the world?'

'We shall have to live in them before we say that!' said Mummy, laughing. 'Now we must have the stoves and sinks put in. They are ready to be done tomorrow.'

Men came the next day, and put a fine little kitchen-range in Mummy's caravan, one that would both cook the meals and heat the caravan. But in the children's caravan was put a closed stove, for heating only. 'I'd like to cook,' wailed Belinda, but Mummy said no, *she* would be the only one doing the cooking!

'But I'd like to cook the bacon and eggs, and put milk puddings into the oven!' said Belinda. 'Oh, Mummy, do let us have a stove that cooks, in our caravan! You always said that I must learn to cook some day!'

'Yes – but not in *your* caravan!' said Mummy. 'You can come and help me cook in mine if you want to!'

'They're ready to live in now. When can we move in, Daddy, say when?' cried Mike.

'Next week,' said Daddy.

'Oh, I simply can't wait till then!' cried Ann. But she had to, of course!

3

Moving-in day

At last moving-in day came. The children awoke at Granny's very, very early. It was a fine day. That was good. Nobody likes moving on a rainy day.

There was very little for the family to take to the caravans, except trunks of clothes, books and toys, for almost everything was now at the caravans.

Men had laid a thick cork carpet of dark red on the wooden boards of each caravan, running it a little way up the walls, to keep out draughts. On top of this were the gay rugs the children had chosen.

'I do love the two little sinks,' said Mike, remembering them. 'Belinda, did you see the big tank near the roof, where we keep the water? Then when we turn the taps, the water comes out of them just as it does here at Granny's.'

'There's a big tank under the caravan too,' said Ann. 'I saw it. We have to keep that full of water as well, and there's a handle thing we have to work when we want to pump the water up into our roof tank.'

'There are three lovely bunks for us in our caravan,' said Mike. 'I shall have the bottom one because

I'm the eldest. You have the middle one, Belinda, because you are the next oldest. And Ann can have the top one.'

'Oh, I shall like that,' said Ann, pleased. 'I can climb right up to it each night. How lovely!'

Daddy hired a car with a trailer to take the little family down to the place where the caravans were. Into the trailer were put the big trunks, and all the odds and ends – a few chairs, one or two stools, Mummy's work-stand, a few pictures, some extra rugs, and things like that. There was a box full of china, too, and cooking things.

Granny waved goodbye. 'I'll come and have tea with you next week,' she said. 'You'll have settled in by then!'

'Goodbye, goodbye!' called the Caravan Family, and the car drove off, the trailer jolting along behind it.

'I'm the happiest person in the world,' said Ann, her round face red with joy, 'I'm going to live in a house on wheels!'

The children could hardly wait till the car arrived at the caravans. But at last they were there.

And there were the caravans, standing in the field corner, looking so new and gay, in their coats of red and yellow! The children tumbled out of the car to open the gate, and the car and trailer bumped slowly over the rough field, and came to a stop near the two caravans.

Daddy gave Mike the keys, and the boy sped off to unlock the doors. There was rather a strong smell of new paint, but that would soon pass off. Mike peeped into the caravans with delight.

How simply lovely they looked – so shining and spotless and gay! Mike's heart jumped with joy. What dear little homes to have!

Belinda looked in too, and gave a gasp of delight.

'Aren't the bunks lovely with their blue and yellow bedding! And look at our sink with its two bright taps! And don't you love the gay rugs on the floor? And oh *look*, Mike! – Daddy has kept his promise and had shelves made for our books. Won't they look lovely arranged there?'

The gay curtains flapped in the wind, as Belinda opened the windows. The sweet summer air came blowing in, and the sound of the whispering trees.

'Come and help, Mike and Belinda!' called Daddy, from the trailer. 'Bring in some of the chairs. Mummy and I will bring the boxes.'

It was the greatest fun in the world, unpacking everything and finding a place for it in the caravan. There were big cupboards flat and long, in each caravan, set with shelves. Mummy and Belinda arranged the china in one of the cupboards in Mummy's own caravan.

Mike and Belinda arranged their books on the shelves, and put their toys into a locker. Then they

helped to unpack clothes and put those neatly into the cupboards too.

'Now,' said Mummy, 'there is one thing we shall all have to remember, especially Mike, who is so untidy – we *must* remember to put everything away tidily. The rule when you are living in a caravan is that everything has a place, and must be kept there.'

'Yes, Mike can't leave his clothes about or they'll be trodden on,' said Belinda. 'Mummy, we promise to keep our caravan neat and tidy and clean.'

'Oh *yes* – we'll shake the mats and polish the cork carpet, and keep the sink clean, and clean the windows too!' said Ann.

'Granny will be very surprised if you turn into such useful, helpful little people!' said Mummy. 'She was always saying you didn't do enough for yourselves. Well, now that you have a caravan of your very own, just see what you can do!'

At last all the boxes and trunks were unpacked, the chairs and stools given a place, the toys arranged, and a few vases set about the caravans.

'I'll fill them with flowers,' said Ann. 'Oh, Mummy, won't it be lovely to sleep in our caravans? I'm really longing for bedtime!'

4

Settling in

The first meal of the Caravan Family was very exciting. Mummy lighted her little fire, and it burned beautifully. 'Mike's job will be to see that we always have plenty of wood to burn,' said Mummy. Mike thought that would be fine. Things like that didn't seem like work. They just seemed fun.

Mummy set her kettle on the bright fire to boil. Ann skipped down the caravan steps to see if the smoke was coming out of the little red chimney.

'It is, it is!' she cried. 'Come and see! It does look nice.'

The others laughed, but they went to see the smoke coming out of the chimney, all the same. 'Now the caravan looks alive!' said Belinda. 'It's breathing. The smoke is its breath!'

Mummy sent Ann to the farm to ask for eggs. She came back without them.

'There are big geese there,' she said. 'They hissed at me.'

'Ann can't say "Bo!" to a goose!' said Mike, and he took his little sister's hand. 'Come on, Baby. I'll say

"BO!", like that, very loudly, and the geese will let us go by!'

So, when they came to the geese, who raised their heads on their long necks, and hissed, Mike faced them boldly. 'BO!' he said. 'Let us pass.'

And the geese, who would not have hurt them, anyhow, waddled off, cackling. Mike and Ann went to the farmhouse, and the farmer's wife gave them twelve eggs.

'Laid by my nice brown hens!' she said to Ann. 'Look – would you like to see a goose egg?'

She showed Ann an enormous egg. 'Goodness!' said Ann. 'That would do for my breakfast, dinner and tea! The geese won't hurt me, will they?'

'Bless you, no!' said the farmer's wife. 'Their hissing and cackling is their way of talking to you.'

'I don't like your cows either,' said Ann. 'They have sharp horns.'

'*They* won't hurt you!' said the farmer's wife. 'Cows are your friends.'

'I don't think they are, really,' said Ann. 'They moo at me so loudly.'

'Well, big animals have big voices,' said the farmer's wife, laughing. 'The cows give you your milk and butter and cheese. You come along here one day, and I'll show you how to milk a cow.'

'I could never do that!' said Ann, feeling quite scared.

20

'Ah, if you live in the country, you must learn good country ways!' said the farmer's wife. 'Now, take your eggs, and tell your mother if she wants any milk tomorrow to let me know.'

Mummy boiled the eggs for tea. Belinda cut bread-and-butter. Daddy ran down to the little village to buy a cake.

Mike set a blue tablecloth out on the green grass. White daisies grew all round, their yellow eyes looking at the children.

'This is the nicest meal I have ever had,' said Belinda, 'and it's the nicest egg I've ever tasted. I wish I could have another.'

'Well, you can,' said Mummy. 'There are plenty. Goodness me, Belinda, I wish Granny could see you eating like this. She was always so upset because she said you played with your food instead of eating it.'

'Well, I'm hungry now,' said Belinda. 'Perhaps people are hungrier when they live in the country than when they live in a town, Mummy.'

After tea, Belinda wanted to wash up. Mummy was surprised. 'But you hate washing up,' she said. 'You were quite a naughty girl at Granny's, trying to get out of jobs like that.'

'Well, it's such a nice little sink, and I do want to turn on the caravan taps,' said Belinda. 'Your fire makes the water hot in the tank, doesn't it, Mummy? I can get hot water *and* cold.'

So Belinda washed up, and enjoyed turning on the taps and seeing the water rush out into the bright little sink.

Then they all sat on the caravan steps and enjoyed the evening air. The sun was sinking. The shadows of the trees grew longer and longer. The daisies closed their eyes. A bat flew close by, and Belinda squealed.

'Don't be silly,' said Daddy. 'It's only a bat. If you live in the country you must learn to like and understand the country creatures, Belinda – yes, even bats and beetles, mice and earwigs!'

'Oh, I never could,' said Belinda.

'It's because you don't know enough about them that you are afraid of them,' said Daddy. 'You will have to learn a lot out here – and it will be very good for you, Belinda!'

Ann suddenly yawned, and Mummy saw her.

'Bedtime!' she said. 'Go along, you two girls. Get undressed, clean your teeth, and brush your hair well. Give me a call when you are safely in your bunks. Mike can stay up till you're ready, as he is the eldest.'

And, for once in a way, no one made any fuss about going to bed. Ah, going to bed in bunks in a caravan, with the green fields outside, and cows pulling at the grass – that was fun, great fun!

'Hurrah for bedtime!' said Ann, and skipped up the steps like a week-old lamb!

Belinda hurried after her, just as anxious to go to bed as Ann.

'Don't be long!' shouted Mike. 'It's so exciting to go to bed in a caravan – I can hardly wait. Don't be long!'

'We shan't be very quick!' called back Belinda. 'We're going to enjoy every single minute – aren't we, Ann?'

5

Going to bed in the caravan

It really was fun going to bed in the caravan. The two girls undressed and washed. They cleaned their teeth at the little sink, and then they brushed their hair well.

They had to give their hair one hundred strokes with the brush, because Mummy had said that made it nice and shiny. Then they said their prayers, kneeling down beside Mike's bunk.

'I said a big thank you to God for our lovely caravan,' said Ann. 'It's funny, I've often prayed to God for lots of little things I wanted, and He didn't give them to me – but the loveliest thing of all that's happened to me, which is having a caravan, I didn't even ask Him for.'

'Perhaps the little things you thought you wanted wouldn't have been good for you,' said Belinda wisely. 'And perhaps living in a caravan *will* be good for you. You may learn to like cows, for instance, and geese.'

'And you may learn not to squeal at bats!' Ann answered back. 'Well, I don't care how good a caravan

will be for me, I'm going to enjoy every minute. Are you ready for bed? You'd better call for Mike.'

'Mike, we're ready!' shouted Belinda, putting her head out of the window.

'I'll come and tuck you up later,' called Mummy, as Mike ran to his caravan.

Ann had climbed up into the top bunk. It was simply lovely to lie there, in the funny, narrow little bed, and look out of the window on the opposite side. Ann could see a big red and white cow there.

Belinda was now in the middle bunk, and she pulled the blue and yellow blanket round her. She bounced up and down a little. The bunk was quite springy and comfortable.

Mike didn't take long in getting ready for bed. He was soon in the bottom bunk. All the windows were open, and the curtains blew in the breeze. One of the taps dripped a little and made a plink-plonk sound. A cow mooed.

'It's lovely,' said Belinda. 'So exciting. Hallo, Mummy! – here we all are, cuddled up in our bunks.'

Mummy tucked them up and kissed them. She had to stand on the side of Mike's bunk to get to Ann.

'Don't fall out, darling, will you?' she said. 'You'd get quite a bump if you did.'

Mummy shut one of the front windows, because the wind blew straight on to the bunks, and she was afraid there was too much draught. But she left

the others wide open and did not draw the curtains across, because the children begged her not to.

'I do like looking at the trees waving, and the cows, and the birds that sometimes fly across,' said Belinda.

'Who has left the tap dripping?' said Mummy, hearing the plink-plonk of the drops falling into the sink. 'Now that's very silly, isn't it? You know there is only just so much water in the tank – and by the time the morning came the tank would be quite empty, and you would have to fill it again. A lot of trouble for nothing!'

'Sorry, Mummy,' said Mike. 'I was the last at the little sink. I can see we'll have to be very careful and tidy here!'

'I wish it was wintertime and we could have a fire in our little stove,' said Ann.

'Well, I'm going to let my fire out at once,' said Mummy. 'It makes our caravan too hot. Now, go to sleep, all of you!'

But who could go to sleep quickly on their first night in a caravan? Not Mike, Belinda or Ann! They lay and talked.

'I can see a cow chewing the cud,' said Mike. 'You don't know what that means, do you, Ann? Well, the cow pulls at grass and swallows it – then she brings it back into her mouth, later, and chews it when she wants to.'

'I wish I could do that with toffees,' said Ann.

'They'd last a long time then. There goes a bat! I heard it squeak!'

'You must have sharp ears!' said Mike. 'Lots of people can't hear the squeak of a bat, you know. I wish one would come in through the window, then we could see it close to.'

Belinda gave a wail. 'Don't say things like that! You know I hate bats.'

'That's because you're just silly,' said Mike. 'They're dear little things, really – like tiny mice with wings.'

The children lay for a long time listening to the evening sounds. They heard a man calling to another in the distance. It was the farmer shouting to one of his men.

Then they heard a dog barking. The light slowly faded and darkness began to creep into the caravan.

'Oh listen, do listen!' suddenly said Mike, in a low voice. 'What's that singing? Oh, isn't it marvellous?'

'It's fairy music!' said Ann, sitting up in delight.

'It's a nightingale!' said Belinda. Mummy put her head in at the caravan door and whispered:

'Are you children asleep? Can you hear the nightingale – and now there's another?'

With the loud trilling song of the nightingale in their ears, the children at last fell asleep. 'How lucky we are!' was Belinda's last thought. 'How lucky we are to have nightingales to sing us to sleep!'

6

Trouble in the night

Mummy and Daddy were asleep in the front caravan. The children were all asleep in theirs. Outside, in the night, the nightingales still sang – not one or two now, but dozens of them.

Belinda dreamt of musical-boxes as she slept. Then suddenly she awoke with a jump.

At first she could not remember where she was. Then she knew. Of course, she was in the caravan! She sat up in her bunk. What could have wakened her?

She heard a strange grunting noise outside, and then something bumped against the caravan and shook it violently. Then there came a harsh rubbing sound.

Belinda was frightened. Whatever could it be? She called softly to Mike.

'Mike! Mike! Wake up! I think there's someone trying to get into our caravan! Oh, Mike, do wake up!'

Mike did wake up, and so did Ann. They sat up in their bunks, and when Ann heard the queer noises, and felt the caravan shaking, she began to cry.

'I want Mummy! What is it? I'm afraid.'

'It's all right, Ann,' said Mike. 'I'll go and see who it is.'

Mike was just as afraid as the others, but he knew that a boy must always look after his sisters. So he swung his legs out of his bunk, and was just about to stand up when something banged against the caravan at the front.

'Oh, it's gone round to the front now,' wailed Ann. 'Oh quick, Belinda, shut the window in case it comes in!'

'I'll peep out of the window and see if I can spot anything,' said Mike. 'If it's a robber, I'll yell for Mummy and Daddy.'

He stuck his head cautiously out of the front window, and drew it back again at once.

'Something breathed hard at me,' he said.

'I heard it,' said Ann. 'Oh, there must be things all round the caravan now – it's being bumped from every side!'

So it was. Bump – thud – bump – biff! Ann clung to the sides of her bunk, and opened her mouth to yell.

Before she could yell an enormous noise boomed into the caravan, and Ann almost fell out of her bunk.

Mike suddenly roared with laughter. 'It's all right, girls,' he said. 'It's the cows!'

'*Cows!*' said Belinda, indignantly. 'What are they trying to get into the caravan for?'

'They're not,' said Mike. 'They're just inquisitive,

that's all. I suppose they didn't like to come and peep round when we were all about – but now that it's dark and quiet they've come to see where we've got to.'

A cow rubbed itself hard against a corner of the caravan, and it shook a little. Then another cow bumped against it.

'*Well!*' said Ann, crossly. 'I do think they are bad cows, coming and waking us up like this. Are they going to bump into our caravan all night?'

'No,' said Mike, 'because I'm going to chase them away!'

He opened the door of the caravan, slipped down the steps, and met a surprised cow face to face in the starlit darkness.

'Moo!' said the cow, startled, and backed away.

'Now you get away from our caravan, please,' said Mike, firmly. 'Go along! Yes, and you too. And is that another cow over there? Well, get away, all of you, and don't come back again till morning. We want to go to sleep.'

The startled cows lumbered off to the other side of the field, where they stood for a long time thinking about Mike and his sudden appearance. Mike went back into the caravan.

'You're very brave,' said Ann, in great admiration. 'They might have put their horns into you.'

'It's only bulls that do that, silly,' said Mike, getting into his bunk again. 'I say, are you girls hot? Shall I

leave the door of the caravan open?'

'Oh *no*,' said Belinda. 'Why, the cows might all come walking in!'

So the door was shut, and the children soon fell asleep again. They slept soundly. Belinda awoke first, and lay lazily looking out of the window.

'It's lovely to go to sleep in a caravan!' she thought. 'But it's even lovelier to wake up in one!'

She slipped out and opened the door. She sat on the topmost step in her nightie, hugging her knees. A nearby thrush sang to her.

'Ju-dee, Ju-dee, Ju-dee!'

'That's not my name,' said Belinda. 'My name is Belinda, not Judy.'

The cows were all lying down now, chewing the cud. The trees whispered secrets together, standing cheek to cheek. A nearby stream made a gurgling sound. 'The world looks so clean and fresh and new,' thought Belinda, 'and the grass is all silvery with dew. The farm dog is up, and so are the birds – and there's a bee too, flying to find some honey. The bee is our friend too. I must tell Ann that.'

Someone looked out of the window of the other caravan. It was Mummy. 'Hallo, Belinda!' she cried. 'Are you enjoying this beautiful morning? Hurry up and dress, and you can help me to cook breakfast!'

Belinda didn't wake the others. She dressed quickly and ran to help Mummy. Soon a smell of bacon and

31

eggs frying crept over the two caravans.

'Breakfast, lazybones, breakfast!' cried Belinda, looking in at the open door of her caravan, and waking up Mike and Ann with a jump. 'come on, do hurry up. I've been up for simply *ages*!'

'You *might* have woken us up too!' said Mike, as he and Ann scrambled into their clothes. 'We don't want to miss a single minute of this caravan holiday.'

7

Davey and Clopper

The happy summer days went by. The children grew used to a caravan life, and became as brown as ripe acorns. Mike collected wood every day for his mother's fire, and stacked it neatly under the caravan for her. Belinda and Ann carried water from the farmer's well to pour into the tank under the caravan. Daddy pumped it from there into the roof tank when it was needed.

Mummy went down to the village to shop, and the children often went with her to help carry back the things. Belinda and Ann tidied their caravan every day, cleaned the little sink, and shook the mats.

'You are really good, useful children now,' said Mummy, pleased. 'And the holiday is doing us all good.'

But one day the Caravan Family got a shock. The farmer came to Daddy and said he was very sorry, but he would have to take the field they were in for two of his bulls.

'This is the only field with a really strong fencing round it,' he said. 'One of my bulls is such a bad-

tempered fellow I must put him somewhere safe now. So I'm afraid I must ask you to go.'

Ann burst into tears. 'We can't go, we can't!' she said. 'We haven't any horses to take us. And the caravans are too heavy for us to pull ourselves.'

'That's all right,' said Daddy to the farmer. 'I didn't mean to stay here all the summer, anyhow. What's the good of having a house on wheels if you stay in the same place all the time? We want a bit of adventure!'

Ann dried her eyes. *That sounded lovely*, she thought. 'But what about horses, Daddy?' she said.

'I can sell you two,' said the farmer. 'Or if you don't like what I've got to sell you, you can go to the next farm and look at the horses there. You want strong, quiet horses for caravans.'

All the Caravan Family went to look at the horses the farmer had to sell – and they loved them at once!

'This is Davey,' said the farmer, patting a strong little horse with a white star on its forehead. 'You could let the children ride on him, he's so good.'

Mike beamed. He had always longed to ride – and now he would be able to!

'And this is Clopper,' said the farmer, patting another horse, dark brown and white. 'Not quite so good-tempered as Davey here, but a good horse, and strong.'

Daddy knew quite a lot about horses. He made

the farmer trot them round and about. He looked at their teeth. He mounted Davey and rode him round the field.

Then he and the farmer bargained together over the price. Daddy knew what he could afford to pay, and he wouldn't go any higher than that. In the end he got the horses for the money he had, and he and Mike led Davey and Clopper proudly to the caravans.

'Now we've got two horses of our own!' said Ann, in delight. 'Davey, I do like you. And Clopper, your big shaggy feet make a noise like your name.'

'When are we going?' said Mike, who, now that they had horses, was longing to be gone. 'Tomorrow? And where are we going?'

'I don't know where!' said Daddy, laughing. 'What do you think, Mummy? Have you any idea where you want to go?'

'Let's go to my brother's farm, the children's Uncle Ned,' said Mummy, suddenly. 'It's almost haymaking time, and the children will love that. They can help. And maybe Davey and Clopper could help too. They could pull the machine that cuts the grass!'

'Oh Mummy – do let's go to Uncle Ned's!' cried the children, who had never been there. 'We'll help in the haymaking. We'd love that.'

'All right,' said Daddy. 'We'll go there. It will take us a day and a half, I should think. Now Mike, I want to show you how to groom a horse, then you can

35

help me each night. We must look after Davey and Clopper well, for they are now part of our Caravan Family.'

The next day there was great excitement. 'No packing up when we move!' said Ann, skipping about as Daddy put Davey between the blue shafts of the first caravan. 'No buying tickets! No waiting about for a taxi or train!'

'We just put in the horses and off we go!' said Mike, laughing as he backed Clopper into the shafts of his own caravan.

In about half an hour they were all ready to go. The farmer's wife gave them a present of twelve new-laid eggs and a pound of butter.

Daddy was to drive the first caravan, and Mike was to drive the other. Mike was wild with delight. Daddy had explained the harness and the reins to him, and exactly what to do. Mummy was to sit beside him at first, in case he did anything silly.

'I'm to drive our caravan,' he told the girls, proudly, and how they stared!

'I want to, too,' said Ann at once, but Mummy said no, not yet anyhow.

Daddy sat in front of his caravan, and Mike climbed on to the front of his, with Mummy beside him. Each of the girls put their heads out of the front windows, one each side.

Daddy clicked to Davey, and the little black horse

set off over the bumpy field, the caravan jolting behind him.

Then came Mike's caravan, the boy proudly holding the reins. 'Clopper could go without you driving him,' said Belinda.

'Don't disturb me,' said Mike, 'or I might drive into a ditch.'

'We're off, we're off in our house on wheels!' sang Ann. 'We're going far, far away and our house is coming too! Goodbye, cows; goodbye, geese; we're off and away!'

And down the winding lane went the two red and yellow caravans, with Ann singing at the top of her voice.

8

Off to Uncle Ned's

What fun it was to travel for miles and miles in a caravan! Davey and Clopper did not go fast, but they went very steadily.

The countryside was very beautiful just then. Sometimes the children could smell honeysuckle on the wayside hedges. They heard the little yellowhammer singing, 'Little bit of bread and no *cheese*,' as loudly as he could.

The corn was growing well, waving sturdy and green in the wind. Some farmers were already haymaking as the two caravans passed by.

'Oh, I do hope Uncle Ned won't have finished his haymaking by the time we get there,' said Belinda, who had set her heart on helping.

Daddy had a map to show him the way to Uncle's farm. It was fun to look at it with him and see the way.

'By a wood, down a hill, along by this river,' said Daddy, reading the map, and pointing with his finger. 'Yes, we should be there by tomorrow afternoon.'

Down long dusty lanes went the two caravans,

the horses' hooves making a clip-clopping noise as they walked. Daddy kept off the main roads when he could. The lanes were so much prettier.

Sometimes the girls sat in their caravan, and sometimes they ran beside it. Once there was a great scare because Ann disappeared!

'Ann! Where's Ann?' suddenly said Mummy. 'She was running beside the caravan a few minutes ago. Belinda, where's Ann?'

Belinda was now sitting beside her father in the front of the first caravan. 'I don't know, Mummy,' she said. 'Isn't she in the road? That's where I saw her last.'

'Oh dear – we must have left her behind somewhere!' said Mummy. 'I'll turn this caravan round and go back to find her. You can stay here and give Davey a rest, Daddy.'

So Mummy and Mike turned their caravan round and went back to look for the missing Ann. But they couldn't find her anywhere!

They didn't know what to do. Mike felt alarmed. Poor little Ann! She would be so frightened. Had she wandered off and got really lost?

'Well, I don't know what to do,' said Mummy, at last. 'We've gone back a long way. Oh look – there's Daddy coming with his caravan – and how fast Davey is going!'

Daddy shouted out as he came near: 'We've got

Ann! She was fast asleep curled up under your eiderdown in your bunk!'

Well, Mummy and Mike *did* feel glad. Ann was surprised to find what a fuss everyone suddenly made of her when she sat sleepily in the bunk.

'Well, after that shock, I think we'll draw up on this bit of common, and have a meal and a bit of a rest,' said Daddy. 'The horses want a drink and a rest, too. Take them to that pond, Mike, and then tether them loosely to some post or tree.'

They spent a lazy time over their meal. Davey and Clopper pulled at the grass, and then lay down in the sun. The caravans gleamed gaily in the bright sunshine, and the windows winked and blinked.

'Well — off we go once more,' said Daddy. 'And mind — if anyone thinks of going to sleep under eiderdowns again, will they please warn us before they do?'

Everyone laughed. Daddy took his place behind Davey, and Mike took his place behind Clopper. Mummy went inside her own caravan to wash up the few picnic things. Mike was quite able to drive Clopper himself now.

That night they camped in a field full of big moon-daisies and red sorrel. The horses, well-fed, watered and rubbed down, lay contentedly in the shadow of the caravans.

'Last night we were somewhere different, and tomorrow we'll be somewhere else too,' said Ann,

sleepily. 'I do like living in a caravan with horses to take you wherever you want to go.'

They set off again the next day, and the children got excited when at last they drew near to Uncle Ned's big farm.

'Won't he be surprised to see us!' they said. 'Oh, let's hope he hasn't done his haymaking yet!'

'That's the boundary of Uncle's farm,' said Mummy, suddenly, pointing to a wood in the distance. 'Now we are nearly there.'

They came to a big field, where long grass, clover and buttercups waved together. Two or three men were there, talking. Mummy gave a call.

'Ned! Hi, Ned! Hallo, there! Hallo!'

In the greatest surprise Ned turned – and when he saw the two gay caravans, with Mummy, Daddy, and the three children waving to him, he could hardly believe his eyes!

'*Well!*' he said at last, and ran to the lane to welcome them all. '*Well*! What a wonderful surprise! Won't your Aunt Clara be astonished? Where did you come from? How long are you staying?'

'As long as you'll have us,' said Daddy. 'We've come to help with the haymaking. I see you haven't begun yet.'

'No, not yet,' said Uncle Ned. 'I wanted to begin it last week because the weather was so fine, but I've had a bit of bad luck.'

'Why, what's wrong?' asked Mummy. 'I hope it's nothing serious, Ned!'

'I've two of my horses ill,' said Uncle Ned, 'so I can't cut the grass yet.'

'We'll lend you Davey and Clopper!' cried Mike. 'They'll pull the machine for you. They're proper farm-horses, really they are!'

'Come along to the farmhouse,' said Uncle Ned. 'Well, well, this is a bit of good news, to be sure. A whole family to visit me – and two horses to lend me! We'll all start the haymaking tomorrow!'

So off they went to the farmhouse, all talking at the top of their voices!

9

A lovely time in the hay

Uncle Ned and Aunt Clara were simply delighted to welcome the Caravan Family. They gave them a glorious tea, and then went to see the two gay caravans.

'This is *my* sleeping-bunk, the topmost of all,' said Ann, proudly.

'And look – our taps have running water!' said Mike, and he turned one on. 'And in Mummy's caravan there is hot water from one tap, when she has the fire going. I collect the wood for it every day.'

'It's all lovely,' said Auntie Clara. 'I almost wish I lived in a caravan too. So you've come to help with the haymaking, have you? Well, we want all hands then, I can tell you!'

'We'll begin tomorrow,' promised Mike. 'We will work just as hard as anybody else, because since we've lived so much in the open air, we have all grown strong and healthy.'

Next day the fun began. First of all Davey and Clopper were put to drag the grass-cutting machine.

They pulled it along, and the knives of the machine cut the grass easily, leaving it behind in big piles.

'How funny the hayfield looks now!' said Ann, dancing among the short stems. 'It's had its hair cut! Now can we begin to toss the hay, Uncle?'

'Toss it as much as you like,' said the farmer. 'The drier it gets, the better I shall like it! Hasn't the hay a lovely sweet smell now?'

The long cut grass turned a grey-green colour and smelt delicious. Belinda said she would like some scent made of it, to put on her hanky.

The children tossed it about, threw it at one another, rolled over and over in it, and had a lovely time. Scamper, the farm dog, came to join them. He was a big collie, and he had a fine time, too.

'He's haymaking as well!' said Ann, and tried to bury him in the sweet-smelling hay. But he wouldn't be buried.

Everyone was pleased next day when they were given big hand-rakes and told to turn the rows of hay over, so that the sun could dry the wet bits underneath. The children worked very hard.

The sun shone down hotly, and Uncle Ned was pleased. 'Just right for the hay!' he said. 'It will dry beautifully, and I shall get it quickly away and built into haystacks before the rain comes.'

'Then your cows will have lots to eat in the winter, won't they?' said Belinda.

When the hay had been well raked and turned the farmer said it must be got into neat wind-rows – big long rows all the way down the field.

'Fetch Davey,' he said to Mike. 'Put him in that big horse-rake machine, Mike, then lead him up and down the field. The girls will love to see how the enormous rake at the back of the machine puts the hay into long neat rows.'

The girls did like watching, as Mike proudly led the horse-rake up and down the field. 'Mike, the big steel teeth slide under the hay and get hold of it!' cried Belinda.

'Yes,' said Mike. 'And now see what happens. As soon as the rake is full of hay, I pull at this handle, which lifts up the steel teeth – and then the hay is neatly dropped in a long row. Isn't it clever, Ann?'

Before the evening came the hay was all collected into wind-rows by the horse-rake, and Mike's legs were quite tired of walking up and down the field.

'Now to build the haycocks!' cried Auntie Clara, who was helping. The children liked her very much. She was pretty and jolly, and she had brought them out a really lovely picnic lunch.

The children helped to build the haycocks all down the field. How pretty they looked in the evening sun, with their shadows slanting behind them!

'I do think a hayfield looks lovely with its haycocks

standing so quietly there,' said Belinda. 'Mike – look, there's Ann, fast asleep in that corner! Let's bury her in hay!'

So they did, and soon there was nothing to be seen of Ann at all. She was just another haycock! Mummy was astonished to see no Ann, and went hunting and calling for the little girl, while Mike and Belinda ran away, giggling.

Ann heard her mother calling, and woke up. What was this all round her? What a funny blanket, thought Ann, trying to sit up. She called to her mother.

'Mummy! Mummy! Where am I?'

'Bless the child, she's a haycock!' said Mummy, laughing, and picked her out of the hay. 'Come along, darling, it's time for supper and bed. You're tired out.'

'It's been such fun,' said Ann, sleepily. 'What do we do next with the hay?'

'As soon as I can I shall take it in the big hay-wagon to the rickyard,' said her Uncle. 'Some I shall store in my sheds, and what is left I shall build into hay-stacks.'

'Can we ride home on the hay-wagons?' asked Mike. 'It's such fun to do that. I shall lie on the very, very top of the hay in the wagon, and look up at the sky, and smell the sweetness of the hay.'

'You shall do all that and more!' said Mummy. 'But come along home to your caravan now – you are almost falling asleep on your feet!'

So back to the caravans they went, and fell asleep at once, with the sweet smell of the hay drifting in at the caravan windows. What a lovely time they were having!

10

Learning to milk

It was great fun living near Uncle Ned's farm. He told Daddy the best place to put the caravans.

'Go into that field,' he said, pointing. 'It's not too far from the farmhouse, you'll be sheltered from the wind, and there's a clear stream nearby for washing water. Drinking water you can get from the well outside the farmhouse.'

So the two caravans were placed there, and a very cosy, sunny spot it was. Cows lived in the field, and Davey and Clopper lived there too. They helped Uncle Ned, and he was glad of them.

'They're fine horses for work,' he said, fondling their big noses. 'When you're tired of caravanning, I'll buy them from you!'

'We shall never, never be tired of living in a caravan!' said Ann. 'And I don't want to sell Davey and Clopper. I love them. Davey always gives me a ride when I ask him.'

Each morning and evening the cows were taken to the sheds to be milked. The children went to watch, and they loved to hear the splish splash of the milk in

the big pails. Mike wanted to try his hand at milking.

'All right, you can try,' said Auntie Clara, and she gave him a milking-stool to sit on. 'That's right – get close up to the cow. Have you got strong hands? Yes, you have – but you want to be gentle, too, not rough.'

Mike began to milk the cow, but he wasn't very good at it. He got some milk, but it took him a long time to get even half a pail full.

'There isn't any nice froth on it like yours, Auntie,' he said.

'No,' said Aunt Clara. 'That's the sign of a good milker, you know – froth on the top. You try, Belinda!'

So Belinda tried, and she was really very good indeed! Her strong little hands worked away, and the swish of the milk in the pail was a pleasant sound to hear. There was plenty of froth too! Belinda felt very proud.

Then Ann wanted to try. 'But you're afraid of cows, silly!' said Mike.

'Oh, I'm not now,' said Ann, and she wasn't. Living in the country and doing all kinds of jobs had made her much more sensible. She didn't think cows would run after her and toss her now! She sat down on the stool beside a big, gentle cow called Buttercup.

But Ann's hands were too small for milking, and she soon gave it up. 'Belinda's the one!' she said. 'Mike and I are no good at milking.'

'Yes, Belinda is good,' said her aunt. 'Now Belinda,

be sure to get every drop of the last milk from your cow – that is always the richest!'

'Are you going to make butter from the cream you get off the top of the milk?' said Ann. 'Can I help you when you do that, Auntie? Do let me!'

'All right, you shall,' said Auntie Clara. 'I make butter every Friday. You come along to the dairy then, and you shall help me!'

Mike took the cows back to the field when they were milked. One of them opened its mouth to moo, and Mike had a great surprise. He called to his Uncle.

'I say, Uncle – this cow, Buttercup, opened her mouth wide just now – and, do you know, she's lost all her top teeth! Poor, poor thing – she won't be able to eat!'

Uncle Ned gave a big roar of a laugh. 'What things you do say!' he said. 'A cow never has any upper teeth, silly boy! Didn't you know *that*?'

Mike went rather red. Ann and Belinda came skipping up to see what Uncle Ned was laughing at. He opened the cow's mouth and made them look into it.

'Do you see what she has instead of upper teeth?' he said. 'There's a bare fleshy pad there – no teeth at all. You see, a cow just pulls at the grass and breaks it off – then she swallows it down into one of her four stomachs—'

'*Four* stomachs!' cried the three children together. '*Four!*'

'Well – four stomachs, or one stomach with four rooms in it, whichever you like,' said Uncle. 'The cow pulls the grass, and swallows it down straight away into stomach number one. Then, when she is resting, she brings back the grass again to her mouth, and spends a very happy time chewing it!'

'Yes, I know,' said Mike. 'That's called chewing the cud, isn't it?'

'Right!' said Uncle. 'Then, when the grass is chewed, the cow sends it down to her second stomach, and from there it goes to the third and to the fourth.'

'What a funny animal a cow is!' said Belinda. 'Not a bit like a horse! A horse has strong upper teeth. Davey has and so has Clopper. Have they got four stomachs too, Uncle?'

'No, only one,' said her uncle. 'And their hooves are different too. Look at Buttercup's hoof, Mike.'

Mike lifted it up, and gave a cry of surprise. 'It's split in two! Not a bit like Davey's, who has his hoof quite whole.'

'The cow always has a split hoof,' said Uncle Ned. 'It helps her when she walks on damp ground, as she often does. All right, Buttercup, we've finished with you! Go and join the others!'

Buttercup, surprised at having her mouth and hoof looked at so closely, lumbered away with a moo.

'I like cows now,' said Ann. 'I used to think they were so fierce – but they are gentle and slow and friendly. I say – won't it be fun to help to make the butter on Friday?'

11

A great time in the dairy

On the next Friday the children did their caravan jobs quickly, because they all wanted to rush off to the farm and watch butter being made.

They made their beds and tidied their caravans. They cleaned the sink, and pumped up water from the tank beneath the caravan to the roof-tank, so that there would be plenty to run down to the taps when they were turned on.

Mike shot off to collect wood for his mother's fire, and stacked it neatly under the caravan. Belinda and Ann ran down to the village to buy a few things their mother wanted.

'Is that all, Mummy?' said Belinda, when she brought back the things and put them into her mother's cupboard. 'Can we go to the dairy now, and watch Auntie Clara?'

'Off you go!' said Mummy, pleased to see the children's rosy-brown faces, and to know how much they were learning of good country ways. They would have to go to school in the autumn – but meanwhile they were learning country lessons they

54

would never, never forget.

The children rushed to the dairy as fast as they could go, hoping that Auntie Clara hadn't begun her butter-making without them. Ann's legs weren't as long as the others' so Mike waited for her.

Belinda got to the dairy first. She looked round the big, cool, whitewashed place, with its stone floors and shelves. It was lovely!

'Auntie! Oh Auntie, you've begun to make the butter!' she cried in dismay. But her aunt shook her head with a smile.

'Oh no, I haven't. This isn't the butter-churn I'm using. This is the milk and cream separator I'm working – it separates the milk from the cream for me. Then I can use the cream for my butter.'

Ann and Mike came in, and they watched with Belinda, as their aunt turned the handle of the separating-machine. 'Watch the two pipes that come out there from the side of the machine,' said Auntie Clara.

The children watched. They had seen their aunt pour fresh milk in at the top of the separator – and now, lo and behold, out of the two side-pipes came milk and cream, quite separate!

'The top pipe has got cream coming out of it!' said Belinda. 'And the bottom pipe has milk. Oh Auntie, isn't it clever?'

'Can I turn the handle, please?' asked Ann. 'Do let

me!' So Ann turned the handle, and was delighted to see the milk and cream flowing separately out of the two pipes.

The cream was added to some cream already in a great big crock. 'Now for the butter,' said Auntie Clara, rolling up her sleeves. 'That always makes me hot. The butter-churn isn't so easy to use as the separator!'

The butter-churn was a big beechbarrel mounted on a wooden frame. It had a handle too. Auntie Clara poured the cream into the churn. It did look thick and yellow and delicious. Ann poked her finger into it and got it covered with cream, which she licked off.

'Naughty!' said her aunt. 'You're as bad as the farm cat. She's always hanging round taking a lick at the milk-pails and a lick at the cream-crock!'

She took hold of the handle and began to turn it. To the children's surprise the whole barrel turned over and over.

'Oh, hark at the cream, splashing away inside!' cried Belinda. 'What a lovely sound!'

'Auntie, how does the churn make butter?' asked Ann, puzzled.

'Cream goes solid when it's whipped, or when it's shaken about like this,' said Auntie Clara, her face getting red, for the churn was heavy. 'It's being shaken about well inside this churn – the butter will soon come.'

'I want to turn it,' said Ann, but it was too heavy for her. It was too heavy for Belinda too, but Mike's strong arms turned it quite well.

'Ah – the butter's coming!' said Auntie Clara, when she took the handle again. 'I always reckon it takes about twenty minutes. Some folks take longer – but butter comes quickly for me, thank goodness!'

Their aunt took the lid off the churn and let the children look inside. Where was the thick cream? It was gone! Instead they saw lumps of yellow butter swimming in what looked like thin milk.

'That's the buttermilk,' said their aunt, putting the lid on. 'Now – just a minute or two more and the butter will be ready!'

She swung the churn over and over again, and then stopped. The lumps of butter were taken out and washed. Then with a wooden butter-roller clever Aunt Clara made the butter firm and hard.

'Let me help you make it into half-pound and pound pats!' cried Mike, who was clever with his hands. Soon the shelf was piled with the neat butter-pats, all wrapped up in the printed farm paper.

'Auntie Clara, I'd like to help you to make the butter each week, and separate the milk and cream too,' said Mike, suddenly. 'Belinda is helping to milk the cows each day, and Ann says she wants to help to feed the hens. So I'll help with the butter. I'm strong, and I can easily swing the churn.'

'Thank you, Mike,' said his aunt, gratefully. 'There's so much to do on a farm just now – I'd be glad to have your help.'

'We *love* helping!' said Ann.

'In return for helping to milk the cows, I shall give Belinda four pints of milk a day,' said Auntie Clara. 'And for helping me with the butter, you shall have two pounds of it each week, Mike – and for helping with the hens you shall have two dozen eggs, Ann!'

Well, wasn't that simply lovely!

12

A wonderful surprise

The summer days went by far too quickly. 'Oh dear!' sighed Mike. 'I wish these lovely, exciting days wouldn't fly so fast!'

'Well, we've done a tremendous lot of things since we became a Caravan Family,' said Belinda. 'And I've made up my mind about one thing – and that is that I will always live in the country if I can. It's much nicer than town.'

'Yes – real, proper things happen in the country,' said Mike. 'Things grow – and calves and lambs are born – and hay is cut – and sheep are sheared – and cows are milked – and—'

'And the harvest is brought in!' said Ann, remembering how she had helped with that. 'Oh, weren't the fields of corn lovely, Mike, when they were tall and golden and ripe?'

'I liked watching that wonderful self-binding machine at work in the fields,' said Mike. 'It certainly had been amazing to watch. It had cut the corn, gathered it into sheaves, tied each sheaf neatly with string, and then had thrown the sheaf on to the ground!

'Harvest-home was fun,' said Belinda. 'I liked going with the wagons to the rickyards – and wasn't the harvest-home supper grand fun, Mike?'

Everyone, from the oldest farm worker, Tom, to little Ann, had sat down to a grand supper given by Auntie Clara, when the last wagon of corn had been taken to the yard, ready for cornstacks to be built later on. Ann had fallen fast asleep in the middle of the feast.

But now those lovely days were past, and September was in. Blackberries were beginning to ripen on the hedges, and Mummy had already made a blackberry tart.

Mike's heart was sad. He knew that he and Ann and Belinda were soon to go to school again. They had already missed a whole term. They could not do that any more.

'Now I suppose we'll have to go and live in a house,' he groaned to the girls, as they sat on the steps of their caravan, waiting for Mummy and Daddy to come back from the station.

'Mummy might not have found a school that would do for us,' said Belinda hopefully. 'Perhaps we shall live in our caravan all the winter.'

'I can't bear to think we'll have to say goodbye to Davey and Clopper,' said Ann, looking ready to cry. 'I do love them so.'

'There's the smoke from the train,' said Belinda.

'Mummy and Daddy will soon be here. Let's go over the fields and meet them.'

So the three little caravanners, all as brown as berries, hurried off to meet their mother and father.

'There they are!' said Ann, and waved. Two people, coming over a field, waved back. Mike rushed ahead to meet them.

'Did you find a school? Say you didn't! Say we can still live in our caravan and not in a house!' Mike almost shouted his questions.

'We'll tell you when we get to the caravans,' said Mummy. 'Have you got the kettle boiling for tea, Belinda, as I asked you?'

Belinda nodded. 'Yes, Mummy – and the bread and butter is cut – and there's a fresh lettuce or two – and some of Auntie's strawberry jam, and a chocolate cake she made for us.'

'Good!' said Daddy, and looked forward to such a nice tea, eaten sitting on the soft grass, with cows nearby, and Davey and Clopper nosing up for tit-bits.

'Well,' said Mummy, when they were seated at their picnic tea, 'well – we've found a school, a fine one too, that teaches gardening and riding and swimming and allows you to keep pets, and has cows to milk and pigs and goats and hens!'

The children cheered up a little. 'And no proper lessons at all?' said Ann, hopefully.

'Of course there will be lessons!' said Daddy. 'You

must learn how to use your brains, or they won't be any use to you or to other people.'

'When do we go?' said Belinda, gloomily.

'The school begins next week,' said Mummy.

The children looked gloomier and gloomier. Only a few days more, and they would have to say good-bye to Davey and Clopper and the two gay caravans.

'But Mummy and I have decided that we will live near the school in our caravans,' said Daddy, smiling. 'And we have arranged that you shall be school children all the week – and caravan children from Friday to Monday! How will that suit you?'

'Oh! OH!' yelled the children, and got up and danced round in delight. 'Can we really live in our caravan every weekend? All the winter too? Aren't we going to have a house after all? Shall we still be the Caravan Family?'

'Yes,' said Mummy and Daddy, laughing at the children's surprise and joy. 'And we had better set off tomorrow in the caravans, because it will take two or three days to get to the school, and we want to be well settled in before you start.'

'Davey! Clopper! Do you hear?' called Ann, running to the two horses, who lifted their heads to listen to her. 'We're going travelling again tomorrow with you! Oh, won't it be fun?'

So, the next day, they said goodbye to Auntie Clara and Uncle Ned, and thanked them for a lovely time.

They put Davey and Clopper between the shafts, and Daddy and Mike took the reins. Then off they went, rumbling over the field to the gate.

'The Caravan Family is off again!' cried Ann. 'Our wheels are turning fast, and soon we shall be miles away. Goodbye, goodbye!'

Goodbye, little Caravan Family. We hope you'll have lots more fun!

The
Saucy Jane
Family

Contents

1

A Most Exciting Idea

Mike, Belinda and Ann were three lucky children. They were at school all the week – and from Friday to Monday they lived in a caravan!

Mummy and Daddy lived in one caravan and the three children had the other. It was such fun. In the holidays they went to visit Uncle Ned and Aunt Clara. Then their two good horses, Davey and Clopper, pulled the caravans down many little winding lanes to Uncle Ned's farm.

'It's lovely to have a house on wheels!' cried Mike, when he sat at the front of his caravan and drove Clopper steadily on. 'I wouldn't like to live in a house that always stood still.'

When the summer holidays came, Daddy wondered whether they should all go to the sea. 'Our caravans want cleaning and painting,' he said. 'The stove wants something done to it, too.'

'Oh, Daddy – must we go and stay in a *house*!' said Ann, who, now that she had lived in a caravan on wheels, didn't like living in a house at all. 'Can't we take the caravans with us?'

'No. We really must get them properly cleaned up,' said Daddy. 'I'd like to take you to the sea, because you must learn to swim, and to handle a boat. All children should know how to swim.'

'I'd like to,' said Mike. 'I'd like to dive as well. And swim under water like a fish. I've seen people doing it.'

It was very difficult to get rooms by the sea anywhere, because Daddy had left it rather late. He tried to hire a caravan by the sea, too, but they were all taken. It really seemed as if the children wouldn't be able to go.

And then one day Mummy had a most exciting letter. She read it to herself first, and her eyes shone. 'Listen!' she said. 'I wonder how you would like this, children?'

'What?' cried the three of them, and Daddy looked up from his newspaper.

'It's a letter from an old friend of mine,' said Mummy. 'She has a houseboat on a canal not very far from here – and she says she will lend it to us for the holidays if we like.'

'A houseboat?' said Ann, in wonder. 'What's that? Does she mean a boathouse – where boats are kept?'

Everyone laughed. 'Isn't Ann a baby?' said Mike. 'Silly, it's a proper boat that people *live* in – they make their home there, just as we make ours in the caravan.'

'*Do* they?' said Ann. 'Do they really live on the boat all day and night? Oh Mummy, I'd like to see a houseboat.'

'And I'd simply LOVE to live in one!' said Belinda. 'Oh, I would! To hear the water all day and night, and to see fish jumping – and the little moorhens swimming about. Oh, Mummy!'

'Where's this houseboat?' said Daddy. 'It certainly does sound rather exciting.'

'It's at Mayberry,' said Mummy. 'On the canal there. It's a very pretty part, I know. It's a lovely houseboat – big enough to take all of us quite comfortably.'

'What's the boat called?' asked Mike. 'Does the letter say, Mummy?'

'Yes. It's called the *Saucy Jane*,' said Mummy, smiling. 'What a funny name!'

'It's a *lovely* name!' said Belinda. 'I like it. The *Saucy Jane*. We shan't be the Caravan Family – we shall be the Family of the *Saucy Jane*.'

'Let's go today,' said Ann. 'Mummy, can we?'

'Of course not,' said Mummy. 'You can't do things all in a hurry like that. Daddy has got to arrange about the caravans being done – and we must find out what we can do with Davey and Clopper.'

'Oh, Mummy – we can't leave Davey and Clopper behind,' cried Mike. 'You know we can't. They would be awfully miserable.'

'Well, we can't have horses living on a boat,' said

Daddy. 'Be sensible, Mike.'

'They could live in a nearby field,' said Mike. He loved Davey and Clopper with all his heart, and looked after them well.

'We'll see,' said Daddy. 'They might perhaps be useful to us if we wanted to go up the canal a little way in the houseboat.'

'Oh – would Davey and Clopper pull our boat?' cried Ann. 'Wouldn't they feel odd, pulling a boat instead of a caravan?'

'Well – what about it, Daddy?' said Mummy, still looking rather excited. 'Shall we try a holiday on a houseboat? The children could learn to swim and dive, and they could learn to handle a little boat too. Just what we want them to do.'

'It does seem as if we were meant to go,' said Daddy, smiling. 'We can't get in anywhere by the sea – so a river or a canal is the next best thing. Yes, write to your friend and tell her we'll go and see the *Saucy Jane*.'

'And we'll make up our minds whether to live in it for the holidays or not when we see it,' said Mummy.

'I'm going to tell Davey and Clopper all about it,' said Ann, and she ran off to where the two big horses stood close together in the field.

'Don't be long,' called Mummy. 'It's almost time to go to bed.'

But when they were in their bunks in the caravan that night, the three children couldn't go to sleep for

a long time. They talked about the *Saucy Jane*, they planned what they would do – and when at last they did fall asleep they dreamt about her too.

The *Saucy Jane*! What would she be like? Just as nice as a caravan – perhaps nicer!

2

The Saucy Jane

Next morning at breakfast-time all the family talked about when they could go and see the *Saucy Jane*.

'The sooner the better, I think,' said Daddy. 'What about today? There's a bus that goes quite near Mayberry. We could catch it and walk across the fields to the canal.'

'Oh, Daddy — today!' said Belinda. 'Yes, let's go today. It's such a lovely day.'

So when they had washed up the breakfast things, tidied the caravans, and locked the doors, they all set off. They caught the bus at the corner of the lane and settled down for a fairly long ride.

'What is a canal, Daddy? Is it a river?' asked Ann.

'Oh, no,' said Daddy. 'A canal is made by man — cut out by machinery, and filled with water. It is usually very straight, but if it meets a hill it goes round it.'

'Doesn't it ever go through it?' asked Mike.

'Yes, sometimes. Some canals go through quite long tunnels,' said Daddy; 'a mile, two miles or more.'

'Do fishes live in canal water — and wild birds?' asked Belinda.

'Oh, yes,' said Daddy. 'They are old now, these canals we have made all over the country, and to you they will look just like rivers. They have weeds growing in them, fish of many kinds, wild birds on the banks. Trees lean over the sides, fields come right down to the canals, though where they run through towns there are houses by them, of course.'

'Why did we build canals, when we have so many rivers?' asked Mike.

'Well, many goods were sent by water in the old days, when goods had to be taken about all over the country, and the roads were bad, and the railways were only just beginning,' said Daddy. 'But rivers wind about too much – so straight canals were cut.'

'I see,' said Mike. 'I suppose big boats were loaded in the towns, and then they were taken across the country to other big towns – by canal.'

'Yes,' said Daddy. 'I'll show you the boats that take them – canal-boats and barges. You'll see plenty going by if we live on the houseboat.'

'*If!* You mean *when*!' cried Belinda. 'Are we nearly there, Daddy? I want to see the canal and the *Saucy Jane*. I can't wait another minute.'

But she had to wait, because the bus was not yet near Mayberry. At last it stopped at a little inn and the bus conductor called to Daddy.

'This is where you get out, sir. You'll find the canal across those fields there. You can just see it from here.'

They all got out. They climbed the stile and walked across a cornfield by a narrow path right through the middle of the whispering corn. The corn was as high as Ann, and she liked looking through the forest of tall green stalks.

They crossed another field and then came to the canal. It was, as Daddy had said, very like an ordinary river. Trees and bushes overhung the opposite side, but the cornfield went right down to the edge of the side they were on.

The canal stretched as far as they could see, blue and straight. A little way up it, on the opposite side, were two or three big white boats – houseboats, with people living in them. Smoke rose from the chimney of one of them.

'There are the boats,' said Mummy, 'I wonder which is the *Saucy Jane*! Dear me, Daddy, how are we going to get across?'

'Borrow a little boat and row it!' said Daddy. 'Come along!'

They were soon just opposite the houseboats. One was very colourful indeed, with red geraniums and blue lobelias planted in pots and baskets all round the sitting-space on the little roof.

'I do hope that's the *Saucy Jane*,' said Belinda to Ann. 'It's much the nicest. It's so shining white, too!'

There was a small cottage by the canal, and a woman was in the garden hanging out clothes. Daddy called

to her. 'Is the *Saucy Jane* over there? Can we get to her in a boat?'

'Yes, that's the *Saucy Jane*,' said the woman. 'The boat with the geraniums. She's got a little boat belonging to her, but I expect it's moored beside her. You're welcome to borrow my boat, if you like. It's the little dinghy down beside you.'

'Thank you,' said Daddy.

Everyone got in, Daddy united the rope and took the oars. Over the water they went to the *Saucy Jane*. Somebody came out on deck, appearing from the cabin-part in the middle.

Mummy gave a cry of delight. 'Molly! You're here! We've come to see the boat!'

'Oh, what fun!' cried Mummy's friend. 'I never expected you so soon. Look, tie your dinghy just there – and climb up.'

In great excitement the children climbed up on the spotless deck. So this was the *Saucy Jane* – a house on a boat! They looked at the cabin-part; proper doors led into it, two doors, painted white with a little red line round the panels.

There were chairs on deck to sit in and watch the boats that went by. There were even chairs on the roof-part, up by the geraniums and lobelias. Ann didn't know which to do first – climb up on the roof by the little iron ladder, or go into the exciting-looking cabin.

'Come along and I'll show you over the *Saucy Jane*,' said Mummy's friend, smiling. 'You can call me Auntie Molly. When you've seen everything, we'll sit down and have some biscuits and lemonade, and talk about whether you'd like to have a holiday here.'

'We would, we would!' said all three children together. 'We've made up our minds already!'

3

What Fun to be on a Houseboat!

It was very exciting to explore the big houseboat. Down in the cabin-part there were two bedrooms and a small living-room. There was even a tiny kitchen, very clean and neat, with just room to take about two steps in!

In one room there was no bed, though Auntie Molly said it was a bedroom. In the other room there were bunks for beds, just as there were in the caravan – two on one side of the wall, and a third that could be folded up into the wall on the other side.

'I call that bunk my spare room,' said Auntie Molly, with a laugh. 'I can sleep three people in this bedroom and two in the other.'

'But where do they sleep in the other room?' asked Mike, puzzled. 'I didn't see any bed at all.'

'Oh, I forgot to show it to you,' said Auntie Molly. 'It's really rather clever, the way it comes out of the wall. Come and see.'

She took them back into the other cabin bedroom, and went to the wall at the back. There was a handle there and she pulled it. Out came a double

bed, opening itself like a concertina! Auntie Molly pulled down four short legs, and hey presto! there was the bed. Tucked away in another cupboard were blankets, sheets and mattress.

'It's like magic,' said Ann. 'And isn't it a good idea? It would take up a lot of room if you had the bed standing all day in this little room. Can I push it back, please?'

It was as easy to push back into the wall as it was to pull out.

'That will be Mummy's and Daddy's bed,' said Belinda. 'Auntie Molly, this houseboat is just right for our family, you know – you've got beds or bunks for five people.'

'Yes,' said Aunt Mollie. 'I knew you had been used to living in a caravan, and I thought you would be just the family to enjoy my houseboat. I was sure you would keep it clean and tidy, because I've heard how beautiful your caravans are.'

'Oh, yes – we'd keep your boat spotless,' said Belinda. 'I would scrub down the deck each day. I'd love that. That's what sailors do, isn't it, Mummy?'

There was a stove in the tiny kitchen for cooking, and a chimney stuck out at the top of the roof for the smoke. There were neat cupboards all round the kitchen, and mugs and cups hung in neat rows.

'You can wash up in the canal water,' said Aunt Mollie, 'and any other washing you want to do you

can do in the canal too. Drinking-water you can get from Mrs Toms' well at the cottage opposite. I fetch it in a big water-jar.'

'I can see that our jobs here will be quite different from our jobs in the caravan,' said Mike, 'but they will be very exciting. Daddy, can I fetch the drinking-water each day, please?'

'As soon as you can handle a boat, and can swim, you may,' said Daddy.

Aunt Molly suddenly looked rather alarmed. 'Oh – can't the children swim?' she said. 'Then I really don't think you ought to come and live here. You see, it's so easy to fall into the water, and if you can't swim, you might drown.'

The children stared at her in dismay. How dreadful if they couldn't come and live on this lovely boat just because they couldn't swim!

'We're going to learn,' said Mike at once. 'We're going to learn the very first day we get here. You needn't worry.'

'But can the little girl learn?' asked Aunt Molly, looking doubtfully at Ann. 'Really, I think if you come you'll have to tie her up with a rope, so that if she does fall into the water she can drag herself back to the houseboat.'

'Tie me up? Like a little dog? I won't be tied up!' cried Ann indignantly. 'I've never heard of such a thing!'

'My dear child, a great many of the canal-people tie their children up until they can swim,' said Aunt Molly. 'Now, just look what's coming by. I believe it's a canal boat called *Happy Sue*. If it is you will see the two babies of the *Happy Sue* tied up with ropes. How could their parents possibly risk letting them fall in and be drowned?'

A long canal boat came chugging by. In the middle of it was a built-up cabin, where the people lived. In the hold, where they carried goods, were great boxes which the boat was taking to the next big town. On these boxes played two small children, about two years old. They were so alike that the children guessed they were twins.

'Yes – they are tied to that post by a rope,' said Belinda, in surprise. 'Oh, Aunt Molly, what a pretty boat – it's all painted with castles and roses.'

'All the canal boats are painted like that,' said Aunt Molly. 'The canal people have their own ways and customs. You must make friends with some of the children and let them tell you all about their unusual life. They are always on the move, sailing up and down the canals they know so well.'

The canal boat went by, and behind it were two barges full of coal, which the first boat was pulling along. The *Saucy Jane* bobbed up and down a little as the big boats went by and sent waves rippling to the banks.

'Oh! – now the *Saucy Jane* really *does* feel like a boat!' said Ann, delighted. 'She was so still before, she might have been on land. But now she's bobbing like a real boat. I like it.'

'Now for biscuits and lemonade,' said Aunt Molly. 'And we'll decide when you're to come. I move out tomorrow. You can come any time after that.'

'The very next day!' shouted Mike. 'Mummy, can we? The very next day!'

And Mummy nodded her head. 'Yes, we'll come on Thursday. We really will.'

4

Settling In

The children went back to their caravans in great
excitement. It really seemed too good to be true, to
think that they were actually going to the *Saucy Jane*
on Thursday!

Daddy went to see a man in the village about
painting and cleaning the caravans. A nearby farmer
asked if he might borrow Davey for the holidays, to
help in the harvesting. He didn't want Clopper.

'Yes, you may certainly borrow Davey,' said Daddy.
'He's getting too fat. He could do with some hard
work. We will take Clopper with us, in case we want
to go up the canal in the *Saucy Jane*.'

On Thursday a car drew up in the lane outside the
field where the two caravans stood. Mummy and
the children got into it with their luggage. Daddy
said goodbye to them, standing by big Clopper, who
looked in surprise at the waving family.

'It's all right, Clopper. Daddy is riding you all the
way to the *Saucy Jane*!' called Ann. 'You'll take longer
than we do. We'll have everything ready for you,
Daddy, when you come.'

Off went the car. Daddy jumped up on Clopper's broad back, and the two jogged off down the lane. Daddy knew some short cuts, but even so it would take a long while to get to Mayberry on slow old Clopper. But who minded that on this lovely summer's day, when honeysuckle grew in the hedges, and red poppies glowed in the corn! Daddy felt very happy, and he whistled as he rode on Clopper, thinking of the *Saucy Jane*, and wondering how his little family would like their new life.

'The very first thing I must do is to teach them all to swim,' he thought. 'Ann doesn't like the water very much. I do hope she won't make a fuss about it. I wonder if they have reached the *Saucy Jane* yet.'

They had! They were even then climbing up on her spotless deck, calling happily to one another.

'Here we are, in our new home! I hope lots of boats and barges go by so that the *Saucy Jane* bobs up and down all the time!'

'I'm going to have the top bunk. Mummy, can I have the top one? I like climbing.'

'I'll always pull your bed out of the wall, Mummy, and get it ready for you at night.' That was Belinda. She loved to be useful. Living in a caravan and having to do so many odd jobs had taught her to be a very sensible little girl indeed.

Auntie Molly had left blankets, linen, crockery, knives and forks – in fact, everything they would

need. Mummy said that it was even more important to keep Auntie Molly's things nice than their own.

'It is so very kind of her to lend them to us and to trust us with them,' she said. 'We must be extra careful not to break anything, or spoil any of her belongings. If people trust us, the least we can do is to be trustworthy!'

It was such fun unpacking their things and putting them into the drawers that lined the walls of the little cabin-bedrooms. There was even space to hang coats and dresses. Belinda went on shore to pick some flowers to fill the vase on the little table in the sitting-room.

Mummy began to cook a meal on the small stove. She had already packed away into the neat larder the food they had brought with them. She was used to the ways of a caravan, where every bit of space was used. It was just the same on the houseboat.

Soon the smell of bacon frying filled the air, and the children sniffed hungrily.

'Where's Daddy? Isn't he coming yet?' said Ann, and she went out on the deck.

Mummy called to her warningly.

'Now, Ann – don't go near the edge of the boat, in case you topple over! You're not tied up, you know.'

'I can see Daddy and Clopper!' shouted Ann. 'Mike! Belinda! Here he comes! Look at old Clopper; he's as proud as anything to carry Daddy. Hi, Daddy, DADDY!'

Daddy had arranged with Mrs Toms to let Clopper stay in a little field opposite the boat, where she kept a cow and a few geese. He jumped down from the big horse's back, called to Mrs Toms, gave Clopper a friendly smack and ran to the little dinghy by the bank. Clopper stared after him. 'Hrrrrumph!' he said, in surprise, as he saw Daddy rowing off in the boat. Then he went down to the water to have a long drink.

'Hallo, Daddy!' called the children. 'You're just in time for supper. Can you smell the bacon?'

'Welcome to the *Saucy Jane*!' said Mummy, appearing out of the cabin door, her face red with cooking. 'Shall we have our meal up on deck? The cabin is very tiny, and it's such a lovely evening.'

'Oh, yes, yes,' said Belinda. 'I know where a little folding table is. I'll get it and lay it. Hurrah for supper on deck!'

Very soon they were all sitting round the low table, enjoying their first meal on the *Saucy Jane*. A little breeze ran over the water, and the boat lifted herself up and down on the ripples. Two moorhens swam by, and a fish suddenly jumped right out of the water at a fly. Swallows flew low, just skimming the canal, twittering in their sweet high voices.

'This is the loveliest place in the world,' said Belinda. 'Lovelier than the caravan. Oh, listen to the plash-plash of the water against the sides of the boat, Mummy.'

'I do love being right at the very beginning of a holiday,' said Ann, sleepily. 'It's such a nice feeling, I don't want to go to bed tonight, Mummy. I want to stay up on deck for hours and hours.'

'Well, it's your bedtime now,' said Mummy. 'Hurry, and you can have the top bunk! It may be nice out here – but think of sleeping down there, with the *Saucy Jane* bobbing whenever a boat goes by. Hurry, Ann. You're half asleep already!'

5

Belinda Wakes Up Early

The first day on the *Saucy Jane* was one long delight. Belinda awoke first and crept out of her bunk so as not to wake the others. She went up on deck in her nightie, but it was already so warm that she was not a bit cold.

The canal stretched up and down, a soft pale blue, edged with green. The sun was rising, and here and there gold flecks freckled the water. The two moorhens swam by again, and a magnificient swan floated slowly up, his image reflected so beautifully in the water that he really almost looked like two swans, Belinda thought.

'One swan the right way up and the other upside down,' she said to herself. 'Swan, come back at breakfast-time and I'll give you some bread.'

The swan turned his head on his long, graceful neck, gave Belinda a look, and then sailed on again. The swallows came down to the water for flies, twittering all the time. Belinda leaned over to look down into the water itself.

'There are hundreds and hundreds of baby fish!'

she said. 'All going about together. How they dart about! And there's a great big fish. He's made all the little ones hurry away. Oh, here comes a canal boat.'

The gaily-painted boat slid along – but this time it had no motor inside it to chug-chug-chug and send it through the water. Instead, to Belinda's great delight, a big horse was pulling it.

The horse walked steadily along a path on the opposite bank. A rope tied to him ran to the boat, and by this he pulled the long, heavy boat along. A girl sat by the long tiller, guiding her boat easily.

She called to Belinda, 'Nice morning! Going to be hot today!'

'I wish we lived on a boat like yours!' called Belinda. 'Ours stays still.'

'Yours is only a houseboat,' cried the girl. 'It's a play-boat. Ours goes to work. It's a canal boat. We go for miles and miles. Goodbye!'

The canal boat slid right by, sending waves to make the *Saucy Jane* bob again. The horse pulling the boat had not even turned his head. Belinda could hear the sound of his hoofs for a long time in the clear still morning air.

Mummy had heard her calling, and woke up. She looked at her little clock. Half-past five in the morning! Whatever was Belinda doing, up so early? Mummy went up on deck, ready to scold.

'Belinda,' she began in a low voice, 'do you know

that it's only half-past five? How naughty of you to come up here and shout!'

'Mummy – it's so perfectly lovely,' said Belinda, putting her arm round her mother. 'Other people are awake. Look, that long boat has just passed by and the little girl guiding it called out to me. And here comes another boat – without a horse this time, but with a motor inside to drive it. Chug-chug-chug – it makes rather a nice noise, I think.'

Mummy forgot to scold. She sat there in the early morning sunshine with Belinda, watching everything. The water was a deeper blue now, and the golden patches were so bright that Belinda could not look at them.

The big fish went flashing by. More and more flies danced over the water and the swallows skimmed along by the dozen, snapping up the flies for their breakfast. The magnificent swan came back again, and looked at Belinda as if to say, 'Is it breakfast-time yet?'

'Not nearly,' said Belinda. 'Though I'm most awfully hungry.'

Mummy laughed. 'I believe I can hear the others waking up,' she said. 'If so, we'd better all get up and I'll get breakfast. We can always have a sleep in the afternoon if we are tired. But really, this morning is too beautiful to waste even a minute of it.'

Ann and Mike came up on deck, rubbing their

sleepy eyes. Ann cried out in joy when she saw the sparkling water and the waiting swan.

'Oh, you should have woken me too! Mummy, isn't it lovely to know there's water under us, not land? Oh, do let's feed the swan. Where's Daddy? Daddy, wake up! You're missing something lovely!'

Then Daddy too came out in surprise, and sat down to watch the water and the swan and the fish. They all watched the long canal boats too, painted with so many bright patterns. Even the drinking-jars were painted, and the kettles and saucepans.

Some of the smaller children were tied with ropes, and once the children saw a dog on a barge, tied up with a rope too.

'He might fall in without being noticed,' said Daddy, 'and though he can swim, he would soon be left behind. So they've tied him up.'

'Good morning to you!' called the canal-people politely, as they passed in their long boats, and each time the *Saucy Jane* bobbed as if she too was saying good morning.

'How early the canal-folk go to work,' said Mummy.

'I suppose they are up at sunrise and in bed at sunset. Well, if *we* get up at sunrise like this, our bedtime will have to be early too. Get dressed, children, and I'll cook breakfast. You lay the table, Belinda, and we'll have it out here.'

It was a very early breakfast, but the children

thought it was the nicest one they had ever had. The swan came up to be fed, and pecked up the bits of bread from the water. Once or twice he caught them in his beak when Mike threw some, and the children thought this was very clever.

'Well – we must get on with a few jobs,' said Mummy at last. 'And then, my dears, you are going to have a most important lesson. Daddy's going to teach you how to swim!'

9

A Most Important Lesson

The children hurried to do the little jobs on the boat. Belinda helped Mummy to wash up. The dishes were put into the rack to dry. Belinda had to give them a polish with a cloth when she laid the table.

Ann made the beds, or rather the bunks. Mike took out all the bedding from his mother's bed, folded it tidily and put it into its cupboard. Then back into the wall went the bed, folding up neatly.

Daddy went to see if Clopper was all right, and to do a little shopping. Everyone worked happily. It didn't seem to be work, somehow! The sun shone down warmly, and the water glittered and sparkled. The swan sailed about round the boat hopefully, and drove away the two moorhens.

'I wish Daddy would come back,' said Ann. 'I want to swim across to the other side.'

'You won't be able to swim at once, silly,' said Mike. 'It may take you a few days to learn. Look, lie flat on the deck, and I'll show you the strokes to use with your arms and legs.'

But before Ann could do that, Daddy hailed

them from the shore. 'Just coming! Are you ready for a swim?'

He was soon across and changed into swimming trunks. 'Now,' he said, 'I'm going to dive into the water and swim past the boat. I want you all to lean over and watch how I use my arms and legs. I shall use my arms like this . . . they will push away the water in front of me, and my legs will open and shut, so that I drive my body through the water. You must all watch carefully.'

Splash! Daddy dived beautifully into the canal, and the children watched him. They could see his brown arms and legs moving strongly.

'I see how he swims,' said Ann. 'Look, he pushes away the water with his arms, and brings them back in front of him to begin all over again, and he opens and shuts his legs like a frog does when *he* swims. I'm sure I could do that!'

Mike was watching very closely. He lay down flat on the deck. 'Watch me, Mummy,' he said, and he began to do the same arm and leg strokes as Daddy. 'Am I doing it right? Are these the strokes I should use?'

'Yes, Mike. That looks very good,' said Mummy. 'If only you can do that in the water, you'll do well. You lie down and do the strokes too, Ann and Belinda.'

So they did, but Mummy said they were not as good as Mike. Then Daddy called to them. 'Get on

to the bank, and you'll find a nice shallow piece of water to step into. It will only be up to your waists, and you can learn your strokes there.'

The three children climbed on to the bank. Then they slid down into the water. They were hot with the sun and the water was cold.

'Oooh!' said Mike, but he plunged himself right under at once. That was what Daddy always did, he knew.

'Oooh!' said Belinda, and waited a bit. She went in very slowly, bit by bit, not liking the cold water very much but determined to be brave.

'Good girl! Jolly good, Mike!' cried Daddy. 'Come on, Ann!'

But Ann wouldn't go in any further than her knees. 'It's cold!' she kept saying. 'It's too cold!'

'It's warm once you're in!' cried Mike. 'Baby Ann! Doesn't like the cold water! How can you learn to swim if you don't even get in?'

'Go on, Ann,' said Mummy, who was now in the water herself, swimming along strongly. 'Hurry up! You look silly, shivering there.'

It took Ann at least ten minutes to get in up to her waist. Daddy and Mummy began to teach Mike and Belinda, and they took no more notice of Ann.

'If she wants to be a baby, we'll let her,' said Daddy. 'Now, Mike, that's right – out with your arms – bring them back – out again. Good! Now try your legs. I'll

put my hand under your tummy and hold you safe so that you won't go under. You can trust me. I'll be sure to tell you when I think you're doing well enough to take my hand away.'

Mike got on extremely well. Soon Daddy took his hand away from under his tummy, and to his great delight Mike found that he could swim three strokes all by himself without going under.

'You'll soon be able to swim,' said Daddy, pleased, and turned to see how Mummy was getting on with Belinda. She too was doing her best, and Mummy was pleased with her. But she would not let Mummy take her hand away, so they couldn't tell if she could really swim a few strokes or not.

As for Ann, she wouldn't even try! As soon as Daddy made her take her legs off the bottom of the canal, she screamed, 'Don't! Don't! I'm frightened!'

'Well, you needn't be,' said Mike. 'Daddy won't let you go. You can trust him.'

But Ann was silly and she wouldn't even try to use her arms in the way Daddy told her. So he sent her back to the boat.

'I'm ashamed of you,' he said. 'You must try again tomorrow.'

After a while they all got out of the water and lay on the warm roof of the cabin to dry themselves in the sun. It was delicious! Ann felt rather ashamed of herself.

'I'll try properly tomorrow,' she told Daddy. 'I really will.'

'Well, little Ann, you can see for yourself that if you live on the water you must know how to swim,' said Daddy. 'I'll give you another chance tomorrow, and we'll see how you get on. Mike and Belinda will be swimming in a week's time – you don't want to be the only person in the *Saucy Jane Family* who can't swim, do you?'

7

Ann Has a Dreadful Shock

The happy summer days went by, and soon the family felt as if they had been living on the *Saucy Jane* for weeks! The weather was hot, the canal was blue and silver from dawn to dusk, and the swan became so tame that he hardly ever left the boat, but bobbed about by it all day. All night too, Belinda said, for once when she had gone on deck in the middle of the night she had seen him sleeping nearby, his head tucked under his wing.

Mike and Belinda could swim well now. Mike especially was a fine strong swimmer, and Daddy was proud of him. But Ann was still foolish. She squealed when she first went into the water and always made a fuss. And she wouldn't try to swim at all.

But one afternoon something happened that made her change her mind. Mummy was lying down in the cabin, glad to be out of the blazing sun. Daddy had gone to talk to a fisherman up the canal. Mike and Belinda were on the bank at the back of the houseboat, lying in the cool grass.

Ann was playing with Stella, one of her best-loved

dolls. And quite suddenly Stella slid along the deck and fell overboard into the water.

Ann gave a squeal. 'Oh, Stella! Don't drown! Keep still and I'll reach you with a stick!'

She got a stick and, leaning over the edge of the boat, she tried to hook poor Stella up to safety. But instead of doing that, she found herself slipping too, and suddenly into the water she went with a splash! She screamed as she fell, 'Mike! Mike!' Then she could say no more, for she went right under the water and sank down, choking. She struck out with her arms, but she had not learnt to swim, and she was terrified.

'Why didn't I learn, why didn't I learn?' she thought, as she went down deeper. Water poured into her nose and mouth, she couldn't breathe, she couldn't do anything at all!

Mike heard the shout. He shot up from the bank when he heard the splash. He ran on to the boat, looked over the edge and saw poor Ann sinking down into the canal.

'MUMMY!' yelled Mike. 'Ann's fallen in!'

Then the plucky boy jumped straight into the canal himself and tried to reach Ann. He found her, and tried to pull her up. In a terrible fright the little girl clutched him, and began to pull him down under the water too.

Goodness knows what would have happened

next if Mummy hadn't gone into the water too, and somehow got the two of them into the shallow part, where Mike could stand. He was gasping and choking. 'Oh Mummy, she nearly drowned me.'

Mummy carried Ann up on deck. The little girl's eyes were closed, but she was breathing. She had not been in the water long enough for any great harm to be done. She soon opened her eyes, choked, and began to cry with fright.

Mummy was very frightened about Ann's fall.

'We daren't risk such a thing happening again,' she said to Daddy, who was very upset too. 'She won't learn to swim, so we shall just *have* to tie her to a rope.'

Then, much to Ann's dismay, she had a rope tied round her waist all the time she was on the boat. Now, if she fell into the water, she could haul herself out. But Ann hated the rope round her.

'The canal-boat children laugh at me,' she wept. 'Nobody as old as I am is tied up. I feel like a puppy-dog. Untie me Mummy, and I promise not to fall in again.'

'I'm sorry, darling, but we can't risk it,' said Mummy. 'You're too precious. And, after all, you can always get rid of the rope yourself, if you want to.'

'How?' asked Ann. 'I can't untie this big knot.'

'I know,' said Mummy. 'I don't mean that. I mean that you have only to be sensible and learn to swim and you will have the rope taken off at once.'

'Oh!' said Ann, and she began to think seriously about learning to swim. After all, it had been dreadful sinking down into the water and choking like that. She shivered whenever she thought of it. And it did seem easy to learn to swim if only she would be brave and trust Daddy.

'How can you be brave if you aren't?' she asked Mike.

'I don't know,' said Mike. 'You might put it into your prayers, perhaps. You can always ask God for help in anything, Mummy says.'

So that night Ann begged God in her prayers to help her to be brave enough to learn to swim, and made up her mind that she really would try.

And, of course, the very next day she found that once she let Daddy really help her, it wasn't so dreadful after all! She *could* be brave, she *could* try – and soon, she would be able to swim!

Daddy was pleased with her. 'You're just as brave as the others now,' he told her. 'And I do believe that you'll swim as fast as Belinda. You've got such a strong stroke with your legs. That's right – *shoot* your arms out – *use* your legs well. My word, I can hardly keep up with you!'

Ann was pleased. 'I did what you said, Mike, and asked God to help me,' she told him. 'It was much easier after that. I'll soon be able to swim as fast as you!'

Soon she was like a fish in the water, and Daddy

said she needn't have the rope tied round her any more. The whole family went swimming together, and presently Ann could actually swim right to the other bank, have a little rest and swim back again!

'I've a family of fish!' said Daddy. 'Now look out for waves – here come two barges!'

The children liked the waves. They lifted their arms from the water and hailed the barges, and the barge people shouted back.

'I wish we could go up the canal on a canal boat,' said Ann. 'Oh, I really do wish we could.'

'Well, perhaps we can,' said Daddy. 'We'll have to find out!'

8

What Happened to Beauty

Daddy had decided that it wouldn't be possible to go up the canal on the heavy old houseboat, which was moored flat to the bank. The children had been very disappointed.

'We needn't have brought Clopper then,' said Ann. 'He won't have anything to do. He'll be very bored.'

'Well, maybe we can go on a canal boat if we can find someone who will take us just for the trip,' said Daddy.

But somehow it didn't seem to happen. Either the boats were taking coal, and Mummy said she didn't want them to go on a dirty coalboat — or the canal-people didn't want to take them — or they just wouldn't stop long enough to discuss it.

Then one early morning a very strange thing happened just by the *Saucy Jane*. The children were all sitting on the houseboat roof watching the canal. They were waiting for a brilliant blue kingfisher who had fished near there the last day or two.

'He sits on that branch, watches for a fish, then dives straight into the water and catches it,' said

Mike. 'He's got such a strong beak.'

It was while they were watching for the kingfisher that the strange accident happened.

A canal boat, drawn by a slow old horse, came silently up the canal. A boy was guiding the boat, yawning sleepily. No one walked beside the horse, which plodded along the tow-path by itself, its head down.

'Even the horse looks half asleep,' said Belinda. 'He stumbles a bit now and again, look.'

They watched the tired horse – and then, unexpectedly, it left the tow-path and walked straight into the water! It had fallen asleep as it walked, and in its sleep had not known where it was going.

It went in with a terrific splash! Mike leapt to his feet, startled. The boy on the canal boat gave a yell. 'Dad! Beauty's fallen in. DAD!'

Then there was such a to-do! People poured up from the cabin of the canal boat. The boat was guided towards where the horse was struggling in the canal.

'Oh, can he swim, can he swim?' squealed Ann. 'Oh, don't let him drown!'

But the horse had fortunately fallen into a shallow part of the water, and after he had lain in surprise on the mud, wide awake with shock, he decided to get up.

He was very frightened, and it took three of the canal-boat men to quieten him and take him from

the water. They rubbed him down, and one of them fixed a bag of oats on his nose. When he felt it there, he snuffled down into the oats and began to eat. Then the men knew he would be all right.

The children had watched the whole thing in the greatest excitement. Fancy a horse falling asleep and walking into the water! What a good thing he was all right.

The canal boat was drawn up to the side. Everyone waited for the horse to recover himself and go on with his towing. But when he was set on the path again and coaxed to walk along it, he limped badly.

'Wait a minute,' said one of the men, and bent to examine the horse's leg. 'He's strained this leg. He won't be able to walk for a day or two, poor thing. It will never get better if we make him work now.'

'Well, what about our load?' said another man, impatiently. 'We've got to get that up to Birmingham before Saturday. It's important.'

'We'll get a tug to tow us,' said the first man.

Then Daddy, who had been listening and watching too, thought of a grand idea, and he called to the man. 'Hi! Do you want the loan of a good strong horse? I've got mine in the field there. You're welcome to use him for a bit if you like. He's longing for a bit of work.'

The men pushed their boat out from the side, and soon she was lying by the *Saucy Jane*. Daddy and the

men began to talk. The children looked with the greatest interest at the long canal boat.

'Look at all the castles and hearts and roses painted on the sides of the boat,' said Mike. 'We've often seen them before, but we've never been able to look at them so closely as this. I wonder who painted them and why.'

'All the canal boats have them,' said Belinda. 'I wish I could get on this boat and look at everything. Even the tiller is painted, Mike. Just look.'

'I say – listen to what Daddy is saying,' said Mike suddenly, in excitement.

'Well,' Daddy was saying, 'you are welcome to borrow Clopper, my horse, if you like, and leave yours to rest in the field over there. He's a good strong horse, is Clopper.'

'That's kind of you, sir,' said the old boatman. 'Er – how much would you be asking us for the use of him?'

'Oh, I don't want you to pay me anything,' said Daddy. 'I'd be glad to have my horse getting a bit of exercise.'

'Well, sir – I don't rightly like taking your horse and giving nothing back,' said the old man.

'Would you like to do something for *me*, then?' said Daddy, and he smiled. 'See those three youngsters of mine? They badly want to go up the canal for a trip – but this houseboat of ours won't budge. You

wouldn't like to take us with you, would you?'

'Ay, that I would, if you don't mind putting up with our rough ways,' said the old boatman. 'We'll be going through a few locks, and the children will like to see those at work. And we'll be passing through a long tunnel too, bored in a big hill.'

'Daddy, can we really go?' cried Belinda, and she rushed up to her father. 'It would be grand. I *do* so want to travel up the canal and see everything.'

'Well, just for a day,' said Daddy. 'We'll be ready in ten minutes, boatman. You can go and get my horse while you're waiting!'

9

A Day on the *Happy Ted*

Mummy quickly got ready a picnic meal to take with them, and told the children to get their macks just in case they needed them. The old boatman and his son went across to the field to get Clopper. Clopper came back with them willingly.

'I'm sure Clopper must feel as pleased and excited as we do!' said Ann. 'I shall take Stella. She'll want to see everything too.'

'I feel just like an adventure today,' said Mike. 'Goodness, fancy going up the canal – past villages and towns, through fields and woods, locks and tunnels!'

Clopper was tied to the tow-rope. The other horse, patted and petted, was left to graze peacefully in Clopper's field, and get over his shock. Everyone went on to the canal boat.

One of the men went to walk with Clopper, for he had never been a tow-horse in his life. But he seemed to understand quite well exactly what to do, and he plodded along slowly and steadily.

The three children felt a little shy on the canal boat at first. There was an old, rather fierce-looking

woman there, but when she smiled she looked very kind. There were also three children, two boys and a girl, but they too seemed shy and hid among the boxes and crates that formed the cargo of the boat.

'It's called *Happy Ted*,' said Mike, reading the name painted on the boat.

'Happy Ted was my grandad,' said the old boatman. 'He got this boat and my granny on the same day, and he called it *Happy Ted* after himself. Then my father had it, and now I've got it. And my son there will have it one day.'

'Who paints all those lovely pictures everywhere?' asked Belinda, looking at the pretty castles and roses she saw on everything. 'I do like them.'

'Oh, I painted most of them,' said the old man. 'And my son he painted a few. All us canal-boat people paint our boats with hearts and castles and roses. It's our custom, and a very old one too.'

'You've painted your big water-can, and your kettles, and this biscuit-tin too,' said Ann. 'And you've even painted a pattern down the handle of your broom and your mop!'

'Ah, we like everything to be bright and tidy,' said the boatman's wife. 'You should see my cabin.'

'Can I?' said Ann, who was longing to peep into the tiny place where all the family seemed to live.

The old woman went backwards down the steps into the cabin. The children followed. There was

hardly room for them to stand there all together, and certainly Daddy would have had to bend his head or he would have knocked it against the low ceiling.

But what a bright, lovely, little place it was! So tiny – like a dolls' house – and yet so many things in it that the children felt if they looked for hours they would never see them all.

There were a lot of brass knobs and ornaments hanging by the door. These glinted and winked like the sun, they were so bright and well-polished. Ann fingered one of them. 'It's like a brass ornament that Clopper wears,' she said. 'Why do you have so many?'

'Ah, we canal-folk collect them,' said the old woman. 'We like to see those brass things winking at us there. The better-off we are, the more we have. Don't you have any at home?'

'No,' said Ann, making up her mind to collect as many as she could, and hang them just inside her caravan door when she got back to it at the end of the holidays. 'Oh, look, Belinda, there's the little stove for cooking – and a table to sit at – but where's the bed?'

The bed was let into the wall in exactly the same way as the one in the *Saucy Jane*. On the wooden panel that shut it in was painted a bright pattern of hearts and roses. Mike wished he could paint like that. Perhaps Mummy would let him paint castles and things on the caravan door when he went back.

Everything was squashed into the small space of
the cabin. The children could hardly believe that five
or six people lived there all their lives!

'Fancy! You have your dinner here, and you sleep
here, and on wet days you sit here!' said Mike. 'It
must be a dreadful squeeze.'

'We like it,' said the old woman. 'I couldn't live
in a house! What, be in a place that stands still all
the time – that never hears the lap of the water, nor
feels the swing of the waves! No, the canal life's a
grand life. We're water-wanderers, we are. You'll
find us all up and down the canals, with our boats
painted with hearts and roses and castles. We know
the countryside like no one else, we know the canals
and their ways, and we're proud of it!'

She looked at the children as if she was sorry for
people who didn't live on a canal boat. Land-folk!
Poor things! What a boring life they must have, she
thought.

It was hot and stuffy down in the little cabin, and
Ann began to pant. They all went up the steps and
out on deck. The long canal boat was going smoothly
through the water, with Clopper tugging her steadily.

'Good horse that,' said the old man, taking his pipe
out of his mouth. 'Ay, a fine horse. He'll go a good
many miles a day.'

The children gazed ahead, and saw that the country
rose uphill in front of them.

'How can we get the boat uphill?' asked Belinda, puzzled. 'Look, we've got to go quite a long way up.'

'We'll go through a lock soon,' said the old boatman, smiling. 'Then you'll see how a boat can go uphill! Ah, you didn't know such a thing could be, did you? But you'll see, you'll see!'

10

Uphill in a Boat!

How can a boat go uphill? That was the question all the children were asking each other. Ann and Belinda did not know what a lock was, and Mike had only heard of canal-locks once or twice.

The *Happy Ted* went on and on, and Clopper's hoofs sounded just like his name as he plodded along. Then the old boatman pointed ahead.

'There's the lock,' he said. 'I'll tell you what happens, if you listen well.'

The children were all ears at once.

'Now you see,' said the old man, 'the water above the lock is higher than below it. How are we going to get the boat up to the higher water?'

The children couldn't imagine. 'Well, now,' said the old man, 'a lock is a small space, big enough to take one or two boats, between the high canal-water and the low canal-water. There are gates at each end, so that when a boat is in that bit of space, and both the gates are shut, she's sort of *locked* in. See?'

'Yes,' said the three.

'Well, now,' said the old man again, 'the gates at

our end, the low-water end, are open, and we'll go straight into that bit of space there. Then we'll shut the gates behind us and lock ourselves in.'

'What's the use of that?' asked Mike.

'Ah, you wait!' said the boatman. 'Now comes the clever bit! As soon as we're in that locked-up space, we're going to open holes in the gate in front of us. See? And water is going to pour through the holes, down into our locked-up bit of space. And that water is going to fill up the lock, and raise us up higher and higher and higher!'

'But what will happen when the water down in the lock rises as high as the water outside the gate?' said Mike.

'Aha! That's another clever bit!' said the boatman. 'What do we do then but open the gates in front of us and there we are, on a level with the high-up canal, and we can sail out as easy as you like!'

'It's a marvellous idea!' said Mike. 'Really marvellous! Oh, I do want to get into the lock and see it all happen!'

'But what do you do if you're in a boat that's coming down from a high part of the canal to the low part?' said Belinda.

'Easy!' said Mike. '*I* know that! You just go into the filled-up lock, shut the gates behind you, and then open holes in the opposite gate to let the water out and wait till the level of the lock is the same as the

low part; then open the gates and out you go!'

'Right!' said the boatman. 'Now you watch what happens in a minute.'

Clopper walked right up to the lock. There was a steep bit of gravel for him to go up to the higher lock-gate, and up he went. The lower gates of the lock were open, and in went the *Happy Ted*.

She stayed there, held by the tow-rope, which was now fastened round a big stone. The gates behind her were shut by the boatman's son. Then he and the old boatman went to open the holes in the gate in front – the 'paddles,' as they were called.

The children sat in the *Happy Ted*, shut up in the lock, waiting. Above them, behind other tall gates, was a great high wall of water. Somehow they had to get the *Happy Ted* up there so that they might sail out on the level again.

Water began to pour into the lock through the paddles of the gate. What a noise it made! It was like waterfalls, rushing and gushing. The children felt excited.

'We're rising up, we're rising up! The lock is filling!' cried Belinda. 'See that mark on the wall above us – now it's level with us – now it's below us, lost in the water. We're rising up, we're rising up!'

The lock was filled at last. The *Happy Ted* was much higher up than she had been before. She was level with the high part of the canal. She nosed against

the top parts of the lockgate and they swung open. Out she went, drawn by Clopper, who was now once more pulling hard on the tow-rope.

'We're through the lock! We're through! We've taken a boat uphill!' cried Mike. 'It's wonderful! Are there any more locks soon?'

'Oh, yes – there's plenty just here,' said the old man. 'It's slow work, going through them. But if you're not in a hurry, why worry?'

'We're not in a hurry! We'd like this day to last for a whole week!' said Ann. 'Oh, look at those corn-fields! They're getting golden already.'

The canal boat went slowly on through fields and woods, past pretty gardens, past lonely farmhouses. Sometimes it went by a small village where children came to wave. Once or twice it came again to a lock, and the children this time got out to help to open and shut the gates. It was lovely to watch the water pouring fast into the lock, filling it, bringing the *Happy Ted* higher and higher, until at last she could sail proudly out on the level again, much higher up than she had been before.

They went slowly by a dirty town. Here the canal was muddy and smelt nasty. The children didn't like it.

'Do people *have* to live in towns?' asked Ann. 'Do they choose to?'

'Oh, lots of people don't like the country,' said

Daddy. 'I'm glad you love it. Look at that busy yard over there. See the loads being put into the canal boats, swung into them by the big cranes.'

'How useful the boats are!' said Belinda, in wonder. 'What a lot of heavy things they carry, Daddy. There are railroads and ordinary roads, and water-roads, aren't there? But I like the water-roads the best.'

Out beyond the town they went, and in the distance stood a big hill. The canal ran straight towards it.

'We're going inside that hill,' said the boatman. 'Put on your macks. It's cold and wet in there.'

11

A Strange Adventure

'We've taken this boat uphill – and now we're going to take it *through* a hill,' said Belinda. 'It all sounds like magic. I never knew things like this happened before.'

'What happens to Clopper?' said Ann, suddenly. 'He won't like walking through a tunnel. He'll be afraid.'

'Oh, Clopper can't walk through the tunnel, missy,' said the boatman. 'There's no towpath. He'll have to go right over the hill. My son will take him.'

'Are you sure you children want to go through the tunnel?' said Mummy. 'You may be afraid. It's so dark and damp.'

But all the children meant to go. What, miss an adventure like this? Certainly not!

'How's the boat going to get through the tunnel without Clopper?' said Mike. 'It hasn't got a motor to drive it along, like a motorboat.'

'There's a powerboat coming up behind,' said the boatman. 'He'll give us a tug. We'll wait for him. You take Clopper, son!' he called. His son leapt ashore,

untied the tow-rope, and disappeared up a steep grassy path with Clopper. Ann pictured them walking right over the hill and down.

The powerboat came up. ' 'Hoy there!' called the boatman. 'Give us a tug, will you?'

'Right!' called back the other man, and went on ahead. He caught the tow-rope of the *Happy Ted*, and made it fast to his own boat. Then, with a chug-chug-chug, his long canal boat disappeared into the dark hole of the tunnel, and behind it went the *Happy Ted*.

How dark it was! Ann looked back and saw the hole they had come in by. It looked like a far-off speck of light now. Further into the tunnel they went and further. It grew darker still and the air was musty and damp.

The walls were dripping wet. It was somehow rather frightening and Ann cuddled up to Mummy, pulling her mack round her, for she felt very cold.

Suddenly she looked up and saw another tunnel right above her! She jumped in fright. 'It's all right,' said Mummy, 'that was only an air-hole going right up through the hill to the top and coming out into the open air. We have to have a bit of fresh air here and there in this tunnel, you know!'

There were three or four air-holes and they were strange to look through. Far, far away at the top of them was a speck of light. Ann wished the tunnel would come to an end.

Chug–chug–chug–chug, went the motor of the boat in front, sounding oddly loud in the round dark tunnel. Chug–chug–chug–chug! Water trickled off the walls nearby, and the canal looked deep and black. Nobody spoke at all.

Then Mike gave a cry that made everyone jump. 'Look! What's that? That red thing gleaming in front of us, like a giant's eye!'

'Ah, that's only another boat coming towards us!' said the boatman. 'Now listen, and you'll hear him tooting to tell us to keep to our side of the wall.'

'Too-toot-tootooot!' came the call from the tug coming towards them. And the two canal boats answered at once. 'Too-too-too-tootoot!' Ann wished she could blow the strange trumpet that the old boatman blew.

Their boat and the tug that was pulling them kept close to their own side of the wall, scraping against it to let the other boat pass. Behind it came two more boats, full of goods. Bump-bump-bump. The boats scraped together now and again, for the tunnel was narrow.

Then they were gone, and the children saw only a faint light in the distance, getting smaller and smaller.

'I wish this tunnel would end,' sighed Ann. 'I don't like it any more. It's too long. I like the locks better.'

'You look out in front of you,' said the boatman, and he pointed ahead. Ann looked – and to her

delight she saw a round patch of daylight coming nearer and nearer.

'Hurrah!' said Mike. 'We're getting to the end of it. Soon be out now!'

Cold and wet, the children at last came out into the blazing sunshine, and how they loved the feel of the warm sun on their heads and shoulders! They flung off their damp macks at once.

The powerboat in front threw back their tow-rope to them, called goodbye and went off up the canal, chug-chug-chug-chug!

'There's Clopper waiting for us!' said Mike, pleased. 'I guess he wondered where we had all gone to. Clopper, you did better to go over the hill than through it!'

Once again they went on up the canal, with Clopper pulling well. How peaceful it was! How lovely to have a picnic meal on the deck of the long boat, sitting on the cargo, watching the green banks slip slowly by.

'Where are we going to sleep tonight?' asked Mike. 'We'll never all get into that little cabin!'

'We're going back to the *Saucy Jane*, of course,' said Daddy. 'We can easily catch a bus. We'll be back in no time.'

'In *no* time!' said Belinda, surprised. 'But it has taken us all day to get here – and soon the sun will be going down!'

But Daddy was right. When they said goodbye

to the canal boat folk, and got on the bus, they were back at the *Saucy Jane* in an hour's time! How extraordinary.

'A canal-boat is a fine peaceful way of getting about,' said Daddy, 'but nobody could call it fast. Well, here we are at the dear old *Saucy Jane*. She looks pretty and peaceful enough, in the setting sun.'

'We've had a lovely, exciting day,' said Mike. 'We may have gone at only about two miles an hour – but we've had time to see even the smallest flower at the edge of the water. Oh, I wish I lived on a canal boat! I'll buy one when I grow up, and you girls can come with me and live on it. What a time we'll have!'

12

Goodbye to the *Saucy Jane*

The holidays went by too quickly. August slipped away and September came in. Clopper had come back a long while ago and Beauty had gone back to work. All the children could swim like fishes, and each of them could row and steer a boat just as well as Daddy could.

The *Happy Ted* passed them once or twice more, and they always waved and called out their news. They knew other boats, too, and once they had gone off again for the day in another boat – but this time they had gone down the canal instead of up.

'I want to go downhill this time,' Ann had said, so she had her wish. There was a tunnel on the way, but all three children had got out and walked over the hill with the horse. No more long dark tunnels for them! One was enough.

They had learnt many things besides swimming, diving and boating. They had learnt the ways of the wild creatures of the water, and had grown to love the great long-legged herons that sometimes visited the canal, and the white swans who now

came to be fed every morning.

They were all brown and strong. Their legs and arms were sturdy with swimming and rowing. Daddy and Mummy were proud of their three children.

'It was the best holiday we could have chosen for them!' said Mummy. 'The very best. They've been good children, helpful and sensible and kind – and what a lot they've learnt.'

It was sad to have to think of leaving the *Saucy Jane*. But now the evenings were getting chilly, and often a low mist came over the water that made the children shiver.

'I don't want to go, though,' said Ann. 'I want to stay all the year round, Mummy.'

'You wouldn't like it, Ann,' said Mummy. 'You are not a child of the canal. You would shiver and get cold and be miserable. It is all right for the summer – but now that the autumn is coming, we must get back to our cosy caravans.'

'And there's school, too,' said Mike. 'I like school. I want to play games again with the other boys and read my books and do carpentering.'

'I like school, too,' said Belinda. They all went to boarding-school, but each weekend they returned to the caravans. And how cosy those caravans were in the wintertime, when the curtains were drawn, the lamps were lighted, and the stove glowed warmly! Games and books and television – yes,

winter was as good as well as summer.

They cleaned the *Saucy Jane* well. Belinda scrubbed the decks and made them spotless. Ann helped Mummy to turn out all the neat cupboards. Mike and Daddy repainted the little boat that belonged to the *Saucy Jane*.

'Auntie Molly will ask us again if we leave her houseboat better even than we found it!' said Belinda. 'Mummy, do you think she will?'

'I shouldn't be surprised,' said Mummy. 'Well fancy, we have only broken one cup and one plate, and those I have managed to replace. And except for the ink that Mike spilt on the rug I really don't believe we have done any damage at all.'

'I'll pay for the rug to be cleaned,' said Mike, and Mummy said yes, he could. Once that was done, the boat would be as perfect as when they first came aboard.

They packed their things into the two trunks they had brought with them. They locked up the *Saucy Jane*, and Mike took the key across to Mrs Toms She was sorry to see them go.

'I've got fond of the *Saucy Jane* Family!' she said. 'I'll miss you. Come again next year!'

The car came driving up and everyone got in. Daddy had already gone off with Clopper, riding on his back. Everybody felt a little sad.

'Goodbye, *Saucy Jane*,' said Mike. 'We did love

living in your little cabins, sunning ourselves on your white deck, and feeling you bob up and down on the little waves!'

'Goodbye, swans,' said Ann. 'I'm afraid you won't get bread for your breakfast tomorrow. But I expect Mrs Toms will feed you if you go to her.'

'Goodbye, canal!' said Belinda. 'I've loved every minute of you and all the wild things that belong to you, and the long painted boats that slide over you day by day. Goodbye.'

'Now don't let's get miserable about saying goodbye,' said Mummy. 'We may no longer be the *Saucy Jane* Family, but we shall soon be the Caravan Family again – and we shall say "hallo" to the two caravans, and to dear old Davey and Clopper!'

Off they went in the car. Nobody said a word for a little while, because they were all thinking of the happy *Saucy Jane*. But then they began to think of the caravans.

'I can collect the wood each day for our fire, Mummy,' said Mike.

'I can fetch eggs and butter from the farm,' said Ann.

'I can keep our caravan tidy and clean like I used to,' said Belinda. 'Oh, Mummy – won't it be fun to be back again in our houses on wheels! One for you and Daddy and one for us children! I'm longing to see the caravans again.'

And how lovely they looked when they *did* see

them. There they stood in a pretty field, all newly painted, clean and bright. The children tumbled out of the car with a shout.

'Hallo, caravans! We're back again. Hallo, darling Davey, have you missed us? Clopper and Daddy will soon be back!'

Soon the fire was going and Mummy was cooking their first caravan meal. It was good to be back after all. Daddy was pleased to see such smiling faces when he arrived on Clopper.

'Hallo, Caravan Family!' he said. 'It's a funny thing, but you're JUST as nice as the *Saucy Jane* Family!'

And he was right about that, wasn't he?

The
Pole Star
Family

Contents

1

Granny's Good Idea

Everyone thought that Mike, Belinda and Ann were very lucky children. 'Fancy having a caravan to live in each weekend!' said Kenneth, one of their school friends.

'*Two*,' said Mike. 'Painted red and yellow. One for Mummy and Daddy and one for us three. It's fun.'

'And there are taps in each caravan that really turn on, and bunks for us to sleep in,' said Belinda. 'When the night is warm we have our door open so that we can see right out in the field. It's lovely in buttercup time. The buttercups grow right up to the caravan steps!'

'It does sound lovely,' said Kenneth. 'And didn't you live in a houseboat on the river once?'

'We lived in the *Saucy Jane* on a canal,' said Ann. 'We had a glorious time. Oh, I do wish we could go in a boat again!'

'Yes, but I'd like to go in a boat that travels about,' said Mike. 'Our houseboat stayed still. Wouldn't I like to go in a steamer!'

'What, far away to foreign lands?' said Kenneth.

'You don't mean all by yourself, do you?'

'Oh, *no* – with our whole family,' said Mike. 'We do everything together. It wouldn't be fun, somehow, if we couldn't enjoy things with one another.'

'I think you're a lucky family,' said Kenneth, and all the others agreed. 'Lovely things are always happening to you.'

But oh dear – horrid ones happened too. The very next day, which was Saturday, Mummy had a telegram that said Granny was very ill. She called to Daddy.

'Oh, Daddy – look at this. I must go at once. Can you see to the children this weekend?'

'Yes, of course,' said Daddy, 'and Belinda is very sensible now. We can trust her to do the shopping and a bit of cooking, can't we, Belinda?'

'Oh yes,' said Belinda, 'but Mummy – poor old Granny! Do take her some flowers from us all, won't you?'

Mummy went off in a hurry, looking worried. The caravan family set to work to tidy up the caravans, and then Belinda went off to do the shopping.

She did hope that Granny wasn't *very* ill. Granny was a darling. She was kind and generous and liked making jokes. She had been going to come and stay with them in the caravans, when Daddy went away for a week, at the end of summer term. Now perhaps she wouldn't.

When the end of term came Granny was still ill. And then, in August, something else happened! Mike began to cough badly, and then he suddenly made a very odd whooping noise.

'Oh dear!' said Mummy. 'That sounds like whooping-cough to me. What a good thing it is the summer holidays, and you won't miss any school. Daddy, as Granny is now in a nursing-home, I think I'd better take him to her house, and hope that Belinda and Ann won't get it. They can stay here in the caravans with you.'

Belinda and Ann were very sad. Poor Mike. All alone at Granny's in the summer holidays. And even Granny wasn't there!

But in a week's time both Belinda and Ann had whooping-cough too, so Mike was brought back to the caravan, and they were once more all together. Mike had it badly and so had Ann, but Belinda whooped only once or twice.

'What a summer holiday,' groaned poor Mummy. 'Granny ill all the time – though she's really getting on now, thank goodness – and now the children down with whooping-cough!'

'We are certainly not a very lucky family at the moment,' said Mike, gloomily, and coughed.

The holidays went by. The summer was not a very good one, and Mummy was quite in despair, because, she said, the children needed a lot of sunshine, and

were getting hardly any. They nearly left the caravans and went to stay at Granny's.

Soon the autumn term came near. Mummy looked at her three pale-faced children and felt sad. 'They need a good holiday with plenty of sunshine,' she told Granny, when next she went to see her. 'I don't like sending them back to school looking so pale.'

Granny took her hand. 'Now you listen to me, my dear,' she said. 'I've got a great idea. You know that the doctor says I must go away for a holiday in a ship somewhere — on a cruise. Well, I don't want to go alone. I want you all to come with me. It will do the children such a lot of good — and you too!'

Mummy looked at Granny in astonishment. 'A cruise! Oh, Mother! What an idea — why, we couldn't possibly do such . . .'

'Yes, you could. I shall pay for you all. It would please me so much — and think how the children would love to go off in a great steamer, and see all kinds of different countries!'

'Yes, they would. Oh, they'd *love* it!' said Mummy, beginning to feel most excited. 'I must go back to the caravans and see what their father says. Dear me, what *will* the children say when they hear!'

She kissed Granny goodbye and hurried off, her eyes shining. What a holiday that would be! How

Mike would love it – and as for Belinda and Ann, they would go quite mad with joy. If only, only, only it could really happen!

2

Shall We Go?

Mummy hurried back to the caravans with her news. The children saw her coming and flew to meet her.

'How is Granny? Did you give her the heather we sent her? When is she coming out of the nursing-home?'

'Very soon now,' said Mummy. 'Where's Daddy? I've got some news for him.'

'Good news, or bad?' asked Mike. Belinda looked at him scornfully.

'Can't you see Mummy's face? It's *good* news, of course, isn't it, Mummy? What is it?'

'I can't tell you yet,' said Mummy. 'Ah, there's Daddy.' She ran across the field to the stream, where Daddy was rinsing something.

'It would be nice to have some good luck for a change,' said Mike gloomily. 'We've been a very bad-luck family lately. I hated having whooping-cough.'

'Well, you haven't got it now,' said Ann. 'You've stopped coughing. Or almost. And when you do cough it's only just to remind yourself that you've had it!'

'Don't be silly,' said Mike, and walked off. Mike wasn't quite himself. He was rather bad-tempered and moody. Mummy said it was because he'd had whooping-cough so badly, and wanted a change.

Presently Mummy and Daddy both came over to where the children sat in a row on the steps of their caravan, one above the other. Mummy was smiling.

Ann suddenly felt excited. She jumped up and ran to her mother. 'What is it? You look like Christmas-time, all happy and full of good secrets!'

'I feel like that too,' said Mummy. 'Now listen, children – how would you like to miss school for a few weeks and go holidaying with me and Daddy and Granny?'

'Oooh,' said Ann, thrilled. Mike and Belinda looked at Mummy. They had been rather looking forward to going back to school – somehow these holidays had been too long.

'Where to?' asked Mike cautiously.

'Oh, to Portugal – and Spain – and the Canary Isles – and down to North Africa,' said Mummy, airily.

'But Mummy! Mummy, do you mean it? What, right away across the sea – in a ship?' shouted Mike.

'Yes, in a big steamer,' said Daddy, smiling. 'It's what you've always wanted to do, Mike, isn't it?'

'I can't believe it,' said Mike, looking as if he were about to burst with joy. His face went as red as the poppies in the field.

'Well, you haven't told us if you'd like to go yet,' said Daddy, with a chuckle. The three children threw themselves on him and almost pulled him over.

'Daddy! You know we want to go. It would be too super for words. When are we going? How long for? What is our ship? How . . .'

'Let's all sit down and talk about it,' said Mummy, smiling happily. 'Now listen – the doctor has said that Granny *must* go away on a cruise . . .'

'What's a cruise?' asked Ann at once.

'A voyage in a ship,' said Mummy. 'Well, Granny doesn't want to go alone, she wants us all to go with her. In the ordinary way you couldn't, because of school – but as you all look so pale and washed-out with that horrid whooping-cough, Daddy and I think it would be a good idea to do as Granny says – and all go off together!'

'Oh, Mummy – it's glorious,' said Belinda. 'Let's make plans at once. Shall we go tomorrow?'

'Dear me, no,' said Mummy. 'There are tickets to get and clothes to pack, the caravans to store somewhere, and the horses to see to.'

'But I can't possibly wait more than a day,' said Ann. Everyone laughed. That was so like Ann.

'Well, darling, would you like to go off by yourself?' said Mummy. 'I daresay I could arrange it.'

But no – that wouldn't do at all. 'I'll wait,' said Ann, with a sigh. 'I do hope it comes quickly, though.

Oh, fancy – we'll be sleeping on board a big ship, right out to sea! You don't think we shall get shipwrecked, do you, Daddy?' she asked after a moment's thought.

'I shouldn't think so,' said Daddy. 'But there are plenty of lifeboats in case we do, you know. And anyway, we can all swim and float.'

'We're a lucky family again,' said Mike. 'We've been unlucky for weeks – now we're lucky. Shall we start packing this very minute?'

'Darling, we are not going till the beginning of October,' said Mummy. 'Two whole weeks to wait. Granny won't be allowed to go till then. If I were you I'd find an atlas and see exactly where our ship will go. Daddy will tell you.'

So, for the next few hours, Mike, Belinda and Ann studied an atlas harder than they had ever studied one at school!

'We shall start at Southampton – here it is – and go down the Solent, look – and then down south. Here is Portugal – and we'll go round a bit of Spain – and then to Madeira or on to the Canary Isles – what a lovely, lovely name!'

'And then to Africa. Will there be monkeys there?'

'There'll be three extra when *you* arrive!' said Mummy. 'What a lovely time we shall all have!'

3

Off to Southampton at Last!

The next two weeks passed rather slowly, because the children were so impatient, and found it difficult to wait till the day came for setting off. Belinda got the idea that it would be helpful if she and Ann got all their things together to pack.

She found warm jerseys, a thick winter coat for each of them, and even got out their warm vests and knickers. Mummy came to see what she and Ann were doing.

'We've got all our clothes ready for you,' said Belinda, proudly. Mummy stared at the pile of warm jerseys, coats and vests. Then she laughed.

'Darling! We're taking all our summery things! It will be autumn when we leave and come back – but it will be hotter than summer on the trip! We shan't want any of those things; just your thinnest frocks and sunsuits and sandals, that's all.'

'Gracious!' said Belinda. 'I didn't think of that. Oh Mummy, how glorious! Will it really be as hot and sunny as summertime?'

'Hotter,' said Mummy. 'So put all those things away

140

again, silly. I'm going to take you into the nearest town to buy you all a few more cotton things. And myself too.'

Daddy got the tickets for them all. They were to travel on a big ship called the *Pole Star*. He showed them a picture of her.

'She looks simply beautiful,' said Mike. 'She's all white. Daddy, where will our cabins be? Up on deck?'

'Oh, no,' said Daddy. 'I've got three cabins for us just below water-level; they will be nice and cool.'

'Shan't we have any portholes to look out of?' said Belinda, disappointed. 'I did want to look out of those round holes you see in the side of big ships.'

'Yes, you'll have a porthole!' said Daddy, laughing. 'It will be just above the level of the water – the waves will sometimes splash against it!'

That sounded good. The children gazed at the picture of the big ship. There were two decks, one above the other. There was a high part that Daddy called the bridge.

'That's where the captain stands, at the wheel,' said Daddy.

'Where's the engine-room?' asked Mike. 'I shall want to see the engines make the ship go.'

'Down below the water-level,' said Daddy. 'You shall see everything when we get on board. There will be plenty of time, for there will be days when we don't touch land at all.'

'Oh dear, I wish it would come,' sighed Ann. 'How many more days? Tomorrow, and the day after – and then, THE DAY!'

It came at last, of course. The caravans had been pulled into the town the day before and left in a big garage. Davey and Clopper, the two horses, had been lent to a farmer. Mummy, Daddy and the children all went to spend the last night at Granny's.

Granny was home now, looking a bit thinner, but very cheerful and excited. 'Well!' she said, kissing the children, 'aren't we going to have a lovely holiday together? I hope you've all made up your minds not to fall overboard. It's such a nuisance if the ship has to keep stopping to pick up children from the sea!'

They laughed. 'We won't fall over,' said Mike. 'You forget we lived for quite a long time on a houseboat, Granny. We're used to being careful.'

'When do we start?' said Ann.

'Early tomorrow morning,' said Daddy. 'We go up to London in a car, and catch the train to Southampton. We shall be on board at half-past two. The *Pole Star* is due to leave at four o'clock.'

'Oh, it sounds lovely,' said Ann. 'I shall go to bed almost directly after tea today, to make tomorrow come sooner. Oh, Mummy, you don't think anything will happen to stop us going, do you?'

'I don't see why anything should,' said Mummy. 'Now you eat your tea, Ann. You've had that bit of

142

bread and butter on your plate for ages.'

'I can't eat anything,' said Ann. 'I feel full up with excitement – yes really, Mummy, as if I'd eaten a whole lot of excitement and couldn't eat any more.'

At last THE morning came. Everyone was awake early. All the trunks were ready. The sun shone down brilliantly, and made it real holiday weather. There was a sudden toot-toot in the drive.

'The car, the car! Quick, Daddy, the car!' yelled Mike.

'Well, it won't vanish in thin air if we keep it waiting a moment,' said Daddy. 'Now you take this bag, Mike. Tell the driver to come in and help me.'

And then in a few minutes they were all speeding off to London. Then they were in a big railway station, packed with people – and then in the train to go down to Southampton. They were off to the sea!

Lunch in the train, then a gathering together of bags. The train slid slowly into a big station and stopped.

'Southampton!' yelled Mike, making everybody jump. 'Our ship's here somewhere. Come along, let's go and find it! Hurrah, hurrah!'

4

All Aboard the Pole Star!

'We must go to the docks to find our ship, the *Pole Star*,' said Daddy. 'Mike, come back. You won't find it just outside the station, silly boy! It's a long way away.'

So it was. And when they did at last arrive at the docks, the children fell silent in awe. The steamers were so very, very big – much bigger than they had ever imagined!

'Oh, Daddy – why, they're ENORMOUS!' said Mike, almost in a whisper. Their porter smiled at him.

'You look over there, sonny – you'll see the finest ship there is!' he said. 'The *Queen Elizabeth*. She's just in.'

They all stared at the *Queen Elizabeth*. Mike felt a lump coming into his throat. He felt so very proud of that beautiful British ship. There she lay beside the dock, towering high, gleaming with paint, her funnels topping her grandly.

'Oh – I didn't dream we should see *her*,' said Mike at last. 'I never in my life thought I'd see such a big ship. Why, she must take thousands of people!'

'She does,' said the porter. 'She's a floating town.'

Grand sight, isn't she? Ah, there's nobody can beat us Britons at ships. Now then – we'll find the *Pole Star*.'

'There she is, there she is!' shouted Belinda, suddenly. 'Just nearby.'

So she was. The children looked at her in delight. She was small compared with the *Queen Elizabeth* – but all the same much, much bigger than they had expected. She was gleaming white from top to toe.

'A beautiful ship too,' said Daddy. 'Fast, comfortable, and with lovely lines. Well, we'll go aboard. Come, Granny, I'll help you up the gangway.'

There was a kind of little wooden bridge stretching down from the *Pole Star's* second deck to the dock where they stood. 'So that's the gangway,' said Belinda. 'I always wanted to go up a proper gangway. Bags I go first!'

Up she went, and Mike and Ann followed. Daddy was helping Granny. A sailor came behind, his hand on Mummy's elbow, for sometimes the ship moved, and the gangway moved with it.

And now at last they were on board ship. Ann gazed up and down the deck. It seemed very long indeed. There were scores of people, carrying bags and packages. Sailors in their dark blue suits went about their business. Ann thought they looked very nice indeed.

'We'll go and find our cabins first, and put our odds and ends there,' said Mummy. A sailor took her

down some steps into a big room that looked like a lounge. Then down some more steps still.

'We're going down into the heart of the ship!' said Belinda. 'Gracious, are our cabins right down here?'

They went down a passage lit by electric light, and came to three doors in a row. Numbers 42, 43, 44. The sailor opened the first door.

'Oh!' said Ann, looking in, 'what a lovely place. But look – we've got proper beds to sleep in. I thought we'd have bunks. And there's a wash-basin too. And a little dressing-table with drawers – and even a wardrobe! Goodness, it's like a proper bedroom.'

'It's got a porthole!' cried Mike, in delight, and ran to it. 'Oh, look – the water's just below it. Do look! Can we open it, sailor?'

'If you like,' said the man, smiling. 'As long as we're in calm water, it's all right. Shut it when we leave, or you'll get a wave splashing on to the bed!'

It was strange, looking out of the round window. The glass was very, very thick, not a bit like ordinary window glass. No wave could possibly break it. The children could hear the water lapping outside. It was a lovely sound.

'Put all your things down for a while,' said Mummy. 'We must go up on deck. You'll want to be there when we move off, won't you?'

They left the cabin. They peeped into numbers 43 and 44, which were just exactly the same. There

were two beds in each. Mummy and Granny were to share a cabin, and Mike and Daddy, and Belinda and Ann. Mike felt very grown-up to be sharing with Daddy. What fun it would be to go to bed in a cabin just below water-level!

They all went up on deck. What a noise and bustle there was! Steamers were blowing their sirens, gulls were screaming, sailors were shouting, and there was a terrific noise of creaking and winding, as all kinds of luggage was hauled up by a crane and dropped into the hold.

The children found a place by the deck-rail and looked over. People were still streaming up the gangway. The crane placed a great pile of luggage in the hold and then swung itself out over the dock-side again to pick up the last lot.

An enormous noise made the children almost jump out of their skins. 'It's all right,' said Daddy, amused, 'that's our own ship's voice – her siren. It's to warn everyone that we're going soon. Look, they are going to pull in the gangway so that nobody else can board us.'

Then the children noticed a rumbling noise that seemed to come from the heart of the ship – the engines were starting. They would soon be off!

'We're moving, we're moving!' shouted Mike, suddenly, in excitement. 'Look, the dock-side is going away from us. We're off, we're off!'

Everyone shouted and waved. 'Goodbye, goodbye!' The children yelled too. 'Goodbye. We're really off! We're really OFF!'

5

Goodbye, England!

The great ship moved slowly along the dock towards the open sea. Mike saw some little tugs that appeared to be joined to her by ropes. Could they be pulling her?

'Oh, yes – they're guiding her out and helping her,' said Daddy. 'Look, there's the sea. Now look back at the docks and see the masses of ships there, of all kinds – some unloading cargoes, some taking in goods, some waiting for passengers, some wanting coal and water, others waiting for repairs.'

'It's all wonderful,' said Mike, who looked happier than he had ever been in his life. 'All those ships and steamers and cranes. To think that the ships have been all over the world and back many, many times. Oh, I wish I was a sailor. Daddy, can I be one when I grow up?'

'If you badly want to,' said Daddy. 'You must wait and see. You wanted to be a bus-driver the other day. You might change your mind again.'

'I shan't, I shan't,' said Mike. 'I want to be a sailor with a ship of my very own. I shall call it the *Belinda Ann*.'

'Very nice too,' said Daddy. 'Now look – here we are out on the open sea. You'll feel the swell of the waves in a moment.'

'Oh, yes!' said Belinda. 'The ship isn't only moving forwards – she's moving a bit from side to side – rolling a little. I like it. She's come alive!'

'Yes, she's come alive,' said Mike. 'I say, I hope we get a storm. How grand to feel the *Pole Star* riding enormous waves, going up and down, and from side to side!'

'Well, I hope we don't,' said Granny. 'I shouldn't like that at all. I should probably be very seasick.'

'We're none of us going to be seasick,' said Mike. 'We've made up our minds not to be. We don't want to waste a single minute of this trip in being seasick.'

'Now the little tugs have gone,' said Ann. 'Goodbye, little tugs. I liked you. You were such busy, clever little things, fussing around.'

'I'm hungry,' said Mike. 'And yet I don't feel as if I can possibly leave my place to have tea.'

'Well, you must,' said Mummy, firmly. 'Come along. We'll go down to the dining-room and have tea. I'm sure Granny is dying for some!'

They went down the stairs to the second deck, and then down steps to the lounge. A steward brought them a lovely tea, with plenty of little cakes.

'Do we have nice food on board ship?' asked Belinda.

'Very nice,' said Daddy. 'Ann, do eat. Or are you still full up with excitement?'

'I am rather,' said Ann, with a huge sigh. 'But these cakes do look so nice. I really must have some. Oh, Granny, do you like our ship?'

'I love it,' said Granny. 'Wasn't it a good idea of mine?'

'The best idea you ever had in your life, Granny,' said Belinda. 'Mummy, what can we do when we've finished? May we go on deck again? On the top deck of all? I want to see the land we pass.'

'Yes, if you like,' said Mummy. 'I need not tell any of you to be careful, not to play any silly tricks on board ship, and to come back to us every now and again so that we know you're all right.'

'I'll look after the girls, Mummy,' said Mike. 'Daddy, are we going down the Solent? Shall we soon see the last of England?'

'Yes,' said Daddy. 'The very last. Go on up now if you want to. We'll come later.'

The *Pole Star* was now well out to sea. Southampton had been left far behind. The children could see the Isle of Wight on one side and the mainland on the other. The *Pole Star* seemed to them to be going quite fast.

'See that long white tail behind her?' said Mike. 'That's called the wake. It's the sea-water all churned up till it's white.'

'We've still got gulls all round us,' said Belinda. 'I like them. I like the funny mewing noise they make too.'

'It sounds as if they were laughing sometimes,' said Mike. 'Oh, look – is that the end of the Isle of Wight? We're going quite near it.'

Dusk was now beginning to come over the sea. Lights sprang up on the big ship. Little lights twinkled here and there from other boats in the distance. Mummy came up behind the children.

'It's goodbye to England now,' she said. 'We're going swiftly away from her. Tomorrow we shall be in the Bay of Biscay, and it may be very rough. I hope not, though.'

'I shan't mind!' said Mike. 'Are we going to France?'

'No. Our first stop is at Lisbon, in Portugal,' said Mummy. 'Now, if you want to stop up here you must put coats on. It's a bit chilly tonight – though very soon we shall feel so hot that we shall want to take our clothes off and bathe all day long!'

'What I want to do,' said Ann, 'is to go to bed in one of those cabins. Oh, Mummy – fancy going to bed under the water, and hearing the waves lapping against the side of the ship. Do you know, I really think I'll go now!'

6

Bedtime on Board Ship

Excitement had made Granny tired too. She said that she didn't think she would stay up to dinner that night. She would go to her cabin and have it there.

'May *we* stay up to dinner?' said Mike, excited at the thought of being with the grown-up people in the big dining-room each night.

'Certainly not,' said Mummy. 'You can't do that till you're much older. You can have a nice supper in your cabin. The cabin steward will bring it to you. I'll choose something good and have it sent down.'

'What about baths?' said Belinda. 'Do we have baths on board ship?'

'Of course!' said Mummy. 'There is a bathroom at the end of our little passage, just for us six to use. You must have a bath every night, just as you do at home. You can have your supper in the girls' cabin with them each night, Mike, if you like, and go along to your own afterwards.'

It all sounded very thrilling. They went to find the bathroom. It was very tiny, but very nice. The bath was green and had huge shining taps. The water

came out scalding hot. There were thick green towels too, marked P.S.

'P.S. How funny – that's what you put at the end of a letter, isn't it, if you want to add a bit more,' said Belinda.

'P.S. stands for *Pole Star*, silly,' said Mike. 'I say, I wonder if the bath-water runs away into the sea.'

'Of course it does,' said Belinda. 'Goodness, the ship rolled quite a bit then. I almost fell into the bath.'

'Yes, you'll have to get your sea-legs,' said Daddy, putting his head into the bathroom. 'If she rolls much more you must be careful to hang on to the hand-rails.'

They each had a bath in turn. Then Ann brushed Belinda's hair a hundred times and Belinda brushed Ann's. Mummy always made them brush their hair one hundred times. She said that made it shine brightly.

They cleaned their teeth at the little basin, and then the steward arrived with their supper.

'Ooooh!' said Ann, looking at the trays. 'What a wonderful supper. Thank you very much.'

'Grapefruit with cherries on top!' said Mike.

'A cup of the most delicious-smelling soup in the world,' said Belinda. 'And look at these little squares of toast.'

'And a pink jelly,' said Ann. 'My favourite. Oh, jelly, are you cold? You do shiver so. Never mind,

you'll soon be warm inside me!'

Everyone laughed. They sat on the beds to eat their supper. They were very happy. It was all so new and strange and lovely. And it was only just beginning!

'The nicest part of a holiday is the beginning,' said Mike. The ship gave a roll as he said that, and his jelly ran off the plate. 'Oh, goodness – look at my jelly! It's on your bed, Ann.'

'Well, spoon it off then,' said Ann. 'I say, I hope we don't roll off our beds at night.'

'We might if it was very, very rough,' said Mike, spooning up the jelly. 'The beds are clamped to the floor, look – *they* won't move.'

Ann climbed up on to her bed and looked out of the porthole window. It was tight shut now, and the children had been told that they were not to try and open it till they were in port again. She could see nothing through it at all, except darkness.

'Do you suppose we say our prayers on board ship?' she said, slipping down to the bed again.

'Why ever not?' said Mike, astonished. 'What difference does it make where we are?'

'Well – it will seem a bit odd to kneel down on a floor that keeps moving about,' said Ann. 'I shall have to hold on to my bed.'

'I've got a lot of prayers to say tonight,' said Belinda. 'I shall say thank you for this lovely holiday, and ask for all of us to be kept safe, and for there to be no

shipwreck, and for Davey and Clopper to be happy while we're away, and . . .'

'Well, let's all be quiet and say them at the same time,' said Mike. So for a few minutes there was no sound in the little cabin except for the waves slapping against the side of the ship. Then Ann scrambled into her bed and Belinda into hers. They were soft and springy, and the two girls cuddled down into them with delight.

Granny came in to say goodnight. She was in her dressing-gown ready to get into bed too. 'Did you have the same supper as we did?' asked Ann. 'Oh Granny, isn't it *fun* to be on board ship? I'm longing to wake up tomorrow morning and remember where I am!'

Then Mummy and Daddy came in. They had dressed for dinner and looked very grand. 'You're beautiful, Mummy,' said Belinda, hugging her. 'Goodnight! I don't want to go to sleep for ages, but I'm afraid I shall go at once. My eyes keep shutting.'

Mike went off to his cabin. Mummy had told him he could read for half an hour, as he was older than the girls. But he didn't want to. He just wanted to lie in his little bed and feel the movement of the ship. To and fro, to and fro, and then a little bit forward and backward.

'It's lovely,' said Mike to himself. 'I shall be a sailor when I grow up. I shall be the captain of a ship like this . . .'

But by that time he was asleep – and in his dreams he was captain of the *Pole Star*. What a wonderful dream!

7

Land Ahoy!

It was lovely waking up next morning, and remembering everything. Ann sat up and reached over to Belinda's bed. She gave her sister a poke.

'Belinda! We're on the sea! Do wake up.'

Then Mike came in, beaming. 'Are you awake? It's a gorgeous morning. I've been up on deck in my dressing-gown, and the sea's lovely. Do get up.'

They got up and washed and dressed. They went on deck, and felt the sun pouring down on them. The sky was blue and the sea was blue-purple. Everything was glorious.

There was no land to be seen at all. It was an extraordinary feeling to stand there by the deck-rail, and see nothing but water round them, stretching for miles and miles. There was not even another ship to be seen.

'If this is the Bay of Biscay it's jolly calm,' said Mike, half-disappointed. 'I say — let's explore the ship, shall we?'

'After breakfast,' said Mummy, coming up behind them. 'Come along, there's a lovely breakfast waiting

for you – six different kinds of cereal to choose from, more grapefruits if you want them, and about twelve different dishes to choose from: bacon and eggs, ham, fish . . .'

'I certainly *shall* be a sailor when I grow up!' said Mike. 'You make me feel awfully hungry, Mummy.'

They explored the ship from top to toe after breakfast. They ran down both the upper and lower decks. There were countless deck-chairs there, and many people were sitting in them reading or snoozing in the sun.

The children found a swimming-pool at one end of the ship and were delighted. 'Fancy a swimming-pool on a ship! We can bathe every day!' said Mike.

They found a nice sun-deck too, just under the captain's bridge. Mummy thought it would be lovely to sit there with Granny.

'There's everything you can possibly want on this ship,' said Mike to his mother. 'Games to play on deck, places to sit, a swimming-pool, places to eat, a reading-room, that big dining-room where we have our meals, a ballroom for dancing . . . Oh, Mummy, there's everything!'

'May we bathe?' asked Belinda. 'In that lovely pool, Mummy?'

'Yes, if you like,' said Mummy, and the three went off to change. What fun they had swimming and diving and going down the chute! Ann wouldn't go

down at first, but she did at last, and loved it. Splash! She flew down into the water and gasped.

'This is a lovely holiday,' said Mike. 'I love the *Pole Star*. She's a jolly good ship.'

The children swam, and played deck tennis, throwing the rubber ring over the net to one another; they went down into the engine room to see the engines, and came back hot and dirty.

And then suddenly Belinda noticed something. 'Look!' she said in surprise, 'all the sailors have changed out of their dark-blue suits into white ones! Oh, how nice they look!'

So they had. Daddy laughed at the children's astonished faces. 'Oh, that shows we're leaving the cold weather behind and coming into hot days. You'll have to change into your coolest things soon too.'

One afternoon, when they were all sitting on the sun-deck, something made them jump suddenly. The ship's siren was near the deck, and it suddenly blew a loud, mournful note. 'OOOOOOOOOOOOOOOO!'

'It's like a giant cow mooing,' said Ann. 'Oh Daddy – whatever did it do that for?'

'Look out to sea,' said Daddy. 'There's a thick sea-mist coming up. We'll soon be in it. What a pity! We shall soon be coming into Lisbon, and I would have liked you to see Portugal coming nearer.'

But the sea-fog thickened, and the siren hooted continually. Nothing could be seen from the deck.

The sea-mist made it chilly, and the children went down below to play games.

'Is it dangerous?' asked Ann, thinking of ships moving blindly in the fog. 'Shall we bump into something?'

'The captain is up on the bridge, at the wheel,' said Daddy. 'He won't leave it until the fog has cleared and he has brought the ship to safety. He'll be up there for twenty-four hours on end, if need be.'

But when at last the ship steamed into the beautiful harbour at Lisbon, the fog had cleared. Night had come, and the harbour gleamed with lights. The big ship moved to her place in the dock.

'We're staying here for the night,' said Mummy, looking over the deck-rail at all the ships in the harbour, each with its lights showing brightly. 'You'll quite miss the roll of the ship, won't you! Tomorrow we will take you to see the royal palace of Pena, set on the top of a steep rugged hill.'

'Oh – a palace! Did kings live there?' asked Ann. 'Oh Mummy, do you know, it will be quite exciting to walk on land again. I've forgotten what it feels like!'

When the children went to bed that night they opened the porthole of their cabin and gazed out into the quiet harbour. Many big ships were there, and many little fishing-boats too, with red sails. It was lovely to look at them all, rocking a little on the dark water, where all the lights were reflected.

'It even smells different here,' said Ann, sniffing. 'It smells foreign! Oh I say – fancy going to see a palace tomorrow. I'm sure it won't be as grand as our Windsor Castle, though!'

8

Going Ashore

The harbour was even lovelier in the morning, when many boats were moving out. The children liked the bright-sailed fishing-boats most of all. They were quite sorry when Mummy came to say that Daddy was ready to take them to the royal palace at Sintra.

Off they went in a taxi that went much faster than any English one. In about three-quarters of an hour's time they came to a very steep, rugged hill, with a winding road that went up and up to the top.

And there, on the summit, was the palace. 'It *does* remind me just a bit of Windsor Castle,' said Mike. 'Isn't it lovely? Can we go in?'

It was strange to wander through a palace that had once belonged to many long-ago kings. After a while Ann began to worry about the ship.

'Mummy, we'd better go back! Suppose it went without us. Do let's go.'

They went at last, and tore down the hill at breakneck speed in the taxi. Belinda shut her eyes in terror and hoped they would soon be at the bottom.

'Are those palm trees?' asked Mike, as they sped

through the beautiful countryside. 'And what are those mournful-looking trees? Oh, cypresses. And look, I'm sure those are orange trees. And what's that big grove of trees with great green leaves? I've never seen trees like that before.'

'Olive trees,' said Daddy. 'You've heard of olives and olive oil, haven't you?'

'I'm quite longing to be on board ship again,' said Ann. 'I do hope she hasn't gone without us.'

She hadn't, of course. There she lay in the harbour, gleaming in welcome. They ran up the gangway, feeling as if they had come back home!

'We go to Spain next,' said Granny, welcoming them. She had not been to the palace, because she was still feeling tired. 'To Seville. I know a place there called the House of a Thousand Shawls. Daddy, would you like to go there and choose one for Mummy?'

'I certainly would,' said Daddy. 'And I should like to go to the wonderful cathedral there – yes, and see a bull-ring, though I don't want to see a bull-fight.'

'Oh no,' said Mike. 'The poor horses! They haven't any chance against the bulls at all. I should like to see the bull-fighters, though; they must look very grand, and be very brave men.'

The ship sailed on to Spain. It went up a wide river to the old town of Seville.

'Do the Seville oranges you make marmalade of come from this district?' asked Belinda.

'They do,' said Mummy. 'Oh, look at the bulls in those fields, Mike. What big creatures they are!'

Seville was a beautiful town, and the most beautiful thing in it was the cathedral. All the children crept in quietly, awed by its grandeur and beauty. They gazed at the great stained- glass windows.

The sunshine seemed very bright indeed when they came out again. Belinda blinked. 'You know,' she said, 'ordinary little churches are just houses for God – but a cathedral is a palace for Him.'

'And now,' said Granny, 'we'll go to the House of a Thousand Shawls. Come along.'

They went to it. It was a great shop, full of nothing but magnificent shawls. They were spread everywhere, and hung down from the roof and over the walls. Oh, the colours – red and green and blue and orange and black, all embroidered most beautifully.

'Which one will you have?' Daddy asked Mummy. 'What about this deep red one? That would suit you beautifully.'

'Oh yes, have that one, Mummy,' said Belinda. 'I do like the great dark roses embroidered all over it. Isn't Seville a beautiful place, with beautiful things!'

But the bull-ring wasn't so beautiful. They all went to have a look at one. It was quite empty, and was

strewn with sawdust. Ann didn't like the smell.

'Let's come away,' she said, pulling at her father's hand. 'I don't like to think of the bulls hurting the horses, and the bull-fighters hurting the bulls, and everyone cheering. Let's go back to the ship with your lovely shawl, Mummy.'

So back they went again, wandering through the Spanish streets, stared at by black-eyed, black-haired girls, who wore little black shawls over their heads. Nobody wore a hat, and they all looked happy and lively, and talked very fast to one another. The children wished they could understand what they said.

Mummy bought each of the girls a tiny gold Spanish bracelet. Mike chose a wooden carving of a bull. They took them proudly back to the *Pole Star*.

'She's hooting, she's hooting,' said Ann, in alarm, as they drew near. 'She's telling us to hurry up!'

'It's all right. There's still half an hour,' said Daddy, laughing. 'Got your shawl, Mummy? Up the gangway, all of you!'

'Now we're off to Madeira, and the Canary Isles,' said Granny. 'We shan't see land for a while. But maybe we shall see a few interesting things – flying-fish, for instance!'

'Flying-fish!' cried Belinda. 'Oh, are there *really* such creatures! I thought they were like unicorns, and only belonged to fairy tales.'

'I'm going to stand at the deck-rail all day tomorrow and look for them!' said Ann. 'Oh Mummy – do you think I could catch one and take it home with me? I *would* like it to fly round the caravan!'

9

Flying-fish, Dolphins – and Bullocks!

The next day the children asked one of the sailors if there was any chance of seeing flying-fish on the trip.

'Oh yes!' said the sailor. 'You watch out, the next day or two. We often see them when we go down south.'

But it was not until two days later that Belinda heard someone shouting loudly, 'Look – flying-fish! Look!'

All the children rushed to the deck-side. Then they saw a strange sight. Rising right out of the sea was a small shoal of gleaming fish! They flew through the air for about half a minute, spreading their great front fins.

They went very fast indeed, and then dived back gracefully into the sea. But in another moment out they flew again, glittering in the sunshine.

'Oh, aren't they lovely!' cried Ann. 'I never, never thought I'd see fish flying, Daddy, how do they fly?'

'Well, they haven't any wings, of course,' said Daddy. 'They swim tremendously fast under water, and then, to escape an enemy, they fling themselves

above the surface, and use their long fins to help them.'

'Is there an enemy making them fly now?' asked Mike. 'Oh yes, look – what are those things showing here and there in the water, chasing the flying-fish?'

'Dolphins,' said Daddy. 'See, there they go, leaping right out of the water, a mile a minute! They belong to the whale family. There are few creatures that swim faster than a dolphin!'

The children watched the curious dolphins, with their long, beak-shaped mouths, leaping along after the flying-fish. It was really most exciting. 'I *think* the flying-fish got away,' said Ann, at last. 'Dolphins and flying-fish – I never in my life thought I'd see those.'

The sun grew hotter and hotter as they went more and more south. The children wore as little as they could. The passengers became one big family, for now that there was no land to be seen they had to find their interests on board, and talk and play with one another.

There was lifeboat practice. That was fun. Everyone had to learn where he or she was to go in case of danger. The children knew exactly which lifeboat they were to make for, and how to put on a life jacket quickly, so that if danger came to the *Pole Star* at any time, they would be saved.

'If everyone knows what to do and where to go to, there is no panic or muddle,' Daddy said. 'And

we have to remember that, just like whooping-cough, fear is catching, and we must always be brave, especially when we are with a lot of people in danger.'

'Is bravery catching too?' said Mike.

'Oh yes,' said Daddy, 'and it's a very good thing to catch. You want to give it to as many people as you can!'

The days began to slip by too quickly. The sun shone down all the time. And then they came to their next port of call!

'We shall come to the island of Madeira soon,' said Mummy. 'You'll like that. We'll take you for a ride in a bullock cart, down very steep, narrow little streets, lined with small cobble-stones!'

'A *bullock*-cart!' said Belinda. 'I shall like that. Why don't we have bullock-carts at home? I think they would be much nicer than buses.'

Madeira was lovely. The *Pole Star* came nearer and nearer to the sun-drenched island, and at last sailed into harbour there, while many jabbering people ran about ashore, excited and welcoming.

The children were eager to go on shore. It seemed such a long time since they had seen land! They felt peculiar when they walked on the dock. 'The earth seems so solid somehow, after the swing and sway of the ship,' said Mike. 'I've got sea-legs now instead of land-legs!'

Bullock-carts were waiting to take the travellers

for trips. What fun it was to ride in one!

'Why, they have no wheels!' cried Ann, in surprise. 'Look – they have runners, like sledges, instead of wheels Can we get in?'

Some of the streets were very steep indeed, and the cobble-stones bright and slippery. The runners of the bullock-cart slid easily and quickly over them. The big, sleepy-eyed bullocks were strong, and pulled them swiftly along. The children were full of delight.

'Oh Mummy! I wish we had bullock-carts at home, I really do. Oh, why are we stopping?'

'Mummy wants to buy some handmade cloths, said Daddy. 'Look, we'll go into this little shop. You can each choose six handkerchiefs, embroidered by the people of this island – perhaps sewn by children as young as you, Ann.'

It was fun shopping in the unusual little hut. They bought a lot of things and then stepped back into their bullock-cart.

'To the ship, bullocks, please!' said Mike grandly, and down the cobbled street at top speed went the bullocks. Ann gasped. What a pace!

'It's funny to think they may be having cold, rainy weather in England now,' said Mike, fanning himself. 'Look at all those brilliant flowers out – just like summer. And I never felt the sun so hot before. I'm sure I should get sunstroke if I took my hat off!'

'You certainly would,' said Daddy. 'So don't try it.

Now, here we are, back on board again. Where do you think we go to next – to the Canary Isles!'

'Do canaries live there?' asked Ann.

'Of course!' said Daddy. 'You'll see them flying all round you, as common as sparrows!'

'Flying-fish, dolphins, bullocks, canaries,' said Belinda. 'Whatever next!'

10

Everything is so Exciting!

On went their good ship, the *Pole Star*, on and on over the southern seas. And when they came to the Canary Isles, it was just as Daddy had said – there were plenty of wild canaries flying about, and singing loudly!

'But they're not bright yellow like ours at home,' said Mike, disappointed. 'They're green. Still, they sing just as beautifully. Daddy, are there any Parrot Isles? I hope we shall go to them too. I'd like to take home a parrot and teach it to talk.'

'Three parrots in one family are quite enough,' said Mummy. 'Oh, look at those little boys swimming round the ship. They're like fish, they're so much at home in the water.'

Some of the passengers threw pennies into the clear water. A horde of small boys at once dived for them. They did not miss a single penny. It was marvellous to watch them.

'We'll do that in the swimming-pool,' said Mike. 'We'll practise it. It looks quite easy, but I suppose you have to keep your eyes open under water.'

A boy yelled something from the water below. One of the sailors told the passengers what he had said.

'He says, for a shilling he will swim right under the ship and come up the other side,' said the sailor.

'I'll give him a shilling then,' said one of the passengers, and threw one into the water. It circled downwards. The boy swam after it and caught it. He came up to the surface, and waved his hand to everyone at the deckside.

Then down he went and down, at the side of the ship. Soon he was lost to sight. The passengers left that side of the ship and went to the other side to watch the boy coming up there.

Ann was rather scared. 'He can't swim under the ship – it's a long long way down, into the very deep water, where it's dark,' she said. 'Oh Daddy – he won't get caught under the ship, will he? He'll come up, won't he?'

'Of course,' said Daddy. 'He does it a dozen times a day! Now, stand by me and watch for him to come up.'

All the same, it seemed a long time before a little dark speck appeared far down in the water. And then the boy shot up to the surface, gasping, and waved his hand merrily. He had done it!

'Bravo!' shouted the passengers. 'Well, well – right under the ship! How did he have the breath?'

Little boats came out and surrounded the ship,

selling fruit of all kinds – bananas, peaches, oranges, even pineapples. The dark-faced, bright-eyed people shouted their wares, and even climbed up the side of the ship with them.

It was all very exciting. The three children, burnt brown now by the hot sun, enjoyed every new and strange thing they saw. There seemed no end to them. When they went ashore, they found that many of the wild canaries had been caught and put into cages for people to buy.

'Few of them will live to reach England,' said Daddy. 'They are so used to this hot climate, poor little things.'

All the same, many people bought them in little wicker cages. They gave them to the sailors on board ship to keep for them, and the children went to see them every day. They sang their hearts out in the little wicker cages, and Ann longed to set them all free.

'They've not been born and brought up in cages as our cage-canaries have,' she said to Belinda, sadly. 'I'm sure they are unhappy.'

The sailors had put up a rope-line in their quarters, and had hung the little cages all along it. It was an unusual sight to see. The children went along each day to make sure that the birds had water to drink.

The good ship went on again over the bright blue sea. The days seemed to run into one another. The only day the children really knew was Sunday. Then

there was a service held on the deck, and all the sailors came too.

The captain read from the Bible, and led the prayers. The children stood there in the sun and the breeze listening. They liked it very much.

'I've never been to church on board a big ship before,' said Ann. 'Mummy, didn't the hymns sound nice sung to the sound of the sea and the wind?'

'Tomorrow will be Monday because this is Sunday,' said Mike. 'I don't know the days any more! By the time tomorrow comes I shall have forgotten it's Monday. That's the extraordinary part about a holiday. You just don't know which day is which – they're all so nice.'

'Where are we going next?' asked Ann.

'To Africa!' said Mummy. 'To French Morocco. And then, my dear – home!'

'Oh, dear – shall we go home so soon?' said Ann, in dismay. 'Can't we go right round the world, Mummy?'

'Good gracious, no,' said Mummy.

'I'll take you and Belinda all round the world when I'm a sailor,' promised Mike. 'We'll stop at any port we like for as long as we want to.'

'There's no land to be seen anywhere now,' said Belinda, looking over the sea. 'Just blue water. Let's go and have a game of deck-tennis. I'll take you on, Mike. Then we'll have a bathe in the swimming-

pool. Daddy, will you come and throw pennies for us, please? We're going to be diving-boys!'

'Right,' said Daddy. 'Who'll swim under the ship for a shilling?' But nobody would!

11

A Different Kind of Shopping

The *Pole Star* went on to North Africa. The children stood at the deck-rail and watched the land gradually coming nearer and nearer. They saw a big city spreading before them, a city of gleaming white buildings and wide streets.

'This is Casablanca,' said Daddy. 'If you are good I'll take you ashore and let you go shopping in the bazaars – little streets of native shops where you can buy almost anything!'

'We'll buy presents to take home,' said Mummy. 'We won't go to any of the big shops in the wide streets. We'll go, as Daddy says, to the little native ones.'

So, feeling very thrilled, the three children stepped ashore at Casablanca, their money in their purses. A taxi took them to the streets of little shops. But almost at once Ann turned to her mother in disgust. 'Mummy! There's the most awful smell. I can't bear it.'

'Oh, there's always an awful smell in these places,' said Mummy. 'Look, here is my bottle of smelling-salts. Hold it to your nose.'

Poor Ann was nearly sick with the smell of the dirty streets. The others put their handkerchiefs over their noses. They looked with interest at the unusual little shops. They sold all kinds of things – hand-made brooches, rings and bracelets, beautiful pottery, slippers with turned-up toes, bags, baskets, brass pots . . .

'They're all quite cheap,' said Daddy. 'But you have to bargain for them.'

'What's bargain?' asked Ann, still sniffing Mummy's smelling-salts.

'Well, I say a low price, and the shopkeeper says a high price, and he comes down a bit, and I go up a bit, and in the end I pay about half what he asks,' said Daddy.

'But why don't they put a proper price on, like we do at home?' asked Belinda. 'It seems such a waste of time.'

'Ah, but they enjoy their bargaining,' said Daddy. 'And they have plenty of time to waste. Now, watch me!'

Daddy wanted to buy some lovely dishes, patterned in all colours. He asked their price, but he spoke in French, because everyone spoke in French in Casablanca.

Then the man said a price and Daddy looked shocked. Daddy said a price, and the man looked horrified. So it went on, and the children laughed to

see Daddy and the shopkeeper arguing and haggling vigorously.

At last Daddy paid over some French money and the man gave him the dishes, all smiles. The bargaining was over. The man had got the price he wanted, and Daddy had paid the price he meant to pay, so both were pleased.

'Can I do some bargaining too?' asked Ann. She badly wanted a tiny brooch shaped like a flying-fish.

'Of course you can, silly,' said Mike. 'You can't talk French.'

'No – I can't,' said Ann. 'Well, I'm going to learn it as fast as I can when I get back to school. I can see it would be very useful. Daddy, please bargain for that flying-fish brooch.'

So Daddy bargained again and got the brooch. Ann was delighted. Then Belinda got a pair of slippers in red, with silver-edged turn-up toes, and Mike got a curious brass pot, carved with little ships.

'I like the lovely things they sell, but oh, how very dirty everything is,' said Ann. 'Look at that meat – and those sweets – all crawling with flies! Why don't the people clean?'

'Perhaps because they haven't been taught to!' said Mike. 'Well, we often grumble at having to wash our hands and put on clean clothes, but I'd rather do that too often than not enough. I shan't grumble about having to clean any more, now I see what happens

when people don't.'

'Mummy, stop! Look at this darling little baby,' said Belinda, suddenly. 'But oh, Mummy, it's got flies crawling all round its poor eyes!'

'Poor little thing,' said Mummy, trying to brush them away. But they came back again at once. 'I'm afraid a good many babies go blind because of these dreadful flies. Oh dear, such a beautiful city, and such lovely things in it – but at the back of it all, so much poverty and so many horrid sights.'

'I didn't know before how lucky we are to be born in Britain,' said Mike. 'Why, we might have been born one of these poor little babies, in all this dirt and smelliness!'

'I think I'm going to be sick,' said Ann. 'I want to go back. It smells so bad. I don't want to come here again, not even to buy these lovely things.'

They went back to the ship. Daddy looked at Ann. 'Poor Ann! Well, I wanted you to see how some people have to live. Now, cheer up – I'll take you for a ride over the countryside in a motor-coach, and you can look out for monkeys!'

So off they went that afternoon, and to Ann's joy they saw hundreds and hundreds of monkeys, chattering gaily, swinging from tree to tree. Then they came to a white-walled house, set by the water, and there they drank mint tea from little cups without any handles.

'Mint tea!' said Belinda, sniffing it in delight. 'Mummy, can you make some when we go home? It's *much* nicer than ordinary tea.'

'Smells, and monkeys, and mint tea,' said Ann solemnly. 'We never know what we're going to have any day now!'

12

There's No Place Like Home!

And now the trip would soon be over. The *Pole Star* turned northwards, and left the great white city of Casablanca behind. The next land the children would see would be England!

They began to long for their own country.

'Going to other countries only seems to make our own all the nicer, somehow,' said Belinda. 'I feel as if I really *loved* England now. I keep thinking of things like primroses, and rainy days in April when the sun shines out suddenly, and buttercups all shining gold.'

'So do I,' said Mike. 'We've had a most glorious time, and I'll never forget it, but it's England for me every time! All the same – I shall certainly be a sailor when I grow up. I must see more of the world!'

'There's only one thing we didn't have,' said Ann, 'and that's a storm.'

'Well, there's time for that, Missy,' said a big sailor nearby. 'We're running into one tonight! I can feel it coming. I'll be changing out of my white things into my warm blue ones before many hours are gone!'

'Oooh,' said Ann, her eyes round, 'a storm at sea!

Do you really mean it? Will it be dangerous? Shall we have to take to the lifeboats? What a good thing the *Pole Star* has so many.'

'We won't need the lifeboats this trip,' said the sailor, laughing. 'But you may feel a bit seasick – and don't you come up on deck when the ship starts rolling about!'

The sailor was right. The storm came that night, when the children were in bed in their cabins. The wind began to howl dismally, and big waves blew up. The *Pole Star* began to roll tremendously.

Ann felt a bit scared. 'I don't mind so much when the ship rolls from side to side,' she said to Mummy. 'But I don't like it when it goes up and down the other way. It gives me a funny feeling. I think I might be seasick.'

'Granny's feeling a bit funny too,' said Mummy, smiling. 'A lot of people will get a touch of seasickness if this goes on. But you lie down and suck these barley sugars, and you won't feel so bad.'

The storm went on all night long. Ann screamed when something began to slide about the floor. Belinda put the light on. 'Something's sliding over the floor,' wept Ann. 'What is it, what is it?'

'Oh Ann – it's only that suitcase under your bed,' said Belinda, with a giggle. 'Look, there it comes from under your bed – and now it's gone under mine – and when the ship rolls the other way, it'll come out

again and go to yours. Yes, there it is. It'll go to and fro all the time.'

Ann gave a giggle through her tears. It was funny to think of the case popping backwards and forwards like that.

Next morning the sea was still very rough, and the children found it difficult to walk, and very difficult indeed to climb up the stairs. They hung on to the hand-rails and tried to keep their balance as best they could.

'Everything will slide off the breakfast table,' said Mike, but it didn't, because the stewards had put up wooden edges called 'fiddles' at every table, and these stopped the dishes and plates from sliding off.

It was quite a puzzle to eat and drink without spilling anything, when the boat was rolling so much. The children laughed to see people doing their best to stop their plates from rushing away from them.

Daddy took them up on deck to see the angry waters. What enormous waves reared up their grey-green heads! How they slapped against the ship! Some broke on deck and water ran everywhere. It was very thrilling indeed.

But by the time the *Pole Star* was due back in England the storm had gone, the sea was calm, and the October sun shone down serenely. The children had all put on warm things once more, because it had become much colder as they went northwards.

They stood watching for their first glimpse of England. 'There, over there!' yelled Mike, suddenly, his sharp eyes catching a very faint line on the horizon. 'Oh Daddy, there's dear old England.'

He had a lump in his throat as he watched the faint line grow bigger and stronger. He seemed to know and love his own country much more now that he had been to others. He would always always love it best!

'Well, our trip is over,' said Granny's voice. 'And how lovely it has all been. How brown and well we are! And now children, school and hard work to make up all the weeks you have missed!'

'Yes,' said Belinda. 'I shall like going back. I'm ready for school now. What a lot we shall have to tell the others!'

'I hope we do Portugal and Spain and all the rest in geography this term,' said Mike. 'I feel I know a bit of *real* geography at last!'

England was clearly to be seen now. Mummy squeezed Daddy's hand. 'Home's all the nicer for having been away from it, isn't it?' she said. 'Dear old England! We're coming back to your autumn mists, your yellowing trees and falling leaves – and we're glad!'

'Won't it be fun to live in the caravans again, and see Davey and Clopper, and hear the rain on the caravan roof when we're cosily inside?' said Belinda.

'Oh hurry, *Pole Star* – we want to be home again!'

'There's no place like home!' sang Ann, suddenly. 'Goodbye, bulls and flying-fish and dolphins and diving boys and bullock-carts and monkeys – and smells! Goodbye! There's no place like home!'

The
Seaside
Family

Contents

1

Summer Holidays Again

'School's over for two months, thank goodness!' said Mike, and he slammed his books down on the table. The vase of flowers there nearly jumped off the table. 'Mike! Be careful,' said Mummy. 'There now – Belinda has done the same – and off goes the vase.'

'Sorry Mummy,' said Belinda, and picked up the vase. Mike went to get a cloth to wipe up the water. Ann picked up the flowers. They were all laughing. Mummy couldn't help laughing too.

'Well I know how you feel, when school is ended for a time,' she said. 'The summer holidays are so lovely and long for you too, aren't they – almost eight weeks. Goodness me – what shall I do with you for eight weeks?'

'I know what I want to do,' said Mike. 'I want to go to the seaside. We've been in a houseboat on a canal . . .'

'And we've been on a big ship for a trip,' said Ann.

'And now we want to go to the seaside,' said Mike. 'Don't we, girls?'

'Yes,' said the girls at once, and Mummy smiled.

'You've been planning this together on the way home from school!' she said. 'Well, it's no good asking *me*. It's Daddy you must ask. It costs money to go to the seaside, you know, and we don't have very much to spare.'

'Mummy, we don't see why it should cost very much to go and stay at the seaside,' said Mike, earnestly. 'Can't we go in our caravans? Then we don't need to take a house anywhere, or to go to a hotel. We'd just live in the caravans as usual.'

Mike's family had two caravans that stood in a green field where cows grazed. Sometimes the cows bumped against the vans at night and woke the children – but they didn't mind little things like that! That was all part of the fun.

The caravans were painted red and yellow. They had little red chimneys out of which smoke came when Mummy lighted her fire, or got the stove going in the children's caravan.

Mike, Belinda and Ann slept in three bunks, one above the other in one caravan. Mummy and Daddy slept in bunks in the other caravan. It was fun.

The children lived at school from Monday to Friday in the term-time, and came back to the caravans for the weekends. How they loved that! What fun it was to have a home on wheels, one that had no roots, but could be taken anywhere they liked.

'We'll ask Daddy as soon as we see him,' said Mike.

'We'll *make* him say yes. He'll love it too.'

So they lay in wait for Daddy, and hurled themselves on him as soon as he walked in at the field-gate.

'Daddy! We've something to ask you.'

'Something very important!'

'Something you've *got* to say yes to!'

'Is it something about the summer holidays?' asked Daddy thinking that three children could be very very heavy when they all hung on to him at once.

'Yes,' said everyone.

'Well, before you begin, let me break the news to you,' said Daddy firmly. 'Whatever ideas you've got in your head have got to come out. I've no money to spend on a summer holiday by the sea! That is – if you want to go to a hotel. The only thing I can do for you this summer is to let you go away somewhere fresh and new in the caravans. Nothing else at all.'

The three children squealed loudly.

'But *Daddy!* That's what we WANT! We want to go to the sea in the caravans. It's what we wanted to ask you.'

'Well, well, well – great minds certainly do think alike!' said Daddy. 'I must ask Mummy about it first.'

'We've asked her, we've asked her!' chanted Ann. 'And she said we must ask you. And we've asked *you*. So is it settled?'

Daddy began to laugh. 'What a lot of little pests you are! Yes, yes – it's settled. We'll choose a nice

seaside place, and we'll all go off there together. I shall enjoy it too. But wait a minute – I've just thought of something.'

'What?' said all three alarmed.

'It's this – I've asked Ben Johns to come and stay with you here,' said Daddy. 'I meant to put him up in the farmer's cottage and let him play with you all day. Oh dear – what shall we do about that?'

By this time Mummy was with them. 'Oh – little Ben Johns?' she said. 'Yes, I remember we said we'd have him for a time. Poor child, his mother's very ill, isn't she? Well – we can't very well go to the seaside then.'

'We can! We can take him too!' said Belinda. 'Just another bunk put up in our caravan, that's all! We've three already. Can't you get another one just for these holidays, Daddy?'

'Yes – I suppose we could,' said Daddy, and everyone cheered. 'Now – I want my TEA! Who's going to get it? And afterwards we'll settle everything.'

'More fun!' cried Belinda, running to make the tea. 'More fun for the Caravan Family!'

2

Benjy Comes Along

It was great fun planning the seaside holiday. They got out maps and pored over them.

'Let's go to the east coast,' said Mummy. 'It's so healthy.'

'Too cold for me,' said Daddy, 'Let's go to the west coast.'

'What's this little place down here?' said Belinda, pointing to where a bit of land curved out and made a small bay. 'It looks lovely here – on the south coast.'

'That's Sea-gull Cove,' said Mike, reading the name printed in very small letters. 'What a lovely name!'

'Sea-gull Cove!' said Daddy, suddenly looking excited. 'Why, I know that. I went there three times when I was a small boy – just for the day only, it's true, but I never forgot it. It's the dearest little cove you ever saw.'

'Let's go there then,' said Mike, at once.

But Mummy wanted to know more about it. 'Is the bathing safe? Does the tide come in too fast? Is the beach sandy or shingly?'

'The bathing's safe, the tide comes in quickly, but

that doesn't matter, and the beach is golden sand – with shells all over it. Does that please you, Mummy?' said Daddy.

'And is there a good place for the caravans?' asked Mummy. 'Is there a farmhouse near for food? Is there . . .'

'Oh Mummy – just let's go, and we'll soon find out,' said Belinda. 'Sea-gull Cove – it sounds just right.'

'I'll pop down there and see if it's still as I remember it,' said Daddy. 'I'll go this week. In the meantime I'll arrange for another bunk to be put into the children's caravan for Benjy – he'll be coming tomorrow.'

The next day two men came along with some wood and went into the children's caravan. Mike, Belinda and Ann followed them in, staring. The caravan was quite crowded out then!

'We'll put the new bunk here – opposite the other bunks,' said the first man.

'Put it under the window, then Ben can look out,' said Belinda. 'Will it fold down to be out of the way in the daytime?'

'Oh yes,' said the man. 'Now – you'd better all get out of here, because when we start hammering and sawing we want a bit of space! My, these caravans are nice, aren't they? I wouldn't mind living in one myself. I suppose you wouldn't sell me this one, miss?'

'Oh *no*,' said Belinda. 'It's our home. We're the Caravan Family!'

'But we'll soon be the Seaside Family,' said Ann, going down the steps outside the caravan. 'Mike, Belinda – who's this? Is it Benjy?'

A small boy, a bit younger than Mike, was standing rather forlornly at the gate of the field, a large bag beside him. He was looking over at the caravans.

'Yes. It must be Benjy,' said Mike. None of the children had seen him before. He was just the son of a friend of Daddy's, and his mother was ill. That was all the children knew about him.

They went over to him. He didn't look very strong. He had straight fair hair and rather pale blue eyes, and a nice, sudden smile.

'Are you Benjy?' said Mike, and the boy nodded.

'Well, I'm Mike – and this is Belinda – and this is Ann – they're my sisters,' said Mike. 'Come along and I'll take you to our mother. You're going to live with us for a bit, aren't you?'

'In our caravan. And we're just getting a bunk put in for you,' said Belinda.

'Don't you think you're lucky to be going to live in our caravan – a house on wheels?' said Ann.

'Well – I don't know,' said Benjy. 'I always thought it was gipsies who did that. I don't know that I'm going to like it. I'd rather live in a house.'

This was such a surprising remark to the three

children that they stared at Benjy without a word. Ann felt cross. How could anyone possibly prefer a house to their colourful caravan?

Mike saw that Ann was going to say something that might sound rude to a visitor, so he spoke hurriedly.

'Come and see our mother. And I say – isn't it grand – we're all going off to the sea in two days' time!'

Ben's face brightened. 'Oh – that's better. We'll be in a hotel then, I suppose?'

'No. In our caravan,' said Ann. 'But if you don't like sleeping inside, you can sleep underneath!'

Benjy was just going to answer back when the children's mother came over to welcome him. She was so nice that Benjy was all smiles and politeness at once.

'You're just in time for a meal, Benjy,' she said. 'Such a nice one too – hard-boiled eggs and salad, and raspberries and cream! Will you like that?'

Benjy clearly thought that this was quite all right.

Belinda pulled Ann aside. 'Oh dear – he'll *spoil* the holiday! How I do wish we were going by ourselves. And I'll hate him in our caravan! What a pity!'

3

Off to the Seaside

After their good meal of eggs and salad, raspberries and cream, the children went to show Benjy the caravan he was to share with them. The men had now put in the new bunk, and Mummy had put bedding on it. It looked very nice.

'Come on Benjy – we'll show you everything,' said Belinda. They all went into the caravan. Belinda ran up the steps first. She showed Benjy the door – it was cut in halves in the middle, so that you could have just the bottom half shut if you wanted to, and the top half open, or both halves shut at once to make a door.

The caravan looked so nice inside. It had highly polished cork carpet all over the floor, with red rugs on it. There was a little stove at one end for heating the caravan in winter. There was a small sink with taps, so that washing-up could be done.

'Isn't it marvellous, to have a sink and taps and water in a caravan?' said Ann, and she turned on a tap to show Benjy that real water came out. But he didn't think it was very wonderful.

'What's so grand about *that*?' he said. 'Water comes out of our taps at home too. I suppose you've got a water-tank on the roof, haven't you? Most caravans have.'

It was all very disappointing. Benjy hardly looked at the bunks. He patted his and made a face. 'A bit hard. Hope I shall sleep all right at night.'

'You ought to be thinking yourself jolly lucky to be sleeping in a bunk in a caravan,' said Ann, quite fiercely. Mike nudged her. This was Benjy's first day and he was still quite a new visitor. You didn't talk like that yet!

Nobody showed him the cupboards where things were kept so neatly. Nobody asked him to admire the row of cups and saucers and plates. Benjy didn't want to live in a caravan, so he wasn't going to admire anything about theirs at all. It was really very disappointing.

'You'll have to share our jobs,' said Mike, as they went down the caravan steps again. 'You know – help to get the wood in, and wash up . . .'

'And make your own bunk and keep it tidy,' said Belinda.

'Goodness – can't you girls make the bunks by yourselves?' asked Benjy, rather scornfully. 'That's not a boy's work – making beds.'

'Our Daddy often makes up his own bunk, and if he can do it, so can you,' said Ann at once, and

she put on a really terrible glare. Mummy was most astonished to see it when she met them round the corner of the caravan. Dear, dear – didn't her three want poor Benjy?

Two days went by very quickly. There was such a lot to do that the children didn't bother about Benjy and his ways very much. They had to go with their mother to buy beach clothes and swimming costumes, and they had to spend a day with Granny, who wanted to see them before they went. They had to go and fetch their two horses, Davey and Clopper, from the farmer, because they were to pull the caravans all the way to the sea.

Fortunately for Benjy he liked both Davey and Clopper! Ann really felt she might have smacked him if he had said something horrid about them.

'This is dear old Davey,' she said, patting the strong little black horse, that showed a white star on his forehead. 'He is awfully good and quiet – you can ride him.'

'And this is Clopper,' said Mike, leading up a dark brown and white horse. 'He's a very good horse – but he won't stand any nonsense. They're both darlings.'

'Oh, I like them,' said Benjy, and he stroked the velvety black nose that rested on his shoulder. 'Davey, I like you. And Clopper, you're a beauty. I love your shaggy feet. I say, Mike, let me drive your caravan, will you? I can make Clopper go as fast as anything.'

Daddy overheard him. 'Well, you won't drive old Clopper then,' he said, firmly. 'He's not a race horse! I shan't let you drive till I can trust you. Now, can you all be ready in an hour's time? I want to start for Sea-gull Cove then.'

Could they be ready? Of course they could! Ann was ready in five minutes! She could always be quick when she really wanted to. Mike got the horses into harness. They stood patiently between their shafts, glad to be on the move once more.

Belinda went round picking up every scrap of litter. Mummy would never let one tiny bit of paper, or even a bit of egg-shell, be left in the field. Every corner had to be tidy and neat.

At last they were all ready. Daddy got up on the driving-seat of Davey's caravan. 'I'll go first, Mike, and show the way,' he called. 'Follow after me, Benjy, wait and shut the gate behind us.'

They were off – off to Sea-gull Cove by the sea! First went Daddy's caravan, with good old Davey pulling it – and then came Clopper, driven by Mike, pulling the children's caravan.

'We shall soon be the Seaside Family!' sang Belinda. 'Hurrah, hurrah, for the Seaside Family on its way to Sea-gull Cove!'

4

Sea-gull Cove

It was exactly the right day to set off for the seaside. The sun shone down hotly, and the sky was bright blue except for little white clouds here and there.

'I'm sure those clouds are made of cotton wool,' said Ann, and that made everyone laugh. They really did look like puffs of wool.

Davey and Clopper went steadily down the country lanes. Daddy had looked up the best way to go on his big maps, and he had chosen the winding lanes rather than the main roads, because then they wouldn't meet so much traffic.

'And anyway the lanes are prettier than the roads,' said Belinda. 'I love the way the red poppies nod at us as we go by, and the blue chicory flowers shine like little stars.'

'It takes longer to go by the lanes, Daddy says,' said Ann. 'But who minds that? If it takes longer than a day we can easily take our caravans into a field for the night and camp there!'

'Dear me, yes,' said Benjy. 'I hadn't thought we could do that. That might be rather fun!'

'You couldn't do that with a house,' said Mike, clicking to Clopper. 'A house has to stay put. It hasn't got wheels it can go wandering away on for miles and miles.'

'Still – I do prefer a house,' said Benjy, obstinately. 'I say, Mike, you might let me drive Clopper for a bit now.'

'No,' said Mike, firmly. 'Daddy said you can't until he can trust you. I'm driving Clopper all day – unless I give the girls a turn.'

They went slowly down the little sunny lanes all day long. Daddy called a halt at teatime. 'We can't get to Sea-gull Cove today after all,' he said. 'We must camp in a meadow for the night. I can see a farmer over there. I'll ask him if we can stay here, in this field nearby.'

The farmer was nice. 'Yes, of course you can put up in my field,' he said. 'I can see you're the sort of folks I can trust not to set things on fire, or leave gates open. I'll send my boy out with eggs and milk, if you'd like them.'

They all spent a very happy evening in a field where big brown and white cows grazed, whisking their tails to keep away the flies.

'I wish I had a tail like a cow,' said Ann, flapping at the flies over her head. 'I think it would be so very useful!'

Davey and Clopper kept together away from the

cows. They went to drink at the stream, and then they pulled at the juicy grass nearby. They looked happy and contented. They were tired after their long walk, pulling heavy caravans – and it was nice to eat and drink and rest in a shady green field.

Ann came to give them each a lump of sugar. Benjy went with her. The horses nuzzled him and Ann, and blew down Benjy's neck. He was delighted.

'I wish they were mine,' he said to Ann. 'Fancy having two horses of your own like this. You *are* lucky!'

'You're nice when you talk like that,' said Ann. 'Instead of turning up your nose at everything!'

'Ann! Benjy! I want you to come and get into your bunks!' called Mummy. 'We're going to start off very early tomorrow morning, at half-past six. Come along quickly.'

Everyone was fast asleep before it was dark that night, even Mummy and Daddy! They were tired with their long drive and the sun and the breeze. Nobody heard the cows bumping into the children's caravan in the middle of the night, nobody even heard the screech owl that screamed and made Davey and Clopper almost jump out of their skins!

Daddy was awake at six o'clock. He looked out of the open door of the caravan. What a perfect morning! The sun was up, but still rather low, and the shadows of the trees were very long. Dew lay heavily on the grass.

Soon the whole family was having breakfast. Mummy had boiled the eggs from the farm, and there was creamy milk, new bread and farm butter with homemade strawberry jam. Everyone but Benjy ate two eggs each.

'What a poor appetite you've got, Benjy!' said Ann. 'No wonder you look so pale.'

'I think you're greedy!' said Benjy. 'Two eggs for breakfast! I can't think how you manage to eat them!'

'You wait for a few days - then you'll be like Mike, asking for *three* eggs, not two!' said Belinda.

They set off once more in the caravans. Davey and Clopper plodded along steadily - clippity-clop, clippity-clop.

Up hill and down hill, along pretty valleys, round the honeysuckle hedges, past green woods - and then, what a surprise!

They rounded a corner on a hill - and there stretching below them was the sea - miles upon miles of brilliant blue water!

'Oh - the SEA!' yelled Ann, and all the children shouted for joy. The first sight was always so exciting.

'And there's Sea-gull Cove!' cried Mike, pointing. 'Look - it must be. Isn't it, Daddy?'

Yes, it was. There it lay, a little bay of yellow sand and blue sea. On the beach sat a crowd of sea-gulls. They rose into the air and came gliding over the children's heads, calling loudly.

'They're saying, "Welcome to Sea-gull Cove",' said Ann, pleased. 'They really are pleased to see us! Oh, what a lovely little place!'

Settling in at Sea-gull Cove

The caravans went slowly down the hill to Sea-gull Cove. It was a steep hill, and the road wound round and about. Daddy and Mike had to put on the brakes of the caravans or they would have run down the hill of their own accord and bumped the horses along too fast!

The cove looked nicer and nicer as they came nearer. 'The beach is simply *covered* with shells!' called Mike.

'And look at the rockpools shining blue,' said Belinda. 'How lovely to paddle in those. They'll be as warm as anything.'

'We can have baths every single day from morning to night,' said Ann.

'*I* shan't,' said Benjy at once. 'I'm not keen on bathing at all. Horrible cold water – and I can't swim, so I hate going in deep.'

'Can't *swim!*' said Ann, astonished. 'Why, I've been able to swim for ages and I'm much younger than you. You *are* a baby!'

Benjy went red and looked cross.

'Now he'll sulk,' said Belinda. 'Well, let him! He'll just *have* to learn to swim if he's going to enjoy himself here. My goodness, isn't the water blue!'

'Mike!' yelled back Daddy from his caravan in front. 'We'll take the caravans right down to the cove. There's a stretch of sandy grass at the back of the beach. If it's all right we'll have our caravans there.'

The children squealed for joy. 'Oh Daddy!' shouted Belinda, 'how glorious! Perhaps the tide will come almost up to our doors. We can leave them open and lie and look at the sea when we're in bed.'

The caravans were placed side by side on the little grassy stretch behind the beach. Davey and Clopper were led into a field behind. Daddy set off to talk to the farmer who owned the land nearby. He had already seen him when he had gone down to Seagull Cove for the day. He knew it was all right to put the horses there. Now he wanted to arrange for food and water for his little family.

The children raced on to the sandy beach. It was firm and golden beneath their bare feet. Ann picked up some of the shells. 'Look – as pink as a sunset! And do look at this one – it's like a little trumpet. Oh, I shall make a most beautiful collection of shells to take home with me!'

Belinda and Mike ran down to the edge of the sea. Little waves curled over each other just there, and ran up the smooth, shining sand. Farther out were

bigger waves, curling over with little splashes. The children yelled for joy.

'We'll bathe all day! We'll paddle! We'll get a boat and row! We'll shrimp and we'll fish! We'll . . .'

Mike leapt into a bigger wave than usual and splashed Belinda from head to foot. Mummy called to him. 'Mike! If you're going to do that sort of thing come and get into swimming costumes! But first, don't you want something to eat?'

'Yes, if we can take it down to the very edge of the sea,' said Mike. He looked round for Benjy. Benjy was dabbling his toes in the edge of the water, looking rather solemn.

'Isn't it *lovely*, Benjy?' cried Belinda, rushing up to him, and giving him a little push that sent him running farther into the sea.

'Don't!' said Benjy, coming back in a hurry. 'My feet are awfully hot and the water's frightfully cold. I was just getting used to it.'

'I said, isn't it lovely!' cried Belinda, who was determined to make Benjy admire Sea-gull Cove.

'Well, it *looks* lovely – but won't it be rather lonely?' said Benjy. 'Shan't we be rather bored here all by ourselves?'

'Daddy says only stupid people are bored!' shouted Ann, in delight, coming up. 'So you must be stupid! Stupid baby!'

'Ann!' called Mummy, really shocked. 'Don't be so

rude to Benjy. Let him get used to things.'

'Well, he must get used to us too, then,' said Ann. 'Mummy, how *can* he ask if we'll be bored in this lovely, lovely place?'

'Ann,' said Mummy, pulling her quietly to one side. 'Do remember that Benjy is very fond of his mother, and I expect that, although he doesn't say much about it, he is secretly very worried about her – she is terribly ill, you know.'

'Oh dear,' said Ann. 'I quite forgot. I'm sorry, Mummy. I'll try and remember to be nice to him. All the same, he's a silly baby.'

Soon all four children were in their swimming costumes. Mummy gave them a basket of food to take down to the very edge of the sea.

'Let's go and sit in the water and have our dinner,' said Belinda, with a giggle. 'I've never in my life had a picnic sitting in the water.'

So they went and sat down in the edge of the sea – all except Benjy, who thought it was a horrid idea. They ate their ham sandwiches and nibbled their tomatoes happily, while tiny waves ran up their legs and all round their bodies.

'Lovely!' said Mike, popping the last of his tomato into his mouth. 'Hurrah for Sea-gull Cove – the nicest place in the world!'

6

Benjy has a Lesson

The tide came in all that afternoon. It crept up the beach bit by bit, and the children watched eagerly to see if it would reach the caravans. But it didn't of course.

'Do you think it might if we had a storm, Daddy?' asked Ann, longingly. 'Oh, Daddy – do you suppose the water would ever get to the top of the wheels, so that the two caravans would float away like Noah's Arks?'

'Oooh – that *would* be fun!' said Belinda.

'That would never happen,' said Daddy, firmly. 'Because if there were a storm I should at once move the caravans farther back!'

'Oh Daddy – you're a spoil-sport!' said Ann, with a laugh. 'Just think of us all floating gaily away on the sea!'

'How horrid!' said Benjy, with a shiver.

'Benjy's afraid of adventures,' said Ann. 'He doesn't even like going into the water up to his knees. He . . .'

'Ann!' said Mummy, sharply. 'Have you already forgotten what I said?'

Ann went red. 'Oh dear – I'm so sorry,' she said.

'Well, please don't forget again,' said Mummy. 'I don't like being cross on a holiday. Now, what are you going to do? Paddle, dig, bathe, or what?'

'Bathe,' said Mike, at once. 'I want a good long swim. Coming, Daddy?'

'Rather!' said Daddy, 'and Mummy will too. I'll give Benjy his first lesson in swimming too, I think.'

Benjy looked up in alarm. 'I don't think I want to learn to swim,' he said.

'Rubbish!' said Daddy. 'All children must learn to swim. Look at Ann here – she swims like a little fish.'

'I can even swim under water,' said Ann, proudly. 'It's easy! I can open my eyes under water too, and see the things on the bottom of the sand.'

'Can you really?' said Benjy, amazed. 'I should like to do that!' He turned to Ann's father. 'All right, sir, I'll do my best to learn. But don't duck me or anything, will you?'

'You can trust Daddy,' said Belinda, at once. 'He'll always tell you what he's going to do.'

So Benjy had his first lesson. He was afraid when he had to walk right into the water up to his waist. He said it was cold, he said it was too deep, he said he was sure there were crabs waiting to bite his toes!

'Yes, it does seem a bit cold,' agreed Daddy. 'And it is quite deep for you. And there may be one or two crabs. But we just won't bother about any of those

things at all. Now then – bend forward – that's right – up with your legs! Don't struggle. I've got you safely. Can't you feel my hand under your tummy?'

Benjy really was very frightened, but he tried his best to do what Daddy said. He worked his arms and legs furiously, and got completely out of breath. The other children roared with laughter at him.

'Daddy, he's trying to go at sixty miles an hour!' squealed Ann. 'You'll have to give him a hooter or something if he goes at that pace!'

That made Benjy laugh too, and he swallowed a mouthful of water and choked. He struck out with his arms in alarm, and clung to Daddy quickly.

'There – you're all right and you did quite well,' said Daddy. 'Now walk into the shallower water while we all go out for a swim.'

Then the Caravan Family all went for a swim together. They went into deep water, and not even Daddy could feel the sand below with his feet. Ann felt very brave indeed. Then she gave a sudden scream and Daddy looked round at once.

'Oh! Oh! Something's nibbling me! Oh!'

Daddy swum up to her and then he turned over on his back and roared with laughter as he floated there.

'Look what's nibbling Ann!' he shouted to the others, and he held up a strand of ribbon seaweed! 'It was bobbing against her – and she thought it was nibbling her! Oh, Ann – how does seaweed nibble?'

It was such fun in the water. But soon Daddy led the way back to the shore, striking out strongly. 'It's the first time we've been swimming for a long time,' he called. 'We won't overdo it – we shall be so stiff tomorrow if we do. Come along to the beach and we'll have some races to warm us up.'

They went to the sandy beach. Benjy was there waiting for them, shivering. Daddy made them all race up and down, up and down, and soon they were warm and glowing.

'The tide's almost up to the caravan steps, it is really, look!' cried Ann, in delight. Everyone looked. It was about twelve feet away from the steps, but the water was already going down. It certainly wouldn't reach the caravans *that* evening!

Belinda gave a terrific yawn. Mummy heard her. 'You're all tired out with excitement,' she said. 'We'll have a light supper – and then off to bed!'

Funnily enough nobody minded going to bed early. 'You see,' said Ann, 'it's going to be *such* a treat lying in our bunks, Mummy, and looking out at the evening sea – and watching it get darker and darker!'

But she didn't see it getting darker – she was sound asleep!

Everything is Lovely

Next morning Mike awoke first. He couldn't think what the noise was just outside. Lap-lap-lap, plish-plash-plash!

And then he remembered – of course, they were by the sea. THE SEA! He sat up in his bunk and looked out. The tide was in again, and was lapping some yards away from the caravan steps. Plish-plish-plash! The sun shone over the great stretch of water and made bright sparkles on it everywhere.

Mike took a deep breath. It was all so clean and new. Surely the world never never looked so lovely as it did in the very early morning.

There came a rush of big wings, and Mike saw a sea-gull standing in the edge of the water. It was facing the caravan. He held his breath because it began to walk towards the steps!

It was a magnificent bird, snow-white and pearl-grey with bright, alert eyes. It walked up to the caravan and then hopped up a step – then another step – then another! And at last it was on the top step of all, peering into the caravan, its head on one side!

'Eeee-ooo, eee-ooo, eee-ooo!' it screamed suddenly, as if it were asking for breakfast. Mike almost jumped out of his skin. The other three awoke in a fright and sat up. They stared in surprise at the enormous sea-gull. It flapped its great wings and soared away into the air. 'Eee-ooo, eee-ooo, eee-ooo!' it squealed, almost as if it were laughing at them.

'Goodness – that did scare me!' said Ann, with a laugh. 'Did it come to say good morning or what, Mike?'

'It's awfully tame,' said Mike. 'We'll feed the gulls today with bread, and see if we can get them to take it from our hands. I really thought that gull was going to walk into the caravan! I say – what about a bathe before breakfast?'

'Horrid!' said Benjy. But the others didn't think so and they scrambled into bathing things and tore down to the water at once. It was cold – but who minded that? Well, Benjy did, of course, but as he didn't put more than his toes into the water, he didn't even shiver.

Mummy called to him. 'Benjy – if you're not going to bathe, come and help me with breakfast. And you might see if you can find some driftwood on the beach, thrown up by the tide. We'll have to find some wood somewhere for the fire, and stack it in the sun to dry.'

Benjy had already found that there were plenty of

odd jobs to do if you lived in a caravan. He had learnt to make his own bed – or rather his bunk – each day. He had been ticked off for leaving the tap running so that the water-tank had emptied. He had had to sweep the floor several times and shake the mats.

He was beginning not to mind doing all these little jobs. Everyone else did them cheerfully, and after all they weren't very much bother. All the same he made up his mind that Mike would have to do his share of hunting for driftwood and bringing it to stack in the sun for the fire!

'I want to buy a boat to sail on the rockpools,' said Belinda at breakfast. They were having it on the beach. Daddy had lighted a wood-fire to boil the kettle and cook the eggs. 'Can I go to the nearest village and see if I can get one, Mummy?'

'And I want a shrimping-net,' said Mike. 'I bet I could catch enough shrimps to cook for tea each day!'

'Oooh, lovely,' said Belinda. 'I do like shrimps with brown bread and butter. Do you want to buy anything at the shops, Benjy?'

'I'll see,' said Benjy. 'I might buy a big ball if I can see one. This is a good beach for a ball.'

'And I shall buy ice-creams for everyone,' said Ann.

'We won't be *too* long at the village,' said Belinda. 'We simply mustn't waste a single hour away from Sea-gull Cove if we can help it. Mummy, can I throw

some bread to the gulls now? You've got half a stale loaf there.'

The gulls were standing not far off, watching the children eating. Mummy broke the stale loaf into bits and gave it to the four children. One by one they threw bits to the gulls.

They came nearer and nearer, squealing angrily if one gull got too many pieces. They pecked one another if they thought one had been unfair. 'Just like naughty children,' said Mummy.

'You know, if we get the gulls much tamer than this, we'll have to lock up all our food,' said Daddy. 'They will be into the caravans before we know where we are! Hey you big fellow, that's my toe, not a bit of bread!'

'Well,' said Mummy, getting up and scaring off the gulls at once, 'it's time we cleared away. Mike, there is a bus you can catch up the hill there in half an hour's time. Girls, wash up for me. Boys, make the bunks and look for wood. I'm going to the farm for food.'

Soon the little family was busy about its tasks, chattering happily. 'Now for the bus!' said Mike at last. 'Come on, or we'll miss it! Run, Benjy, or you'll be left behind!'

8

Benjy's Ball

They just caught the bus nicely, and off they went, jolting through the country lanes to the nearest village of Miminingly. It was a dear little place, with only four shops, a church, a chapel, and clusters of pretty thatched houses.

'It must be fun to live in a tiny place like this and know simply *everybody*,' said Ann. 'I should like that.'

'Look – there's a shop where we can buy what we want,' said Mike. 'It looks as if it sells simply *everything!*'

So it did. It was a little general shop, hung with all kinds of things inside and out – pails, kettles, rope, sou'westers, china, wire-netting, postcards, sweets, ships, toys – everything was there it seemed!

'Is there anything you *don't* sell?' Ann asked the little round woman who beamed at them from behind a counter piled high with yet more goods.

'Oh yes, miss,' she said. 'I don't sell rocking horses and I don't sell cuckoo clocks – so don't you go asking for them now, will you?'

Ann giggled. 'I wasn't going to,' she said. 'I really want to buy some ice-cream.'

'Ah, I've plenty of *that*!' said the plump little woman, and she took the lid from a big ice-cream container. She scooped yellow ice-cream into four cornets. It looked lovely. Ann paid her in delight.

'*Just* what we wanted!' she said. 'Can we look round your exciting shop while we eat them?'

'Of course – and you can poke into any of the corners you like,' said the shop-woman. 'There's no knowing what you might find!'

Belinda found just the ship she wanted – one with a nice heavy keel that looked as if it would help the ship to sail properly and not fall on its side. Mike found a splendid shrimping-net – a good strong one that wouldn't break if he pressed it too hard into the sand when he went shrimping.

And you should have seen the ball that Benjy bought! It really was the nicest the four had ever seen! It was blown up to make it very big and bouncy. It was striped in yellow and red and blue and was twice as big as a football!

'That's a lovely ball to play with in the sea,' said the little shop-woman, when Benjy paid her. 'It bobs on the water like a live thing.'

'Oh, I shan't play with it on the sea,' said Benjy, at once. 'It's too precious. I shall only play with it on the sands.'

'I say – we'd better hurry if we want to catch the bus back,' said Mike, suddenly. 'Look – it's at

the corner there, waiting. Goodbye – we did enjoy your shop!'

Off they went, scurrying to the bus, and it was not long before they were back at dear old Sea-gull Cove again. Daddy was waiting for them.

'Coming in for a bathe?' he shouted. 'And what about your swimming lesson, Benjy? You'll get on fine today!'

'I don't think I want one today,' said Benjy. 'I think I'd rather play with my new ball – isn't it a beauty?'

'Rather!' said Daddy. 'You can play with it after your lesson – we all will, to get ourselves warm. Come along now, into your swimming trunks!'

And so Benjy had his second lesson, and he splashed away valiantly. Daddy was quite pleased with him. 'Now listen to me, Benjy,' he said. 'You want to practise the strokes I have told you. Practise them by yourself in the water each day – three or four times a day.'

'Benjy won't! He never goes in farther than his knees!' shouted Ann. 'He's afraid!'

'Well – if he does not go in farther than that it'll take him a long time to learn to swim!' said Daddy. 'Now come on out, all of you – and we'll have a fine game with Benjy's new ball!'

It certainly was a lovely ball. It bounced as lightly as a feather, and was so light that even the wind could bowl it over the sand. The children had to run fast

after it when the breeze began to join in their game!

They were all terribly hungry for dinner. Mummy had bought a big meat pie from the farm, and it was soon gone. Not even a small piece was left for the gulls! Then plums and greengages were handed out, and if anyone wanted bread-and-butter with them they could have it. Creamy milk from the farm was in a big jug set in a pail of cold water to keep it cool.

'Lovely!' said Ann, when she had finished. 'Now for another bathe.'

'Not after that enormous lunch,' said Mummy firmly. 'You can bathe at three o'clock, but not before. Have a read now, in the shade. That would be nice. Lend Benjy a book.'

At three o'clock Mike, Ann, Daddy, Mummy and Belinda were all out in the water again – they really were a family of fishes! Benjy wouldn't come. He played on the beach with his ball.

And then something happened. The wind took the big ball and blew it down to the edge of the sea. It bobbed on the water. It was taken out a little way. Benjy splashed in after it – but the wind took it out even farther! 'Mike! Belinda! Get my ball!' squealed Benjy. But nobody heard him, nobody at all.

Now what was he to do? He would lose his ball – there it went, bobbing away on the waves! Poor Benjy!

Benjy is Most Surprising

Benjy stood in the water up to his knees and howled dismally. 'My ball! Get my ball! It's going away on the water. MIKE! MIKE!'

But Mike didn't hear him. Mike was trying to swim under water with Ann. Daddy and Mummy were having a race on their own. Belinda was floating peacefully on her back. Nobody saw what was happening to Benjy.

Benjy stared desperately at his bobbing ball. It came back a little way because a wave broke over it and sent it rolling in towards the beach. If only it would come back a little more Benjy might be able to reach it.

He waded in deeper. Oooh – he was up to his waist now. How dangerous, he thought – and how cold! Ah, there was his ball – nearer still! Another few steps and he really might get it. He waded deeper still. Now he was almost up to it – and oh joy, a wave sent the ball almost on top of him. He had it! It was safe!

He felt very proud indeed. He had never been out so deep before. A wave wetted him right to the

armpits. After all, the water wasn't so very cold – it was rather warm and felt silky to the skin. He waded back with his ball and put it in a safe place. Then he turned and looked at the sea.

The others were really having a glorious time out there. It was fun to hear them shouting and laughing. What a pity he couldn't swim!

Benjy waded into the sea again. It still felt warm. He waded right up to his waist. Then he bobbed under to wet his shoulders. Why, it was *lovely*! He stayed under for a little while and then began to make the armstrokes he had been shown that morning.

He suddenly lost his balance and his legs went up into the water. He struck out in alarm – and goodness gracious, he really could hardly believe it, but he swam three whole strokes before water went into his mouth and he choked!

Benjy was full of pride and amazement. He had swum – he really had! His feet had been right up in the water. Should he try again?

And then he saw the others nearby watching him in astonishment.

'Benjy! We saw you then! Were you really swimming?' yelled Ann.

'Benjy, do it again!' shouted Mike, swimming up. 'I say – you didn't *really* swim, did you?'

'I did,' said Benjy. 'I'll show you!'

He let his legs leave the sandy bottom and then

he struck out again. Four strokes this time before he went under, spluttering and gasping.

'Daddy, he's marvellous!' cried Belinda. 'Mummy, look, he's learnt already! If he practises he'll soon be swimming out with us! How lovely!'

Benjy had never felt so proud in his life. He had always been a spoilt timid boy – now for the first time he had been really brave on his own, and he felt grand. He did some more strokes, and then went under so completely that he really thought he was drowning!

'We're going in now,' said Mike helping him up to the surface. 'I say – don't swallow *all* the sea, will you? We do want a bit left, you know.'

'Can we play with your lovely ball, Benjy?' asked Ann, wading out with the spluttering Benjy.

'Yes, of course,' said Benjy.

'Benjy, whatever made you go and swim like that all by yourself?' asked Belinda curiously. 'I never thought you would. You *are* brave!'

Benjy nearly didn't say anything about his runaway ball. He badly wanted to be thought brave enough to go and practise all on his own, without any ball to make him wade into the water.

But he knew that Mike and the others always owned up and never pretended, and he wanted to be the same. So he went red and told them what had happened.

'I wasn't really brave! It was my new ball that made me go into the water. The wind blew it out to sea, and you didn't hear me calling to you to get it for me. So I waded out and got it – and it was so nice out there I thought I'd practise swimming. That's all. I wasn't really *brave*, you see.'

Daddy had heard all this. He clapped Benjy on the shoulder. 'It's nice to see a boy brave enough to own up that it was his ball sent him into the water, and nothing else – and very nice to see that he was sensible enough to stay there once he was in! I'm pleased with you Benjy. You'll be as fine a swimmer as Mike soon!'

Well, of course that was quite enough to make Benjy determined to practise his swimming every single day. He blushed with pride and thought the children's father was the nicest he'd ever met – except his own, of course.

They all had great fun that day. They sailed Belinda's boat on the pool, and it really did sail beautifully and only fell over once on its side, when the wind blew too strongly.

Mike went shrimping and caught seventy-two shrimps and Mummy cooked them for supper. The gulls came round and ate up all the heads and tails that nobody wanted!

'They're quite useful, aren't they?' said Ann, throwing them a few more heads from her plate.

'Good as dustmen, the way they clear up our litter! No, shoo, gull – you are *not* to peck Belinda's boat!'

'What fun we're having!' said Mike. 'I wish these holidays would never, never end!'

10

Ann and Benjy

Now the days began to slip by too quickly. 'I never know *what* day of the week it is now,' said Mike. 'I really thought today was Tuesday – and now I find it's Friday! Goodness knows where Wednesday and Thursday went to!'

'We know when it's Sunday, anyway,' said Ann, 'because then we hear the church bell ringing from the village of Minningly – and we go to church.'

'Yes – I liked that,' said Belinda. 'It's the dearest little church I ever went into – the sort of church that God really does feel near in.'

'We never go to church at home,' said Benjy, 'but I liked going with you. God never feels very near to me though. I'm sure He doesn't bother about a boy like me. I say "Our Father" at night, but I never ask Him for things like you do. I can't really feel that He's listening.'

'Well, you can't feel very safe then,' said Ann. 'I mean – we always feel that God really *is* a Father and loves us, and is always looking after us, so we feel safe. But you can't feel at all safe.'

'Well, I don't,' said Benjy. 'I'm always afraid something awful is going to happen, and – well, don't let's talk about it.'

'But I want to,' said Ann. 'Mike and Belinda, you go away. I do really want to talk to Benjy. I don't like his not feeling safe.'

Mike and Belinda went off. They were rather bored with this anyway. They just thought Benjy was being silly, as usual.

But he wasn't. Something was frightening him very much. He told Ann what it was.

'It's my mother,' he said. 'You know she's awfully ill, Ann. I haven't always been very kind to her, and now what's worrying me all the time is that she might – she might *die*, Ann, and I wouldn't even have been able to tell her I was sorry.'

'Oh Benjy!' said Ann. 'Might she really die? And you're away here with us and can't even tell her you love her and didn't ever mean to be horrid? Oh Benjy, I'm sorry I've been horrid to *you*. I ought to have been kind. I shall pray for ever so long tonight to ask God to make your mother better. You must too. God will know it's very important if we both pray for exactly the same thing for a long time.'

'Well, I will,' said Benjy. 'Don't tell your father and mother about this, Ann. You see, I heard them talking yesterday when they didn't know I was

near – and they said my mother was worse. I couldn't help hearing.'

'Ann! Benjy! Whatever are you talking about so earnestly?' called Mummy. 'Not planning any mischief, I hope!'

'No, Mummy,' said Ann. She gave Benjy a quick hug. 'Don't worry any more. You needn't now.'

'ANN! Come on – Daddy's got a boat and we're going out on it!' shouted Mike. 'Do come.'

Ann was thrilled. She raced down to the sea, where Daddy had the boat. Benjy went too, looking much more cheerful. He hadn't liked Ann a bit before – but now he felt as if she was his best friend. He got into the boat with the others.

'Can you row?' Mike asked him. Benjy shook his head.

'But I'd like to learn,' he said, rather surprisingly.

'Good boy!' said Mike, and grinned at him. 'You're not nearly such a mutt as you were, are you?'

Rowing was hard work, Benjy found. All the others rowed well, even Ann. It really was astonishing, the things these three could do! They were always willing to try anything and go on trying till they were good at it.

They had a bathe from the boat itself. 'Ooooh! *Really* deep water here!' said Mike, and dived over the edge of the boat. Splash! He was up again at once. Belinda dived in too, but Ann let herself down over

the side. Benjy looked at Anne's father.

'Shall I go in too, sir?'

'Yes, if you like,' said the children's father. 'If you get into trouble I'll dive in and get you. You can swim now – it doesn't matter whether you're in deep or shallow water, you can still swim!'

So in went Benjy, and although it gave him an odd feeling at first to know that the bottom of the sea was rather far down, he soon forgot it. He forgot his troubles too, and Ann was very pleased to hear him squealing with laughter.

Then back they went to the shore again, and the day slipped by as quickly as usual. It seemed no time at all before it was bedtime.

Benjy and Ann were sent to bed first because they were the youngest. 'Hurry, Benjy,' said Ann. 'Then we can have a long time to say our prayers before the others come. You know how important it is tonight.'

And so, if Ann's mother had looked in ten minutes later she would have seen two washed and brushed children kneeling down beside one of the bunks, absolutely still. How hard they were praying!

'Please, dear God, think how sad Benjy is and make his mother better,' prayed Ann. 'You always want to be kind, so I know You'll help poor Benjy. Please, please make his mother better!'

It was the longest prayer Benjy and Ann had ever made. 'Goodnight, Benjy,' said Ann, when she

climbed into her bunk. 'God was listening, as he always does. Here come the other two – we only *just* finished in time!'

11

About Sea-creatures – and a Telegram!

Next day Benjy waited eagerly for the postman. Would there be good news? He had no letter, but there was one for the children's mother.

'Yes, Benjy,' she said, when she saw him looking anxiously at her. 'It's about your mother. She's just the same, neither better nor worse.'

'There you are,' Benjy said miserably to Ann, when they were alone. 'I told you so. God doesn't really care about a boy like me.'

'It's wicked to say things like that,' said Ann. 'Don't let's talk about it if that's what you think. Look, what's that – it's a starfish! Daddy, come and look!'

Everyone came and looked at the unusual five-fingered creature. 'It's just five legs and a tummy!' said Daddy. 'Its mouth is in the middle of it.'

'How does it get along?' asked Mike, seeing the creature dragging itself down the sand.

Daddy turned it over. The children saw dozens of white tube-like things sticking out of the five fingers. 'Those are its legs,' said Daddy. 'Look at the way it puts them out. It takes hold of the ground with the

first rows, pulls itself up, takes hold with the back legs, and so it gets along. Very clever!'

The starfish got into a pool and disappeared. A crab ran out as if it was afraid. It sank itself into the soft wet sand and vanished.

'That's another clever little creature!' said Mike, with a laugh. 'I wish I could make myself disappear like that. Daddy, how do crabs grow? Their hard shell can't grow, surely?'

'Oh no,' said Daddy. 'The poor crab has to creep into a dark corner and hide himself when he grows too big for his shell. Then his shell splits – and out he wriggles! He hides away quietly for a day or two – and hey presto, a completely new shell grows on his body!'

'It's just like magic,' said Ann. 'I wish I could see it happening. Daddy, I'm going shrimping if Mike will let me borrow his net. Then you can tell me about shrimps and prawns too!'

She went off with Mike's net, and soon she and Benjy were hard at work catching shrimps and prawns in the big rockpools.

They looked at their peculiar eyes on stalks, and their funny little bunches of swimmeret legs. 'Daddy told me that the shrimps and prawns are the dustmen of these rockpools.' said Ann. 'They clear up all the rubbish. Did you know that, Benjy? Oh, do look – there are some sea-anemones!'

They both looked at the different jelly-like lumps
growing in red and green on the rock in the water.
'Watch!' said Ann. 'They will put out things that look
like petals soon, and wave them about in the water.
Mummy, look! What are those sea-anemones doing?'

'Ah, they are trying to trap tiny shrimps or other
creatures in those waving petals,' said Mummy.
'Once they have caught them with those unusual
arms of theirs they will drag them into their middles
– and that's the end of the little shrimps! They're not
flowers, of course, they are jelly-like creatures that
are always hungry!'

'Can I give this one a bit of bread?' asked Ann.
'Here you are, anemone. Take that! Mummy, he's got
it – his petals caught hold of it – and he's dragged it
into his middle part. Goodness, I'm glad I'm not a
shrimp in this pool!'

'Yes, it would be dangerous,' agreed Benjy, and he
gently touched the petals of the sea-anemone. 'I can
feel this one catching hold of my finger! No, anemone
– you're not going to gobble it up!'

The day went quickly by and soon it was teatime.
Belinda set the tablecloth out on the beach, and she
and Ann put out the tea – two loaves of new bread,
a big slab of farm butter, a chocolate cake from the
farm, made that morning, and an enormous jar of
homemade jam. What a tea!

They all sat down to enjoy it. In the middle of it

238

Benjy looked, and gave an exclamation.

'The telegraph boy! Oh dear – do you think he wants *us*?'

Everyone's heart sank. Daddy and Mummy looked at one another. They were afraid of what the telegram might say.

Poor Benjy went very pale. Ann squeezed his arm. 'It's all right,' she said. 'You'll see, it will be all right.'

The boy came up on his bicycle. Daddy took the telegram. Everyone watched him tear it open, his face grave. Then he suddenly smiled.

'Benjy! Your mother's better! She'll get well!'

'Oh!' squealed all the children, and Benjy sat smiling with tears running down his cheeks.

'You do look funny, Benjy, smiling and crying too,' said Ann. 'Oh, Benjy, I was right, wasn't I? Benjy, I'm so glad for you. Mummy, do look at him – I've never seen anyone laughing and crying at once before.'

'Don't be horrid, Ann,' said Mike.

'She's not,' said Benjy, in a shaky voice. 'You don't know how good and kind she is. It's all because of Ann that I'm happy again. Now I shall *really* enjoy my holiday!'

12

Goodbye to Sea-gull Cove!

Benjy was so full of high spirits after the good news that he made everyone laugh. He shouted, he paddled up to his waist, he turned head-over-heels in the water, he even swam fifty strokes out to sea and back, a thing he had never done before.

'Poor Benjy,' said Mummy, watching him. 'He must have been very miserable about his mother – and we didn't guess it.'

'Ann knew,' said Mike. 'Good old Ann. Hallo, here comes Benjy again, with his ball. All right Benjy, I'll play with you. Race you to the cliff and back, kicking the ball all the way!'

Benjy didn't say much to Ann about his feelings, because he was shy. 'I just want to say that I feel as if God's given me another chance now,' he said. 'I shall be awfully good to my mother to make up for my horridness before. Ann – wasn't it marvellous that our prayers were answered like that?'

'Yes, but I really did believe they would be,' said Ann. 'And that's important too, Benjy, don't forget. Benjy, do you like living in a caravan now? You

didn't at first.'

'I love it,' said Benjy, promptly.

'Do you like sleeping in a bunk?' asked Ann.

'I love it,' said Benjy.

'Do you mind making the bunks and getting in the wood and things like that?' went on Ann.

'I love it,' said Benjy. 'Go on, I shall say "I love it" to everything you ask me, silly – don't you know I'm happy here?'

'Do you like polishing the floor of our caravan?' asked Ann, slyly. This was always her job.

'I love it,' said Benjy, of course.

'All right – you go and do it then for a change!' squealed Ann. And oddly enough, Benjy took the polishing duster and went off like a lamb. Well, well – he really was a different boy, there was no doubt about that!

And now the holidays really did seem to fly past. There were two days of rain, when the children sat and played games in the caravan and really enjoyed the change. They bathed in the rain too, and that was fun. There was one day that was so hot that nobody dared to sit out in the sun, and Ann expected to see the sea begin to boil! But fortunately it didn't!

Benjy astonished everyone by his sudden appetite. He demanded two eggs at breakfast-time – and one day he asked for three!

'Aha!' said Mummy, 'what did I tell you? Yes, you

can have another – but don't ask for *four* tomorrow, or there won't be enough.'

Then the last week came. Then the day before the last, when the children did simply everything they could so as not to miss anything.

'We'll dig and paddle and bathe and sail the little boat, and shrimp and go rowing and collect shells and seaweed,' said Belinda. 'Oh, I do hate it when holidays come to an end – it's just as horrid as the beginning is nice!'

And then the last day came. Oh dear! Come along Davey and Clopper, your holiday is over too. What – you are glad? You want to get back to the old field you know so well – you will enjoy the long pull home?

Seaweed hung in long strips from the outside walls of the caravans. The children were taking the fronds home to tell the weather.

'If the seaweed's dry the weather will be fine; if it gets damp, it shows rain is coming,' said Ann to Benjy. 'You can take the very nicest bits home with you to show your mother, Benjy.'

'I've had a lovely time,' said Benjy. 'I thought at first I was going to hate it, and I didn't much like any of you – but I've loved it, and I feel as if you were my very best friends.'

Then Mike made them jump. 'Football!' he said suddenly. 'I've just remembered – it'll be the Christmas

term now, with football. And there'll be gym. I like that.'

'And we shall have hockey,' said Belinda. 'And we're going to do a play – aren't we Ann? We're both going to be in one at school.'

Everyone suddenly cheered up. Holidays were lovely – but there were things at school that you didn't have at any other time. There were so many others there too – there was always something going on. It would be fun to go back.

Davey and Clopper were put into the shafts. Daddy called to Benjy. 'You and Mike can take it in turns to drive Clopper, Benjy. I can trust you all right now.'

'I can trust you all right now.' What lovely words to hear. It was the nicest thing in the world to be trusted. Benjy would see that his mother could trust him now, too. He looked round at the golden beach. He was sad to leave it – but all good things come to an end.

'Come on, Benjy!' called Mike. 'We're going.'

Up the hill went the two caravans, pulled by good old Davey and Clopper. The sea-gulls came swooping round them. 'Eee-ooo, eee-ooo, eee-oooo!' they called.

'They're shouting goodbye,' said Ann, in delight. 'Goodbye! We'll come again. Don't forget us, will you, because we'll come again. Goodbye!'

The
Buttercup Farm
Family

Contents

1

An exciting plan

Everyone at school called Mike, Belinda and Ann the Caravan Family, because they lived in two caravans. They thought it would be lovely to do that.

'I wish *I* went home to a caravan every Friday like you do,' said Susan to Ann.

'It must be such fun,' said Tom to Mike. 'I suppose when you get tired of being in one place, you just put in your horses and wander away!'

'Do ask me to spend a weekend with you!' said Hilda to Belinda. 'I've never even been inside a caravan. I do so want to see what it's like.'

Mike, Belinda and Ann loved the two caravans they lived in with their mother and father at the weekends. They were yellow, painted here and there with red. Davey and Clopper were the two horses that pulled the caravans along, when the family wanted to move somewhere else.

'Once we went to Granny's in our caravans,' said Ann, remembering. 'She let us have them in her back garden. I liked that.'

It was at the end of the Christmas holidays now. The

Caravan Family had been to Granny's for Christmas Day and Boxing Day. After that the snow came, and Mummy said that living in caravans wasn't so much fun then. The children loved the snow, and had built a most enormous snowman outside their own caravan, which quite scared the two horses when they first caught sight of it.

One afternoon the children went to their parents' caravan and saw Daddy and Mummy sitting there, talking excitedly to one another.

'But what about the children?' Mummy was saying. 'We can't possibly take them with us. What shall we do with them?'

'Granny will have them,' said Daddy.

Belinda burst into the caravan at once.

'Mummy, Daddy! What are you talking about? Where are you going without us? Oh, please, please don't go!'

'Oh, dear – did you hear what we were saying?' said Mummy. 'I didn't want to tell you till everything was decided.'

'What? Tell us what it is,' said Mike. 'I don't want you to go away and leave us.'

'Well, we'll tell you,' said Daddy. 'Come in and sit down, all three of you – and don't look so upset, it's nothing dreadful!'

Mike, Belinda and Ann came in, shut the door, and sat down in the caravan. Daddy waved a letter at them.

'I've just had a most exciting letter. It's an invitation to Mummy and me to go to America for six months, from my brother out there – your Uncle Harry. A holiday like that would be so lovely for Mummy.'

'But – but – would you leave us behind?' said Ann, looking very unhappy.

'Yes, we should have to,' said Daddy. 'But you are all big enough to look after yourselves now, and if anything happened Mummy and I could fly back and be with you in a day. So you needn't worry about anything.'

'Would you like to go very much, Mummy?' asked Mike.

Mummy nodded. 'Yes. Daddy and I haven't had a proper holiday alone together for years and years. I don't want to leave the three of you – but I'm sure you'd be all right with Granny.'

'Well, then,' said Mike, suddenly putting on a very brave look, 'you go, Mummy. We won't be selfish and make a fuss. You deserve a holiday. Doesn't she, Daddy?'

'She certainly does,' said Daddy, and he put his arm round Mummy and kissed her. 'Thanks, Mike, for being so nice about it.'

'I'll be nice too,' said Ann, though she looked as if she was going to burst into tears at any moment.

Belinda hugged her mother.

'I'll look after the others,' she said. 'You needn't

worry a bit about them, Mummy.'

'Thank you, darling,' said Mummy. 'Now we'll go and ring up Granny and see if she can have you.'

But oh dear, Granny couldn't have them after all! Daddy came back from telephoning looking quite upset.

'Granny can't have the children,' he said. 'She has asked her two little great-nephews to stay this year, because their mother is very ill and can't look after them for months.'

'Well, I know what I should like to do,' said Ann. 'I know where I'd like to go.'

'Where?' asked Mummy.

'To Buttercup Farm, of course – Uncle Ned's farm,' said Ann. 'Fancy you not thinking of it, Mummy! It's a lovely place.'

'Oh, yes – we went there a year ago,' said Mike. 'I like Uncle Ned and Auntie Clara. Oh, Daddy, if we went for six months we could really help properly on the farm. There'd be all kinds of things to do.'

'That really is a splendid idea,' said Mummy.

By the next day everything was arranged. Uncle Ned said he and Auntie Clara would love to have the children for six whole months and they were to come right away!

'We'll set off on Thursday,' said Daddy. 'Maybe the snow will have cleared by then, and Davey and Clopper will get a foothold on the roads. Ned will

be glad to have both horses to help on the farm, I'm sure. The caravans can stand in a barn somewhere at the farm till we come back again.'

So on Thursday the little family set off to Uncle Ned's. The children were all excited. To live on a farm for six months – what could be better than that, with the springtime just coming on?

'We're going to Buttercup Farm!' sang Ann, as they went jogging along in the caravans. 'Buttercup Farm, Buttercup Farm! We're going to Buttercup Farm!'

2

Buttercup Farm

On the way to Buttercup Farm Clopper slipped on the frosty road and fell down with a crash. Ann screamed in fright.

'Clopper! You've hurt yourself!'

Daddy leapt down and ran to poor old Clopper. Clopper looked up at him out of puzzled brown eyes that seemed to say, 'What has happened? I'm frightened.'

'Get up, then, old fellow,' said Daddy, gently. 'Let's see if you're hurt. No – you haven't broken your leg, old boy. You're all right.'

But Clopper simply wouldn't get up. He lay there on the road, and wouldn't move. Daddy and Mike tugged at him, but he was much too heavy.

He lay there for almost three hours, and Daddy was quite in despair. 'We'll have to go to the nearest farm and get ropes and a couple of men and pull him up,' he said. 'He really must have hurt himself somewhere, poor old boy.'

Daddy got two men and a strong rope – and then, as they hurried over to Clopper, a surprising thing

happened. Clopper heaved himself over, gave a funny groan, and stood up! He seemed a bit wobbly, but certainly he had no broken legs.

'Look at that, now!' said one of the men. 'Just thought he'd lie down for a rest! Nothing wrong with *him*. Bit scared, I expect, after slipping like that. You walk at his head, sir, for a while.'

So Daddy walked at Clopper's head, and he seemed to be quite all right. But how late it made them all in arriving at Buttercup Farm!

'Instead of arriving at half-past two, we shan't be there till half-past five, in the dark,' said Mummy. 'And we shall all be so cold and hungry. Oh dear, whatever will Auntie Clara say when we arrive so late!'

It was quite dark when the two caravans reached Buttercup Farm. There was the farmhouse, with lights shining out of all the downstairs windows. A dog came bounding to meet them, barking loudly.

'Oh, Gilly!' cried Ann, pleased. 'You know us, don't you, and you're so pleased to see us.'

Gilly was a spaniel, with lovely long, drooping ears and a silky coat. She licked each of the children in turn and then ran barking indoors to tell Auntie Clara that the family had arrived.

Auntie Clara gave them a lovely welcome. She stood at the door, plump and beaming, and a most delicious smell came from the house. The hungry children sniffed it eagerly.

'Oooh – bacon and eggs, isn't it? Just what I feel like!' said Mike. 'Hullo, Auntie Clara! We're late because Clopper fell down on the frosty roads, and wouldn't get up.'

'Oh, you poor things – you must be so cold and hungry,' said kind Auntie Clara, and she took their cold hands in her warm ones, and pulled them into the house.

'Ned, Ned!' she called to her husband. 'See to the horses for them – they're all so tired and hungry!'

'I'm going to love living with you, Auntie Clara,' said Ann, pleased to be in the warm farmhouse kitchen with its big red fire.

'That's right,' said Auntie Clara. 'Now, if you're not too tired, there's hot water in the bathroom, and then there's a hot meal down here, just waiting to be served. So hurry!'

They hurried. They were soon downstairs again, sitting round the big wooden table. Ann liked it because it was quite round. 'Nobody can sit at the top or the bottom, because it's round,' she said to Belinda.

Bacon and eggs. New bread and honey. Hot scones with creamy farm butter. A great big fruit cake with almonds on top. Big mugs of creamy milk. What a meal! Mummy looked round at the hungry children and smiled.

'Clara, if you feed them like this all the time, I

shan't know them when I come back. They'll be so big and fat!'

'Like Uncle Ned,' said Belinda, and they all laughed. Uncle Ned was very big indeed, and getting rather fat, but all the children loved him because he was so jolly.

'Where are Davey and Clopper?' said Ann. 'Are they having a meal too?'

'Of course,' said Uncle Ned. 'Let me see, Clara, did we send bacon and eggs out to them – or was it scones and butter?'

'Uncle Ned, you always make jokes,' said Ann. 'Nobody would give horses bacon and eggs.'

'Well, you're a clever little girl, so I dare say you're right,' said Uncle Ned with one of his booming laughs. 'You needn't worry your head about Davey and Clopper, little Ann. They're in the stables along with my horses, eating a fine meal of oats. And the caravans are put into the big barn, where they're saying how-do-you-do to the wagons and the carts!'

'It's lovely to be at Buttercup Farm,' said Belinda. 'Oh, Auntie Clara, you really *will* let us help, won't you? I want to feed the hens.'

'And I'm going to milk the cows,' said Mike.

'And I shall look after the piglets if you've got any,' said Ann.

'You shall all help,' said Auntie Clara. 'But mind, now – farming is hard work, and you'll have to stick

to your jobs and do them well, week in and week out! Just like real farmers do.'

'Oh, we will,' said Mike earnestly. 'It's very kind of you to have us, and we'll be sure to do all we can.'

'Now – if you've all finished, I think it's time Ann went to bed,' said Mummy. 'And then, Belinda, you come along with Mike.'

'So *early*!' said Mike, surprised.

'Ah,' said Uncle Ned, 'early to bed and early to rise is the farmer's motto, young man. There are no lie-abeds here! Breakfast at seven o'clock sharp!'

'I don't care if it's at six!' said Mike. 'So long as I'm at Buttercup Farm!'

3

First day at the Farm

It was lovely to wake up in the morning at Buttercup Farm. It was still dark, but all sorts of noises were going on outside the windows.

'Clank, clank! Clipper-clop! Hrrrumph! Mooooooo-ooo! Quack, quack!'

It was a quarter to seven. Mike got up and went to the window, but it was still too dark to see anything. He put his head into the girls' room.

'Oh, you're getting up! I'm just going to,' said Mike. 'Doesn't everything wake up early on a farm – even before it's light!'

'Yes. I heard the cows mooing,' said Ann, dragging on her jersey. 'I suppose they're being milked. And I heard Clopper *hrrrumph* like he always does when he wants to get out of the stable.'

They all had breakfast in the great big farmhouse kitchen. There was a bright wood fire burning, and it looked very cheerful and cosy.

'What a big breakfast you eat, Uncle Ned!' said Belinda, in surprise.

'Ah – there's hard work to do,' said her uncle. 'We're

getting potatoes out of the clamps today, to send to market. That's hard, cold work out there in the frost. We need a good breakfast to get down to that!'

Auntie Clara laughed. 'Don't you listen to your Uncle Ned making excuses for eating so much! He eats as big a breakfast on Sunday, when he leaves most of the outside jobs to the men!'

They all tucked into the porridge, cold ham, toast and marmalade.

Belinda looked at her mother. 'When are you going away, Mummy?' she asked. 'Not yet, are you?'

'Well, Daddy and I have to go to London to get some clothes for our American trip,' Mummy said, 'and to do a few other things. We thought we'd go today, and then stay in London till it's time to leave by plane.'

'Oh, I *wish* I could fly over with you!' said Mike at once. 'That would be almost better than living on a farm.'

'What about school?' asked Belinda, suddenly thinking of all kinds of things. 'And what about . . .'

'You needn't worry about anything, darling,' said Mummy. 'It's all arranged. You are so near to your school here that you can go there by bus each day, which is very lucky. You can sleep at Buttercup Farm each night.'

'That sounds lovely,' said Ann. 'I don't want to miss school, but I don't want to miss a minute of

Buttercup Farm either. Mummy, won't it be lovely? – we shall be here long enough to see exactly what goes on at the farm right up to summertime.'

'Lovely!' said Mummy. 'You must write and tell us all about everything each week, and we'll write and tell you about New York and the buildings that are called skyscrapers because they almost touch the clouds.'

'I'd like to climb up to the top of one and catch a cloud,' said Ann. 'I'd tie it to my wrist and fly it like a balloon.'

'Isn't she a baby!' said Mike, and everyone laughed.

After breakfast the children went in the car to the station with Mummy and Daddy. They said goodbye quite happily, because they knew their parents were going to have a lovely holiday, and they knew that they themselves were going to have a splendid time at Buttercup Farm.

'Now mind you're good and helpful,' said Mummy. 'And be kind to everyone, and remember to say your prayers every single night, and be sure to put Daddy and me into them.'

'Well, of *course*,' said Belinda, 'Oh, here comes the train. And now, oh dear, I don't want to say goodbye!'

'Don't say it then,' said Daddy sensibly, and that made Belinda laugh. She yelled goodbye with the others, and waved madly. The train went out of the station and the children turned to go back to the farm.

'I vote we go all over the farm, and see what animals there are, and find out where everything is,' said Mike.

The others thought that was a very good idea, so they spent the day having a 'good old wander', as Auntie Clara called it. They were very tired and rather dirty by the time teatime came – but, dear me, they knew a great deal more about the farm!

'We saw Jamie and Jinny the sheep-dogs,' said Mike, 'and all the sheep on the hills.'

'And we saw all your hens. You've got thirty-three, Auntie,' said Ann. 'I counted them when they went in to roost.'

'Well, fancy that!' said Auntie Clara. 'I never knew how many hens I had before!'

'And fifteen ducks,' went on Ann, 'and six geese. I don't know how many turkeys, because they gobbled at me and I didn't like to go too near.'

'There are seventeen,' said Mike. 'And we saw all the cows, Uncle Ned, and we know all their names – Clover, Buttercup, Daisy, Sorrel, Blackie, Whitey . . .'

'Thank you – I know them too!' said Uncle Ned. 'Did you see the horses? Fine creatures they are.'

'Oh, yes – lovely!' said Mike. 'I like the ones with shaggy heels, Uncle. They're so enormous, and I like their big manes and shining coats. They're proper farm-horses, aren't they?'

'Yes – strong as giants,' said Uncle Ned. 'Best workers I've got.'

'And we saw the old sow,' said Ann. 'She's enormous too. And did you know you've got about nine cats, Uncle?'

'I hope we have!' said Uncle Ned, with his booming laugh. 'We've got about a thousand mice and as many rats – so nine cats are none too many, little Ann! Well, well, you've certainly been round the farm today. Did you like it?'

'We *loved* it!' said all three at once. 'It's the nicest farm in the world!'

4

The little lamb

It was such fun spending the days at Buttercup Farm, even though it was wintertime. There was always something to do. The hens to feed, the cows to bring in, the hay to be fetched, and the firewood to be brought to the kitchen door for Auntie Clara.

One day Ann went to see the old shepherd, who lived in a little hut up on the hills with his sheep. He was a bent old man, with a wrinkled, smiling face, and eyes that twinkled merrily. His name was Willie. Willie beckoned to Ann to come close to him. Near his hut he had built a little sheep-pen, fenced in with stakes. It was spread with straw.

'Lookee here, Missy,' he said. 'See what I've got today. They came in the night.'

Ann looked. She saw a big mother sheep, and beside her two tiny lambs – so small that they almost looked like big toy ones.

'Oh! Are they real?' said Ann. 'Do, *do* let me go in and stroke them.'

'No – the old mother wouldn't like it,' said the shepherd. 'They're the first lambs of the season on

Buttercup Farm. We'll soon be having plenty more. You must come and see me every day, little Missy, then I can show you all the new-born lambs I've got.'

'Oh, I will,' said Ann, earnestly. 'I'd like that better than anything. Can I play with them when they get bigger, Willie?'

'Oh, yes – they'll love to have you skipping about with them,' said the old shepherd, and his eyes twinkled at Ann.

'Willie – I suppose you couldn't *possibly* give me a lamb for my own, like the one Mary had in the rhyme that goes "Mary had a little lamb" could you?' said Ann, her eyes shining at the thought.

The shepherd shook his head. 'Oh no, Missy, I couldn't take a lamb away from its ma. It would fret. Look, here are Jamie and Jinny come to talk to you. They're my dogs, you know – hard-working sheep-dogs.'

'Do they work for you, then?' asked Ann, surprised. 'What do they do?'

'They be wonderful dogs,' said Willie, and he stroked Jinny gently. 'My old legs are getting tired and bent now, and I can't go chasing the sheep uphill and downhill like I used to. So Jamie and Jinny do all that for me. When I want to move the sheep to another hill, these dogs take them for me. I'll show you them at work one day.'

'How clever they must be,' said Ann. 'I must go

now, Willie. I'll come tomorrow and see if you've got any more new lambs to show me.'

She ran off to tell Mike and Belinda what she had seen.

Every day after that the little girl went trudging up to the hill to see old Willie and to look at the new-born lambs.

One day he showed her a weakly little lamb.

'Poor mite!' he said. 'Looks as if it will die. Its mother won't feed it, and the other ewes won't have anything to do with it either.'

'Poor little thing!' said Ann. 'I wish I could feed it, Willie. Wouldn't it drink out of a spoon, if I gave it milk like that?'

'No, Missy. But it would drink out of a baby's bottle,' said Willie. 'You ask your aunt if she'll let you have this lamb down at the farmhouse to feed. She'll give you an old bottle and a teat for the lamb to suck through.'

Ann stared at Willie as if she couldn't believe her ears. '*Willie!* Oh, Willie – are you *giving* me this lamb? For my own – to feed and look after?'

'Well – it sounds like it!' said the old shepherd, laughing. 'See you don't get tired of the little mite, now. You'll have to feed it many times a day, with any milk your aunt has to spare.'

Ann held out shaking arms as the shepherd put the tiny lamb into them, and then, almost crying with

joy, she went carefully down the hill.

'Mike!' she called. 'Belinda! Look what I've got – for my very own. A lamb! A real live lamb whose mother doesn't want it.'

Mike and Belinda stared in amazement. Ann took the lamb into the kitchen.

'Auntie Clara! Dear Auntie Clara, look what Willie's given me – a poor lamb without a kind mother. He says I can keep it and feed it if you'll let me. Will you?'

'Well, well, well!' said Auntie Clara, and she fetched a bottle from the cupboard, and put a rubber teat on it. 'Poor wee thing! Yes, of course you can feed it, child, and care for it. Many's the little lamb I've fed and brought up myself! Belinda, get the warm milk off that stove. I'll give it to the lamb.'

'Let *me*, let *me*,' said Ann. 'It's my lamb. *I* want to feed it, Auntie.'

Auntie Clara let her, of course. The tiny lamb smelt the milk as Auntie Clara squeezed a little out of the teat, and nuzzled at it. In a moment he was sucking away at it, drinking the warm milk as fast as he could! He stood up on his tiny legs, looking just like a big toy lamb.

'He's beautiful! Look at him!' said Ann in joy. 'Auntie, he's swelling up fat already with the milk. He'll soon be well and strong, won't he? Oh, Auntie, fancy, I've got a lamb of my very very own!'

'What will you call him?' asked Mike 'I should call him Wobbly. Look how wobbly he is on his legs!'

'What a horrid name!' said Ann. 'No – I shall call him Hoppetty, because soon he'll be hopping and skipping all over the place!'

'You love him so much that I expect you'll put him into your prayers,' said Belinda. 'You always put Davey and Clopper in, don't you, our two horses?'

'Yes. And now Hoppetty too,' said Ann. 'Oh, I'm so happy. I never, never thought in all my life I'd have a lamb of my very own.'

5

Belinda and the hens

The three children were very sorry when the holidays came to an end, and they had to go to school. But after a day or two at school they decided it was great fun to be back again with all their friends.

'And it's lovely to go home at the end of the day to Buttercup Farm,' said Belinda. 'I keep wondering how many eggs the hens have laid, and if there are any piglets yet.'

'And I keep thinking of Hoppetty,' said Ann, 'and hoping he hasn't got into mischief, and wondering if Auntie Clara's given him his milk.'

'Well, you needn't wonder *that*,' said Mike. 'You know she'd never never forget. Anyway, Hoppetty's so cheeky now that he'd be sure to go and remind her if she did forget. He'd go and put his front hooves up on her skirt, like he does to you.'

'Yes. He's *sweet* when he does that,' said Ann.

The weeks went by and February came in with snowdrops and hazel catkins blowing in the wind.

'They shake and wriggle on the hedges just like Hoppetty wriggles his tail when he drinks his milk,'

said Ann. 'I suppose that's why the catkins are called lambs' tails!'

Belinda had got very interested in the hens. She wanted to look after them for Auntie Clara, who, now that she suddenly had three children to see to, found that her hands were very full indeed. So she was glad to let Belinda help.

'Now,' she said, 'I want to know first if you mean to help properly, every week, and every day of the week – or if you only want to try looking after the hens for a few days, just for fun. You must tell me honestly, and then stick to what you say.'

'Auntie, I want to help properly,' said Belinda. 'I won't get tired of it and give up. I promise I won't. Well – if I *do* get tired, I still won't give up! Will that do?'

'Yes, I'll trust you,' said Auntie Clara. 'You see, Belinda, when we have animals or birds in our care, we have to be very, very trustable, because if we are not, they go hungry or thirsty, or may be cold and unhappy.'

'I wouldn't let that happen,' said Belinda. 'I really am trustable, Auntie.'

'Yes, I think you are,' said Auntie Clara. 'You have certainly never forgotten anything I asked you to do, and, what is more, you have done all your jobs well. Very well, then – you may have the hens to look after!'

'Oh, *thank you*!' said Belinda. 'I think I know all I have to do, Auntie – feed them with hot mash in the morning – feed them again when I come home from school – always give them fresh water – see that they have straw in their nesting-boxes – put fresh peat on the hen-house floor when it needs it. That's all, isn't it?'

'What about cleaning the house out three times a week?' said Mike, who was listening. 'You don't like *that* job, Belinda. You say you hate the smell in the hen-house when it wants cleaning. I bet you won't do that!'

'No, she won't,' said Uncle Ned, joining in suddenly. 'You'll do that, Mike! It's a boy's job, that.'

Mike went red and wished he had offered to clean the hen-house himself, before Uncle said anything about it. But Belinda had other ideas.

'Oh, *no*! I'm going to do everything, thank you!' she said. 'Cleaning the house out too. I know I don't like it much, but I'm not going to be the sort of person who just chooses the bit she likes and leaves the nasty part to other people.'

'Well, there now!' said Auntie Clara admiringly. 'That's the way to talk, isn't it, Ned? We can easily find Mike some other job. I'm sure Belinda will do the cleaning just as well as Mike or anyone.'

Belinda took the hens very seriously indeed. She even wanted to lift the heavy pail of cooked food

down from the kitchen stove each morning, to take to the hens, but Auntie Clara wouldn't let her do that. 'No. It's too heavy. You just think what's in it – all the bits and pieces and scraps, all the old potatoes we don't want, all the peel, everything that's over from the food prepared for this big household! I'll lift it down for you. You can stir in the mash to make it nice for the hens.'

So Belinda stirred in big spoonfuls of mash, and she put a dose of cod-liver oil for the hens each day too, because Auntie Clara said it was very good for them in the cold weather. Belinda never forgot.

She always saw that the hens had clean water, and if by chance it had frozen hard, she put in fresh water. She gave them plenty of fine soft peat in the hen-house, and stuffed their nest-boxes with straw.

The hens soon grew to know Belinda, and came running to her as soon as she appeared, clucking excitedly. Auntie Clara complained that they came walking into her kitchen to find Belinda when she had gone to school!

'I'll have to shut them up in their yard, and not let them run loose,' she said, jokingly.

'Oh, no!' said Belinda at once. 'They wouldn't like that, Auntie. They do so like to run loose and scratch over the ground everywhere. Please don't shut them up.'

At night, when dusk came down on the farmyard,

Belinda went out to her hens. She called to them in her clear little voice. 'Chookies, chookies, chookies! Bedtime! Come along then! Out of the hedges and out of the field. Chookies, chookies, chookies!'

And obediently all the hens came rushing from every direction, and Belinda took them to their house. Up the slanting boards they ran, and settled on the perches to roost, cuddling close up to one another sleepily.

'Good chookies,' said Belinda, shutting and locking the door. 'Lay me plenty of eggs tomorrow!'

'Cluck, cluck,' answered the hens, almost asleep.

And will you believe it, the very next day they laid twenty-seven eggs for Belinda to take proudly into the house. She had to take two baskets to carry them in. How pleased Auntie Clara was!

'Well! You're doing better with the hens than I ever did!' said her aunt. 'I really do feel proud of you!'

9

The wonderful dogs

One day, when Ann went to tell Willie the shepherd the latest tale about Hoppetty the lamb, who was growing fat and very mischievous, he told her something exciting.

'You won't be at school this afternoon, will you?' he said. 'It's Saturday. Well, how would you like to come along and see Jamie and Jinny do some real good work for me?'

'What sort of work?' asked Ann, thrilled.

'Well, I want to move the sheep away from this hill,' said Willie. 'I want them to go over to that hill yonder, where there's some good grass for them. My old legs won't walk fast enough to do work like that now – so I'm going to get Jamie and Jinny to do it for me.'

The two big sheep-dogs heard their names and wagged their tails hard. They looked up adoringly at Willie, their long pink tongues hanging out.

'But Willie – can they really take the sheep all by themselves?' asked Ann, astonished. 'And what about that bridge down there, over the stream – will

they make the sheep cross that? I'm sure they won't want to.'

'Ah, it won't matter if they want to or not,' said Willie, with a smile. 'They'll go, just the same. You be along at two o'clock, Missy, and bring your brother and sister too.'

So, at two o'clock sharp, Mike, Belinda and Ann were up by the shepherd's hut. All around were the sheep, grazing peacefully. A few little lambs frisked about, kicking up their heels and making themselves a real nuisance to their mothers.

'Jamie! Jinny! Bunch them up!' said Willie suddenly to the two listening collies. In a trice they jumped up and ran to the sheep. 'You watch them bunch them for me,' said Willie, proudly. 'They'll do it quicker than you could!'

And he was right. The two dogs ran round the sheep, barking loudly, and the startled animals ran together in alarm. They stood and looked at the dogs wonderingly.

One or two sheep didn't like being made to bunch together with the others. They trotted off, and some little lambs followed them in delight. Jamie went after them immediately. Wherever those sheep turned, there was Jamie, head down, barking, and at last in despair the runaway sheep and the naughty little lambs ran to join the big bunched-up flock.

'See? He's bunched them for me,' said Willie. 'Now

they've got to take them down the hill and up the other side. Jamie! Jinny! Take them then! Down you go!'

The two clever dogs listened to Willie's orders, their tongues hanging out. They watched his arm as he waved it down the hill.

'They've understood you!' cried Mike. 'Oh, Willie, aren't they marvellous? But I guess they won't find it easy to make the sheep cross that tiny bridge. Why, it's only a plank or two set across the stream!'

'Don't you worry!' said Willie. 'The dogs will have them across in no time. Once they can get the first two or three sheep on the bridge they're all right. The rest will follow as sheep always do.'

The three children watched eagerly. Down the hill in a big flock went the hurrying sheep – down, down, towards the water. They came to the bank and stopped. They didn't want to wade into the water, and they certainly couldn't jump across!

Jamie set to work to keep the sheep from scattering up and down the bank. Jinny wriggled through the crowd of sheep and got behind one that stood near the little bridge. The sheep suddenly found Jinny there and was scared. It turned to the left. Jinny was there too. It turned to the right. Jinny was at once on the right. The sheep didn't know what to do.

'Go over the bridge, silly, go over the bridge!' shouted Ann, almost beside herself with excitement.

Jinny gave a sharp bark, and the sheep, in the greatest alarm, trotted right across the bridge to the other side. The sheep behind at once followed it – and the next one and the next.

The children laughed and laughed.

'It would be more difficult to stop them now than to make them go across,' said Mike. 'How silly sheep are! Look – they're nearly all across. Oh – two or three think they won't go.'

But Jamie was behind the last few sheep, and over they went, their little hooves making a clip-clip-clip sound on the bridge.

'Now watch,' said Willie. 'The dogs have bunched them, and taken them safely across the water. They remember that there are two good grazing grounds up there, one to the north and one to the south of the hill. They're looking at me to see which way I want them to go. Watch!'

Jamie and Jinny were both gazing hard at the old shepherd. He put his fingers to his mouth and gave a shrill whistle. Then he whistled again and waved his left arm. With one accord the dogs took the sheep to the south side of the hill, bunching them together first, and then running round and round them, forcing them the way they wanted them to go.

'See?' said Willie. 'They know exactly what I want done, and they do it. I couldn't do without my dogs.'

'They're wonderful!' said Ann. 'Oh, Willie – I never

never thought dogs could be so clever. I do love Jamie and Jinny. Don't you?'

'My best friends they are,' said Willie gruffly. 'You should see them go hunting for sheep lost in the snow, too. They won't come home till they've found them.'

'There can't be any cleverer dogs in the world than Jamie and Jinny,' said Mike.

'Oh, there are,' said Willie. 'You go to the sheep-dog trials, and see what other sheep-dogs can do with *strange* sheep. Wonderful good dogs they are.'

Jamie and Jinny came running up. Willie took down a bag and shook out a heap of meaty bones for them.

'They deserve their wages,' he said. And the three children thought so too!

7

A litter of pups

The children often talked about the two wonderful sheep-dogs, and marvelled at all they could do.

'There's only one lamb that won't take any notice of Jamie and Jinny,' said Ann, proudly, 'and that's Hoppetty. He just skips round them and says cheeky things in that funny little bleat of his.'

'You're lucky, Ann,' said Mike, who envied Ann her pet lamb. 'So's Belinda. She's got heaps of hens that lay eggs for her, and you've got Hoppetty. I've got nothing of my own.'

'Well, have a piglet when the old sow has her family,' said Auntie Clara.

But Mike didn't want a piglet.

'I'd like a horse or a dog,' he said. 'Something that would follow me round like the hens follow Belinda, and like Hoppetty follows Ann. Auntie, did you know that Hoppetty came all the way to the bus the other day, when we went to school, and Ann wanted to let him get on, but the conductor wouldn't let him?'

Auntie Clara laughed. 'I expect Ann wanted Hoppetty to follow her to school, like Mary in the

nursery rhyme,' she said. 'That's a bad little lamb you've got, Ann. He came into my dairy the other day and drank a whole pint of my cream!'

'Oh dear!' said Ann. 'Don't make me put him in the field with the other sheep yet, Auntie. I do love him so.'

Uncle Ned came in. 'Heard the news?' he said.

'No, what?' cried the three children at once.

'Well – it's Willie's news really,' said their uncle. 'You'd better go and ask him what it is.'

The children tore out of the house like wind. Up the hill they went to Willie. Jamie the sheep-dog came to meet them eagerly.

'Where's Jinny?' said Ann, missing the second dog. She was nowhere to be seen.

Willie came out of his hut when he saw the three children. He was smiling all over his brown, wrinkled old face. He beckoned to the children, and pointed inside his hut. They ran up to him.

'Got some news for you,' he said, mysteriously. 'You look in there.'

They crowded into the little hut. Lying on some straw in the corner was Jinny. She looked very happy indeed. Ann gave a loud squeal of delight.

'Look! She's got some puppies! Oh, Willie, are they hers?'

'Hers and Jamie's,' said Willie, proudly. 'And a wonderful fine litter they be, Missy. Five of them,

strong and healthy. Did ever you see such a sight?'

The children knelt down by Jinny, who didn't in the least mind their loud cries of admiration. She gave each pup a lick as if to say, 'They're all mine! Don't you envy me?'

'The darlings!' said Belinda. 'Oh, Willie, won't it be lovely to see them all grow up!'

Mike was looking at the tiny pups with shining eyes. He turned to Willie and put his hand earnestly on the old shepherd's arm. 'Willie,' he said, 'please, please, Willie, could I have one of these pups for my own?'

Willie laughed. 'Oh no, sonny. They are very valuable dogs, and they've all got new homes to go to. Soon as your uncle knew these pups were coming, he put the news around, and he's got orders for every one of them. When they're two months old they'll leave Jinny, and go to their new masters to learn their trade.'

Mike was bitterly disappointed. 'I never wanted anything so much in all my life,' he said sadly, and Ann felt very sorry for him. So did Belinda. But if the pups were already sold, there was nothing more to be said.

They certainly were beautiful puppies. They seemed to grow bigger each day, and when they at last had their eyes open they were really adorable.

'They roll about everywhere now, Auntie,' Ann

told her aunt some weeks later, 'and one of them tries to walk, but he's very wobbly. Oh, I do wish they hadn't got to go away when they're so young – I wish we could see them grow up into fine big sheep-dogs.'

'If I'd kept all the pups that the dogs here have had, I'd have about a hundred dogs running around,' said Uncle Ned. 'Jinny's pups are always good. They make wonderful dogs for the sheep on the hills round here, and there's many a dog you'll see at the sheep-dog trials that's been one of Jinny's youngsters.'

When the pups grew old enough, they had to go to their new homes. The children had given all five of them names, and were very sad when the new masters came to fetch them.

Farmer Gray came for the pup called Tubby. Farmer Lawson came for Tinker, and a farmer's wife for Whiskers. Then a boy came for Scamp, and after that only little Rascal was left.

'He's the one I love most,' said Mike, and he picked the puppy up and hugged him. The tiny thing licked his nose and gave a small whine.

'Uncle, who's having Rascal?' asked Ann at dinner-time that day. 'Nobody has come for him yet.'

'No, I know,' said Uncle Ned. 'The farmer who wanted him is leaving the district after all, and taking up fruit farming. He doesn't want a sheep-dog now. I don't know what to do with Rascal – can't seem to get anyone to buy him.'

Mike was listening with all his ears. He went very red. 'Uncle,' he said, 'I've got ten pounds saved up in the post office. *I'll* buy him. Please, please, do let me. I'll always love him and look after him well.'

Uncle Ned and Auntie Clara looked at one another. Auntie Clara nodded. 'Give him Rascal,' she said. 'He's been a good hardworking boy, Ned – cleaned out the dairy for me, fetched all my wood, done lots of jobs. He deserves a pup of his own.'

'Right!' said Uncle Ned. 'He's yours, Mike.'

What a picture of joy Mike's face was. 'A dog of my own,' he said, in a funny low voice. 'Oh, Uncle – it's the loveliest thing that's ever happened to me. A dog – of my very own!'

8

The twins

One morning Belinda came tearing into the kitchen, where Ann and Mike were doing their homework.

'Ann! Mike! The calves are born! Oh, they're so sweet. Do, do come.'

The homework was forgotten. Mike and Ann raced after Belinda to the cow-sheds. Calves! New calves for Buttercup Farm! It really did sound very exciting. After the children scampered Hoppetty, Ann's lamb, and fat little Rascal, Mike's pup. Jake the cowman was in the shed, and he grinned as all the children came flying in.

'Now, now – what's the hurry? Anyone would think you'd never seen calves before!'

'We've never seen such new ones,' said Belinda. 'Oh, aren't they small – and what long legs they've got! Sorrel, are you pleased with them?'

Sorrel was the calves' mother, a big red and white cow with a very peaceful-looking face. She looked up at the children, and then bent her head down and licked one of her calves.

'She's got twins!' said Jake. 'Your uncle's pleased

284

about that. Two fine, strong calves they are, that anyone would be glad to have. Well, Sorrel, my beauty, you can be right proud of them!'

The twin calves soon grew to know the children, because they came a dozen times a day to see them. They marvelled at the way the tiny things could stand on their long legs, and it even seemed wonderful to Ann that they knew how to whisk their tails properly.

Auntie Clara said she would be very busy now, with two calves to feed and look after. 'They will have to have milk to drink,' she said, 'but not milk with the cream on it – we can't spare that. They must have the separated milk, and I must put in cod-liver oil to make up for the cream.'

'Like I give my hens,' said Belinda at once. 'Auntie, do the calves know how to *drink*? I thought new-born animals could only suck.'

'Well, you come along tomorrow morning and watch me teach the calves to drink,' said her aunt. 'It's Saturday, so you'll be at home.'

'We'll all come,' said Ann. 'I wouldn't miss a thing like that for anything!'

Next morning, all three children followed their aunt as she got ready the calves' meal. She filled two buckets with milk that had the cream taken from it, and shook some drops of cod-liver oil into the pails. Mike took one pail of milk for her and she took the other.

They went up to the cow-shed. Sorrel was out in the yard, with her calves near by. They were red and white, just like her. All three stared at Auntie Clara as she came along with the pail.

'The calves can suck, Auntie,' said Ann. 'I know that, because when I put my hand up, they take it into their mouth and suck my fingers hard!'

'Well, I shall use their sucking to help me to teach them to drink!' said Auntie Clara. She set down her pail by one of the calves. She dipped her hand into the pail and held it out to the little calf.

He stared at Auntie Clara in surprise, but didn't try to lick her hand, or even to suck it. So Auntie Clara pushed her milky fingers against the calf's soft nose. He smelt the milk at once and sniffed at it. Then he took Auntie Clara's fingers right into his mouth and sucked hard, getting every drop of milk.

'Oh, Auntie – what a long time it will take to feed the calves like that,' said Belinda. 'It'll take all day.'

'No, no,' said Auntie Clara. 'Watch me.'

She dipped her hand into the pail again, and held it out to the calf. He came nearer to smell the milk on her fingers. In a trice he was sucking at them again. Auntie Clara drew her hand towards the pail. The calf followed it, sucking hard. Auntie Clara put her hand right down into the pail of milk.

The calf's nose went down too, and in a moment his mouth was right in the milk! He went on sucking

at Auntie Clara's hand, but because his mouth was in the milk he couldn't help *drinking* some too! He made a lot of noise about it and Ann laughed.

'Doesn't he sound rude? Oh, Auntie, that's very clever! You made him suck first, and then because he liked the sucking, his mouth followed your hand into the milk, and he found himself drinking too!'

'Yes,' said Auntie Clara. 'He'll soon be drinking well. And in a few days' time he'll be listening for the first clink of the pail, and will come tearing to meet me!'

'Can I teach the other twin?' begged Belinda. 'Do, do let me! I know just how to.'

'Very well,' said Auntie Clara. 'But don't let him upset the pail!'

Belinda dipped her hand in the milk and rubbed it gently against the other calf's mouth. He sniffed eagerly and began to suck her hand. She took it away and dipped it into the milk again. Once more the calf sucked her fingers, and this time she did just what Auntie Clara had done – lowered her hand gradually into the pail – and so the hungry calf was half-sucking at her fingers and half-drinking out of the pail!

'I've done it!' said Belinda. 'Oh, I do feel clever! Look at my calf, Auntie.'

'It's been a most exciting morning,' said Ann when the pails were empty. 'There's always something lovely happening on a farm. I don't know why

anybody bothers to live in a town when there are
farms to live on.'

Belinda helped her Aunt to feed the calves every
day – and before a week was up the twins raced to
meet Belinda as soon as they heard the jingle of her
pail-handle!

'You're lovely!' said Belinda. 'I don't know who's
the loveliest – you – or Hoppetty – or Rascal!'

9

Cluck, cluck, cluck!

'Auntie Clara,' said Belinda one day, when she came in from feeding the hens, 'Auntie Clara, it's such a nuisance, there are two of my hens that won't stop sitting in the nesting-boxes. I keep shooing them out to run with the others, but back they go again as soon as my back is turned!'

Auntie Clara laughed. 'Why, they're broody,' she said.

'What's broody?' asked Ann.

'They want to sit on clutches of eggs and brood over them till they hatch,' said her aunt. 'Belinda, we'll get a clutch of thirteen eggs for each of them.'

'Thirteen! What a funny number!' said Belinda.

'Not really,' said her aunt. 'It's just about as many as a hen can manage.'

'I wish one of the *ducks* would go broody, and then we could put her on a clutch of duck eggs,' said Mike. 'I do love baby ducks.'

'Well, if you like we'll put thirteen hen eggs under one broody hen and thirteen duck eggs under the other,' said Auntie Clara. 'Then you'll have plenty

of young chicks and plenty of young ducklings too!'

'Oh – I *should* like that!' said Belinda at once. 'It's the Easter holidays now, Auntie, so I shall have plenty of time to look after the hens. Where can I get the clutches of eggs?'

'Your uncle will get them,' said Auntie Clara. 'Mike, do you think you can go and look out two old coops to put the hens in? See if they want mending at all. They should be in the old barn.'

Mike found them. One wanted a nail or two, but the other coop was all right. He carried them to Belinda. 'Here you are,' he said, 'cages for your two broodies! Poor hens, they won't like being shut up in them.'

'Oh, they won't mind,' said Belinda. 'You should see how they sit for hours and hours on the nesting-boxes! They will be very pleased to have nice coops like this to sit in. I've asked Auntie what to do, and it's very easy.'

Uncle Ned brought home two clutches of eggs. One clutch was made up of brown hen eggs. The other was of greeny-grey duck eggs, a little larger than the hen eggs.

Belinda arranged each clutch on some straw in a coop. Then she fetched a hen. She pushed her into the coop and shut her in. Then she went to fetch the other broody.

Mike and Ann watched the first hen. She stood in

the coop and squawked. She looked at the clutch of eggs with her head on one side. She rearranged one or two with her beak, then she sat herself down very carefully on the whole thirteen and fluffed out her feathers so that she covered every single egg.

'She's sitting!' cried Ann to Belinda, as she came back with the other hen. 'Look! She's happy.'

Belinda put the second broody hen into the other coop. The hen stood for a minute or two as if puzzled and annoyed. She poked her head out between the bars of the coop, and then she sat herself down. A peaceful look came over her hen-face, and she fluffed herself out well.

'She likes the feel of all those eggs under her,' said Belinda. 'Auntie Clara, look! Both my broodies are sitting on eggs. Thirteen each. I shall have twenty-six new little birds!'

'Belinda's counting her chickens before they're hatched,' said Mike with a grin. 'Auntie, how long will it be before the eggs are hatched?'

'Three weeks for the hen eggs, and four for the duck eggs,' said his aunt. 'See that you look after the two hens well, Belinda.'

'Of course, Auntie,' said Belinda. And she did. She opened the coops every morning and lifted each squawking hen off the eggs. She gave them a good meal and let them run about for twenty minutes. Then back they had to go into the coops again.

'The eggs mustn't get cold,' she told Ann. 'If they do, they won't hatch. A hen mother is much better than a duck mother, because ducks often leave their eggs to get cold.'

The day that the three weeks were up, the hen sitting on the hen eggs gave a loud cackle. Belinda rushed up in excitement. 'A chick is hatched, a chick is hatched!' she squealed in delight. 'Come and see!'

Mike and Ann rushed up. Yes, there was a tiny yellow chick – and then another egg cracked and a second chick came out – and then a third and a fourth! The old hen kept putting her head on one side, and listening and looking. She was very pleased.

Eleven chicks hatched out of the thirteen eggs. They were a week old, and running about all over the place, before the duck eggs hatched. And oh, what dear little waddly things the ducklings were! All of them were yellow, except one black one. Ann couldn't imagine how they could have been packed into the eggs because they looked so big when they uncurled themselves and waddled about, cheeping.

'There are ten,' said Belinda. 'Only ten! I did hope there would be thirteen.'

'Well, you have twenty-one new birds, so you can't grumble,' said Ann. 'I think it's marvellous. Oh, aren't the ducklings *lovely!* I like them much better than the chicks.'

'What I like is to see the chicks rush to their

mother hen when one of the cats comes near,' said Mike. 'Look – here's one of them now. Watch what happens!'

The hen saw the cat and called loudly to her chicks. 'Danger! Come here! Cluck; cluck, *cluck*!'

And at once every tiny chick raced to its mother and hid in her fluffed-out feathers. Not one could be seen.

'There! She's hidden them all,' said Mike. 'I say, Belinda – what's the other hen going to say when her ducklings go into the pond?'

Ah, what! There's going to be some fun then!

10

Something is always happening

'There's hardly a day goes by without something happening on a farm,' said Mike. 'Especially a farm like this that keeps so many animals and birds.'

He was right. Day after day something exciting happened. One day the sow had twelve piglets, and it was the greatest fun to go and watch them rush round the enormous old mother sow at top speed, their absurd little tails curled over their backs.

The mother sow was a lazy, fat old thing. 'She lies there all day long, and only gets up to eat,' said Mike. 'Oh, I really *must* get into the sty and tickle some of those piglets. They're so round and pink and comical!' He climbed over the gate and tried to catch one of the piglets. They were frightened, and ran about all over the place, squealing.

'Look out, look out!' shouted Belinda suddenly. 'The old sow is getting up!'

Sure enough she was. She didn't like to hear her piglets squealing like that. She lumbered up on to her short thick legs – and then she rushed headlong at Mike! He was so surprised.

She hit him at the back of the knees and he sat down very suddenly indeed. The sow put down her head to bump him, and Mike shot up at once. In a trice he was climbing over the gate, his shorts very muddy and dirty!

Ann and Belinda laughed till they cried.

'Oh, I never thought the old mother pig could move so quickly!' said Ann. 'I guess you won't try to catch one of her piglets again, Mike!'

Rascal, Mike's puppy, tried to lick his master's legs clean. He had grown into a bonny little fellow, and followed Mike about like a shadow. Hoppetty played with him a lot, and it was lovely to see the puppy and the lamb frisking round one another.

The twin calves had grown well, too, and no longer had to be fed on milk from the pails. They were out in the fields now, eating what Ann called 'grown-up cow food' – hay, turnips, and things like that.

'I wish animals and birds didn't grow up so quickly,' complained Ann. 'It seems no time at all since Hoppetty was as tiny as a toy lamb – now he almost looks like a sheep, his coat is so thick and woolly.'

Auntie Clara at last said firmly that Hoppetty must not run loose any more, but must go and live in the field, or up on the hills with the sheep.

'He's a scamp,' she said. 'I caught him going up the stairs to look for you this morning, Ann. And *somebody* ate a whole cake that stood cooling in the

kitchen. I'm sure it was Hoppetty.'

'He won't like living with the sheep,' said Ann, with tears in her eyes. 'He won't really.'

'He'll love it,' said Auntie Clara. 'But he won't forget you, Ann. He'll always come running when you call him, so don't fret about it.'

Auntie Clara was right. Hoppetty liked being with the other growing lambs and the big sheep. He played wonderful games of chase-me, jump-high, and frisk-around with the other lambs, and was always the ringleader when any trouble was about. And he never forgot Ann.

Whenever the little girl came by and called him, Hoppetty came scampering over to her, nuzzling against her, bleating in a little high voice, just as he used to when he was tiny.

'I'm glad you love me still,' said Ann, 'but oh dear, I do wish you wouldn't grow up into a silly sheep!'

Another excitement was when the ducklings were a few weeks old, and discovered the pond for the first time. All the children were in the yard, having just brought back a big cart-horse from the blacksmith. That was one of their nicest jobs – to take the horses down to the smith to be shod.

They had handed over big Dobbin to their uncle, when he suddenly gave a chuckle and pointed to the pond.

'See there?' he said. 'Those new ducklings have

seen the pond – now watch old mother hen!'

The hen had no idea at all that her chicks were ducklings. She hated the water. She would not get even a toe wet, and whenever the chicks or ducklings went near the water all the hens nearby set up a warning squawk – 'Cluck, cluck, come back, naughty chicks. Cluck, cluck, don't go near that water!'

And, as soon as the ducklings wandered near that day, their mother hen gave a loud, angry cluck. 'Danger! Come back!'

One duckling thought the pond looked fine. He paddled in the water. The hen went nearly mad with fear and rage. She stood at the edge and scolded the daring duckling loudly.

He suddenly went in deeper. He launched his little yellow body on the water like a boat and swam off in the greatest delight, his tiny legs paddling him as if he had done it for years.

Another duckling did the same – and then a third. The mother hen ran up and down, angry and frightened, making a tremendous noise. All the other hens ran up to join in. The children were helpless with laughter, and Uncle Ned let out one of his booming laughs.

Soon all the ducklings were on the pond, bobbing up and down, enjoying themselves with delighted little quacks. What fun they had! 'Why, we're ducklings, not chicks!' they told one another. 'Think

of that! Aren't we lucky! We'd better tell the old hen that when we get back.'

So they did. But she didn't believe them, and rushed them all away from the water at once.

'But that won't be any good, old hen!' called Mike after her. 'They'll be in again tomorrow, splashing with joy. You just see!'

They were, of course, and at last the old hen gave them up in despair, and went off to scratch with her friends.

'Something is always happening here,' said Mike. 'I just *love* Buttercup Farm!'

11

A very exciting day

'Children, the sheep are to be sheared tomorrow,' said Auntie Clara. 'Do you want to watch the shearers at work?'

'Oh, of *course*!' said all three at once.

'I've always wanted to see a shearer cut the wool off a sheep,' said Mike. 'Auntie, is uncle going to have men do it with shears, by hand, or is he going to have a clipping-machine?'

'It's to be done by hand,' said his aunt. 'It's lucky tomorrow is Saturday, or you wouldn't be able to watch.'

'Will Hoppetty be sheared?' asked Ann, looking very solemn. 'I don't think I'd like him all shaven and shorn. He wouldn't look like Hoppetty.'

'No, he won't be done,' said her aunt. 'Lambs are allowed to keep their coats for a whole year. Hoppetty will be shorn next year.'

'I should think he'll wish he could be done this year,' said Belinda. 'It's very hot for May, and I'm sure I'd hate to have to wear a woolly coat like Hoppetty in weather like this!'

As soon as they woke up the next day the children heard the sound of baaing and bleating. They looked out of their windows.

'Look! Look! Jamie and Jinny are rounding up the sheep to bring them to the shearing-sheds,' said Mike in excitement. 'And oh, I do believe Rascal is with them! He's learning to round up the sheep. Oh, isn't he going to be clever!'

'Yes, he'll be a very valuable sheep-dog one day,' said Belinda. 'You'd be able to sell him for a lot of money!'

'Oh! As if I'd ever, ever sell Rascal!' cried Mike, looking so furious that Belinda laughed.

'I didn't mean it,' she said. 'Not one of us would ever sell Rascal.'

The children went out to the shearing-sheds directly after breakfast. There were four men there, all shearers. The children had never seen them before. What a noise of baaing and bleating there was, as the three dogs brought the sheep around the sheds.

One of the shearers caught a sheep, threw it quickly on its side, and tied its legs together, so that it could not struggle and hurt itself on the big shears when its coat was being cut.

Then, as soon as the sheep was quite quiet, the shearer began his work. Clip, clip, clip, went his big sharp shears, and to the children's amazement the sheep's thick woolly coat fell off smoothly and cleanly.

'Oh, look – he's peeling the sheep!' said Ann, and the others laughed at her. But it did look as if the sheep were being 'peeled', their coats came away so very neatly.

'Good wool, this,' said the shearer, looking up at the children. 'Fine heavy coats your sheep have got. Ought to fetch a lot of money.'

'I'm glad,' said Mike. 'Uncle Ned wants to buy a new tractor, so he'll be glad of the money. How quick you are, shearer!'

'Well, we've got plenty of work to get through today,' said the man. 'All those sheep to do! We go to another farm on Monday. Good weather this, for shorn sheep – hot sun, warm wind, mild nights. I've known the poor creatures be shorn just before a bitter-cold spell of weather, and how they must have missed their warm coats then!'

'I expect they're glad to be rid of them now, though,' said Belinda watching the gleaming shears snip, snip, snip at the wool. 'It's so very hot today. Oh – whatever are you doing to that sheep now it's done?'

The shearer had dipped a big brush into a bucket of tar and had daubed something across its shorn back.

'It's a letter B,' said Mike. 'Oh – B for Buttercup Farm, I suppose.'

'That's right,' said the man. 'Now if they wander, you'll know they're yours. Get along there!'

He had undone the sheep's legs, and sent it out of the shed with a gentle smack. It trotted off, looking very bare and comical.

'I don't suppose they know each other now,' said Ann, as sheep after sheep was sheared and sent out into the sun. 'I do think they look queer. I am glad that Hoppetty and the other lambs aren't going to be shorn. I'm sure I wouldn't know Hoppetty from the rest if he didn't have his coat on.'

Willie the shepherd looked into the shed. 'What are the fleeces like?' he asked.

'Good and heavy,' said one of the shearers. 'Your sheep are healthy, every one of them, shepherd. A fine lot. Best lot of fleeces we've seen this season.'

Willie looked pleased. 'Oh ay. They're a good lot of sheep,' he said. 'And we didn't lose a single lamb this year. We've seventeen running in the field.'

Hoppetty came sidling into the shed to look for Ann. The shearer caught hold of him. Ann gave a wild cry and flung herself on Hoppetty, pulling him away.

'No, no! That's my pet lamb. He isn't a year old yet. You're not to shear him!'

'It's all right, Missy,' said the shearer with a smile, 'I was only going to play with him. I could tell he was a pet, the way he looked at us all – in that cheeky way pet lambs always have. He's growing a fine coat already. I'll shear him for you next year.'

'Yes, I'd like that,' said Ann. 'Will you put an A on him, though, for Ann, because he's mine.'

'That I will,' said the shearer. 'And you tell your uncle to have a nice warm coat made for you out of your lamb's wool. That'll keep you warm all winter!'

'Oh, I *will*,' said Ann, her face glowing. 'That's a lovely idea! Fancy, Hoppetty, you're wearing your coat this year – but *I* shall be wearing it next year!'

12

Harvest home

The summer went by. It was sunny and warm and full of colour. The may spread along the hedges like snow. It faded, and buttercups came to fill the fields with gold.

Then they went and poppies danced by the wayside in bright scarlet petals. They were in among the corn too, and though Ann knew they should not be there she couldn't help thinking how nice the brilliant red was, peeping out of the golden corn.

The corn had been short and green at first. Then it grew taller, and waved about. Then it gradually turned yellow and the ears filled and were heavy.

'You know, I thought Daddy and Mummy would be back by now,' said Mike. 'They went for six months – and they've been gone for almost seven. It's the summer holidays now. I wish they would come back.'

'They've been having a wonderful time together,' said Auntie Clara. 'They will be very glad to get back to England, though, and to see you again. They *will* be pleased by the look of you – you've grown as fast

as the corn, and your faces are as red-brown as the corn in the field!'

'We've had a lovely time here,' said Mike. 'I loved the hay-making in June. That was fun.'

'We shall be here for the reaping of the corn, shan't we?' said Ann anxiously. 'I do want to help with that. I want to see a reaper-binder at work, Auntie – what does Uncle call it? – the self-binder. I do want to see that.'

'And so you will,' said Auntie Clara. 'We're going to begin reaping next week. Uncle's borrowing a self-binder from a friend. My word, it's a wonderful machine! It cuts the corn, bundles it into sheaves, and ties each sheaf up before it tosses it back into the field.'

'Does it really?' said Ann. 'It sounds like magic.'

It looked like magic too! All three children were out early in the cornfield to watch the self-binder at work. Uncle Ned sat in the seat of the machine, and it set off with a great noise. In wonder the children watched it work.

'Look!' said Belinda. 'It goes into the waving corn – it cuts it – it binds it into sheaves – ties a bit of string round each sheaf – and throws them back behind it for us to pick up and stand into shocks!'

The children watched for a long time. It was wonderful. In front of the machine was the field of waving corn – but behind it was nothing but sheaves in a row!

'Well, well! What about a little work?' said Auntie Clara, coming up. 'Look – we must stand these sheaves upright, and make shocks of them. Watch me.'

Soon their aunt had made a fine shock, and the children set to work to make shocks of the fallen sheaves too.

'Sixteen sheaves to a shock,' sang Mike. 'Sixteen sheaves to a shock! I've done twelve shocks. How many sheaves go into twelve shocks!'

'Goodness! Who wants to know a thing like that!' cried Ann. 'Oh dear – I can't build my shocks nearly as quickly as you can. Get away, Rascal. You keep knocking my sheaves down!'

'He only wants to help you,' said Mike. 'Come here, Rascal!'

When Uncle Ned's corn was all cut, and the sheaves were neatly set up in shocks, the fields looked very lovely and peaceful. Each shock had its own shadow, and as the sun went down, the shadows grew longer and longer.

'Thanks for your good work, my dears,' said Uncle Ned, coming up. 'Now it won't be many days before we cart the corn to the rick-yard – the corn's very dry already.'

'Carting the corn to the rick-yard is called harvest home, isn't it?' said Belinda. 'Bringing the harvest home. It sounds nice.'

The day came when the corn was to be taken to the

rick-yard at the farm. Wagons were sent to the field, and Uncle Ned and Jake began to fork the sheaves up into the cart.

'Oh, look! – the wagon's getting very full,' shouted Mike. 'You've put so many sheaves in, and they're piling higher and higher!'

'We know that!' panted Uncle Ned. 'We're having to throw up the sheaves a long way now – it's hard work.'

When the cart was full, and no more sheaves could be put into it, Clopper and Davey had to pull it out of the field to the rick-yard.

'Up you get on the top!' shouted Uncle Ned to Ann and Belinda. 'Mike, you can drive Davey and Clopper, can't you? Off you go, then, and we'll begin filling this other wagon.'

The heavy wagon moved off, pulled by Davey and Clopper. Mike sat on the front, proud to be taking the harvest home. The two girls sat right on top of the golden sheaves, clutching at them as the wagon swayed down the lane.

'Harvest home!' sang Ann in her little high voice. 'Harvest home! We're bringing the harvest home!'

The wagon went slowly into the yard. Belinda saw two people waiting there. She gazed at them, and then gave a great shout of joy.

'Mummy! Daddy! You've come back!'

She and Ann flung themselves down from the

wagon, and Mike leapt down from the front. They
threw themselves on their father and mother.

'Oh, Mummy, we've had such a wonderful time!'
cried Ann. 'Have *you*? We've got a puppy and a lamb,
and twin calves and heaps of piglets, and . . .'

'And I've got something much better than all
those!' said Daddy lifting Ann high above his head so
that she squealed like a piglet. 'I've got three children
again!'

'You've come on the right day,' said Mike. 'It's
harvest home. We've brought the corn home – and
you've come home too.'

'What a lovely harvest home!' said Mummy,
hugging them all. 'What a lovely harvest home!'

The
Queen Elizabeth
Family

Contents

1

Home for the Weekend

'Cuckoo!' called Belinda, Mike and Ann, as they opened the gate leading into a field.

'Cuckoo!' called back their mother, waving to them from the steps of one of the colourful caravans there. 'So glad you're back again!'

It was Friday afternoon. Mike, Belinda and Ann went to board at school all the week – but they came back to their caravan homes for the weekend. How they liked that!

'It's such fun to have school-life from Mondays to Fridays – and then home-life in our caravans from Fridays to Mondays,' said Belinda, as they walked over to the two pretty caravans. Then Ann ran on in front and hugged her mother.

'Mummy – I was top in writing!' she said.

'And I got one of my drawings pinned up on the wall,' said Belinda, proudly. 'I couldn't bring it home because it's got to stay there all next week.'

'And what about you, Mike?' asked his mother.

Mike grinned. 'Oh – I shot three goals yesterday afternoon,' he said. 'So our side won.'

'What a very successful week!' said Mummy, and she sounded pleased. 'Well – I expect you'd like to know what I've done too. I've made new curtains for your caravan – and I've made some lovely blackberry jelly!'

'Top marks, Mummy!' said Mike, and hugged her. 'Are we having the jelly for tea?'

'We are,' said his mother, and led the way into her caravan. There was one caravan for her and Daddy and one for the three children. Mummy had laid tea in her caravan, and it looked lovely. Blackberry jelly, cream in a little jug, new bread and butter, ginger biscuits, a chocolate cake and tiny buns made by their mother.

'Nicest tea in the world,' said Mike, and sat down at once.

'You must go and wash your hands,' said Ann. 'Just look at them!'

'My hands are clean, and anyway I only go if Mummy tells me,' said Mike at once. 'Wash your own!'

'Where's Daddy?' asked Belinda. 'Will he be late or early?'

'Late,' said Mummy. 'His firm is doing a lot of business with America just now, and he has to have a good many meetings with the men who are going over there.'

'I wish we could go to America,' said Belinda. 'We're

learning about it in Geography. Did you know you had to cross an enormous ocean called the Atlantic, Mummy, to get to America?'

'Well, yes, I did happen to know that,' said Mummy, pouring out mugs of milk.

'And did you know that there are two great ships called the *Queen Elizabeth* and the *Queen Mary*, that go across it in just a few days?' asked Ann. 'Goodness, how I'd like to go in one. They're supposed to be the finest ships in the world.'

'They are,' said Mummy. 'Well, perhaps one day we will all go to America, and you'll see what it's like.'

'Only if we could come back afterwards,' said Mike suddenly. 'I expect I'd like America very much – but I should always, always like England best.'

'Well, of course,' said Mummy. 'All the same you'd be astonished to see the food the Americans have – much better than ours!'

'But I don't think there could be a nicer tea than this,' said Ann at once, with her mouth full of bread and butter and blackberry jelly and cream.

Mummy laughed. 'Well, so long as you're satisfied, that's all right. Now – save some of the cream for Daddy. I've made him a blackberry tart for his supper, and he likes to pour cream all over it!'

'He'll get fat,' said Belinda. 'Why – here he is!'

And sure enough, there he was, coming in at the field-gate, waving to his little family, who were now

crowding out of the caravan to meet him.

'Daddy!' yelled Ann, and almost fell down the steps. Mike reached him first. Daddy always liked his Friday welcome. He said he felt such an important person when four people rushed at top speed to meet him!

'Why are you home early?' asked Mike. Mummy said you'd be late.'

'I'm home early for a very important reason,' said Daddy. 'I've got an invitation for you all to see the *Queen Elizabeth* tomorrow! She's at Southampton, and sails on Saturday night. How would you like to have tea on board?'

'Daddy! *Really?*'

'Oh, how super!'

'It can't be true!'

Everyone spoke at once, and Daddy put his hands over his ears. 'Good gracious, I shall be deaf. It really *is* true. Look – here are the cards. We get on board with these, and we can see over quite a lot of the ship – and have tea on board too.'

'Did you say tomorrow?' said Mummy. 'That will be *lovely!* What a good thing it's Saturday and the children are home. It would have been so disappointing if it had been on a school-day. How are we going?'

'I rang up Granny and she's lending us her car,' said Daddy. 'She wants to come too. So do you think

you could take Ann on your knee in front, Mummy, and let Granny go behind with Mike and Belinda.'

'Oh, easily,' said Mummy. 'It would be lovely to have Granny too. What a treat! The children will hardly believe a ship can be as big as the *Queen Elizabeth*!'

'I shall never go to sleep tonight,' said Belinda, and the others said the same. But when bedtime came they were all as sleepy as usual, of course.

Mummy came into their caravan to kiss them goodnight.

'I do like the new curtains,' said Belinda sleepily. 'Thank you, Mummy, for making them. They're all over buttercups and daisies and cornflowers and marigolds. It's like looking at a field.'

Ann kissed her mother goodnight too. 'Mummy,' she said, in her ear, 'the ship won't sail off with us on board, will it? It'll wait till we've gone, won't it?'

'Oh yes – don't you worry about that!' said Mummy. 'Go to sleep now, and the morning will come all the sooner. You're going to have a really lovely day!'

2

A Very Big Ship

Mike woke first the next morning, and he remembered at once that it was Saturday – and that they were all going to see the big ship, *Queen Elizabeth*. He sat up and rubbed his hands in joy.

'Wake up, girls! It's *Queen Elizabeth* day!' he called, and Belinda and Ann woke with a jump. They too remembered what was going to happen, and they leapt out of their comfortable little bunks like rabbits springing from their holes.

Belinda flew down the steps of the caravan to help with the breakfast. Mike ran to see if there was plenty of wood for the fire. Ann made the bunks very neatly and tidily. There wouldn't be much time for jobs after breakfast today!

They didn't even have time to wash up the breakfast things before Granny's car arrived at the field-gate!

'Honk! honk!' the horn sounded. 'Honk, honk!'

'There's the car!' cried Ann, in excitement, and nearly knocked the milk over. 'Mummy, Mummy, we aren't ready!'

'Well, we soon shall be – but not if you knock

everything over,' said Mummy. 'Belinda, just pack all the things into the little sink so that we can wash them when we come back. Ann, Mike, go and get your hats and coats.'

Soon everyone was running over to the field-gate. Granny was in the car, looking out anxiously for them. Daddy opened the door and gave her a kiss.

'Hallo, hallo!' he said. 'Punctual as always. Good-morning, James. I hear you are going to be good enough to look after the caravans and the two horses for me today.'

The driver touched his cap. 'Yes, sir, I'd be delighted. Nice to have a day in a caravan in the country! And I'll see to the horses, sir. Davey and Clopper, aren't they?'

'Yes,' said the children. Ann touched his arm. 'You *will* go and talk to them, won't you?' she asked. 'They don't like it when we all go off for the day and nobody comes near them.'

'Don't you worry, miss – I'll ask them all their news,' said the driver, and he helped Mummy into the front seat.

Daddy got into the driving-seat. Ann sat on Mummy's knee in front. Mike and Belinda got in at the back, trying hard not to squash Granny too much. But she was a very little person and didn't really take up much more room than they did.

'Well, what a treat this is going to be!' said Granny.

'I was so surprised when Daddy rang me up last night. I've always wanted to see the *Queen Elizabeth* – our most magnificent ship!'

This time they drove the whole way to Southampton. They stopped for lunch, sitting in the sun on a grassy hillside, looking down over a valley. Little fields separated by green hedges spread out before them.

'It's rather like a patchwork quilt,' said Belinda. 'All bits and pieces joined together by hedges. Is America like this, I wonder?'

'Oh no!' said Daddy. 'You wouldn't see any tiny fields like this, with hedges between. You'd see miles upon miles of great rolling fields, as far as the eye can reach. One field in America would take a hundred of our little fields – sometimes a thousand or more!'

'It must be a very, very big country then,' said Ann. 'I should get lost in it.'

'You probably would!' said Granny. 'But as you're not going, you can feel quite safe here with me. Now – have we all finished our lunch? We ought to be setting off again.'

After a while they arrived at a big, familiar town.

'It's the port of Southampton,' Daddy declared, 'where big ships – and little ships too – come to harbour.'

'What a lot of cranes everywhere!' said Mike, watching a crane in the distance pulling up a great

package. 'I suppose they're used to unload ships, aren't they?'

'Yes,' said Daddy. 'Do you see that little box-like house near the bottom of the crane? Well, a man sits in there all day long, and works the crane.'

'I'd rather like to do that,' said Mike. 'I once built a little crane with my Meccano, and it worked just like that big one.'

'Look! Aren't those the funnels of the *Queen Elizabeth*?' suddenly said Mummy, and she pointed beyond the crane. Daddy slowed down the car.

Two enormous red funnels showed above the tops of the buildings beyond the crane. 'Yes,' said Daddy. 'That's the *Queen Elizabeth*.'

The children stared in awe. She was even bigger than they remembered from their holiday on the *Pole Star*. 'Are those her *funnels*?' said Ann, hardly believing her eyes. 'Good gracious – if her *funnels* are higher than houses, what a *very* big ship she must be! Why, you could almost drop a house down one of her funnels!'

'Not quite,' said Mummy. The car went on again through the crowded streets of Southampton, and at last came to the docks. What a wonderful place!

Mike couldn't take his eyes from the ships there. Great big ships – smaller ships – quite small ships. Fussy little tugs bustling here and there. Boats everywhere. Hootings and sirens, and hammerings

and shouts! What a wonderful place to live!

'I wish we lived at Southampton,' said Mike. 'I'd be down at the docks every day. I think I shall be a sailor when I grow up, Daddy.'

'Not an engine-driver after all?' said Daddy, stopping the car at a gate, and showing some tickets to the policeman there. 'Can we go through? Thank you.'

'The *Queen* is up beyond,' said the policeman, and saluted.

The car ran through the gateway, and Daddy put it in a parking-place where there were many other cars. Then they made their way to the *Queen Elizabeth*. Ann didn't even know the *Elizabeth* when they came in sight of her. She hadn't expected anything so enormous. But the other two children gasped in surprise.

'Mummy! She's the biggest ship that was ever built!' cried Mike, as his eyes went up and up the sides of the great ship, past deck after deck, to the topmost one of all – then to the funnels that now towered far above him, higher than any house.

'She's grand,' said Daddy, proudly. 'I'm glad she's British. No one can beat us at ship-building. We've been ship-builders for centuries – and here's our grandest ship so far!'

'Let's go aboard – oh, do let's hurry up and go aboard!' cried Belinda. 'I want to see what she's like inside!'

3

Tea on the *Queen Elizabeth*

'Gangway for the *Queen Elizabeth*, sir? That one over there,' said a nearby sailor, and pointed to where a slanting gangway ran from the ship to the dock-side. Up they all went, and into the ship.

'We have to find Mr Harrison,' said Daddy, looking at his tickets. 'He will show us as much as he can.'

Mr Harrison was a very jolly man indeed. He wore officer's uniform, and greeted Daddy like an old friend.

'Good afternoon, sir. I was told you were coming. Now, how would you like to see over our little ship?'

Well, of course, it was anything but a little ship! The children were soon quite bewildered by all the different decks they were taken on – each deck seemed to stretch for miles! They went on the games deck too, and Mike wished they could have some games.

'Deck-tennis – ooh,' he said. 'And quoits – and shuffle-board. Oh Daddy, do people have time to play all these games on the way to America? There's such a lot of them.'

'Plenty of time,' said Daddy. 'Look – these are the lifeboats, slung up there ready for any emergency.'

'What's an emergency?' asked Ann.

'Oh – something like a terrible storm that might harm the ship and make it necessary for people to get off her in the lifeboats,' said Daddy. 'Or a fire aboard. You never know. All big ships have lifeboats.'

'Daddy, I can't somehow think that we're on a ship,' said Belinda, as they walked down another big deck. 'It's so very big. Why, when I look over the deck-rail the ships down below look like toys!'

'And we can't feel any movement either, because the ship's too big to feel any waves in the dock,' said Mike. 'I'd like to feel what it's like when she rolls, though – or don't big ships like this roll?'

'My word, young man, you wouldn't like it if you were on board when the *Elizabeth* really *does* roll!' said the officer who was showing them round. 'Sometimes it seems as if she's never going to stop heeling over to one side – it feels as if she's going to go right down below the water before she rights herself a bit, and then rolls back and over to the other side! Ah, you want to be in a bit of a gale on this ship.'

'I wish I could be,' said Mike. 'I'd like that.'

'Well, what about tea?' asked the officer. 'It will be ready for you. I'll take you down to the dining-room in the lift.'

'In the *lift*?' echoed the children in astonishment. 'Is there really a lift on this ship?'

'Good gracious, yes – quite a lot,' said the officer,

and led them into a big lounge between the fore and aft decks. At each side there were lifts. The doors of one slid open, and the children gazed into what looked like a little room.

'What a big lift!' said Ann. They all stepped in and down they went, past one, two, three floors – and then stopped.

'Fancy going down and down in a lift inside a ship!' said Mike. 'How many floors down does this lift go?'

'Fourteen,' said the officer. 'And after that there's yet another lift that goes down into the bowels of the ship.'

'Oooh – what an enormous dining-room!' said Belinda, as they went from the lift into a great, empty room.

'Yes – it holds hundreds and hundreds of people,' said the officer. 'You should see it when it's full of diners – and the band is playing – and great mounds of food are being carried about all over the place!'

But the dining-room was empty now and silent. The officer led them to a table in an alcove, set ready for tea. 'Here you are,' he said. 'Tea on the *Queen Elizabeth* for you! I hope you'll enjoy it!'

The children gazed in awe at the tea. 'What's that?' asked Ann, pointing to a plate of snow-white slices of what she thought must be cake.

'Bread and butter!' said Mummy. 'They have white bread aboard ship and in America. You'll like it.'

They did! They couldn't believe it was only bread and butter. It looked so beautifully white! And the cakes were amazing – all sugary and creamy and the prettiest shapes.

Belinda looked towards what were like two oblong cakes in the middle of the table.

'What are those?' she said. 'Can I have a slice, Granny?'

'Yes,' said Granny, and cut her a big one. It was in layers of three colours – pink, yellow and brown.

'Eat it with a spoon,' said Granny.

'Why?' asked Belinda in surprise. 'I don't eat a slice of cake with a spoon, do I?'

But she picked up her spoon and broke off a piece of the cake. Her eyes opened wide and she rolled them round at Mike and Ann in delight. She swallowed her mouthful.

'It's *ice-cream* cake!' she said. 'Would you believe it – we've got two great big cakes of ice-cream all to ourselves! Are we meant to eat them all, Mummy?'

'You won't be able to,' said her mother, laughing. 'Isn't it lovely? They have an enormous amount of ice-cream in America, you know – and these big ships must make tons of it for their passengers.'

'I wish we were passengers then,' said Belinda. 'I *wish* we were going to America. Do they have ice-cream every single day like this? I wouldn't eat anything but that, Mummy, have some!'

Everyone laughed at Belinda. She made up her mind not to leave a single scrap of the ice-cream cakes – but alas, they were so rich that nobody could possibly manage more than one slice. It was very sad.

They were sorry when they had to leave the big *Queen*. 'She's beautiful,' said Mike, as they went down the gangway and then stopped to look up at her great steep sides. 'How I wish I could live in her when she's really out on the sea!'

'Yes – she doesn't somehow seem like a real ship when she's here in dock,' said Mummy. 'But out at sea, when she's rolling and tossing – ah, that would be a wonderful thing!'

Mike and Belinda stood still to have one last look. 'I'm afraid it will be a long time before we see you again!' said Belinda, to the big ship. 'A very, very long time!'

But it wasn't. Surprising things were going to happen to Mike, Belinda and Ann!

4

It Can't Be True!

The three children went back to school again the next week, full of their visit to the *Queen Elizabeth*. The boys and girls listened, and wished they had gone too, especially when they heard about the marvellous lifts and the wonderful ice-cream cake.

Then, when Mike, Belinda and Ann went home the next Friday, what a surprise they had! Daddy was home before them, his face one big smile. Mummy was smiling too, and looked very excited indeed!

'Why is Daddy home so early?' asked Mike. 'And why do you look so excited, Mummy?'

'We were waiting to ask you something,' said Mummy. 'It's this – how would you all like to sail away on the *Queen Elizabeth*, and spend two weeks in New York?'

There wasn't a sound from the three children. They stared as if they couldn't have heard right. Mike opened and shut his mouth like a goldfish.

'Tongue-tied!' said Daddy, with a laugh. 'Say something, one of you, or you'll most certainly burst!'

Then all three yelled at the same time.

'Do you really mean it?'

'Is it really true?'

'When do we GO?'

Ann flung herself on her father. 'Tell us about it, Daddy. It isn't a joke, is it?'

'No,' said Daddy. 'It's quite true. The man who was going is ill – and so the firm have asked me to go instead. I'm allowed to take Mummy – and Granny says she will pay part of your fares if I like to take you as well for the trip.'

'She says it would do you a lot of good to see America – it will be like living in a geography lesson,' said Mummy. 'What do you think of that?'

'Mummy! I can't believe it,' said Mike. 'When do we go? And what about school?'

'You'll have to miss school for two or three weeks, I'm afraid,' said Mummy. 'But it will really be a great experience for you – a real education! Fancy Granny saying you ought to go – and helping to pay for you!'

'Good old Granny,' said Belinda. 'She's the kindest person in the world – except you and Daddy!'

'You still haven't said when we *go*,' said Mike.

'We go when the *Elizabeth* comes back,' said Mummy. 'She will be back here again next week. She's at New York now – and she leaves there tonight or tomorrow morning. We shall sail next Friday, or very early the next morning rather.'

'Next Friday!' said Belinda, her eyes shining.

'Next Friday! We'll have to come back home to the caravans then.'

'Yes – you must come home on Wednesday,' said Mummy. 'Then I can get your clothes and things ready, and pack. We have to be on board Friday night.'

'Shall we have to go to bed on board while she's in Southampton?' asked Mike. 'I would have liked to see her slipping out of the port by daylight. Shan't we see her leaving England?'

'Don't look so solemn!' said Mummy. 'The *Queen* has to be guided by the tide. You'll be fast asleep when she leaves – and you'll wake up to find her far out at sea in the morning!'

'And we shan't see land again for days!' said Belinda.

'Oh yes, you will,' said her mother. 'The *Elizabeth* goes to Cherbourg in France before she goes to America – so you'll see land the very next day.'

'Oh – shall we see France too, then?' asked Ann, in delight. 'Can we go ashore?'

'Dear me, no,' said Daddy. 'We shall probably stay outside Cherbourg, and watch the little steamers chugging out from the port with new passengers for the *Elizabeth*. You can watch that. You'll like it.'

'I can't believe it's true,' sighed Belinda. 'I thought last Saturday was wonderful enough – having tea on board – but *next* Saturday we'll be sailing over the ocean in the biggest ship in the world.'

'Can I take my doll Josephine?' asked Ann. 'It

would be an education for her too.'

Daddy laughed. 'Yes – you take her – she shall meet the American dolls and see how she likes them. Some of them don't only go to sleep, and talk, but they can walk too. We'll see what Josephine says to that.'

The children could hardly do any lessons at all the next week. They kept thinking of the *Queen Elizabeth*, and seeing her great red funnels towering high above her spotless decks.

'I know I shall get lost on such a big ship,' said Ann to Belinda. 'It's as big as a small town! I'll never know my way about.'

'We'll soon get used to it,' said Belinda. 'Did you know there was a swimming-pool, Ann? We couldn't see it when we went, because it was shut up – but there is one. We can go swimming in it.'

'Don't tell me any more,' begged Ann. 'It's beginning to sound like a fairy-tale – and I do want it to be true.'

It was true, of course. Wednesday came, and the children caught the bus to go home to the caravans.

'We've come!' cried Ann, seeing her mother waiting at the gate. 'It's Wednesday at last.'

'And soon it will be Friday,' said Mike. 'Only one more day – then Friday!'

Thursday was a busy day of washing clothes and packing lots of things. Ann wouldn't let her doll be

packed. 'No — she wants to *see* everything,' she said. 'I'll carry her, Mummy.'

Thursday night came — the last to be spent in the caravans for some time. Then Friday morning dawned, fair and bright — a really lovely October day.

'It's Friday, it's Friday!' sang the three children as soon as they woke up. It didn't take them long to get dressed *that* day!

'We must say goodbye to Davey and Clopper,' said Ann. So they went to find the two horses and hugged them.

'We're going to America,' said Ann. 'But we'll come back. Goodbye, Davey, goodbye, Clopper. Be good, and I *might* perhaps send you a postcard!'

5

On Board at Last!

Granny lent them her car again, to drive down to Southampton. She didn't come with them because there wasn't room for her and all the luggage too. As it was, the children had to sit with suitcases all round their feet!

'Have you got our tickets, Daddy?' asked Ann, anxiously. 'Shall we get there in time? Suppose we have a puncture? Will the boat wait for us?'

'We'll be all right,' said Daddy. 'Yes, I've got the tickets, and I know which cabins we've got and everything.'

It didn't really seem very long before they were in Southampton again. Daddy took them to a little hotel to have supper. It was all very exciting.

They could hardly eat anything. Mike was anxious to go. 'We might be too late to get on,' he said. 'We really ought to go.'

'Mike – the boat doesn't sail till about half-past one at *night*,' said Daddy. 'Or rather, in the very early morning, long before dawn, while it's still pitch-dark.'

'Oh,' said Mike, and decided to eat something after all.

'Shall we be seasick?' said Ann, suddenly.

'Not a bit,' said Mummy, at once. 'And if you are, it soon passes. Now do eat that pudding, Ann.'

At last they were at the dock again, and at last they were walking up the gangway. But this time there seemed to be hundreds and hundreds of people walking on too! The children stared at them in wonder.

'Are they all going to America?' said Mike.

'Most of them,' said Daddy. 'Some are just going to see their friends off, of course. The ship looks different now, doesn't she, since the Saturday we saw her with hardly anyone on board?'

She did look different. It was night now and there were lights everywhere. The round portholes glittered like hundreds of eyes, and there was such a noise that Mike had to shout to hear himself speak.

'Keep close to me,' said Daddy. 'Our cabins are together, so we shall be all right once we've found them.'

They did find them at last. Belinda looked at them in awe. They were quite big, and had beds, not bunks. The big round porthole looked out over the dock, and she saw thousands of twinkling lights out there. She imagined what it would be like when she looked out in a day or two's time and saw nothing but sea.

'There's every single thing you want,' said Mike, looking round his mother's cabin. 'Wash-basin – dressing-table – wardrobe – drawers – and look, when you put this flap down, Mummy, it makes a little desk for you to write on!'

The three children had a cabin with three beds in. They were delighted. 'Can I have the one by the port-hole?' begged Belinda. 'Oh Mike, do let me. I want to be able to stand on the bed and look out of the port-hole any time in the night that I wake up.'

'Well, you won't see anything if you do,' said Mike. He looked longingly at the bed by the porthole. He badly wanted it himself, but he was very unselfish with his two sisters.

'All right,' he said, with a sigh. 'You can have the bed by the porthole going to America, Belinda, and Ann can have it coming back.'

'I don't want a bed by the porthole,' said Ann. 'I don't like to be as near the sea as that. I'm afraid it might leak in on me.'

'You're silly,' said Mike, cheering up. 'Well, if that's what you're afraid of, you can have the inside bed each time. I'll have the porthole bed coming back from America.'

A nice bright face with twinkling eyes popped round the door. 'Ah – I've got three children in this cabin of mine this time, have I? That's nice.'

The children stared at her. She looked very nice

and crisp and clean – rather like a nurse, the children thought. She laughed at their faces.

'I'm your stewardess,' she said. 'I look after you. If ever you want me, just ring that bell over there – and I'll come trotting along to see which of you is sick, or wants a hot-water bottle, or some more to eat!'

The children laughed. They liked this stewardess. 'Would you like something to eat now?' she said. 'I expect you've had your supper, haven't you? But would you like some nice sugary biscuits, and a big glass of creamy milk each – or some orange juice?'

All this sounded very nice. 'I'd love the biscuits and some orange juice,' said Belinda and the others said the same. Then Mummy came in, and smiled to hear that they had ordered eats and drinks already!

She began to unpack a few things for them. She laid their night things on the beds and set out their tooth-brushes and washing things.

'You behave exactly as if you were at home,' she said. 'Cleaning your teeth, washing, brushing your hair and everything.'

'And saying our prayers,' said Ann. 'I'm going to ask God to keep us safe when we're on the deep sea. I'd like him to keep a special lifeboat for me if anything happens.'

'You've got a special lifeboat already,' said Mummy. 'I'll show you yours tomorrow. And in that cupboard you've each got a special cork life jacket. You will

have to learn how to put it on tomorrow.'

Belinda sighed. 'Everything is so lovely and exciting,' she said. 'Fancy having cork jackets of our own, too. I shall love to put mine on.'

'Now you must go to bed,' said Mummy. 'It's long past your bedtime. And here comes your nice stewardess with biscuits and orange-juice – and what biscuits!'

They certainly were wonderful ones. The three children hurriedly undressed, cleaned their teeth, washed, and brushed their hair, and hopped into bed.

'I shall say my prayers last of all,' said Ann. 'Then I can say thank you for these biscuits too. Oh dear – I'm sure I shall never go to sleep tonight!'

'I'm going to keep awake,' said Mike. 'I want to hear the anchor come up – and hear the fussy little tugs pulling away at the big *Queen* to get her out to sea. I want to feel her moving as she leaves Southampton.'

'Oh, so do I!' cried Belinda. But she and Ann fell fast asleep. Only Mike lay awake, waiting.

9

Goodbye to England

More and more passengers came on board the big ship, and found their different cabins. Cranes worked busily and loaded the enormous holds with luggage. There was a great deal of noise and bustle and excitement.

Belinda and Ann slept through it all. They were tired out with excitement. Mike kept awake for two hours, and then he felt his eyelids closing because they were so heavy. He propped them up with his fingers. But then his fingers felt heavy, and slid down from his eyes. His eyes closed. He slept too. Poor Mike – he had so much wanted to be awake when the time came for the *Elizabeth* to leave the big port of Southampton.

Half-past one came. The tide was right. Little tugs fussed up in the darkness, and ropes were thrown from the big ship over to them. How was it possible for such tiny tugs to move such an enormous ship? But they did. Gradually the *Queen Elizabeth* moved away from the dock-side. Gradually she left Southampton docks behind.

Mike awoke with a jump. He felt a peculiar movement far below him. He sat up, wondering what it was. Then he knew! The *Queen Elizabeth* was moving!

'She's away!' he thought and got out of bed. He groped his way to Belinda's bed, which was by the big porthole. He wondered if he would wake her if he stood up on her bed and looked out.

He cautiously got up on the bed. Belinda woke at once. 'Who is it?' she said, in a frightened voice. 'Where am I?'

'Sh! It's me, Mike! Belinda – the *Elizabeth* is moving! I felt her just now. Can *you* feel her? She's not keeping still any more. You can feel the water running under her!'

Belinda was thrilled. She knelt up to the porthole and the two of them looked out. They whispered together.

'Yes – we've left the dock-side. We must be right in the middle of the harbour. Look at all the lights slipping past.'

'Doesn't the water look a long long way down?' said Mike. 'And so awfully black! And look at all the lights twinkling in it, reflected from the dock-side.'

'Now she's left the dock,' said Belinda. 'Is she going backwards, Mike? She must be, to get out of the dock. Soon we shall feel her stopping – and then going the other way, shan't we?'

Belinda was quite right. The *Elizabeth* stopped when she was well out of the dock, and then began to move the other way. The little tugs hooted in farewell and chugged off by themselves. They had done their job.

'There goes a little tug,' said Mike, seeing one dimly in the starlit darkness. 'Aren't they clever, Belinda, the way they push and pull, and get a big ship like this safely out of the docks? I wouldn't mind having a tug of my own.'

'Now we're really going,' said Belinda, softly. 'I suppose we'll keep along the coast a bit – but by the time morning comes we'll be out of sight of land.'

'Till we reach France,' said Mike. 'And then we'll be days on the enormous Atlantic Ocean, hundreds of miles from anywhere.'

They were silent. The *Elizabeth* was big – but the ocean was vast. Belinda shivered a little. Then she thought of the big lifeboats and the life jacket and felt more cheerful. She watched the line of far-off lights that gradually passed behind them as the big ship ploughed on through the dark waters.

'I like to feel we're really moving, don't you, Mike?' said Belinda. 'I like the little rolls the ship gives now and again when a bigger wave than usual passes under her. Isn't this *fun*?'

The cabin door opened cautiously, and light streamed in from the passage outside. The two children looked

round. They saw Mummy outlined in the doorway.

'Mummy!' said Belinda, in a loud whisper. 'Mummy, we've left Southampton now – did you know? We're off to America!'

'Sh!' said Mummy. 'You'll wake Ann. I wondered if you two were awake. Yes, we're really on our way now. I hope you didn't keep awake all the time.'

'No,' said Belinda. 'I only woke about twenty minutes ago.'

'Well, cuddle down into bed again now,' said Mummy. 'I won't stay in case I wake Ann. Mike, get back to your bed, dear.'

'Right,' said Mike and slipped down from Belinda's bed. 'Mummy, will you come and fetch us in the morning? We wouldn't know how to find the dining-room.'

'Of course I'll come,' said Mummy. 'Now, good-night, dears. Go to sleep at once.'

The door shut. Mike yawned. He really felt very sleepy indeed. He called softly to Belinda. 'Good-night, Belinda!'

But there was no answer. Belinda had curled up and was already fast asleep!

They all slept very soundly indeed in their comfortable little beds. They were awakened by a loud knocking on the door. Belinda woke in a fright, and sat up. She felt sure the boat must be sinking or something!

Then the stewardess put her head round the door, smiling. 'Sleepyheads, aren't you? This is the third time I've been along. Your mother says, will you get up now, because she will be ready to take you down to breakfast in ten minutes' time.'

'Oooh yes,' said Mike, scrambling out of bed. 'What's for breakfast, stewardess? Do you know?'

'Porridge, cereals, iced melon, stewed fruit, bacon, eggs, steak, fish, omelettes, chops, ham, tongue . . .' she began.

The children stared at her in amazement. 'Do we *have* to eat all that?' asked Mike.

The stewardess laughed. 'You can choose whatever you want, eat as much as you like, and take as long over it as you wish!' she said. 'So hurry up now, and get down to a really fine breakfast!'

They certainly did hurry up – and when Mummy came for them, they were all ready. Down in the lift they went to the enormous dining-room – and found their table. And when the menu came, the children simply didn't know what to choose from the dozens and dozens of things on it!

'If all the meals are like this, I *am* going to enjoy this trip!' said Mike.

7

A Wonderful Ship

That first day on the *Queen Elizabeth* was simply marvellous to the three children. At first they wouldn't go anywhere without their mother or father, because they really were afraid of getting lost!

'Everything's so *big*,' said Belinda. 'The decks are miles and miles long. It takes ages to go all round the ship on just one deck!'

They went to see the big swimming-pool, and Mummy said they might bathe there some time. They went to see the beautiful library with hundreds and hundreds of books waiting to be read. They found the children's corner there, and each of them borrowed a book to read.

'Though goodness knows when we'll have time to read a book on this lovely ship!' said Mike.

There were shops on the *Queen Elizabeth* too! The children went to look at them – all kinds of shops that sold anything the passengers wanted. How odd to have shops on a ship!

It was great fun up on the sports deck. It was windy up there, and the children had to hold on to their hats.

They went to watch the grown-ups playing games.
There were games with rope rings. There were
games with great wooden discs that had to be pushed
very hard indeed with a big wooden pusher. That
was called shuffle-board. The children waited till the
grown-ups had finished playing with the shuffle-
board, and then they had a try.

But they couldn't push the great wooden counters
very far! They tried their hand at throwing the rope
rings on to numbered squares, and Mike was so
good at that, that Daddy had a game with him. Mike
nearly won!

'It's nice up here on the sports deck,' said Belinda,
her cheeks glowing with the strong breeze. 'It isn't
all enclosed with glass windows like the other decks
down below — you can really taste the spray up here,
and feel the wind. I like it.'

The great sea spread out round them for miles.
Always there was the plash-plash-plash of waves
against the ship's sides — a lovely sound. She left
behind her a long white trail of foaming water.

'That's called the wake,' said Daddy. So they
watched the wake forming behind the ship, spreading
away as far as they could see.

'The fishes must be very astonished when a big
ship like this comes by,' said Belinda, looking down
into the water.

'I should be frightened if I were a fish and I suddenly

saw a great thing like this coming towards me,' said Ann. 'I should swim away quickly.'

'We're going fast now, aren't we, Daddy?' said Mike.

Daddy nodded. 'Yes – she's a fast ship, the *Elizabeth*. So is her sister, the *Queen Mary*.'

At eleven o'clock they went downstairs and found their own deck-chairs on the deck below. Mummy said that it was about time that deck stewards brought round little cups of hot soup and biscuits for everyone.

'Good gracious!' said Belinda. 'Do we really have hot soup in the middle of the morning? I do think this is a ship with good ideas!'

Sure enough the stewards appeared with trays of hot steaming soup in little bowls. There were biscuits to go with it. It was simply delicious. The children wondered if they might have another helping each, but Mummy said no.

'You will want to have an enormous lunch at one o'clock,' she said. 'Don't spoil it! It will take you about ten minutes to read all down the menu!'

After that they went to see the gym, where people were doing all kinds of exercises. There was a peculiar-looking imitation horse there, and Mike got on it. Up came the instructor, pulled a handle – and dear me, that horse came alive and began to do such extraordinary things that Mike nearly fell off! He clutched it hard round the neck and tried to stop

himself slipping. Belinda and Ann screamed with laughter.

The horse bucked and reared and rocked from side to side till Mike yelled for mercy. He was very glad when it stopped and he was able to get off. Belinda got on and had a turn, but Ann wouldn't. She was quite certain she would fall off at once.

'This is a wonderful ship,' said Mike, happily. 'There's simply *everything* here – it's like a small town all neatly put together with everything anyone can want.'

They went up on the sports deck again after a lunch that was good enough to eat in a king's palace. 'Even the menu is like a book!' said Belinda, marvelling at the wonderful coloured cover. 'And look at the inside! Mummy, can we *really* choose any of these dishes? I simply don't know what to have.'

'I'm beginning with iced melon – then chicken soup – and two little chops with tomatoes and onions and mushrooms – and an ice-cream called Bombe-something,' said Ann, unexpectedly. 'And I think I'll finish up with iced melon too!'

It really took quite a long time deciding what they were going to have, but nobody seemed in a hurry at all. 'After all, no one's got a train or a bus to catch,' said Mike. 'There's all day long to choose food and games and wander round.'

They all felt rather full after such a marvellous

346

meal, and went up on the sports deck in the wind. It was nice up there. The sun shone, the sky was blue, and the sea was very blue too. Ann sat down in a corner and fell fast asleep!

She was awakened by a most terrible noise. She leapt up in a fright, yelling for her mother. 'Mummy, Mummy, what is it? Are we sinking? Have we hit a rock?'

But it was only the siren of the *Queen Elizabeth* hooting loudly because she was coming near France. It was such a sudden and tremendous noise that everyone looked startled for a moment.

'There's France!' Mike told Ann. 'Daddy says that port is Cherbourg. We're not going right into the harbour because it's a bit rough here. So they're sending out boats to us with new passengers, and taking off passengers that want to go to France.'

Out came two little steamers from Cherbourg, and the *Queen Elizabeth* stayed quite still, waiting.

'Isn't it fun?' said Mike, leaning over the sports-deck rail to watch. 'How small those steamers look! I'm glad I belong to the *Queen Elizabeth*. It makes me feel very important!'

8

Out on the Ocean

That first day seemed deliciously long and full of excitement and surprises. They were all very tired when they went to bed. The *Elizabeth* had left the coast of France, and was now on her way to America! The sea wasn't quite so smooth and calm, and sometimes the children staggered a little as they walked down the passage to their cabin.

'One day gone,' said Mike. 'I hope the days don't go *too* quickly! I wonder what we do tomorrow. It will be Sunday. How can we go to church? I haven't seen a church here, have you?'

'You couldn't build a church on a ship,' said Ann. 'We'll have to see what happens.'

Mummy told them the next morning that there were two things that day that she wanted them to do. 'There is a church service at eleven o'clock,' she said, 'and you must put on your hats and coats just as if you were going to a real church, although the service is only being held in the big lounge. You must each take pennies for a collection too.'

'Fancy going to church on a ship!' said Ann. 'I do

like that. What's the second thing we have to go to, Mummy?'

'Lifeboat drill,' said Mummy. 'We all have to get out our life jackets from the cupboards in our cabins and put them on properly. Then we have to go up to our boat stations . . .'

'Boat stations! Are there stations here, then?' asked Mike. 'I haven't seen them!'

'They're not really *stations*,' said Mummy. 'Just places where we meet for lifeboat drill – or to get our lifeboat if there was any need to.'

'How do we know which is our boat-station?' asked Belinda.

Mummy showed her some directions on a card in the cabin. 'This shows you the way to yours,' she said. 'Up the stairs, and up again. On to that deck. And go to the place on the deck marked with your number. It's quite easy. There are many different stations, and each passenger must know his own.'

'So that if the boat was wrecked, we'd all know where to go at once, and be helped into our life-boats, I suppose,' said Mike. 'That's very sensible.'

They went to church service at eleven o'clock, looking very proper in hats and coats. Ann even put her gloves on.

It was very like a real church service except that there were no proper pews, only chairs, and it seemed extraordinary to look out of the windows and see

miles of green-blue sea outside instead of houses and streets.

Ann was very pleased with one hymn that ended each verse with:

Oh, hear us when we cry to Thee
For those in peril on the sea.

'That's a very good hymn to sing on a ship,' she said afterwards. 'I'm glad there's a hymn that prays for people on the sea.'

The captain gave a short, interesting little sermon, and everyone listened. There were more hymns and prayers and a collection. Belinda thought it was the nicest church service she had ever been to in her life. It was peculiar to feel the ship moving all the time, and to see the white clouds racing by as the ship moved along.

'Now for lifeboat drill,' said Mummy, and took them to their cabin to get their life jackets. A loud bell rang out and made them jump.

'That's to warn everyone to go to their lifeboat stations,' said Mummy. 'If ever we hear that in the middle of the night, up we must get, snatch at our life jackets and run to our stations as fast as ever we can.' This sounded very exciting, but none of the children wanted it to happen!

They got their life jackets and Mummy showed them

how to tie them round them. They began to laugh.

'We look *enormous*!' said Mike. 'Do look at Ann. She's as broad as she's long!'

'Hurry up,' said Mummy. 'This is a thing we always have to be quick about, even if it's only practice.'

Soon they all had their life jackets on, and Mummy and Daddy took them to the deck where their boat-station was. About fifty people were with them. Farther along there were other groups of people. Every passenger had his own boat-station, and now he knew where to go for it.

'And, you see, in a real emergency, when the life-boats are lowered for us to get into,' said Daddy, 'everyone gets into his own lifeboat, and there are just the right number. Then down the boat goes into the sea, and is cast off to safety.'

'All the same, I hope it won't happen,' said Ann, looking rather scared.

'No, it won't,' said Mummy. 'But it's good to know what we must do if it *should* happen.'

When everyone was at his boat-station, an officer came up to Daddy's group. He went round to see that everyone's life jacket was on properly. Then he talked to them all, and told them exactly what to do if the ship met with an accident.

The children were glad to go back to their cabins and take off their bulky life jackets. 'Is it dinner-time yet?' asked Ann. 'I had an enormous breakfast,

351

and soup and biscuits at half-past ten, and now I feel hungry all over again.'

'I suppose you'll start off with iced melon again?' said Mike, with a grin. 'So far, you've begun every single meal with iced melon. You'll turn into a melon yourself if you go on like this.'

'And do you know what *you'll* turn into?' said Ann, as they went to get into the lift to go down to the big dining-room. 'You'll turn into a chocolate ice-cream – and you'll be lucky if I don't eat you!'

9

A Gale Blows Up

The days began to slip away, but on the fourth day things suddenly changed. Great clouds came over the sea, and huge waves began to form in the strong wind that blew.

Then the *Queen Elizabeth* showed that, big or not, she was a ship that took notice of big waves! She began to roll from side to side. First this side a little, then back to the other side.

The children began to stagger a little as they went about the ship, which they now knew very well indeed. 'I hope she doesn't roll any farther over,' said Mike. 'I'm not sure I like it very much.'

'Why? Do you feel sick?' asked Ann.

'No. But I just don't *want* her to roll any farther over,' said Mike. However, she took no notice of Mike's wishes, and began to roll more than ever.

When night came ropes had been put up on the decks so that people might hold on to them as they went. The children were quite glad when bedtime came. At least their beds felt firm and safe!

But it was most peculiar to lie on a bed that slanted

353

sideways when the ship rolled! I feel as if I ought to hold on to the sides in case I fall out,' said Ann.

When the light was out, it seemed as if the ship's rolling felt worse than ever. Down – down – down – to one side, until the children really thought they must be touching the water – then up, up, up, and over to the other side – down – down – down again, lower and lower till Ann sat up.

'I don't like it,' she wailed. 'Suppose it rolled so far over that it didn't come back!'

The stewardess put her head round the door. 'Who's this shouting out?' she said, and switched on the light. 'Dear me, surely you're not making a fuss about a bit of a gale like this? You want to be in a *real* storm to have something worth shouting about!'

'Isn't this a real storm, then?' asked Ann.

'Good gracious no. It'll be gone by the morning,' said the stewardess. 'A big ship always rolls a bit in a gale – she can't help it. But you want to be out in a small boat to know what pitching and tossing and rolling are really like!'

All the children were relieved to feel that there wasn't much likelihood of the alarm bell's sounding for them to put on life jackets, rush to their boat-stations and get into a lifeboat!

'Now you just listen to what I say,' said the stewardess. 'The gale's beginning to die down even now – we're only touching the fringe of the storm

and we'll soon be out of it. You must enjoy the rolling instead of getting scared of it! You want a ship to behave like a ship, don't you?'

She said goodnight and went. 'Well, we shall certainly have something to tell the children at school about when we get back home,' said Mike, sleepily. 'I'm going to pretend I'm in a rocking-bed and enjoy it!'

'So am I,' said Belinda. 'That's a good idea.'

Ann didn't say anything. She had suddenly remembered something. What did a storm matter? What did a rolling ship matter? Hadn't she prayed to God that very night to keep them all safe – and here she was thinking He couldn't manage to protect them in even a *little* gale!

'That's very bad of me, and very untrusting,' she thought. 'I'm not afraid any more now.' And she fell asleep thinking of the hymn they had sung on Sunday, which now seemed an even more sensible hymn than ever,

> Oh, hear us when we cry to Thee
> For those in peril on the sea.

The stewardess was right. The *Elizabeth* sailed right out of the gale by the morning, and when the children woke up, what a difference! The big ship hardly rolled at all – all the guide-ropes had been

taken down – and people who had felt seasick came down to make a good breakfast.

And now the great excitement was the arrival at New York! The gale had slowed down the *Elizabeth,* and instead of arriving that night she would not arrive till ten o'clock the next morning.

'Which will be very nice,' said Daddy, 'because you will be able to watch the coastline all the way up the big river to New York. And we shall pass something that the Americans are very proud of – the colossal Statue of Liberty, holding a great torch aloft.'

'All the same – I feel quite sad now to think we're going to leave the *Queen Elizabeth,*' said Belinda, looking solemn. 'I've got used to her, and I love her.'

'Well, we're going *back* in her, in two or three weeks' time, aren't we?' said Mike. 'You'll have another trip just like this.'

'Except that the clocks will have to be put forward each day, instead of back,' said Mummy. That had been a very funny thing to happen, the children thought.

Every day their clocks had been set back an hour, because they were travelling westwards, so they had gained an hour in their day. But when they returned eastwards they would lose an hour each day – the clocks would be set an hour forward! It seemed funny to meddle about with time like that – but – as they already knew, the time in New

York wasn't the same as the time in England at that particular moment!

They were all excited to see land again. They passed into the great river and watched the enormous buildings on each side. 'Much, much bigger than ours,' said Mike.

'You wait till you see some of the high buildings in New York!' said Daddy. 'You won't believe your eyes!'

'There's the Statue of Liberty!' said somebody, suddenly, and everyone craned their necks to see the enormous and magnificent statue, guarding the entrance to New York harbour. Only the stewards did not bother to look – they had seen New York before.

'America at last!' said Mike, excited. 'The newest country in the world – and one of the finest! When do we land, Daddy? I can hardly wait!'

But he had to wait, of course, and at last their turn came to walk down the gangway and on to American soil.

'America!' said Ann, holding up her doll Josephine. 'Take a look, Josephine – you've come halfway across the world – and now we're in America!'

10

America at Last

New York was a most extraordinary city to Mike, Belinda and Ann. They stepped off the *Elizabeth* and marvelled to see how the big ship stretched herself right over the street. Her huge bows rose above some of the buildings, and this looked very peculiar.

They took a large yellow taxi to their hotel. The taxi-driver spoke exactly like they had heard many people speak on the films.

'He said "twenny-four" instead of "twenty-four",' whispered Ann to Mike. 'Like Mickey Mouse talks on the films. Is that the American language?'

The taxi drove very fast indeed, and whenever they came to red traffic lights it pulled up with a terrific jerk. Then all the taxis waiting began to hoot loudly without stopping.

'Oh dear,' said Mummy. 'Does this go on all the time?'

'You'll soon get so used to the noise of New York streets that you just won't notice it after a day or two,' said Daddy. 'Look, children – do you see those skyscrapers over there?'

They looked – and gasped. The buildings were so tall that they had to crane back their necks to see the tops of them as they raced past. Floor after floor after floor – however many storeys were there?

'You wanna see the Empire State Building,' said the taxi-driver, joining suddenly in the conversation. 'That's what you wanna see. Over a hundred floors. Yes, *sir*!'

'*Can* we, Daddy?' asked Mike, eagerly. 'Do we go up in a lift? Can we go to the very top?'

'You've got to take more than one lift if you wanna get to the top of the Empire State building,' said the taxi-driver. 'You go right to the top and have a looksee round. You'll see little old New York all right then, and a lot more too!'

Some of the streets were very dark because the walls of the very tall buildings rose opposite one another and kept out the sun. Lights burned in many of the windows in those streets, though it was full daylight.

'Why don't *we* build skyscrapers in London?' asked Belinda. 'It certainly does save a lot of space.'

'New York is built on hard rock,' said Daddy. 'It will bear tremendous weights. We couldn't build enormous buildings like this in London – they would gradually sink with their weight!'

'It's a very good name – skyscrapers,' said Ann. 'They do really look as if they must be scraping the sky, Daddy.'

'New York's not a *bit* like London,' said Mike. 'The streets are so wide and straight – and quite straight streets run off the main avenue. There aren't any winding streets, or higgledy-piggledy ones, as there are in London.'

'Ah, London grew, but New York was planned,' said Daddy. 'They are both beautiful in their own way. Now look, this is Broadway. At night the lights here – the advertisement signs – are wonderful. I'll bring you out to see them.'

They came to their hotel at last. It was a skyscraper too, though not a very big one. Mike looked at the number of floors marked on the lift – thirty-two! Goodness, no wonder the lift shot up at such a speed. It would take all day to go from the bottom to the top if it didn't go so quickly!

They unpacked their things and settled in. They thought their bedrooms were enormous after the ones on the *Elizabeth*. They looked out of the window and gave a gasp.

They were so high up that the people down in the road looked like ants! The children stared in amazement.

'Look at those cars!' said Mike. 'Honestly, they don't look as big as my dinky-cars at home!'

'No, they don't,' said Belinda. 'They just don't look real. They're so small they make me feel as if I must suddenly have become a giant – so that everyone

looks tiny to me!'

'I don't like the feeling very much,' said Ann. 'Nor does Josephine. I shan't look out any more.'

Meals in America were enormous. The menus seemed even longer than those on the *Elizabeth*. The children gazed at them in astonishment, when they went down to a meal in the restaurant.

'Waffles! What are they?' asked Ann. 'They sound like the name for a rabbit or something. Hamburgers – Mummy, are they nice? And oh, look – hot-dogs! Can I have a hot-dog? Not if it's *really* dog, though. I wouldn't want to eat a dog.'

Everyone laughed. Ann looked round and her eyes opened wide when she saw the enormous platefuls of food that the waiters were setting in front of the guests.

'Have we got to eat so much?' she said to her mother. 'We had big helpings on the *Queen Elizabeth*, but these are even bigger.'

'I'll ask for small helpings for you,' said Mummy. So she did. But dear me, they were still so big that the children could do no more than nibble at them!

'Oh Mummy – will it all be wasted?' said Belinda, who knew how careful her mother was with food at home. 'What will happen to it?'

'It'll go into the pig-bucket, I expect,' said Mummy. 'The Americans waste far more than we eat – but it's America, and that's the way they like to live. I

daresay if we had as much food as they had, we'd be the same!'

'Oh dear – I don't like to leave so much,' groaned Belinda, 'but I shall be ill if I eat all this.'

'English people no eat much,' said the waiter, taking her plate and smiling. He was an Italian American.

'Let's go out on Broadway now,' said Mike, looking out of the windows. 'It's dark. We could see the lights, Daddy. I'd like to do that.'

So out they went on Broadway to see one of the sights of the world – the masses of twinkling, racing, jigging, blazing, brilliant lights on all the tall buildings everywhere. What a sight it was.

'Better than fireworks on Bonfire Night!' said Ann.

And it really was!

11

A Wonderful City

The Americans were very friendly. As soon as Daddy met the people he had come over to see, they asked to meet his little family.

They made a great fuss of the children, and said they had wonderful manners. Mummy thought secretly that they had much better manners than the American children, who spoke loudly and were often rude to grown-ups. She felt proud of her three.

Nobody could have been nicer or more generous than their friends in New York. Every day Mummy found fresh flowers in her room sent by one friend or another. If she was asked out to dinner a beautiful box would arrive, tied up with magnificent ribbon – and inside would be a lovely buttonhole or shoulder-spray of flowers.

The children were not forgotten either. 'Look,' squealed Ann, coming into her mother's room with a parcel she had undone. 'Did you EVER see such a box of sweets in your life! Mummy, LOOK!'

Mummy looked. So did the others. It was certainly magnificent. The box was covered with bits of ribbon

made to look like flowers, and had a big sash of ribbon round it – far better than any hair-ribbon Ann had!

Inside were layers upon layers of wonderful sweets. 'Candies, the Americans call them,' said Mike. 'Oh, Ann – what a *magical* box. They look too good to be eaten.'

'Have one?' said Ann, and soon they were all eating the candies, which were certainly nicer than any they had ever had in their lives.

Belinda had a doll sent to her, and Mike had a wonderful pistol. It could shoot water, but if you fitted a bulb to the tip, it would light up like a torch when you pulled the trigger – and if you took out the bulb and put in a little paper of cartridges it would go off pop-pop-pop at top speed when the trigger was pulled.

Belinda's doll could walk. Belinda could hardly believe it when she saw it walk rather unsteadily over the floor, one foot after the other.

'Oh!' she cried, 'just look. She's far, far better than Josephine, Ann.'

'She's not,' said Ann, hugging Josephine. 'Anyway, I don't want Josephine to walk. Her legs aren't strong enough yet.'

Flowers, candies, fruit, chocolate, toys, books – everyone showered presents on the little English family. Surely there couldn't be more friendly or generous people in the world? Invitations poured

down on them too – dinner-parties, afternoon parties, all kinds of parties. Mummy had to buy the children new clothes, because they really hadn't brought enough with them!

'I don't know *how* we're going to return all this friendliness,' said Daddy, in despair. 'The Americans are rich, and English people are poor – I haven't enough money to repay all this kindness.'

But the Americans didn't want any return. It was just their way. They liked Daddy and his family, and they wanted to show it.

The children lived in a whirl. There was hardly time to go sight-seeing at first. Mummy took them to see the shops, which were full of the most beautiful things in the world. She took them to a cake-shop too, and the children blinked when they saw the wonderful cakes. Were they real?

'It's *such* a pity, Mummy – I'd like to eat dozens of those cakes,' said Belinda, longingly, 'but when I've had one, I'm so full I can't eat any more. But American children can eat four or five at a time. I've seen them.'

'Well, I expect you enjoy your one as much as they enjoy their four or five,' said Mummy.

Another thing that the children found very strange was the number of people from many different cultures. Daddy said that because America was a much newer country than Britain, people had come

from lots of other countries to make her their home.
It was so interesting. They made many new friends.

The Afro-American woman who cleaned the
corridor had twinkling eyes and dazzling white teeth.
'You been up to the top of the Empire State,
honey?' said the friendly old cleaner. 'Tell your Ma
to take you along!'

And so one day Mummy and Daddy took them to
the Empire State Building, the highest in New York.
It was so high that Ann felt sure it really did touch
the clouds.

Up they went in the lifts, shooting skywards so
quickly that Ann clutched her tummy.

'What's the matter?' asked Daddy, smiling. 'Have
you left your tummy behind?'

'It felt like it, when we suddenly shot up,' said
Ann. 'Oh Daddy – what a fast lift!'

The liftman spoke to them. 'Better look out for
the pop in your ears now, sir,' he said. 'We're getting
pretty high, and some people's ears go pop, and they
feel funny. But it's nothing.'

Sure enough, their ears did go pop with a curious
little noise in their ear drums. Ann felt a bit giddy, but
it soon passed off.

They got into the last lift, to go up the top dozen
or so floors. Up they went, and then, click! The door
opened and they stepped out on top of the Empire
State Building.

'OH!' cried Mike, in amazement. 'Mummy! We're right on the very top of the world!'

And really it did seem like it. Far, far below lay the earth, stretching out for miles and miles and miles all round the tower. An aeroplane flew by – below them! How extraordinary! People down in the far-off street were tiny dots – cars were smaller than even Mike's dinky-ones at home.

'What a building!' said Daddy. 'What a height! What a view!'

'We must be very near to Heaven up here,' said Ann, and the others smiled. Ann looked up as if she expected to see an angel or two around. But there was nothing but a few fleecy white clouds.

Then back they went down to earth again – down, down, down in the express lift, almost gasping at the way the lift seemed to fall down. Ann clutched her tummy again.

'I do like America,' said Belinda. 'It's full of the most wonderful things – it's *almost* magic!'

12

Time to go Home

Their time in America fled away fast. '*Every* thing goes fast in America; the taxis, the lifts, the parties – and even the time!' said Mike.

'Yes, no sooner is it morning than it seems to be night again,' said Belinda. 'I do really begin to wonder if time *is* different here – I mean, perhaps an hour isn't really an hour: perhaps it's only half an hour.'

'Oh, it's an hour all right,' said Mummy. 'It goes quickly because everything is strange and new and exciting, and the days go whizzing by.'

'I don't want to leave America,' said Ann. 'I like it.'

'Well, shall we leave you behind?' said Mummy. 'I've no doubt one of our American friends would love to keep a nice little girl like you.'

Ann looked alarmed. 'Oh *no!*' she said. 'It's just that I'm loving everything so much. I love England too. I couldn't *bear* not to go back.'

'I shan't mind going back at all,' said Mike. 'I love America and the Americans – but somehow they make me feel more English than ever, and they make me feel I belong to England. I want to get back

to England, though I wouldn't mind staying a few weeks more here, Mummy.'

'Well, we've got our return tickets for home now,' said Mummy, 'and anyway we've very little money left to spend here. When the *Queen Elizabeth* docks in New York on Wednesday, off we go in her, back home!'

The last day or two Mummy spent shopping with the children. They wanted to take little presents home for all their friends. The difficulty was what to take!

'There are so many things to choose from,' said Belinda, looking round a big store in despair. 'I just can't make up my mind. I mean, there are *thousands* of things here I'd like to take back. Don't Americans have a lot of everything, Mummy?'

'They do,' said Mummy, 'but then America is a rich country. She can afford to have everything.'

'Next time we come, don't let's stay in New York all the time,' said Belinda. 'Let's go and stay somewhere in the country, Mummy. I want to see what the trees and the flowers are like – I've hardly seen a tree in New York! And I've hardly seen a dog either.'

'Yes, it would be nice to stay somewhere in the country,' said Mummy. 'After all, we haven't really seen much of America if we only stay in New York – any more than Americans would see much of England if they only stayed in London.'

'That's true,' said Belinda. 'England's made up of

a lot of things, isn't it, Mummy, not just towns. It's —
well, it's primroses in springtime . . .'

'And taking the dogs for a long walk,' said Mike.

'And sailing down the river,' said Daddy.

'And watching the first green blades come through
in the fields of corn,' said Mummy, 'and seeing all
our lovely little patchwork of fields, with their odd
shapes and sizes.'

'It's Davey and Clopper the horses,' said Mike,
remembering suddenly.

'And treading on the first patches of ice when we
go to school in the winter,' said Belinda.

'Oh do stop,' said Ann. 'I'm getting so dreadfully
homesick. How could we *ever* have left England?'

'It's good to travel,' said Daddy. 'We see how
other people live and make themselves happy – and
we love our own home and country all the more
for seeing other people's. Each of us loves his own
country best, and his own home best and his own
family best.'

'When are we going to pack?' demanded Ann.
'I suddenly feel I want to. Oh Daddy – think how
pleased Davey and Clopper will be to see us again!'

'I wonder if the caravans are all right,' said Mummy.
'I wonder if . . .'

'What a lot of home-birds you are, all of a sudden,'
said Daddy, but he looked pleased. 'Well,' the *Queen
Elizabeth* sails at midnight tomorrow, so you can

begin to pack as soon as you like.'

They packed – and dear me, Daddy had to go out and spend some of his last precious dollars on a new suitcase, because they had so many presents there just wasn't room to pack them all in!

'I shall carry Sadie, my walking doll,' said Belinda.

'Better put a bit of string on her, or buy her some toy reins, then,' said Mike. 'She might walk overboard!'

They said goodbye to all the friends they had made. They promised to come again for a longer stay. They took a last look at the wonderful lights on Broadway. And then they taxied to the *Queen Elizabeth*, which had now arrived once more and was down at the docks, waiting for them.

'There she is!' cried Mike, as he saw her enormous bows sticking up over the street. 'Good old Lizzie!'

'British, not American,' said Belinda, proudly. 'Britain is very tiny compared with America, isn't it, Mummy? But even a small country can do grand things!'

'Of course,' said Mummy. 'Now, here we are – up the gangway you go!'

And up they went, the girls clutching Josephine and Sadie, and Mike carrying his marvellous pistol. What a surprise when they got to their cabins!

Their American friends were generous to the last. Great sprays of flowers were there with friendly messages, boxes of magnificent roses, beautiful

buttonholes to wear at dinner the next night, boxes of candies for the children!

'What a people!' said Daddy, as he looked at the enormous collection. 'I wonder we can bear to leave America, and go back to England!'

But the little island far away across the ocean, set in its own silver sea, was their home – the home they loved and wanted.

'Speed the ship!' said Daddy, as at last the *Elizabeth* began to move. 'Speed the ship home!'

'Home to England, dear old England,' chanted the children. 'Speed the ship, Captain, speed the ship!'

And away went the great ship, ploughing through the waves, eager to get back to England – it was her own home too!